"Taut, darkly humorous and heartbreaking, with an unforgettable narrator, *Sweet William* packs a real emotional punch." LISA GRAY, DAILY RECORD

"A compassionate novel imbued with a deep knowledge of mental health issues … Tense and insightful … A heart-stopping thriller with a powerful denouement." PAUL BURKE, NUDGE BOOKS

"Tense … astounding … dark and chilling … and shockingly realistic. Gripping and immersive … an intelligently written thriller that deals with the intricacies of the human brain, mixed up with the emotional ties of the family." ANNE CATER, RANDOM THINGS THROUGH MY LETTERBOX

"A story of danger, delirium and devastation … absolutely electrifying." ALIX LONG, DELIGHTFUL BOOK REVIEWS

"Enthralling … makes us cold to our bones … a stunning novel." BURIED UNDER BOOKS

Praise for Out of the Madhouse:

"An excellent exploration of the phenomenology of mental illness and its wider impact." JOSHUA FLETCHER, PSYCHOTHERAPIST

"I love this book; profoundly moving, beautifully written … incredibly important …wonderfully hopeful." JAMES WITHEY

"Confronts the shocking bleakness of mental illness head on." CHARLIE MORTIMER

"The overriding ingredients … are the warmth of his connections, … and the power of communication." DR NIHARA KRAUSE

Praise for Dear Michael, Love Dad:

"A wonderfully entertaining and moving book, with lessons for every parent." DAILY MAIL

"A moving read – honest, funny and sad." WOMAN AND HOME

"Raising the issue of men's mental health is important and *Dear Michael, Love Dad* is to be praised for that … [a] loving and well meant mix of letters and commentary. DAILY EXPRESS

Also by Iain Maitland:

Mr Todd's Reckoning

Sweet William

Out of the Madhouse (with Michael Maitland)

Dear Michael, Love Dad

"*The Scrib...* ...illiantly creepy cr... ...spense." BARBARA

"A brilliant read [… on] LGBTQ+ crimes that traditionally were underreported ... Thankfully, times have changed." NEIL BOAST MBE, former ... be returned or renewed former head of t... ...ed below.

Praise for Mr Todd's Reckoning:

"Splendidly creepy." Geoffrey Wansell, DAILY MAIL

"Maitland conjures madness from the inside, looking out … a brave book." JEFF NOON, SPECTATOR

"With stylish economy and a remorseless eye for detail, Iain Maitland's Mr Todd lures us in to his moral abyss. The banality of evil … drip feeds us its shockingly tense story of unending horror … Riveting, terrifying." PAUL RITTER

"Hurls you through the secret underground tunnels of an insane mind bent on destruction … phenomenally dark and utterly compelling." CHRIS DOLAN

"A dark chilling read, but I have to say a lot of fun too. There is a clever poetic ending that restores balance to the world but it's a long journey down a dark tunnel before the light. *Mr Todd's Reckoning* is gripping and gritty, exciting and scary." NB LITERARY MAGAZINE

"Superbly crafted … spellbinding and gripping … brilliantly observed … The setting of an ordinary two-bedroomed bungalow in suburbia is genius … the possibilities presented in *Mr Todd's Reckoning* are quite terrifying. … Sparkling, mesmerising … absolutely magnificent." LINDA HILL, LINDA'S BOOK BLOG

"The characters are brought to life so vividly I could see and smell them … genius … You can't stop turning the pages … a jaw dropping, atmospheric, creepy and uncomfortable read." TRACY FENTON, COMPULSIVE READERS BLOG

"Truly scary ... a fabulous dive into the mind of a classic, self-justifying psychopath ... A fantastic book." BARBARA NADEL

"Chilling ... compelling ... extremely thought provoking and shocking." JERA'S JAMBOREE

"A sinister novel with a build that [is] totally unexpected ... A quite unique thriller." A KNIGHT'S READS BLOG

"The kind of creepy disturbing read that stays with you ... It's dark psychological crime fiction with no ground rules or boundaries ... don't get too comfortable." CHERYL MM'S BOOK BLOG

"This novel grabbed me from the very first page and refused to let go ... wonderfully quirky yet frightening ... The atmosphere that Iain Maitland creates with his writing is incredible ... he is a master of suspense." BOOKAHOLIC CONFESSIONS

"Pure creepy gold ... A superb storyline, brilliant characters and subplots that tweaked my adrenaline ... This is a stunner!" BOOKS FROM DUSK TILL DAWN

"A deliciously dark and disturbing read ... incredibly dry wit ... dark to the nth degree ...wonderfully surprising, with a couple of real gasp-out-loud incidents." RAVEN CRIME READS

"Iain Maitland is a genius what a book Mr Todd s Reckoning is ... A really fantastic read." IT'S ALL ABOUT THE BOOKS BLOG

"A very clever psychological thriller ... A really dark, almost claustrophobic story, with some genuinely creepy moments that had me reeling in disbelief." JAFFA READS TOO BLOG

"There is no way the bloke who wrote this isn't some kind of psychopath." ALICIA HARRISON, STREETWISE PUBLICATIONS

Praise for Sweet William:
"A breathless journey through fear and love that explores how interdependent those two extreme emotions are." EWAN MORRISON

"Extremely well written and very frightening." BARBARA NADEL

"A dark, rocket-paced thriller." JON WISE, SUNDAY SPORT

THE
SCRIBBLER

THE FIRST GAYTHER & CARRIE
COLD CASE THRILLER

BY

IAIN
MAITLAND

CONTRABAND ☻

Contraband is an imprint of Saraband
Published by Saraband
Digital World Centre
1 Lowry Plaza, The Quays
Salford, M50 3UB

www.saraband.net

ISBN: 9781912235803
ebook: 9781912235810

Printed and bound in Great Britain by Clays Ltd, Elcograf S.p.A.

10 9 8 7 6 5 4 3 2 1

This is a work of fiction.
All characters are a product of the author's imagination.

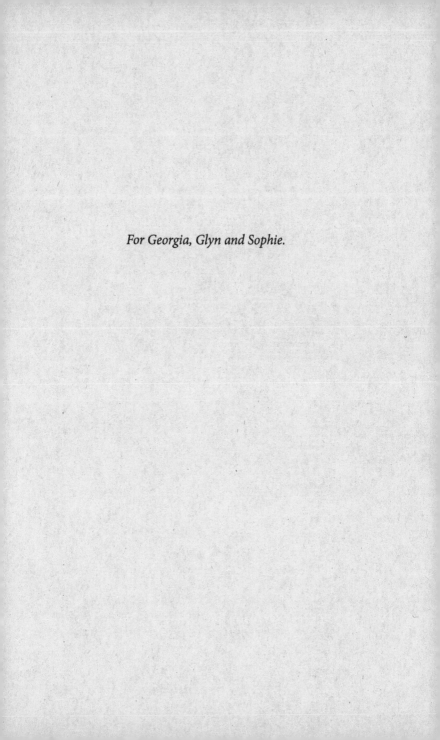

For Georgia, Glyn and Sophie.

PROLOGUE

MONDAY 12 NOVEMBER, 7.25AM

The Carrie family – the 20-something woman, her middle-aged mother and her five-year old son – sat around the kitchen table of a semi-detached bungalow on an estate on the outskirts of Ipswich in Suffolk.

Eating breakfast. Cereal. Coco Pops. Tea. Orange juice. Milk. Toast. Marmalade. Nutella.

Watching the clock on the wall.

The two women both had jobs to go to and the little boy had to be dropped off at school before that, by the older woman on her way to the hospital.

"So, Georgy …" the older woman sipped at her glass of orange juice as she looked across at her slight, crop-haired daughter, "… you're sure this new job's what you really want to do?"

"Bit late to change my mind now, Mum." The younger woman checked the clock. "An hour and a half before I start work." She bit into a corner of her toast.

"It wouldn't be the first time, sweetheart." The mother smiled back.

"Mum!" the young woman shouted in mock exasperation. "I know what I want to do now ... something that makes a difference to people ... changes lives ... and something I can get stuck into. DI Gayther's new LGBTQ+ Cold Case section allows me to put things right from years ago. It's better than spending my time deciding which officer should attend to a dog that's got loose on the by-pass."

The older woman sat quietly for a moment, chewing on her toast and thinking about what she was going to say next.

The younger woman leaned towards the little boy, reaching out her hand to push his hair out of his eyes with her fingers.

The boy moved his head from side to side, giggling, and then shook his hair, which flopped back into his eyes.

"Which one's DI Gayther? Is he the one that kept pestering you?"

"No, that was creepy Greening – he transferred to the Met six months ago. Gayther, Roger Gayther, is the one I worked with when I was a special at uni. He lives up by that little Co-op at the mini roundabout. I pointed his house out to you once, remember? The one with the clematis. He's quite funny in a dry sort of way. You have to tune into his wavelength a bit ..."

"Is he ...?"

"You met him a couple of times before I passed my test. He gave me lifts to work sometimes. Biggish man, he'd be about mid-fifties. Grey suit and tie and grey hair ... receding a little ... balding now probably ... you know the one, you said he'd look quite nice with a wash and brush up. He worked on crime investigations. The heavy stuff."

She looked at her young son, Noah, and smiled widely at him.

The little boy smiled back sweetly as he spooned Coco Pops into his mouth. Some of it went in, most of it didn't. He looked down at the milky mess on the tablecloth and then looked back up at his mum, who pulled a pretend-angry face at him. He wiped at the puddle of milk and Coco Pops with his sleeve.

"He's really nice," the young woman added, taking a mouthful of tea and mopping at the boy's sleeve with a piece of kitchen roll on the table.

She turned away from her son towards her mother and dropped her voice. "His wife passed away earlier this year … it's said she was an alcoholic and took her own life. He then had some sort of breakdown and is now back at work heading up this new section. They're easing him back in, I'm told. At his own pace. I think he might be a bit depressive, too."

"Well, I hope you know what you're letting yourself in for, that's all I can say … if he's not well up here." The older woman touched the side of her head.

"He was always kind to me," the young woman replied as she put her emptied glass of orange and cup of tea on her plate ready to clear away. "I'll learn a lot from him. He's very open … or was, I don't know how he'll be these days. He has a son who did, or does, something terribly hush-hush in the Met. He's based in London, so DI Gayther must be on his own at home and quite lonely, I'd have thought."

"Well, you be careful, don't take any nonsense …" the older woman instructed. "LGBTQ+. Lesbian, gay, bi–"

"Lesbian, gay, bisexual, transgender and queer or questioning and others," the younger woman interrupted. "They've a big cold case team at work that covers all of the unresolved cases – missing people, serious sexual offences, murders – all going back to the sixties and seventies. Massive, it is. All the files. And they've a couple of big cold cases that they're looking into … a tenth and twenty-fifth anniversary … the media will be all over them … it's just got too many cases at the moment."

The younger woman paused before carrying on.

"So, they've set up a separate section for LGBTQ+ cases, going way back, and all across East Anglia, and put DI Gayther in charge. It ticks the politically correct boxes and they've had loads of local publicity in the papers – on the radio and he's been on Anglia TV, BBC and ITV. It gives him a way to come back in at his own pace."

"So," the older woman replied as she stood up and began putting the breakfast crockery onto a tray, "you've no idea what you'll be doing when you get into work this morning then?"

"No," replied the younger woman. " … It could be anything from a hate crime to a murder. Whatever it is, I'm ready …"

They smiled at each other.

The young woman ran her fingers through the boy's hair.

The older woman said, "Good luck."

PART ONE

THE CARE HOME

1. MONDAY 12 NOVEMBER, EARLY MORNING

Newly qualified Detective Constable Georgia Carrie walked slowly up the steps of the temporary portacabin office to the side of the main police station building, balancing two full mugs of tea, one in each hand. She stopped to read the sign, 'DI Gayther, Cold Cases' and the handwritten scrawl above it, 'LGBTQ+'. She put the mugs down on the top step to open the door and then paused for a moment, thinking what she might say.

"Sorry to hear about your wife, sir"? No, not even that cursory sentence of sympathy would be welcomed. His wife's alcoholism was an open secret at the station, but he had never talked of it. "I'm looking forward to working with you again" sounded suitably keen. But she was sure he viewed his sideways move – "a washed-up old has-been shuffling through dead files," as he'd probably put it – without much enthusiasm.

She opened the door. Picked up the mugs. Stepped inside. The older man, in his battered grey suit and brown loafers, looked up as the young woman put the mugs of tea on the desk. One on his side, the other on hers. He smiled briefly and nodded his thanks. She went to say her opening words, "Good to see you again, sir", but as she did so, he turned the papers he was reading round so they were facing her on the desk. Old man in a hurry, she thought.

"Read this, Carrie," he said abruptly, pushing two sheets of A4 paper across towards her.

She took the sheets and sat down at the desk and began reading the first one. He picked up his mug of tea and swung round on his chair, his back to her, looking out of the window towards the back of the main building and what looked like a building site. The police station was being renovated. Ladders, pots and paints and stacked-up scaffolding seemed to fill the whole space. It was a mess. He hated mess.

"*Still At Large,*" she read the front page headline of the local newspaper out loud, "*The Scribbler.*"

"When was this…?"

"Two years ago. Thirtieth anniversary of the first killing," he replied. He gestured towards the two sheets and she carried on reading without speaking.

"*Police are still searching for The Scribbler, the serial killer who murdered six people in Norfolk between 1988 and 1990.*

"*He is described as white British and would now be in his fifties.*

"*The Scribbler met his victims in bars and clubs in and around Norwich and later stabbed them to death.*

"*He carved a cartoon likeness of each victim onto their torso.*

"*The first victim was Donald Worthington, a 53-year-old abattoir supervisor.*

"*The second victim was 42-year-old office clerk Andrew Marven.*

"*The other four victims, middle-aged men from the Norwich area, were found dead in the summer and autumn of 1990.*

"*Police believe The Scribbler may have killed twelve men in total.*"

She stopped, cocked her head at an angle, and looked across the desk at Gayther. "If he drew a cartoon likeness of each victim, should he not be known as 'The Caricaturist' rather than 'The Scribbler'?"

He turned and looked at her. "'The Scribbler' is snappier. And more accurate, although the press, the media, don't know it. He used to criss-cross the body with cuts after he drew the likeness … as if he were scribbling it out in a rage. Read the other page, Carrie. I've started a summary."

She nodded and continued reading. She worked her way down the half-page of bullet-pointed, handwritten notes in his small, neat hand.

The Scribbler. White Male. Early twenties/Now mid-fifties. Slim build. No distinguishing features.

She looked up. "Do we have a likeness ... of this Scribbler?"

He dug into the briefcase by his feet and pulled out one more sheet, which he handed to her. "It's probably the worst I've ever seen in thirty or so years. Mr Potato Head. Your little boy could have done a better job with his crayons." He stopped and thought and then added, "How is ... your little boy?"

"Noah's well. Started school in September ... just round the corner from my mum's. We've moved in with Mum for now. She's helping out, taking him and collecting him from school when I can't."

"Is ... your partner—"

"No," she said, interrupting and shaking her head. "He's gone for good this time. I had enough of it. I'm just trying to sort out the legal stuff. Solicitors are involved. He doesn't make things easy. Do we have an aged version of this?" She changed the subject, holding up the picture of The Scribbler.

"I've just asked for one, for what it's worth. It's in the system, but Christ knows how long that will be. It's certainly not a priority." He leaned forward suddenly, took a fountain pen out of his inside jacket pocket and drew three lines across the forehead of the image and lines between and to either side of the nose and mouth. He stopped and added stray hairs from the nostrils and ears. "There, that's what he looks like now. Old Mr Potato Head."

"Eyes?"

"Blue. Or Blue-grey. Or brown, according to one witness."

Gayther drew a pair of glasses on the image. "He might have glasses these days, unless he's like me and pretends he doesn't need them."

"Height?"

"Five eight, nine. Slight build. Lean. Stringy. Everyone seems to agree on that."

"No distinguishing features at all?"

"None that were recalled by anyone. One witness said he had 'staring eyes' and another 'mad eyes', but someone always says that … especially when the person has just tried to murder them. That's about it."

She stopped and paused. "And who gave us the descriptions?"

"Three of his victims escaped. We also had statements and descriptions from a barmaid at the time. And an old boy who got into a conversation with him … read on, though. My summary. I've not finished it yet. You were here earlier than I expected."

Six victims – forties, fifties, family men, closet gays.

Three got away – teacher, bank manager, vicar. Now aged 65 to 80+.

Three prime suspects: Challis (plumber), Halom (drag act), Burgess (sales rep). All released without charge.

She wasn't sure who to ask about first, but this was one of an endless stream of cold cases they'd be looking at over the coming days, so she decided to come straight to the point.

"And so … " she said, "why are we looking at this case again now? First of all?"

"Because he's back, Carrie. The Scribbler is back."

* * *

DI Gayther eased his old silver Ford Focus out of the police station car park and headed across towards the A12, to go north up the Suffolk coast.

"So where are we off to, guv? A stroll on Southwold Pier? Fish and chips at Aldeburgh? A boat on Thorpeness Mere? I like a nice boat ride, me," Carrie asked cheerfully.

"You'll be lucky," he replied, then paused and added, "You might get a bag of chips on the way back … for now, we're heading just beyond the power station at Sizewell. Near Dunwich … I'll tell you why in a minute. Let me bring you up to speed on the case first, though. I've been working on it all weekend."

He turned to the young policewoman in the seat beside him. "I was about to add, at the bottom of my summary, 'Believed to be responsible for twelve deaths.'"

"So, the six murders? And …"

"Worthington, Marven, Rudd, MacGowan, Fotherby and Davies were the six men who were murdered. White, respectable, middle-aged men, married or divorced, but secretly homosexual … or at least bisexual. White-collar workers, as they used to be called. It was another world back then, of course. There was still a stigma attached to homosexuality.

"The Scribbler picked up his victims in busy city-centre bars in Norwich. Went with them in their cars to secluded places, mostly woodlands, a few miles out. Stabbed them and dumped them in ditches across Norfolk and Suffolk. Drove their cars back to where they started or as close as he could. Went home and disappeared for another few months."

"Always their cars?" she queried. "That's odd."

He nodded his reply. "There were suggestions he may have driven a car or a van that would stand out, be remembered, if it were seen in a layby late at night. An ice cream van, maybe. Imagine that, trying to outpace a police car in an ice cream van."

Carrie smiled, pleased that they were already at ease together.

"Or he may not have had a car. Or not been allowed to drive … because he hadn't passed a test … or on medical grounds. He may have had epilepsy. These were all lines of enquiry that led nowhere. Fact is, we just don't know. It's an odd one, though."

"But … if he drove their cars … he must have left something behind. A muddy footprint? Hair? Fingerprints? Surely? Very,

very risky. Why not torch them?"

He shrugged. "Always dangerous that and, on a more mundane level, maybe he didn't want to walk three miles or whatever back into town. As for traces, nothing. We think he was incredibly thorough. And it was the 1980s," he added, "different days. If it were today, the advances in DNA collection would probably give us a trace however careful he thought he'd been …"

He went on, "Deposition sites weren't protected the way they are now. I remember one, late 80s, where I was standing guard by a corpse, a young woman had been raped and murdered. I found a cigarette stub close by and we all thought we had a good forensic lead. Turned out Hoskins, an old-timer who dated back to Eynsham Hall days, had had a crafty fag before I took over."

"Was there sexual activity?" she asked, taking her mobile phone out of her pocket to open Google Maps.

"Non-consummation, for want of a better expression. They'd be in the early stages of having sex, him supposedly active, the victim passive, often on all fours or laying on their front, legs apart. He stabbed them. Killed them when they were at their most vulnerable."

"And the six other deaths?" she said, resting her phone on her thigh. "No reception," she added.

He nodded. "We don't need it. I know how to get there. I Googled it last night … Hope, Tanner … Bulgin … Hardy, March and one more … Gerry Rhodes. Six more middle-aged men – similar profile to the known victims. All went missing from Norfolk and Suffolk between the first and last murders … no, one, Rhodes, was just after, a few weeks. None of them has been heard of since."

"So, they've never been found," she stated. "Their remains are out there somewhere rotted away in ditches?"

"Maybe," he answered, accelerating the car up to 70mph on a

long, straight stretch of the A12. "That was how the others were left. Dumped in ditches. There was no attempt to bury the bodies. Maybe he found a better place to put them later on."

"What about the ones who got away?"

"There were three of them. That we know of anyway. Alan Wade. Thirty-five at the time, a teacher at a private school in Suffolk. An all-boys school. He went with The Scribbler to a field outside Swainsthorpe, crouched down on all fours and The Scribbler went to stab him with a screwdriver. Somehow, he managed to fight him off and made his way to the main road where he hid by a layby all night, scared out of his wits, and then stopped a passing police car in the morning."

"What do we have from him?"

"Not a lot. He gave a statement. It's in the file. Read it later. And a description. Vague. The Scribbler wore some sort of peaked cap, maybe a baseball cap, throughout. He used the words 'lean' and 'baby-faced' and 'soft-featured'. Said he – The Scribbler – had a bit of a Suffolk accent. Sloightly on th' huh, but not fully. But a local. Maybe second generation."

"And the next one?"

"Much the same. Wilkerson. Bank manager from Diss, forty-two. Picked up in another busy city-centre bar, the other side of the city. Taken to a field on the way to Drayton. The Scribbler stabbed him two or three times before they were about to … supposedly … have sex. He was interrupted by a dog walker. He ran off. Left Wilkerson for dead. It was touch and go, but he pulled through."

"His statement and description?"

"He was the most reluctant to talk. Bank manager. Married man. Two children. All very middle class, respectable. He didn't want it coming out. Marriage. Career. All of that would have ended back then, especially in a bank. Issues of trust and blackmail. We have a statement and a description; similar to Wade's. You could swap them around and not know whose was whose. Identical modus operandi. Only difference was that he said The Scribbler smelt of a farmyard. A farmer's boy? That was followed up without success."

"And the third?"

"The third one who got away – that we know of – was a vicar. Edwin Lodge, fifty-one, from Ipswich. From his statement, The Scribbler made him put on a condom … and then attacked him … stabbed at his genitals with a screwdriver but cut the vicar's thigh instead. The vicar was the stronger man and fought him off, and The Scribbler ended up running away."

"And what did he have to say, the vicar?"

"He came forward some time later. Just after the fourth victim – fourth known victim anyway – was murdered. Wracked with guilt. Clutching the cross of Jesus and all of that. Much the same story as before … That's where we're off to now."

"What, to go over his statement with him again … after all this time?"

"We're off to a care home on the road to Dunwich. Edwin Lodge, eighty-something, lived there these past two and a half years. Completely alone. No family. No visitors, at least not lately. Abandoned by his flock."

"Lived? Past tense. So where is he now?"

"He was the vicar of … one of these old rural churches in the middle of nowhere. Then lived quietly near Dunwich in his retirement. Went into this care home to be looked after, became increasingly demented … sorry, not the PC phrase I know … he suffered from dementia and it got gradually worse."

"Okay, so are we going to get much sense out of him?"

"He suddenly started rambling about The Scribbler and what happened. The staff couldn't make much sense of it, most of them are either too young to remember what happened or are from overseas ... Eastern Europe, the Philippines ... and don't always understand the language too well. Especially the biblical stuff, the lord shall smite thee ... all of that. One of them managed to understand some of what he was saying ... that The Scribbler had come back and was going to kill him."

"So, okay if he's experiencing dementia – and the related hallucinations and paranoia that can go with it – are we going to get any more out of him now than they did thirty-odd years ago?"

"We're not going to get anything out of him, we're going to meet the doctor who's there this morning. Edwin Lodge died six or seven weeks ago. The coroner ruled death by misadventure. It seems Edwin, when alone in his room, and in the later stages of dementia, got himself out of bed unaided, used a frame to walk across to the window, undid the locks and bolts and then climbed up and onto the ledge and threw himself head-first onto the concrete path below. As you do..."

"So you think ..."

"I'd think it an unlikely scenario. But what came out from the coroner's report – and what Ray Wilson, one of our ex-DCs working as a civilian investigator, picked up on and passed to cold cases – was that, before he died ... or possibly after ... a face was etched into his stomach and then scratched out."

Gayther paused for a second, gathering his thoughts, before going on. "No one seemed to give it a second thought. It's not unknown for dementia patients to self-harm apparently, but ... the talk of The Scribbler ... and the serial killer's motif on the deceased's body in the same location as the other victims ... well, two plus two makes four in my book..."

* * *

"You don't have a mobile phone do you, guvnor? You could put it on the dashboard if you did. Use it as a sat-nav."

"Not a fan, Carrie, although I have one here." He gestured towards the side door. "But it needs charging. I forget sometimes … old age … creeping senility, I'm afraid."

"You can get a lead these days to plug into the cigarette lighter. Charges it for you from the battery. Clever, eh?"

He smiled. "Something to think about, Carrie, but it's all a bit hit and miss out here anyway. Reception. In the sticks."

They drove along in companionable silence.

Carrie took out her phone and fiddled with it.

Gayther ignored her and carried on driving.

"I've got reception," Carrie said suddenly. "What's the postcode?"

"No idea," Gayther answered. "Google 'Kings Court Care Home, Dunwich' and see what that brings up. It's about two miles off the A12, we turn right at the pub in Westleton."

"You were saying, guv … there were three suspects. How far did they get?" she asked, tapping away at her phone. "Go on," she added, "I'm still listening."

"Good of you … Three suspects were questioned. Ray Challis was a plumber who frequented at least three of the city-centre pubs where The Scribbler met his victims. He was named several times by viewers calling in after a TV appeal. He had alibis for three or four of the murders. Forensics on his van and at his home didn't turn up anything."

"Did we have DNA in those days? Before my time," she said, looking up from her phone. "Sorry."

"Early days and The Scribbler was very, very careful. He wore a cap at all times, either as a disguise or to make sure his hair didn't get onto the victims' clothes. There's some speculation he may have been bald, which would have been unusual in a man of that age. They did one or two appeals with different images but without success. Or possibly he was having chemo – that was another line of enquiry that was followed up without success."

She nodded.

"And each of the victims … the ones who escaped … said he wore gloves. Ladies' cotton gloves. Supposedly for eczema, according to Wade, although Wilkerson said they were rubber gloves, which would be odd. The latex might have been an issue if he had eczema, so it's likely that The Scribbler was just being careful. I imagine he'd have burned those and his clothes later on."

She asked, "Blood, what about blood? He'd have been covered, wouldn't he?"

"Some," he replied. "From them. Onto him. He stabbed them repeatedly from behind so there would have been something, but if he took off his outer layers of clothes … who knows … he may have been painstakingly careful or just very lucky … or both … either way, it was thirty-odd years ago and things were more hit and miss then."

"Turn up here, for Kings Court. Here …"

"Yes, thank you, Carrie, I do know." DI Gayther signalled and then swung the car across the A12 on to the side road towards the coast.

"And the others. The drag act and the sales rep. What about them?"

"The drag act … Peter Halom … turned himself in and confessed to the murders. That was the biggest waste of time and manpower ever. Seems he had done his act in some of the pubs and clubs The Scribbler had been to. This fellow said he had been suffering from blackouts and had convinced himself he'd committed the murders in some sort of trance-like state. We had psychiatrists and all sorts in to persuade him he didn't. Then he went to the press, who had a field day. Front page of the old *News of the World* newspaper. Nightmare."

She nodded, "It's about a mile down here, on the right ... and the sales rep?"

"Simon Burgess ... a freelance agent for baby and childrens-wear from Sussex. He bought stuff cheap from Indian wholesalers in East London on Sundays and then sold it at twice the price to small independent shops in East Anglia, up as far as Cromer and Hunstanton on weekdays. Not much of a living even then. His ex-girlfriend wrote in, bizarrely, a long and rambling letter saying it was him and how he used to make her dress up as a schoolboy and then beat her and rape her 'from behind', as she put it."

"Wild goose chase?" she replied, and then added, "About half a mile now, guv."

"He was in the area at the time of each murder – and no alibis, or at least nobody recalled him. He stayed overnight when he was in Norwich or higher up on the coast. The old boy who'd got talking to The Scribbler saw Burgess drive by a week or two later and made a note of the number plate. He then ballsed it all up by picking someone else out of a line-up. The ex, his by-now-pregnant ex, then retracted her statement and said he was with her on two of the occasions. Looking at the files, I'd say Challis and Burgess are worth another close look ... if we had then what we have now – CCTV, DNA, all of that – we'd have put one of them away."

"*You have arrived at your destination.*"

"This is it, we're here."

"Thank you, Constable Carrie. Where would I be without you?"

"Driving off Southwold Pier, guv?"

They smiled at each other.

Both thinking that they'd liked each other when they'd worked together before.

And then, that they'd make a good team moving forward.

2. MONDAY 12 NOVEMBER, MID-MORNING

DI Gayther slowed the car, looking along the long row of battered post-war prefabs to his left and the slope ahead of him that seemed to take the road down into an alleyway and woods. Finally, he turned his head towards the tree-lined grounds and building behind the tall brick wall to his right.

"It's in here," Carrie said, pointing to the sign on the wall by the wide driveway: 'Kings Court'. There were times, he recalled from when they had crossed paths a while back, that she spoke to him as if he were half-witted. With most people, it would annoy him, but he had a soft spot for Carrie and so it amused him.

He drove the car onto the driveway and pulled over to the side so they could survey the care home. A big, Gothic-looking house, red-brick and turrets, with a long gravel drive opening out into a tarmac car park with twenty, twenty-four spaces in front of the building and more, 'Staff Parking', further round at the side.

Carrie tapped at her mobile phone, turning it off and slipping it into her trouser pocket. "All neat and tidy," she said encouragingly, studying the care home.

"Fur coat, no knickers, as they used to say, Carrie ... it was actually in special measures, before Lodge's death." He reached for the file tucked between their seats and took out a sheet of paper. "This print-off ... a press cutting from two months or so ago, just before his death ... If you read it, please. I want to sit here and watch the comings and goings for a few minutes."

"*The Kings Court Care Home near Dunwich in Suffolk provides residential and nursing care for up to thirty-two people, some living with dementia,*" she read aloud.

"I've read it," he sighed. "I know what's in it."

She carried on reading, this time in her head...

A care home that has served the Suffolk community for more than thirty years has been inspected by the Care Quality Commission and is now in special measures after being rated as inadequate.

The service was not considered 'safe' ... patients' records were not always accurate and up-to-date ... concerns about staff training in safeguarding and ... whether patients were drinking sufficient fluids ... staff were caring ... but sufficient care was not taken to maintain patients' dignity.

According to the report, the rating for this service is 'inadequate' and is now in special measures ... services in special measures are kept under review and, if we have not taken immediate action to propose to cancel the provider's registration of the service, will be inspected again within six months ... The service will be kept under review and, if necessary, could be escalated to urgent enforcement action.

If not enough improvement is made within this timeframe and there is still a rating of 'inadequate', we will take action in line with our enforcement procedures to begin the process of preventing the provider from operating this service.

"So," Carrie asked, "if it was in special measures before and there's been a death – even an accidental one from their viewpoint – is this ... commission thing ... now beginning the process of ... is it, the home, now being closed down?"

"Lodge's death threw everything into a frenzy," he answered. "A second inspection straightaway. Immediate action. A new management team drafted in to oversee the staff. New structures and systems coming into place. A complete overhaul, but there's still talk of closure. It's not an instant thing anyway. They need to find places for twenty or so residents. The woman I spoke to, Coombes, who told me all this, she is … at least was … in charge. She sounded really bitter. As if she had been blamed for everything and it was nothing to do with her at all."

He watched two young female members of staff coming out of the front door, chatting as they made their way towards the staff car park. He thought they looked happy, carefree even.

"She, Ruth Coombes, as good as says it's all their fault." He pointed to the young women as they got into a car. "It's been down to a turnover of staff … low pay, long hours, her hands were tied, she did her best blah blah blah … problems with getting new employees in and training and then keeping them seems to be the gist of it. More than a touch of the 'bloody foreigners' about it all."

"No CCTV cameras," Carrie pointed suddenly to the building. "Should there be? It would make life a lot easier if we could rewind and see everyone coming in and out at the time of Mr Lodge's death. Might there be some elsewhere? Covert recordings we could check?"

He paused, seeing a grey-haired gardener, carrying a tray of bedding plants and a handheld spade, coming out from around the far side of the building to the left and making his way to the entrance. There, he knelt and started digging out dead plants from two urns to either side of the front doors.

"Guv…?" she said, after a few moments' silence.

"Sorry Carrie, I was just thinking … Big issue, apparently, CCTV in care homes – privacy and dignity and all of that. Anything that's up has to be overt; all out in the open for everyone to see. They've not done it here because of the costs, so Mrs Coombes said."

He stopped for a further second or two, looking at the gardener, before shaking his head and going on.

"The fact is, Carrie, if The Scribbler was here, and he did kill Edwin Lodge, he could pretty much stroll in and out as he pleased at visiting times. I asked Mrs Coombes about security and she didn't seem to know what to say. From what I can make out, a sign-ing-in book's about the be-all and end-all of it – and that seems to be pretty lax. Visitors pretty much come and go as they wish."

He watched as the grey-haired gardener put the old plants into a plastic bag he had in his pocket, then started placing bulbs into the first urn. He could, thought Gayther, be The Scribbler. Same sort of age and build, forgettable, overlooked, maybe a new employee who then came face-to-face with one of his victims and had no choice but to silence him and his ravings. Gayther sighed. If only it were that easy, but he made a mental note to check on him later.

"So, what are your thoughts, guvnor?" Carrie asked. "If Mr Lodge was murdered by The Scribbler, did he recognise a member of staff? Someone who came to visit another resident? A workman fixing a radiator? Did The Scribbler realise and then come and kill him?"

DI Gayther raised his arms and spread his hands out wide as if to say, 'who knows?'.

She went on, "Or could it just be that, in his dying days, Mr Lodge was tormented about his homosexuality, which he saw as an ungodly thing, had visions of The Scribbler and then took his own life … and this is just us …" she hesitated for a second because of Gayther's expression but then went on, "… chasing ghosts?"

"Well that, Constable," replied the older man, "is what we are here to find out. Come on, we've an appointment with Mrs Coombes in …" he checked his watch, "five minutes ago."

* * *

DI Gayther and DC Carrie sat in the reception area of the care home, the entrance behind them. They'd been directed there by a young, stick-thin woman in the office to the right as they went in through the front doors. She slid back the glass pane, asked their names, and waved them through the next set of doors into reception. There was a moment's confusion as Carrie pushed the doors, found they were locked, and had to ask the thin-as-a-rake woman to let them in. She pressed a button on the office wall and the doors opened.

"There is some security then," said Carrie, walking through and leading the way. "Of sorts."

Gayther nodded and replied, "Some, but at busy times, visiting times, when The Scribbler would have come in unnoticed, they'd all just pass straight through."

"They need a CCTV camera up there in the office," Carrie replied as she sat down. "Just there." She pointed. "Solve everything, that would."

He nodded again as he sat down too and looked around.

The reception area's walls were magnolia-painted, the sofa and chairs a brown-and-orange stripe; the floor looked like wood, but was more likely, thought Gayther, laminate. The place smelled of antiseptic and possibly vomit and urine, although that may just have been his over-active imagination.

The reception area was an almost perfect rectangle, with a gated-off flight of stairs to one side, leading up, he assumed, to a floor of bedrooms. Another door led to a long corridor where he guessed most of the patients' rooms were located. He could see, through the windows, a wide garden behind the building. To the left through more doors, he assumed, would be a lounge and other communal areas, and maybe a kitchen.

"I told you, I've been through this before, we all have, weeks ago, with the proper police, just after the reverend's death," said Mrs Coombes in a sharp voice, as she came through the doors towards them. A tall, thin, old-fashioned-looking woman, she seemed harassed, as though she had more important things to do right now. After brief introductions, she sat straight-backed, a file on her knee, half-open with a passport-sized photograph of the deceased Reverend Lodge attached to the first page of papers.

"It's a pain, I know," replied DI Gayther, nodding sympathetically. "But I've just been asked to go over the case one final time … with my colleague … so we can close our file. Not to trouble you further. I just want to go through a few things, get it straight in my mind."

"I don't believe it was a suicide," she answered abruptly. "If that's what you're thinking. Not for a second. I told the last policeman. The Indian gentleman. The reverend was not himself. He would not have taken his own life. He was a man of the cloth. He opened the window for fresh air. In his befuddled state, he must have leaned out too far …"

"Can you tell me a little about … the reverend? When did he come here?"

"Two years ago, give or take. A very nice man. Very nice indeed. A sensible and well-organised man. He sold up, not that he had that much, being a vicar, and came to us. He knew he was suffering from dementia. He declined steadily over that time, mentally rather more than physically. Forgetfulness. Meandering talk. Wanderings. In his mind."

She paused for a moment, as if gathering her thoughts.

"The last day or two before, well, I probably shouldn't say this … he was not himself at all. He was always so polite and thoughtful. But, at the end, he turned in on himself and kept talking, almost arguing with himself, so angry and frightened, about someone coming to kill him."

DI Gayther leaned forward. "The last day or two of his life. Was there a specific moment when he changed?"

"He soiled himself at the fete on the Saturday, which would have been … two days before. I remember that. He was very subdued afterwards. But that's normal. Incontinence. They can feel ashamed and embarrassed … if and when they are aware of what they've done."

She considered what she was going to say, choosing her words carefully, and then carried on.

"It seemed to come on quite quickly after that. The madness. That's what I believe it was. His mind was going, poor old chap. I believe he got quite vocal with Jen, one of our regulars, and with Sally, another of our care assistants. He grabbed her arm so hard he left red marks on it."

"The fete?" interrupted Carrie suddenly. "So, you had people coming in from outside? Do you have a record of visitors?"

Mrs Coombes smiled. "Not for that, no. There's a signing-in book for visitors, but …" she added, seeing the officers look at each other, "… it depends who is on. Kazia's on, at the moment, nice enough girl, but new. Been here a couple of weeks."

"So, the fete …?" said Carrie.

"We have a little old-fashioned fete – tombola, second-hand books, home-made cakes – once a year on the last Saturday in September … quite late really … for the residents and their families and anyone who wants to come and see us. We get a few locals wander in, waifs and strays mostly, looking for something to do, and sons and daughters planning ahead for a place for Mum or Dad. It's all free and easy, donate a pound or two on the way in, that's all."

"So …" Carrie pressed, "was there a big turnout? Were there any passers-by coming in? Was there anyone you didn't recognise? Was there—"

"Goodness …" replied Mrs Coombes, "so many ques–"

"What my colleague meant to ask," interrupted DI Gayther, glancing across at Carrie, "was this: did the vicar come down and join in the fete?"

"Why, yes, of course. He was most keen and had talked about helping out on the second-hand book stall, which he did for a little while. That was his thing really, books and reading. Not that the books would have interested him much. Mills & Boon romances mostly. He was interested in architecture and … I don't know, English Heritage and National Trust–type matters. He was very well-read and interesting, although he would never press his opinions on you."

She laughed unexpectedly. It sounded surprisingly joyful, thought Gayther.

"I remember seeing him later sitting in the shade in a wheelchair – it was quite a sunny day. September can be nice, of course. We always seem to have a sunny fete. Anyway, he didn't really need a wheelchair, but his legs ached after a while. He was eating a 99 ice cream … the chocolate flake first, while all the ice cream ran down his fingers. He knew what was happening and was joining in the fun and laughter. I didn't see him after that but was told later, by Sally, that he had been taken back to his room. Do you know, I can't remember if he soiled himself at the fete or later in his room."

DI Gayther asked, "I wonder if he saw anyone he knew at the fete. Did you notice anyone talking to Mr Lodge, other than staff?"

She shook her head. "No, not that I saw, though I'm sure he must have done. But we had about twenty or more residents there at different times and I was back and forth, to the gate, the refreshments, doing the prize draw later on, so I wasn't really focusing on Mr Lodge particularly. A lot of people locally would have known him, of course, from his church days, and would have stopped to talk if they saw him."

DI Gayther went on, "Did he have many visitors, Mr Lodge? Family, friends?"

"He was a single man, never married, no children. He had a brother I think, an older brother, who had passed away. The brother and his wife, his second wife, I believe, had a daughter and she visited the reverend with her husband earlier in the year, from New Zealand or Australia, one or the other. They took him out for lunch while they were over here. They didn't come back again before they went back home. I don't know why. Perhaps they didn't have time."

She looked around, as if nervous, and then continued.

"There were occasional visitors from his church in the early days. I remember a church warden who came and read the bible with him on Sundays for a while. I don't know what happened to him. He may have moved away. And a couple of lady parishioners visited on and off some weekends, but I think one of them passed over and the other didn't come back after that. I don't think he had any visitors since his niece, thinking about it."

She paused and turned her head and looked around the reception area as if to check she could not be overheard. She then leaned towards them.

"There is something I didn't mention before. To your Indian gentleman. It didn't seem relevant. But there was a young man, in his early thirties, I'd say, who came very often, two or three times a week, for the first few months Mr Lodge was here."

She hesitated for a second or two.

"There was some light-hearted talk that he might be the reverend's secret son. They were both tall and slim and ... I don't know, there was something about the way they stood, slightly bent and stooping almost, that made people stop and wonder. But there was some sort of argument and the reverend was left in tears when the young man stormed out – and he never came back. The reverend never talked of it and, by and large, it was forgotten about."

She looked over her shoulder and then spoke in a low whisper.

"I think he might have been the reverend's, um, special friend … if you know what I mean."

Carrie spoke. "So this … friend of Mr Lodge … he's not been seen for a while now? He wasn't at the fete?"

"Goodness me no, but, funnily enough, Mr Lodge did receive a letter from him, out of the blue, well it must have been a week or two before the fete. Sally or Jen, they were his favourites, so we tried to match them up as often as possible, read it to him. It was just a polite note really, in a little thank you card, saying he was going to France, I think it was, to start a new job and wishing the reverend well. It upset him though. The reverend."

Before either officer could say anything, the doors into the reception area opened, and they all turned to see who was coming through.

Mrs Coombes stopped talking and looked up expectantly as a short Asian man in his forties, immaculate in his dark-grey suit, white shirt and cuffs, came through the doors into reception. He stood there smiling at them.

"This is Dr Khan," she went on, getting to her feet and doing the introductions. "He was here at … after … Mr Lodge's … demise."

Dr Khan looked from DI Gayther to DC Carrie and then spoke in impeccable, clipped English. He sounded as though he was enjoying himself, thought Gayther.

"You're going to ask me if the Reverend Lodge fell out of the window or killed himself? Let me give you the answer."

* * *

Dr Khan sat in the remaining empty armchair and smiled warmly at them all as he put his leather bag down by the side of his feet. He then reached into his pocket, took out his mobile phone and touched several buttons. A long pause, as he read what was on the screen, scrolled down and read further, and then, after a second long pause, smiled again. He looked at DI Gayther and spoke.

"Would you like me to summarise my statement to the coroner? It gives you the key facts."

"No," answered DI Gayther, irritated by the man's theatricality. "I have your statements, both from my colleagues and the coroner's report. I'd just like to ask you, and Mrs Coombes, a few questions, first of all, to get the timeline of the vicar's death straight in my head."

The doctor and Mrs Coombes both nodded and smiled as Gayther continued.

"Mrs Coombes, Reverend Lodge had his evening meal with some of the other residents, as usual, on Monday 1 October and, after sitting in the residents' lounge for half an hour, was taken back to his room afterwards by a Sally Reece at 7.45pm? All very normal."

She nodded her agreement and started to say what it was that Reverend Lodge had eaten, but Gayther hushed her gently – "Please just correct me if I'm wrong or miss something you think is significant" – and moved on.

"Sally helped him to get ready for bed and was joined by Jennifer Coates just after 8.00pm. About 8.10pm. The three of them chatted together, settling him down, and then Reverend Lodge was left alone to read from about 8.25pm, 8.30pm. He seemed calm and relaxed at that time—"

"That's right," interrupted Mrs Coombes. "We'd made a slight change to his medication to calm him, with Doctor Khan's approval, and he seemed much happier."

The doctor nodded his agreement as Mrs Coombes went on.

"He liked to read for about an hour before he went to sleep. The girls had to prop him into place and put his book, a large-print book, on a stand with a lamp light on it. One of them would go and check on him at half-nine or ten and help him put everything away, back in its place. He was a very tidy man. As often as not, he'd be fast asleep when they went back in."

Carrie went to speak, to ask something, but Gayther waved her down with his hand. He noted the flash of irritation that crossed her face as he did so.

DI Gayther carried on speaking to Mrs Coombes and the doctor. "So, Mrs Coombes, he was alone from just before 8.30pm until … Sally went in at 9.55pm. She discovered his empty bed. The window was now open. It wasn't when they left him. She looked out and saw his body on the path below." Gayther noted the lack of emotion in the woman opposite him but thought that she must see death time and again in her job, most weeks probably, and become hardened to it. As he knew he was. Or, as he should put it, "toughened", not "hardened".

"Yes, that's all correct," she replied. "Sally set off the alarm and ran down the corridor towards the stairs leading to … just over there." She pointed to the staircase at the far right of the reception area. "Jen and I were here. I went through those doors there, to the ground-floor rooms, with Sally, to fetch Doctor Khan, who was here attending to a patient."

"That's unusual, isn't it, Doctor Khan?" asked Carrie. "Attending to a patient at that time of night?"

The doctor spread his arms wide and smiled warmly, "It's all part of the service." Gayther thought, but did not ask, that he must be private, not NHS, and on a hefty out-of-hours call-out fee.

DI Gayther turned to the doctor and asked, "So, please tell me what happened from this point."

Dr Khan cleared his throat and leaned slightly towards Gayther. "I believed, from the tone of the care assistant's voice, that this was an urgent matter and so I came out of the patient's room, turned left and made my way down the corridor towards the care assistant and Mrs Coombes."

He looked from one to the other to check that all were paying close attention. Gayther thought that he was little more than a puffed-up buffoon. Sitting there in his peacock finery.

"There was a moment or two's confusion due to the assistant's incoherency. I surmised quickly that the Reverend Lodge had fallen from his window and I led the way through reception and along and out to the path by the back garden. Sadly ..." the doctor dropped his voice in a professionally sympathetic manner, "... he had passed away."

"Cause of death?" asked Carrie.

The doctor smiled at her, and Gayther and Carrie exchanged a glance, both thinking much the same thing at the same time: "patronising bastard".

"The open window ... the nine-metre fall ... the concrete path ... an octogenarian skull ... osteoporosis in the bones ... need I go on?" Dr Khan smiled at them and then added, "Let me put it simply." He paused for effect. "He fell and fractured his skull ... severe intracranial hemorrhage ... death would have been rapid, if not instant ... to a layman. He would have been unconscious on impact."

"Time of death then?" said Carrie sharply.

"Ah, now that is interesting," The doctor replied. "He was alone from 8.30pm until he was found at 10.00pm. From my professional assessment, I would put the time of death at closer to 8.30pm than to 10.00pm. Rigor mortis. What surprises me is ... let us say this happened, for argument's sake, before 9.00pm, why, when he was in full view of anyone looking out of the window, walking in the garden, did no one see him for a full hour?"

"Mrs Coombes?" Carrie turned her attention towards the care home manager.

"Well," she replied, "your colleagues spoke to everyone here and I believe that we were all busy at that time, seeing visitors out, putting the patients to bed, sorting their medication … no one has time to stand around, especially at that time of night. I myself was back and forward from reception to the rooms … a hundred and one things to do as usual. Anyone on the top floor who looked out would have had to have looked straight down rather than outwards to see … him. Those patients on the ground floor tend to need the most care. It was just a very busy time."

"Did anyone hear anything?" Carrie persisted. "The neighbouring rooms? The ones below and to either side? Anything out of the ordinary, anything unexpected? Surely, he must have cried out … or there would have been the sound of impact."

Mrs Coombes shook her head. "The room to the left was empty, has been since Mrs Vincent passed away the month before. The other side had, still has, a Mr Simkins in it. He's a rather lively chap, still quite mobile, wandering hands, even at his age, seventy-eight, but he is deaf as a post. He didn't get along with the reverend, called him the Reverend Todge."

DI Gayther and Carrie exchanged glances again.

"Below, the three rooms, directly and to the left and right, have three dementia patients: Miss Bright, Mrs Howes and Mrs Smith. Two, Miss Bright and Mrs Smith, had music on loudly at the time and Mrs Howes had the television turned up. Two assistants, with Miss Bright and Mrs Smith, thought they heard a thump, about a quarter to nine, and both stopped for a moment to listen, in case someone had fallen from their bed and was calling out. They then carried on."

Carrie turned to the doctor, "Would you not expect a man falling out of the window to cry out as he fell ... or after he had hit the ground?"

"No, not necessarily. He would have been taken by surprise. It would have been over almost instantly. He landed on his head and would have been unconscious immediately."

Carrie pressed on, "If he fell out of the window and landed head-first ... is that not unusual, to fall head-first?"

"Again, not necessarily, he could have tripped over and his momentum and weight could have taken him to the window and out. He may have leaned out to see something that caught his eye and lost his balance. He had mobility issues. And let us not forget he suffered from dementia. You cannot apply logical reasoning to illogical behaviour."

Carrie then said, "So, everything you've seen ... An old man with dementia and who struggles to walk ... crosses to the window ... opens tight bolts and catches ... a frail man, doing all this ... and then goes head-first out ... and that's death by misadventure?"

The doctor nodded and smiled slightly. "It would seem to be the case."

"Not suicide?"

He raised his hands, palms upward, and smiled blandly as if to say, 'it could be, but an accident suits everyone better'.

"Or murder?"

The doctor laughed out loud. Mrs Coombes laughed too, although her laugh, thought Gayther, was a nervous, uncertain one. Carrie ignored the look that DI Gayther gave her as she asked again.

"Could it be murder?"

DI Gayther interrupted before the doctor could answer. "The drawing on the stomach, the criss-cross scratches ... what are your thoughts on those, Doctor Khan?"

The doctor paused and waited for a few moments before replying. DI Gayther thought he enjoyed being the centre of attention, his moment in the spotlight.

"A crudely scratched face possibly, a few lines back and forth – patients like Mr Lodge … it's not commonplace for elderly dementia patients to self-harm, but it's certainly not unique. I have seen other cases during my career."

"And the cuts, were they old or fresh?" pressed Gayther.

"Oh, fresh, there were lines of blood on his pyjama top. From just before his fall."

"Did Mr Lodge have the strength to get out of bed unaided and cross to the window?" asked Carrie.

"I believe so."

"And open it?" added Carrie.

Gayther noted how Mrs Coombes stared fixedly ahead as the doctor answered.

"It's conceivable."

"So that's that, end of," concluded Carrie, a touch of anger in her voice.

Gayther tried to catch her eye, but she avoided it.

"I'm not sure why you persist …" the doctor started to answer Carrie and then stopped before saying, in a calm and steady voice, "Everything I have seen … the coroner has seen … Mrs Coombes and her team have seen … points overwhelmingly … conclusively, I would say … to death by misadventure. If …" He added, looking straight at Carrie, "… you want me to be blunt with you, it is a simple and straightforward matter. The Reverend Lodge died from his own foolish mistake."

3. MONDAY 12 NOVEMBER, LUNCHTIME

"Here's the reverend's room," said Mrs Coombes, unlocking the door for Gayther and Carrie. "If you want to take a look, I'll go and see if I can find Sally and Jen. They're both in today."

DI Gayther nodded his thanks as she left the room.

"What do you reckon, then … Doctor Khan … Mrs Coombes?" Carrie asked.

"They toed the line, said what they were expected to say. The doctor seemed to believe it more than Mrs Coombes … maybe he's just a better actor."

"You don't think … you know, they could be right? That it's just that, a stupid mistake."

"A foolish accident? No, and even without The Scribbler's mark, I'd be hard pressed to accept suicide. No family, see, no friends, no one to fight his corner, ask awkward questions. No one bloody cares … cared … if he lived or died at all. He's old. He's gay. He doesn't matter … well, he does to me."

"The room's still empty?" queried Carrie, looking across to the windows. She noted the anger rising in Gayther's voice and thought it best to move the conversation on.

"I doubt anyone's going to want to send their loved one to a home in special measures, let alone one with patients falling out of the windows willy-nilly," answered Gayther. He scanned the room too, taking in the soft grey carpet, the lemon-coloured walls, the cheap white furniture and the hospital-looking bed. "Not a place I'd want to die. Soulless. Antiseptic."

"You'd think …" said Carrie, crossing to the window, "… in this day and age, all care homes would have locks on windows that allowed them to be opened only a fraction, not the whole way. This isn't good, is it? My friend's grandad's in one on the south coast and when we visited in the summer he was complaining about the heat because he couldn't open his windows enough to let in a breeze … guv, look at this …"

She pointed to a dark, centimetre-long mark on the inside ledge of the windowsill. "Blood? Mr Lodge's as he struggled to stop The Scribbler throwing him out?"

Gayther moved across and looked at it and shrugged, "Could be … anything really. Even if it is blood, it could be the window cleaner's from last week or the fellow who fitted the window however many years ago."

"Forensics? Is it worth asking?"

"For what? To come and check it, and the room, because an old has-been and a new DC working on a file of LGBTQ+ cold cases from ten, twenty, thirty years ago think they're on to something that no one else noticed? It would be a black mark, Carrie. We just need to keep our heads down, do this quietly. If I, we, you and I, can solve this case, well, I think you've probably heard they'd really rather have me out the door. I'm not going to give them any reason to do that. Not until I'm good and ready to go, anyway. And I'd rather go out on a high, bringing in The Scribbler."

As Carrie went to answer, the door behind them was opened and the two care assistants, Sally and Jen, stood there. Late forties, early fifties, thought Gayther. Sally, a small and petite Chinese woman, smiling and open-faced; Jen, a straggly beanpole sort of woman who would not meet his eye at first but who, as the silence lengthened into a sense of tension, spoke first.

"We have been over this with the regular police already … do we need to do it all again? We've so many things to do."

"We'll be quick," replied DI Gayther. "We just have to tick various boxes so we can say we've done what we should have done. Red tape, the curse of us all. You must have it too. Great boxloads of it, I expect?"

Sally and Jen nodded in turn, both half-smiling at Gayther.

"We've established that Mr Lodge had been declining physically and mentally since he'd been here. He took a turn for the worse, at the fete, just before his death. He said he'd seen someone who he called The Scribbler ...?"

Sally and Jen looked briefly at each other. They, thought Gayther, have discussed this and prepared what they are going to say. Sally spoke first.

"He was very quiet, withdrawn and subdued, after the fete, where he'd had a little accident. He said he felt ashamed, although we're used to it here. Many of them have dementia, most of them downstairs are quite advanced, so it's an everyday thing for us. Every hour sometimes."

"Yes," added Jen. "He started ... his wild talk the day after that. Muttering to himself angrily. Shouting incoherently. Now and then the fog would clear and he would whisper things to us ... about a man ... with staring eyes and velvet gloves ... who had come back to kill him ... even when he was rational it made no sense. It was like something off the telly, except he doesn't watch it."

Sally then spoke further, as if this were all rehearsed carefully, thought Gayther. "I remember the day he died, I was tidying his bed-side cabinet and he sat up suddenly, grabbed my arm and squeezed it really hard – so hard it left a bruise. Jen, he said, he always got our names the wrong way round, The Scribbler knows I am here ... he is going to come and kill me ... you must call the police."

"And did you?" asked Carrie.

"Do not go gentle into that good night ..." Sally replied and then added, "Old age should burn and rave at close of day ... Rage, rage against the dying of the light ... they often get like that, angry and frightened, as they realise they are ... at the end of their days.

Paranoid too. Some don't let go easily."

Jen spoke next, "I did Google this Scribbler and there were a few things on there about him, a sort of Jack the Ripper figure from Norfolk years and years ago. It seemed so extraordinary and I couldn't work out the connection with the Reverend Lodge. I wondered, myself, if this Ripper character had confessed his crimes to Mr Lodge and it all eventually came back and haunted him. Perhaps he felt guilty he didn't go to the police at the time?"

"Did he say who The Scribbler was? Someone on the staff here? Someone who had been at the fete?"

Sally interrupted, "I asked the reverend how he knew this Ripper … Scribbler … and he just turned his head away and wouldn't speak. It was like talking to a child. He'd either be shouting at you to call the police – 'Danger! Help! Murder!' – or, when you tried to have a proper talk to him about it, he just clammed up."

"I think we decided," she looked at her colleague and waited for her nodded agreement, "well, we don't know how he came to hear about it, maybe he read something in a newspaper when he was lucid and it stuck in his mind and he started imagining things. They often do."

"Tell me, about the residents, physically, mentally?" Carrie asked. "Did Mr Lodge mix much with them … Did they visit each other's rooms?"

Jen sat on the bed and answered. "No, not that we know of. There are usually about twenty residents, over the two floors. We tend to have those with dementia issues on the ground floor, those with mainly just physical needs … I say 'just' … on the top floor. There are stairs at either end, gates too, of course, and a lift at the far end. Mr Lodge would have been moved to the ground floor soon, once a room became available … because he was worsening so much."

"Did any of the residents fall out … ah, have an argument … with Mr Lodge those last few days?" Carrie queried. "Or visit him unexpectedly … anything out of the ordinary … that might have upset him, disturbed him in some way?"

Sally, sitting down on the bed next to Jen, took over. "No. Generally, they keep themselves to themselves and the ones on the ground floor are not really with us. Their minds are elsewhere. The Reverend Lodge did not mix really, except, well, residents come into the main lounge from time to time when we have an event; a lady brings in her golden retrievers and we have two young girls, Sophie and Frances, who come in to play the piano … and sing and dance to old-time songs … and a chap who does magic tricks and doubles up as Father Christmas in December."

Gayther, standing quietly by the window, listening to them talk, suddenly cleared his throat and spoke.

"Have there been any new members of staff, around the time that Mr Lodge took fright … or anyone who came in, with their dogs or magic tricks, or any unexpected visitors who stood out that you noticed? Men, rather than women, older men, my sort of age … who might have known the reverend before he came here."

Sally and Jen looked to each other. "You first," said one. "No, after you," replied the other. Sally spoke. "Not really," she said, "no new patients, anyway. We've two new care assistants come in, young girls, to replace the girls who were leaving, Karen and Sue. I've not met them yet. Not to talk to properly anyway."

"There is a new handyman, Alan," added Jen. "He joined a week or two before the fete because I remember him putting out tables and chairs and wondering who he was."

"Would he have mixed with Reverend Lodge?" Carrie asked.

Sally shrugged. "It's possible, they would have both been at the fete. And he … Alan … is here and there, doing bits and pieces as needed. Mostly weeding. Planting bulbs for the spring, things like that. So, yes, I think their paths may have crossed, possibly. I couldn't say for sure, though. I doubt they would have spoken, what with one thing and another."

Jen interrupted. "He's not English. Eastern European, I think, and he doesn't really talk. He says 'Good Morning' if you speak to him and it's a very thick accent. I mean, very heavy. He only does a few days a week. I don't see him every day. He's not on the staff, I don't think. He'd have been checked, though, DBS and all of that, so he'll have passed various checks."

"And there was that man who came and sang songs. From the 1960s," Sally said. "On that Sunday teatime. Mr Lodge was at that because I remember him trying to sing along with some of the songs. The singer, I forget the name, got them all clapping. I hadn't seen him before. He's not a regular. He did one or two Elvis Presley songs and did an impression and jiggled about a bit ... a few of the old folks seemed to remember him, Elvis, and laughed."

"How old was the singer, young, old?" Carrie pressed.

Sally and Jen looked at each other. "Fifty?" said one. "Sixty?" said the other. They both smiled.

"He was in his fifties, maybe?" Jen said, glancing towards Gayther, who gazed back at her with a blank expression. "But he dressed quite young, in denims."

"And this was the day before or the day after the fete?" quizzed Carrie.

"The day after," both Sally and Jen said.

"You haven't told anyone this before?" asked Gayther.

"Well, no," replied Jen. "No one asked."

"Oh, and there was that visitor who came to see Mrs Smith. Do you remember, Jen? Perhaps we should have mentioned him to someone before," Sally said. "That would have been the day after the fete, her nephew, was it? He came to see her out of the blue. It was so sad. She had no idea who he was. I'm not sure he knew her very well either as he went into Miss Bright's room first and was talking to her by mistake. He hadn't seen her for years."

"That's right," replied Jen. "I'd forgotten him. Karen had taken him in and thought it was very funny. She said he then started to ask if there was a vicar in the home who could say a prayer. Karen said there was one in the room above but that he couldn't be disturbed as he'd be taking a nap at the time. He then left and said he'd come back. I don't know that he did, though. Karen left a week or two after, so we can't ask her for you."

There was a moment's silence and then, as Carrie, Sally and Jen all turned towards DI Gayther, expecting him to speak, to ask more questions, the door was opened again and Mrs Coombes was standing there. "All done?" she said. It was more of a statement of fact than a question. She stood in silence as Gayther thought and then slowly nodded his agreement, farewells were said, and Sally and Jen slipped away.

* * *

"All good?" said Mrs Coombes once Sally and Jen had left the room. "Are we finished now?" She smiled, her words sounding more like an instruction than a question.

Gayther nodded again and moved, with Carrie close behind, to the door and out. The three of them walked alongside each other towards the stairs at the far end of the corridor, taking them to the reception where they had entered the building.

As they were about halfway along, an elderly woman, in her late eighties or so, and using a frame, came out of her room, accompanied by a young, dark-haired female care assistant. The old woman stopped and peered at Mrs Coombes.

"Is my daughter dead?" she asked, her voice raised and cracking with emotion.

Mrs Coombes slowed in front of the old woman and then turned towards her. Gayther wondered, from her manner, whether she would have just brushed by and ignored the woman had they not been there.

"Jean says my daughter is dead. Is that true?" The elderly woman was close to sobbing out the words.

Mr Coombes looked at the care assistant. "Jean?" she asked.

The young care assistant shook her head, as if to dismiss the matter, then said quietly, "Miss Baker, Dot's friend, can be …" her voice dropped and she mouthed the last word "… mean."

"Who is your daughter?" asked Mrs Coombes. "What is her name? I will check for you."

The elderly woman stopped and Gayther could see she was thinking, searching for a name or even a word or a phrase, something to say back. Mrs Coombes stood there, waiting, and Gayther could sense the impatience in this dismissive woman.

The elderly woman spoke again at last, bewildered now, uncertain. "I … I don't know …" She thought for a while longer and Gayther could see Mrs Coombes' patience running out. "Is my daughter dead?"

Mrs Coombes smiled tightly and answered her, "I'll go and find out for you and let you know. Don't worry. I'm sure all is well."

As the three of them reached the doors to the stairs, Mrs Coombes pressed 6 9 2 1 on a keypad to let them through and then turned and said, "It's sad, isn't it, that they come to this?"

"Is her daughter dead?" asked Carrie.

Mrs Coombes laughed drily. "I doubt it … I'm not sure she even has a daughter. It's something of a madhouse in here. An Alice in Wonderland world. We have an old headmistress who goes round opening and shutting windows for no apparent reason. Another old lady, strong as an ox, lets off fire extinguishers. Another who heads for the fire escape every chance she gets. That old woman … she'll have forgotten all about it in five minutes, they always do."

"Mrs Coombes," asked Gayther as they walked down the stairs, "before we go, I have a couple of things I want to follow up."

Gayther saw the flash of annoyance, anger even, in Mrs Coombes' eyes as she turned and looked at him. He pressed on.

"I'd like to have some details, a phone number, an address, for the care assistant called Karen who's just left? … and details of the man who came in and did a sing-a-long on the Sunday after the fete … and I'd like to see the DBS of your gard—"

Mrs Coombes looked at him with barely disguised anger. "Yes, we can do all that, that's all in the office, but I don't see why. I thought you were good and done? So you said. Obviously not."

"And I'd like to have a word with Alan, your gardener. Just a quick word if you—"

"Aland, his name is Aland with a d, not Alan," she replied. "Although goodness knows what he has to do with anything. I have his papers in the office."

She stopped as they entered the reception area and, with Gayther and Carrie behind her, she pointed towards the window that looked into the garden.

"That's him there, Aland, the man doing the weeding. If one of you wants to go and speak to him, I'll go to the office and we can also photocopy those details for Karen Williams and the singer who came in. Mr Elsworthy. Hopefully, we can then all get on with what we're supposed to be doing. Our jobs. What we're actually paid for."

As she pointed, the man, the same man Gayther had seen gardening when they arrived, looked up. He glanced slowly and casually from Mrs Coombes to Gayther and on to Carrie. Then looked down, still crouched on his haunches, and continued weeding. Gayther sensed that the man was half-watching them from the corner of his eye.

"You go and get those details, Carrie. I'll go and talk to the gardener … which is the quickest way to get into the garden?"

Mrs Coombes sighed, as if this was all too much trouble for her. She pointed to the doors to the left of reception. "Go through there," she said, "you don't need … go to the far end of the corridor and, just before you get to the kitchen, turn right into the residents' lounge, straight through the doors into the garden and double back up to him."

"Is there another way?" Gayther pressed.

Carrie looked at him, thinking that he maybe wanted her to go one way, him the other.

"No," Mrs Coombes answered. "He's in the corner. There's a window there, but no door," she added, a note of incredulity in her rising voice. "He's not going anywhere. He's weeding a flowerbed."

Gayther nodded and stood there quietly, watching the man. He carried on digging slowly, as if he knew he was being observed.

"Oh, for goodness sake," said Mrs Coombes, "we've all got work to do." She turned and walked briskly towards the office. "Come with me," she snapped at Carrie.

As Carrie followed her, Gayther just watched the man weeding. He was too precise, too mannered in what he was doing, thought Gayther. It just didn't seem natural.

Look up, you bastard, thought Gayther.

Go on, look at me. Give yourself away.

But the man continued weeding, slowly and methodically, as if he were unaware that Gayther was standing there.

Gayther turned, moving towards the doors to the left of

reception. As he put his hand to the door, he looked back through the window, expecting the man to be up and running. The man was still there, but standing now, his back to Gayther.

Turn round and look at me, thought Gayther.

Check I'm coming for you. Then run and give the game away. Show me you're The Scribbler.

Gayther pushed through the doors, striding into the corridor. He saw the kitchen at the far end. To the right, just before it, doors into the residents' lounge.

Ten, nine, eight strides away.

Had to stop himself breaking into a run.

Seven, six, five. Almost there.

An old lady came through the doors of the residents' lounge. She walked unaided but was painfully slow.

She stopped in the middle of the doorway.

Gayther tried to pass on one side, then the other.

Stood in frustration and smiled at her.

"I'm not supposed to be here, you know," she said, looking up at him.

"Can I just …"

"My son knows I am here and he is coming to get me," she said firmly, and then added, "I have to meet him outside. Can you take me, please?"

"Wait here, my love," he said, guiding her slowly by the arm into the corridor so that he could slip through the doorway. "Someone will come and help you in a minute."

She turned to say something back, but Gayther was already moving quickly through the residents' lounge. Four or five semi-conscious old ladies sat in a half-circle of armchairs in front of a quiz programme on the television. The care assistant there, a young girl of seventeen or eighteen, looked up and smiled vaguely at him as he rushed by.

He reached the doors to the garden, turned to the right and saw the gardener was no longer at the far end of the garden. His tools and equipment had gone too.

"Have you seen Aland?" Gayther said to the young care assistant as he turned around. "The gardener, Aland, he must have passed by these doors a moment ago."

The care assistant smiled back and answered in fractured English, "I not know."

"Oh for God's …" Gayther turned and ran back outside. The garden was a long thin rectangle. The gardener could only have gone one of two ways. To the left, by the residents' lounge, out and around into the staff car park. Or he could have gone through the window in the corner, into the main part of the building where the residents' bedrooms were spread over two floors. Either way, he must have been fast, moving the moment Gayther was gone from sight.

Gayther thought for a second; he had only one chance.

Guessed the gardener would not have gone to the car park, as he'd risk coming face-to-face with Gayther by the doors to the residents' lounge.

Through the window, then, somewhere inside the main building now, maybe hiding out in an empty bedroom until Gayther had gone.

Gayther ran back down towards the window, tugged it open wider, and pulled himself through into the corridor where most of the dementia patients had their bedrooms. He stumbled and fell and, as he got to his feet, he noted soil on the floor and guessed it must have come from the gardener – a minute or two ago. That was the giveaway – why would an innocent man scramble through a window to run away?

Somewhere, on these two floors of bedrooms, The Scribbler was hiding.

Gayther knew he had to be quick, act fast, before he got away.

There was no time to go and get Carrie. He had to do this himself, find this man and bring him in. They'd not be able to put him out to pasture then.

* * *

Gayther stood in the corridor, on the ground floor of the main building. Breathing heavily, he knew he would struggle to apprehend The Scribbler. He was too old, too out of condition. And the medication he was on didn't help.

But he had to try. He wouldn't be intimidated. He'd fight if he had to. He'd had his fair share of violent encounters over the years and had won most of them.

This was his chance. To make the capture, show that he wasn't the has-been everyone believed he was.

Behind him were the doors, identical to the ones he'd come through with Carrie and Mrs Coombes on the floor above. He pushed at the doors with his hands, but they were locked and needed a key card to get through rather than the 6921 code used upstairs. He thought it unlikely a gardener would have a key card to enable him to escape that way.

At the far end of the corridor was another pair of doors, again needing a key card to open them. Beyond the doors, Gayther imagined there was the lift and the gated staircase to the upper floor. Again, the gardener would not have a key card to escape that way.

So, he must be on this floor then. The Scribbler. Hiding, skulking in the corner of an old woman's room. Like a bloody coward.

Gayther wished he had his mobile phone on him, had not left it in the side of the car with the file of notes, so he could call Carrie for back-up.

He looked along at twelve or so closed doors. Each, he assumed, had an elderly resident suffering from dementia in it. And one, he was sure, also had The Scribbler inside. So be it. He was ready to take him on.

He moved to the first door, paused, checking the carpet for any tell-tale signs of soil or grass. Nothing. He put his ear to the door. All silent. He hesitated for a moment. An empty room maybe. Or The Scribbler inside ready to attack?

Gayther pushed the door open ever-so-slowly, pushing it right back so he could see across the whole room. And to be certain The Scribbler wasn't hiding behind the door, knife in hand.

He looked in. An old woman, at least he thought it was a woman, lay propped up in the bed in front of him. Her head was little more than a skull. Wisps of white hair covered some of the pink-white scalp. Eyes stared vacantly into space. The jaw hung open. She, he – whatever – had no teeth, just a desiccated, lifeless tongue lolling there. The stuff of nightmares, thought Gayther, that we might all come to this at the end.

He watched as, hearing the door open, the woman tilted her head, slowly, almost painfully, to the side, listening. Her hands, clasped together in front of her on the bed, moved slightly. Signs of life, of a sort. He saw her mouth move, trying to form words, a sound, anything.

He looked around. A wardrobe, too small for a grown man to hide in. The bed, too low for anyone to slide beneath. Windows, with curtains pulled to, hanging lower than the windowsill but not as far as the floor. No one there.

He stepped back, pulled the door closed behind him.

Moved into the corridor.

Open each door, one by one, that's all he had to do, until he found the room with The Scribbler in it.

Gayther moved to the next door. He checked the floor outside for fresh grass or mud stains. Nothing. Leaned in, his right ear close to the door, his hand upon it. Heard voices, two women's, one raised, the other calm and measured.

"Bitch," said the woman with the raised voice. "The bitch comes in my room."

"I'm sure she doesn't, Moira," replied the woman with the calm voice. "Debbie doesn't work here any more."

Gayther heard a buzzing, angry noise coming, he thought, from the woman with the raised voice. It grew into a roar and then the woman shouted at the top of her voice. "She comes into my room … when I am asleep … and she moves my things around."

He moved to the next door. The third of twelve. Could be this one. The odds were shortening. He felt his body tense.

Put his ear to it again. Silence.

This is it, he thought. The moment of truth. In here. The Scribbler. With a knife. I have to be bold and attack. Hard and fast.

As he stood there, hesitating, he heard a door opening, four or five away, further along the corridor. He turned, not sure what to expect. A young care assistant: a big, Eastern European-looking boy of twenty to twenty-five stood there, staring back at him.

"Can I help you?" the boy asked, his voice rising, "Who are you visiting, please?"

Gayther put a finger to his lips and made a hushing sound before pointing to the door.

"What? … What?" the boy said, taking a step towards Gayther. "Wait a minute … who are you? … How did you get in?"

Gayther turned and pushed the door of the room open. Stepped inside quickly, ready to attack.

He saw the room was empty, other than a bed, two piles of folded-up clothing and belongings, and a wardrobe. Again, too small to hide anyone.

As he turned back, he heard an alarm going off in the corridor, the sound of doors opening, people running.

The boy stood there blocking the doorway as other care assistants came up behind him.

Gayther breathed heavily, "I'm a police officer, doing my job. I'm looking for Aland, the gardener. I just need to have a word," he added wearily.

The boy did not seem to know what to say. He looked at Gayther, down at the floor, and then at the care assistants gathering around him before he finally spoke. "You shouldn't be here. These are our residents' rooms. You're not supposed to be here."

"I know," Gayther replied slowly. "Yes, I know." He edged towards the boy and the care assistants, realising that he needed to get by them to search the other rooms. The boy shifted slightly to fill the doorway. The alarm kept ringing and Gayther wished someone would switch it off. "But I need to speak to Aland. Have you seen him … any of you?"

He looked at the group of care assistants, waiting for one of them, some of them, any of them to say something. An older woman with a 'Tracey' name badge put her hand up, was about to say something. But then the doors at the end of the corridor opened and they all turned in unison to look towards them. They stepped back from the door and Gayther took the opportunity to step forward and through.

"Detective Gayther?" Mrs Coombes walked briskly towards him, with Carrie a step or two behind. "What is going on here?"

He noticed the look of suppressed laughter on Carrie's face. Really, it was too much.

She treated him as if he were simple.

"I wanted to speak to the gardener, Aland. He ran away from me. Climbed through the window where he was weeding into this corridor. He's hiding in one of these rooms."

She looked at him with something close to open-mouthed disbelief.

Gayther realised suddenly how foolish this must appear, feeling somehow that he needed to explain himself further in some way but without revealing too much.

He ignored the expression on Carrie's face as he spoke.

"We're looking for a man who matches Aland's description very closely … for crimes … serious crimes … going back a while."

Mrs Coombes laughed in his face, an embarrassing, scornful noise. "He's only been in the country for four months. For goodness sake. He's on a VPRS … vulnerable persons resettlement scheme – displaced by the Syrian conflict."

"Ah," said Gayther, nodding, as if fully understanding what Mrs Coombes was saying to him.

"I'm not at liberty to discuss his case with you … but he's here perfectly legally and he has all his papers. He's a refugee, not an asylum seeker. I had them in the office for you … we were taking copies if you remember … your colleague left them there when we heard the alarm."

"Yes," Gayther replied, "Carrie will pick them up on the way out … now that we're leaving." He started to move away towards the doors, hoping Mrs Coombes and Carrie would follow. They did and Mrs Coombes continued talking.

"You're clearly from the police … your whole manner. The way you dress. I imagine Aland saw you coming towards him … assumed you were the secret police … an immigration officer … or some such. He took fright and ran. And who could blame him?

Look at yourself," she added witheringly.

He looked instead at Carrie.

She looked him up and down.

Clearly thinking this was hilarious.

As they got to the door and Mrs Coombes reached for the key card in her pocket, Gayther saw her turn and look back along the corridor. He followed her gaze, past the care assistants going back into different rooms and saw Aland, standing at the far end, by the final door.

"I need to speak to Aland … reassure him … if you'll pick up the copies from the office and then see yourself out …?" said Mrs Coombes, turning off the alarm before opening the door for them and showing Gayther and Carrie through. "Oh, and one more thing, if I see you here again, I shall complain to your Chief Constable, for harassment."

Gayther nodded as she moved away, back down the corridor.

He turned to Carrie, "Don't say anything, Georgina, just don't. I'm really … not in the mood."

They walked in silence side by side, across the reception area towards the office.

"By the way, guv. It's not."

"Not what?

"Not Georgina."

Carrie led the way into the office, smiling at the assistant sitting in the corner, and picking up a sheaf of photocopied papers.

"Georgie?"

"Friends and family, guv."

"George, then? I've heard you called that."

Carrie shook her head as they headed for the way out.

He looked at her with a long-suffering expression on his face. "Georgina … Georgie … George … I've called you all of those on and off for the past eighteen months. And you're none of them? So, what are you then ...?"

She laughed. "You're the detective, guvnor, see if you can find out ..."

                                    * * *

"So, how would you rate that then, guv ... on a scale ... from a result to a complete balls-up?" said Carrie as DI Gayther drove the car around in the car park and headed for the exit.

He ignored her, pointing to the glove compartment by her knees. "Pass me the bag of mints in there please, Carrie ... or at least one of them anyway."

"Sugar-free?" she said, taking them out. "On a diet, are we?"

He took a mint from the bag and gestured for her to take one too. "Diabetes, Carrie. It's caught up with me. My GP says I'm in the shallow waters, whatever that's supposed to mean. I thought you either were or you weren't. The cigarettes have gone. The alcohol too ... I lived off those for years. And now I have to get rid of all the sugar I can. There's not much pleasure left, I can tell you."

She nodded and they drove along quietly for a few minutes, sucking mints and reflecting on the visit. She then reached for the file between the seats and started flicking through papers, as if searching for something. DI Gayther drove the car in silence along the twisting road that led back up to the A12, and down south to the police station. As they approached the A12, Gayther spoke.

"There are three options, Carrie, so far as I can see. Play devil's advocate with me. One, Lodge simply decided, whether in the fog of his mind or a moment of clarity, that he was going to take his own life for whatever reason and going through the window was the quickest, and possibly the only, way to do that."

"Okay," Carrie replied, "so, um, I've lots of questions about that.

On the one hand, he seemed happy, up until a day or two before. There's no reason to suggest he would do that. He is … was … a religious man, so suicide would be against his principles, surely? On the other hand, everything – the undisturbed room, no sign of a struggle – suggests he went out of the window without a fight. If he believed he saw The Scribbler, whether he did or not, that could be enough to frighten him. And he was suffering from dementia, so we have no idea what was going on in his mind at the time. Could be anything."

DI Gayther nodded. He looked across at her as he turned the car to the left and on to the A12. "Okay, so the second option is the one that the care home, the doctor and the coroner and everyone else seems to accept … to want to be true. The one that's most convenient and tidy and easiest to sweep away under the carpet. He got up, decided he needed some fresh air, went over to the window, opened it and, oops, somehow managed to fall out. How likely is that?"

Carrie thought for a minute and then replied, "The thing is, we need to bear in mind that he was, as Mrs Coombes put it when we arrived, 'befuddled'. So, a rational person is not going to go up to the window and fall out. Mr Lodge, it says in the file here, is, was, 1.80 metres. A fair bit taller than me but even so …"

He nodded, "And …?"

She paused, thinking, and carried on. "When you were talking to the assistants, I stood with my back to the window and I would have had to lift myself up with my hands to get my bum onto the ledge, let alone over the edge. You could not, accidentally, go out head-first. But if he sat on the ledge, I don't know why, he would then fall backwards, landing on his back, and possibly surviving, rather than falling slap-bang on his head. He could not have fallen accidentally. He either lifted himself or was lifted."

"They seem to be sticking to the line that he lifted himself up, as if to sit and look out ... backwards? ... and lost his balance ... anyway, option three, Carrie. He really did see The Scribbler. The Scribbler knows it and came and silenced him as soon as he could. He visited when the home was at its busiest. Walked into the room ... opened the window. Crossed to the bed, lifted up a dozing, medicated Lodge, dragged him to the window and threw him out. Then left, as if he were a visitor who was a little slow to leave ... so, is that possible?"

Carrie shut her eyes in thought. "Yes ... let's suppose The Scribbler was at the fete ... or was the singer, maybe ... they saw and recognised each other after all these years? Is that possible? Maybe. The Scribbler ... I don't know ... would he come back? How would he know there wasn't CCTV everywhere? And the sketch and the scratches – does he hold Lodge down and keep him quiet while he cuts him with a knife ... it's possible I suppose, but it's more likely, for me anyway ... I don't buy the accident line either ... that Mr Lodge did it himself in torment and, although no one wants to say it, took his own life ... there, case closed, done and dusted."

Gayther thought before speaking. He then said, "That all makes sense, Carrie. All of it. Except for one thing ... well, two actually ..."

Carrie turned towards him, a sudden look of 'here we go again' on her face before she masked it with a smile.

"... two things that tell me it's murder and it's The Scribbler."

"Oh yes?"

"One, Lodge might have known about the cartoon likeness from the papers, whatever, but he would not have known about the criss-cross scratching out. It's far too much of a coincidence that he'd self-inflict the exact same wounds as The Scribbler. Millions and millions to one chance, that."

"Okay, and the other thing?"

"The knife, Carrie, the knife." Gayther laughed loudly. "If he'd done it to himself and then killed himself, where the bloody hell is the knife?"

4. MONDAY 12 NOVEMBER, AFTERNOON

Gayther sat in his Silver Ford Focus in a layby on the A12, undid his seat belt and turned to Carrie as she climbed back into the passenger seat.

"So…" she said, "I was wondering—"

"Chips first," he interrupted, before she could go on. "I'm starving."

She passed him his wrapped chips before sitting back and opening her own.

"That's good," she murmured. "You can't beat cheesy chips."

He looked at her, went to say something and then thought better of it; instead he pushed three fat chips into his mouth all in one go.

"Tartare sauce," he said after a few minutes.

"What?"

"Tartare sauce … it's what we used to have with chips when I was young."

"What was that like then?"

Gayther laughed. "Horrible, actually. I can't believe you've not had it, let alone not know what it is." He looked at her but wasn't sure whether she was winding him up or not. "It sort of looked like mayo with bits in it … green bits I think … it tasted of … I don't know …"

"Snot?"

"Um well, I was going to say fish and vinegar actually."

"I'll stick to cheesy chips … or curry sauce … or ketchup … I love a bit of ketchup, me – if it's proper ketchup … Heinz."

They sat there, comfortable together, eating the rest of their chips.

As they finished, and both screwed up their wrappers, Gayther sighed happily and passed his wrapper to Carrie.

"Tuck it down the side, Carrie, I'll empty the car later. Did you get some water?"

She passed him one of the two bottles of water she had bought with the chips. Then waited as he took one, two and then three swigs of it.

"So …" said Carrie.

"So … oo …" echoed Gayther, mimicking her Suffolk accent.

"So, what next, what are we going to do this afternoon? Write up our notes, add them to the file?" asked Carrie, ignoring his impression.

"Okay, I want to spend some time on this case … the victim's own words … the criss-cross scratches … the absence of a knife … it's, well, let's assume it's murder and see where it takes us. It would be good to crack this, for a number of reasons."

"What have we got so far then, guvnor? That's useful."

"Well, we have our timeline. We know exactly when Lodge died and that's not something we've had with The Scribbler so far – rotted bodies, much later, for the most part. And where and how he died. So, when we have a suspect, we can narrow things down pretty quickly if he doesn't have a solid alibi. DNA, of course. Is there CCTV footage from a camera where he stopped for petrol before or after the murder? Is there speed camera footage? Is there anything from the care home in his car? On the tyres? In the foot-well? Remember Locard's Principle, every contact leaves a trace."

"Okay, yes, and …?"

"We need to follow all the leads we have. We'll sort those this afternoon. You never know where they will take us. We know – we assume – that Lodge saw The Scribbler, possibly at the fete, and that he came back to silence him, to kill him. If we have a suspect, and can get a photo, it's possible Mrs Coombes or Sally or Jen might look at it and say, 'Ah yes, that's the fellow who came in first, last or whenever that night. Asked directions, whatever.'"

"But Mr Coombes said …" Carrie queried.

"Don't worry about that for now," Gayther waved his hand in the air as if to say, 'no matter'.

He went on, "We need to speak to this Karen, to talk about that visitor for … Miss Bright was it? Smith? … that's a big flag to me … and this Elvis look-a-like singer; he's less likely, someone would have recognised and remembered Elvis if he had turned up out of the blue swivelling his hips and thrusting his crotch in their faces … but I guess you never know."

He then said, "And we have two other would-be victims who got away from before. Let's track them down and have a word, see if we can turn up something new. And there are other leads from the original killings. The three suspects … where were they the night of this killing? We need to follow everything up, find the red herrings and the clues and decide which is which."

"So," asked Carrie, "what now?"

"For you? When we get back, I want you to find a quiet corner somewhere and start going over everything that's in the files on The Scribbler, the notes, the witness statements, photos, everything. Just read it all through, nice and slowly, take it home if need be. See if you can find me the needle in the haystack … it's there somewhere. You just have to spot it. There's always a needle."

Gayther paused and then added, "My first case, years ago, when I was starting out like you, was a little boy … Christopher … he was eleven years old … he was killed. Strangled. We got the killer four months later, after he did the same again … another little boy, Alex, twelve. Thing is, when we went back through the files for the first boy, there was an interview with a neighbour who named various people she'd seen hanging about in the run-up to the murder. We interviewed them without success."

He stopped for a moment, working through his thoughts.

"She also described but could not name another person who she had seen hanging about, who wore a distinctive hat. Like a Russian hat. What with one thing and another, he was never traced and interviewed … it slipped through the net … even though he lived just three streets away … and he turned out to be the killer. It was a throwaway remark, noted down properly, but not followed up correctly … well, not at all. If we had only … the line between success and failure is …"

He shrugged and then stopped again. Carrie could see that he was moved and was struggling to find the right words. A surprisingly emotional man.

"Fact is, Carrie, we now have, for The Scribbler, all of this information, lots of it from before and a little bit now and, well, when it's murder, you can never have too much information. Not really. Thing is, we will almost certainly have the answer in there somewhere right in front of us. A clue. An overlooked lead. Once we see it for what it is, things will start to fall into place. We just haven't seen it yet."

He turned and smiled at her.

"And we have more on our side these days. The bits of evidence that we've kept all these years maybe will yield DNA that, if we can get forensics involved, might match DNA in Lodge's room that has no right to be there. And relationships change. That Burgess fellow, his wife flip-flopped ... did she cover for him because she became pregnant? Are they still married or divorced now? Will she sing the same tune these days if we go and talk to her again? My wife always said ..." Gayther's words tailed away.

"Your wife, guvnor?" Carrie asked, after a moment or two's silence.

"Annie," he sighed. "You remember her. I think you met once or twice?"

Carrie nodded, not sure what else to say.

"She worked for the taxman for much of her working life. Until, you know, things got too much. She always said that most of their most successful enquiries ... investigations, whatever, came from ex-spouses or partners dishing the dirt ... for revenge."

"Heaven has no rage like love to hatred turned," Carrie said. "Nor hell a fury like a woman scorned."

"Shakespeare?"

"William Congreve, Restoration playwright."

"Oh yes, slipped my mind. That English degree of yours ... glad to see it's come in useful for something after all."

He smiled at her and she smiled back.

"Time to go, guv?"

He nodded and then said, "We need to get moving on this as fast as we can. In fact, look, we'll go back to the station, spend the afternoon going through the papers between us. See if you can pull in one or two other new DCs who can give us an hour or two. Then we can get that big whiteboard out. Allocate tasks and start following through properly, get stuck in, in the morning."

"We've a couple of new direct-entry detectives doing their training at the moment, guv. And they'd be well-suited to this cold case. They're ... you know."

He looked at her. "Gay? Say so, Carrie; it's not like you to go all coy. And we're a modern police force these days, aren't we? We even take 2.2 university graduates with degrees in Elizabethan poetry."

"Ooh, low blow. I had glandular fever in my third year ... and I think it was a William or a Mary, not Eli—"

"What worries me, Carrie, is this," interrupted Gayther, as if struck by a sudden, urgent thought. "Is this a one-off murder to silence a witness, which is bad enough and we need to solve that anyway, or is it ... quite possibly ... the start of another killing spree? If it is, we've no time to lose."

* * *

Gayther stood at one end of the portacabin, in front of a big white-board, black marker pen in hand. He wrote 'Rev Lodge' in the middle, circled it, and then turned to Carrie, sitting at the desk at the other end of the portacabin alongside two young men, early twenties, Thomas and Cotton.

Gayther was struck by how similar they looked, dark-haired, slim ... 'nerdy', although he wasn't sure that was a word used so much these days and knew he probably wasn't supposed to think it, let alone say it out loud. Someone, somewhere, would be offended. Or be offended for someone else who they thought should be offended.

"Direct-entry detectives, great things expected of them, guvnor," Carrie had said to him, as they were waiting for the two young men to arrive. "I've known them both a while, they're good lads. I gave them a quick summary along with copies of the papers and they've had a look over them, too. They're sharp, up to speed already."

"They're all direct-entry these days, Carrie. No police experience whatsoever and, zoom, straight into being a detective. Took me bloody years. You were three or four years in uniform, weren't you? They don't even need that any more … just whizz straight in on the back of a cycling proficiency certificate. There's no substitute for experience in my opinion."

"A cycling what, guv?"

"It doesn't matter, Carrie," he said, shaking his head as the two young men came through the door. They both look about twelve, he thought, and so white and pasty that they must spend hours playing computer games in their bedrooms with the curtains drawn.

He half expected them to offer their hands to high-five, but they both shook his hand in turn, respectfully enough, and took their seats at the desk before turning towards him. Gayther thought they looked like eager children ready to take part in a spelling test. He resisted the urge to spell the letters 'C U P B O A R D' out loud very slowly. Instead, after smiling to himself, he turned back to the board.

"So, the three of you, from what you've seen, the connections to Lodge, who could have murdered him?"

"Sally and Jen," replied Carrie with a straight face.

"Are you being serious?" asked Gayther looking at her.

"Well, we're always told not to rule anyone in or out at this stage, sir. Just to list them all and then work through them one by one … in order of probability … but not discount anyone who could have done it."

"Okay … well on that basis, I imagine the window cleaner or the postman or the fellow delivering an Amazon parcel could have …" Gayther stopped himself and sighed, adding their names first together and then, after rubbing them out with the sleeve of his jacket, separately. "But do you really think that's likely? Really?"

"Well they were the last, officially, to see him alive. So that puts them in the frame, surely? Who's to say Sally didn't go back at 8.45 instead of 9.55 and tip him out the window?"

Gayther put the lid back on the black marker and looked straight at Carrie. "Why," he asked, "would she do that? What possible motive could she have?"

Carrie shrugged. "I don't know. We were always told … by instructors." She gathered her thoughts and then added, "Who knows, maybe The Scribbler was her brother … or Jen's … and one of them heard Lodge's ramblings and decided to silence him."

"Sally's Chinese, in case you hadn't noticed. That won't be her real name because her proper name would be harder to pronounce …" Gayther hesitated for a moment and then went on, "Chinese people usually choose their own names when they arrive here. So she'd have picked Sally probably because she liked the sound of it."

"Jen, then … or maybe Sally was adopted by The Scribbler's family?"

"Pushing the coincidence a bit far, Carrie."

"More than The Scribbler happening to turn up where one of his victims lived?"

"Yes, because for it – your supposition – to have been possible, The Scribbler would have had to have confided he was a serial killer to his supposed sister and – and – she would then have had to stumble across Lodge, the talkative victim. That's two big ifs. The latter's conceivable, the former isn't, not in my book."

Carrie nodded.

"But look, it does no harm … if you do some digging and, later today or tomorrow, if you want to see if you can talk to them again separately … that's fine by me. Do what you need to do to discount them. Low profile though … I don't want Mrs Coombes complaining about harassment. I'm due a meeting with the boss man – Bosman – later this week. I don't want to be hauled before him to explain myself before that."

"So, who else do we put in the magic circle?" piped up one of the young men. Gayther did not look up fast enough to see who it was. No matter, they were identical twins to him.

"Okay, Thomas, Cotton … We also have the man who visited Miss Bright and asked about the vicar. Did Carrie cover that? So, we put Karen Williams, the care assistant who dealt with him, on the board for him. Elsworthy is the singer who came in to entertain the residents. He's on the list, too."

Gayther added 'Bright?' and 'Karen Williams' and 'Elvis Elsworthy' to the board, then thought better of it, and rubbed out 'Elvis' with the corner of his sleeve. "We've got their details and I'm going to pay a visit to them, one this afternoon, one in the morning."

"And us, sir?" one of the young men asked. Gayther could not remember which was which. The one on the left. "What can we do?"

"We'll also go back to the original three suspects," said Gayther. "Challis the plumber, Halom the drag act and Burgess the sales agent. We want to know what they were doing the night of Lodge's death. You never know. See what you can find out about them first – bring me updates and addresses as soon as possible and we can take it from there. But online only at this stage. I don't want you to get ahead of yourselves, alert them to the investigation. Can you can start now?"

"We'll get straight on to it, sir," one said.

"Right away," echoed the other.

"And then," said Gayther, writing on the whiteboard, "we have 'Mr X, The Scribbler'. He may not be … Bright or Elsworthy … Challis, Halom or Burgess. He may be someone we can find in the files … or someone who's not on the radar at all."

He stopped and pointed at the two young men.

"As well as following through on the suspects, I want you to go through all of the files, see if anything catches your eye, that might have been missed. Suspects first, then files. And the two victims who got away, see what you can find on them too."

They looked at each other, ready to go.

He waved them down, just for the moment.

Then turned to Carrie.

"And you, Carrie. I want you, as well as seeing Sally and Jen … and looking at the files … to find me a list of men in their twenties who died within a month, three months, maybe six of the last murder. Why did he stop killing? They sometimes keep going until they're caught. Why did this one, with all that blood and death, suddenly stop?"

He went on, talking to Carrie still.

"And then get me a list and details of the other men who have gone missing from Norfolk and Suffolk … maybe Cambridgeshire, too … over the years. Those who have never turned up again. Maybe he hasn't stopped killing. Maybe he's been doing it for the past thirty-odd years in different places and we've just not realised it. If that's the case, God help us, we've one of the biggest serial killers of all time on our hands."

* * *

"Karen? Karen Williams?" Gayther stood in the porch of the neat, semi-detached house in a close in a nondescript housing estate in Saxmundham in Suffolk.

He'd arrived half an hour or so earlier and been told by a truculent teenage boy that she was out at work but should be back just after three-thirty. He had sat in his car at the top of the road since then, waiting for her arrival.

He had spent most of the time Googling her but could not find anything beyond an old entry for her and a David A. Williams on the 192.com site; no Twitter account, Facebook, Instagram, nothing.

And then she'd walked by him, this slight, anonymous, middle-aged woman in her beige blouse and skirt, and he watched as she went into the house. Waited five minutes, then stepped into the porch.

"Yes, yes, that's me," she answered, her hand raised to her forehead, brushing away an imaginary strand of hair. "Kai told me you wanted a word about Reverend Lodge, although I'm not sure how I can …"

She then stopped, as if something had occurred to her suddenly, and she stepped back and added, "… but, where are my manners, do come in and sit down. Can I make you a cup of tea?"

He nodded as he stepped inside the clean but tired-looking house. Not much money, he thought. Just about making ends meet. Struggling, most likely, whenever an unexpected bill came up.

He sat in the living room perched on the edge of an armchair and looked around at the age-old carpet, sofa and chairs and other furniture. There were photos of her, when she was younger and happier, with a handsome, moustached man, one with helmets and skis, smiling, another in swimming costumes on a beach and a final one, with a young boy, the now awkward teenager, all huddled around a birthday cake with an '8' on it.

"Oh," she said, coming back in with two mugs of tea and seeing Gayther looking at the photos. "That's my David. Everyone called him Dave, but he was always David to me. He passed over five and a half years ago. There's not a day goes by I don't …"

Gayther nodded as he took the mug of tea. "I lost my wife, Annie … not so long ago."

She smiled at him and did not seem to know quite what to

say other than "I'm so sorry". She then asked if he took sugar or sweetener or wanted a biscuit. Like most people, he thought, she doesn't want to hear of let alone talk about someone else's loss, only her own.

He smiled back, at this sad, crushed woman, wondering whether the husband had died unexpectedly, without life insurance. He could sense the despair.

"Well, look at me," she said, a little more brightly. "Kai told me I must ask to see your ID card or warrant or whatever it's called. Just in case. I'm sure you're not, er, you know." She flapped her hand, not quite sure what it was she wanted to say.

Gayther reached inside his jacket pocket and handed her his warrant card. She looked at him and then down at the photograph, which she studied carefully.

"It's quite old," he said. "And it's like passport and driving licence photos. You look grim, like a waxwork. At least I do. And I had more hair then. And less flesh." He felt himself gabbling to the woman and wasn't sure why.

"You're still recognisable," she said reassuringly, although, as the photo was little more than five years old, he wasn't sure that was much of a compliment.

"Thank you … I just wanted to talk a little, I won't take up too much of your time, about Reverend Lodge."

"Such a nice man," she answered quickly. "And so sad when he died. Was it …" she lowered her voice and then mouthed the word, "suicide?"

"What do you think?" asked Gayther simply.

"I don't know," she answered, looking at him. She hesitated and then went on. "I didn't really see much of him. I did for him once or twice, that's all. Sally Reece and Jennifer Coates kept him pretty much to themselves. None of the rest of us got a look in."

"Why was that then; why do you think they did that?" Gayther pressed.

She sat back, putting her mug of tea carefully on a table by her side. "I wouldn't like to say for sure but …"

Gayther waited, sensing an explanation was coming. He hoped the teenager would not come in at this moment, or put on loud, thumping music from upstairs, disturbing her thoughts as they formulated into words.

"The residents … well, most were too far gone to … but not all and sometimes they'd … well, they'd pay us for things … to get them little treats from the supermarket, things like that, nothing much, just for a pound or two extra … but every little helps as they say."

"So, these two care assistants … they kept the Reverend Lodge to themselves as he paid them for … what did he pay them for, Karen?"

Gayther looked at her, could see how uncomfortable she felt. She twisted slightly in her seat, almost squirming, uncertain what to say next.

"Nothing … like that. I don't think. I don't know for sure. There was talk that, well, Mr Simkins, one of the other residents, gave both Sally Reece and Jennifer Coates money regularly. Quite a lot of it. I know that for a fact because I heard them talking once, comparing how much he'd given them and it was, well, something like £20 each. I don't know what they did to get that from him, but it wouldn't be for buying a box of Jaffa Cakes from Tesco."

Gayther smiled at her, but then thought maybe he should have shook his head. That she was angry in some way, that she'd been cheated of extra money.

He was not sure money for sexual favours from female care assistants would lead anywhere with the Reverend Lodge, but he made a mental note to charge his phone and then text Carrie, *Sally and Jen. Favours for money with Lodge? And others? Sex?* Then he thought he'd put *Sex?!* and an emoji if he could find one with a surprised face. He knew there was one with tears on it as if crying with laughter, but didn't think that was the right one to send.

"No, quite. Is that why you left the care home, Mrs Williams?"

"Good Lord, no," she replied.

He waited for her to go on.

"Long hours. Eight to eight some days. You have to sign away your rights. It's hard work at times, lifting people, even with the equipment, and I'm not getting any younger."

She held her arms out towards Gayther. "And my wrists and legs, I have arthritis. And you get no pay if you're off sick, not until the third day when you have to go to the doctor and sign on for the state sickness pay." She shook her head in frustration.

"I've got a job in the supermarket in town. Pay's the same, well a bit less, but the hours are better. I do eight until three and then get any bits I need in town and I'm home by half-three most days."

He nodded.

She smiled at him.

Gayther then went on, "The reason I'm here is to ask you about Miss Bright's nephew. I believe he came to see her a day or two after the fete but went to the wrong room and didn't know which resident she was. That must have been funny."

"Oh, it was," she replied. "But no, he was Mrs Smith's nephew, not Miss Bright's. I came in to get Miss Bright ready for her lunch and he was just sat there in her armchair next to her ... she was on the bed ... he was, well, I don't think he was getting much sense out of her. She drifts in and out. I caught the tail-end of what he was saying, asking her if there was a vicar in the home. I think perhaps ... she was religious ... she had a cross and a bible ... and she wanted to speak to a vicar before she, well, you know."

"I'm confused," Gayther said. "This man was in Miss Bright's room. You heard him asking her if there was a vicar in the home. But … he was Mrs Smith's nephew. How do you know that?"

"Well, I said to him, 'Can I help you?' because I didn't recognise him … we have a few regulars we get to know … and he said he was just asking if there was a vicar in the home and he sort of nodded and smiled towards Miss Bright as if it had been her who had been asking him. So, I asked him who he was and he said he was John Smith, a 'long-lost' nephew, that's what he said, and I laughed and said that Mrs Smith was in the next room along and no wonder Miss Bright didn't recognise him."

"And what did he say to that?" Gayther asked.

"He smiled and said something about not having seen her – Mrs Smith – for many years. He then asked again if there was a vicar who could 'say a few words'. That's what he said, 'say a few words'. I remember that and I told him the Reverend Lodge was in the room right above."

"Did you then show him to Mrs Smith's room?" Gayther pressed.

"No, I would have done, but I was running a bit late, and Miss Bright, well, I think she needed changing. So, he showed himself out and that was the last I saw of him."

"Did you ask Mrs Smith about him later, to see if they had had a nice chat."

"I did, but she's another one who's away with the fairies much of the time. She didn't have anything to say about it. I don't think she could remember what she had for breakfast that morning. And I was in at different times and on the other floor, and then I left, so I never did find out how that went or whether the Reverend Lodge said a prayer for Mrs Smith. I don't know where he got the idea she was dying, though, as she's physically quite well for her age."

Gayther finished his cup of tea and placed it carefully on the table by his side. As he thought about his next question, she spoke.

"Why?" she asked, and then added, "perhaps I'm missing something, but why, I mean, what does John Smith have to do with the death of the Reverend Lodge. I don't understand?"

Gayther tried not to sigh, "We just have to tie up the loose ends. It's possible John Smith may have some insight into why the Reverend Lodge died. If they spent some time together."

Before she could think about that, and ask another question he might struggle to answer, he went on.

"Can you describe him for me, Mrs Williams?"

"Mr Smith? I would say he was about fifty, maybe a little older. He had on one of those dark hoodies. He was wearing a cap, a sort of baseball cap, and blue jeans. I remember thinking how he was, well, quite old really, but dressed young. What did make me smile, although it's a bit mean, is that he had these old blue canvas shoes on, with the Velcro strips across the top rather than laces. Hobos. It's what all the old boys with dementia wear. It makes it easier to get them dressed and undressed."

"Did you notice his eyes at all?"

"His eyes? No, not really. He was quite pale, though, with white stubble and, well, I wouldn't say he was, what's the word, um … albino, is it? He didn't have pink eyes or anything like that, but he was very pale, and his skin sort of looked a bit flaky. I did wonder whether he might have been ill."

"Did he wear gloves? Maybe for eczema?"

"I can't say I noticed that."

"And his height and build?"

"I, oh dear, I still think in feet and inches, I'm afraid. He was a bit taller than me, maybe five foot seven or eight. There wasn't much of him. Ten or eleven stone?"

"One last question, because we'd like to trace him, see if he can help us ... what about his voice, how would you describe that?"

"Oh ..." she said, distracted suddenly by the sound of what Gayther assumed was the teenage son running downstairs, "he was from Suffolk. He had an accent, quite nice to hear, quite old-fashioned, it was. Everyone speaks, what's it called, Estuary English these days."

Got him, thought Gayther as he nodded his thanks and rose to his feet to end the conversation and say goodbye. We can forget Sally and Jen ... and Elvis bloody Elsworthy ... and cut to the chase. This man is The Scribbler and the net starts closing on him from now.

5. MONDAY 12 NOVEMBER, 4.10PM

The man with the latex gloves stood beside a copse of trees close to run-down public toilets in Acle in Norfolk. He coughed and wiped his runny nose, which he always seemed to have at this time of year.

He had, one way or the other, spent the best part of three hours in and around the park. Here by the trees for the past ninety minutes and more. Woollen hat pulled down. Fleece collar pulled up. Pocket-sized binoculars in his hands.

Bird-watching, or so any casual passer-by who saw him would think, as he scanned the trees and sky.

He was really waiting, as he had done so many times over so many years, for what he hoped would happen next, the perfect set of circumstances that would give him the opportunity for his next kill.

He noted who had gone into the toilets and who had come out. Two teenage boys, one going in, the other waiting outside, were there for no more than two or three minutes. Two ladies going into adjoining toilets and out as fast they could; he could hear one of them commenting loudly on how dirty the toilets were from where he was. That was it, the only visitors.

And then, as dusk approached and he was close to giving up and leaving, yet another wasted visit, a man walked by him, on the path. A similar age, but shorter and slighter. Balding. Rough and ready in anorak and boots.

The balding man made eye contact, nodded and smiled briefly at him, maybe walked a little slower. A sign of interest.

Stopped again then, at the step up to the toilets, glancing round, before entering. Another tell-tale sign for sure. This would be the next, the man with the gloves decided, his thirtieth kill. Easy to overpower, this one. A manageable corpse. He reached into the left pocket of his fleece, checked the screwdriver and the Stanley knife were there.

Bin bags and black tape in his trouser pockets.

Ready to use.

If he got lucky with this one.

He savoured the moment, counting the seconds. Knew, if he had judged it correctly, that he should give the balding man in the toilet two or three minutes before following him in. He counted down from 180 in his head. Got to 120, 90, close to 60 and then, impatient, started walking across as slowly as he could. He tucked his binoculars into the right pocket of his fleece, checking around to make sure no one was in sight. All clear, and so he went into the toilets.

He paused for a moment, his eyes adjusting to the darkness. He almost recoiled from the stench, although he had known worse.

Wiped his nose with the back of his hand. He drew breath in through his mouth.

Three urinals, all filthy, overflowing. Dirt and tissues and God-knows-what beneath.

Three cubicles, two half-open, the other with its door pushed to. The balding man would be in there, shifting nervously, full of excitement.

The man hesitated. Even after all this time, he never quite knew whether to tap on the door or wait outside for a signal. He coughed, then paused, listening for a response. He could hear the man on the other side of the door, waiting for him, breathing heavily in expectation. So, he stepped forward, pushed at the door, which seemed to be sticking, pressed harder as it slipped its latch and opened fast.

The balding man sitting there, his head down.

Moving back, startled, as the door hit him; either on his head or on his knees. He wasn't sure which.

Looking up, face full of fear as he stared at the man with the latex gloves standing there in the doorway.

"What the …?" The man struggled to his feet, covering himself then pulling his underwear and trousers up and buttoning them. "How dare you …" he added angrily, stepping forward now and pushing the man with the gloves back, outside of the cubicle.

The man with the latex gloves stumbled backwards, steadied himself.

Dipped his head down, brought his gloves to his face, as if wiping his brow.

"Sorry," he said, as he turned away. "Didn't know you were in there."

He hurried out of the toilets. Across to the trees and to the path that wound its way towards the exit and his van parked in a quiet street. He cursed himself for rushing forward in his enthusiasm and desire, for not waiting for a clear sign from the man that he was interested.

He had made this mistake before.

Been chased.

And been lucky to get away.

He sat there in his van, coughing, and then slowing his breathing as best he could until it was regular. Watched in the van's wing mirror to see if the man in the toilets was coming this way. Knew that if he had judged correctly, if the man was a secret middle-aged homosexual, he might have changed his mind, come looking for a second chance.

He sighed, knowing too that he dare not wait to find out. He had spent so long checking the park, the entrances and exits, the hiding places, the absence of CCTV, the busy and the quiet areas, that he knew he was safe so long as he left now. Could not risk the man in the toilet seeing him in the van, noting the number, maybe reporting him to the police.

He started the van's engine. Wiped his nose one more time.

Looked back over his shoulder, seeing the road was clear, pulling out and away.

Thinking already of the place he would go tomorrow evening. To find his next kill.

PART TWO

THE SUSPECTS

6. TUESDAY 13 NOVEMBER, EARLY MORNING

The four of them – Gayther, Carrie, Thomas and Cotton – sat around the table in the portacabin the next morning.

Carrie pushed a cup of coffee across the table towards Gayther. He stopped rummaging through his papers and looked at it.

"What ... exactly is that, Carrie?"

"New cups from the new machine, sir. They're called ripple cups. Because of these ridges here, see. Eco-packaging, sir, environmentally friendly. Save the dolphins, sir."

Gayther grunted. "I meant the drink, Carrie, what is it, tea or coffee?"

"Hard to say for sure, sir. I pressed the button for coffee, with milk but no sugar, sir, what with you paddling in the shallows, sir."

Gayther saw Thomas and Cotton exchange puzzled glances over their coffees. "Ignore Carrie," he said, "you'll only encourage her." He smiled at them and then continued. "Look, okay, let's get ourselves up-to-date on this Scribbler case."

Gayther shuffled his notes, put them to one side and pulled the cup towards him. He looked across at Carrie as she sipped hers first. She mock-shuddered. Gayther laughed.

"Okay, as I texted you all last night," he looked at them in turn and they nodded to confirm, "I had a chat with Karen Williams, the woman at the care home who met Miss Bright's ... Mrs Smith's alleged nephew. Her description of him matches how I think The Scribbler would look now, so ... yes, Thomas?"

Thomas put his raised hand down. "Sorry, sir, but if Mrs Smith had a nephew, would her nephew be Smith as well ... if she'd married? Wouldn't they have different surnames."

"I assume The Scribbler just picked the name Smith on the basis that it, or maybe Jones ... possibly Patel these days ... was a really common surname and there was likely to be someone of that name at the home. Maybe he caught one of the foreign care assistants on the way in and talked to them about residents, who knows? Anyhow, the name Smith gave him his entry point. That then gave him his chance to ask about a vicar and where he was, which room he was in."

"But could he, this man, actually be her nephew, sir?" Thomas pressed. "Perhaps he might just be that and not be anything to do with anything else at all?"

"I suppose so, possibly," Gayther replied slowly. "If he were her husband's blood nephew and hers by marriage. Or if she had never married and the Mrs became a sort of courtesy title over the years. Carrie, make a note … that's something you can check please. I want you to go back and talk to Mrs Smith, see if you can get any sense out of her … did you get to see Sally and Jen yesterday afternoon?"

Carrie shook her head. "I got waylaid, sir. Did a bit of desk research … some background reading … then ran out of time. I had to pick Noah up from after-school club at five. Going to do it today, sir."

Gayther nodded but then added, "Just hold fire on Kings Court for now, then; let's see if we can get a decent sketch from Karen Williams first. I want to get someone round there. Then see if Mrs Smith recognises her so-called nephew … or Sally or Jen. Who knows, they may turn round and say he's the local odd-job man."

"Did anyone say he actually called himself John Smith?" Thomas persisted.

"Yes," sighed Gayther, "Karen Williams referred to him as Smith … John Smith, I think. Not a very imaginative name, that. Anyway, look, let's move on for now." With that, he stood up and moved to the whiteboard at the other end of the portacabin.

"I'm sure this man ... let's call him John Smith ... as good a made-up name as any ... is The Scribbler." He turned to the board and wrote 'John Smith' at the top, circling it two and then three times for emphasis. "In fact, let's put 'John Smith' in the middle and work outwards from there."

After rubbing out the name and writing 'John Smith' again, Gayther continued. "I'm going to have a word with Peter, the new artist, to see if I can get him over there ... to Karen Williams ... to do a sketch. That will be useful. I want to see if upstairs will let us put something out ... a press release ... if we need to ... down the line. Thomas, Cotton, how did you get on with tracing Challis, Halom and the other one ... Burgess?" Gayther wrote the three names, with question marks, in a circle around 'John Smith' on the board.

"Three suspects. Ray Challis was the first. A plumber ... frequented some of The Scribbler's pubs ... had alibis for some ... but not others ... anything on him on the PNC, the Police National Computer?" Gayther added.

Thomas shook his head. "Not for the father, no. He's a builder these days. Saxmundham-based. Works with his two sons. One of the sons, Tobias, was arrested but not convicted of a burglary last year. Interestingly, it was up Dunwich way. An ordinary house, not the vicarage. A solicitor from London applied to have his information removed from the files, DNA, fingerprints, on the grounds that there was corroborative evidence that he had a proven alibi."

Gayther grunted, "Unusual, that. I'd maybe expect a lefty-liberal type from London to want to have DNA and fingerprints removed, civil rights and all that, but a hairy-arsed builder's boy from Suffolk? That's odd. We'll follow that up."

"We were thinking of familial DNA searching, sir," Cotton said. "If the father was The Scribbler, he'd not want his son's DNA on the database in case it was a close match for any DNA found at any of The Scribbler's murder scenes."

He looked at Thomas and went on. "We did this course, see, sir, the two of us. And there was a case where … if you compare twenty DNA markers, most people, like any two random people, just by chance, would have maybe half a dozen markers in common. But close relatives can have maybe a dozen or more."

"I take your point," said Gayther and then added, "although we don't have any, do we, Carrie, on file? DNA?"

Carrie shook her head. "I'm amazed at how little we have sir, just notes … in what you gave me anyway."

"Different age, Carrie." Gayther stopped for a second and then added, "I think there are some clothes kept somewhere. From the murders. God knows where they'd be now. But there may be something. Can you …"

"Noted sir," Carried replied, writing in her notebook. "I'll get that checked today."

Gayther addressed Carrie, Thomas and Cotton together. "Unless … until … it may be until … The Scribbler strikes again and conveniently leaves his DNA somewhere for us, we'll crack this case the old-fashioned way. Plod. Plod. Plod. Check. Check. Check. And then a lucky break. But we have to work hard to create that break. Cross-referencing. Spotting something odd. Following it up. Proper policing. Like it used to be done, without technology and predictive algorithms and all of that shi … stuff."

Carrie laughed.

The other two smiled politely.

Gayther turned back to Thomas and Cotton.

"Anyway, Halom? The drag act fellow. Is he still playing at being Danny La Rue?"

Thomas and Cotton looked blankly at him.

"Oh, forget it. What have you got on him? Is he still doing his act?"

Cotton spoke this time. "He's got a record as long as your arm, sir. Handling stolen goods going way back, also credit cards in his parents' names, fraud too. All low-level, petty stuff. Most recently, past couple of years, he set up fake profiles on Facebook and sold non-existent goods. Took money from people and then tried to disappear. Not very successfully. He was sentenced to twelve months' suspended in May and a hundred hours of community service."

"So, we've got his DNA and fingerprints then, in case we need them. Do we know where he's doing his community service?"

"No, sir, not yet, but he's based up the road in Wickham Market and does a karaoke evening at a caravan park in Great Yarmouth Friday evenings. We made a call, sir, and he's on this Friday … if you want to have a word. He's up and down the A12 fairly regularly. His mother, who gave a statement about the credit cards and then withdrew it, lives in sheltered housing in Leiston. We were wondering, sir …" Cotton turned to Thomas, "… whether, given her age, she's in her eighties, Halom might have been looking at Kings Court for her, sir …"

"Yes, good work, one to follow up, too. And Burgess, what about Burgess? Looking at the case history, if I had 50p to spare, he'd be the man I'd put it on. What's on the computer?"

"Nothing on the PNC, sir," Thomas answered. "But, and this is odd, sir, certainly a coincidence anyway. He … from Google … appears to have moved from wherever he was, Sussex, to Aldeburgh in the early 1990s and became a wedding photographer for a while. Bit of a shift, but we've cross-referenced and it's definitely him."

"Go on," said Gayther.

"He then seems to have retired recently, sir, past year or two, and has vanished off the radar as far as we can see. Nothing online we can find. But his wife, Angela, appears to be still living just outside of Aldeburgh on her own."

Carrie leaned towards Gayther, pushing his cup to one side. "So, it should be easy for us to start by checking to see where Challis and Halom were on the night that Reverend Lodge died ... then get their DNA and see if we can match it with what we can find at the care home, sir."

Gayther turned back to Cotton and Thomas. "Well, one step at a time, before we think about interviewing anyone, trying to get DNA, checking cars and CCTV and so on. We can sort this quickly. Are there photos anywhere of Challis, Halom or Burgess? On social media? Facebook? A poster of Halom dancing about at the caravan park? If so, we can show them to Karen Williams and see if she recognises any of them as this John Smith character. Job done. Can't get simpler than that."

"Is that legal, sir? Doing that?" Thomas asked.

"PACE. Aren't we supposed to follow some sort of procedure on that, sir?" Cotton echoed.

Gayther sat down, tapping his fingers, thinking of the right words to put into his next sentence; a sentence that, ideally, he thought, should not include the words 'snowflakes', 'millennials', 'PC bloody crap', 'balls' or 'bollocks to all that'.

After an awkward pause, he concluded, "We're trying to catch a serial killer ... Thomas ... Cotton ... kindly go and find a computer and see if you can, somehow or other, get photos of the three of them. Print them off, just the photos, no names or identifying material, and bring them to me as soon as you've done that. Thank you ... Carrie, you wait here please, I want a word with you..."

* * *

"Kids, eh, guv?" Carrie smiled at Gayther. "Fifteen-year-olds. What can we do with them?"

"My thoughts exactly," Gayther caught Carrie's eye. "Oh, you're quoting my own words back at me … from … whenever … so many possibles … yes, very good, well done, Carrie. Very droll."

"They're good lads, guv – clever, smart, that's why they've been fast-tracked. They know how to do desk research." She paused, a worried look on her face. "What about PACE, though, guv. This is hardly by the book, is it?" She looked at Gayther, clearly not happy.

"Carrie," he said forcefully. "We have a serial killer on our hands … who may kill again at any moment. So, we can do this by the book, line by bloody line, and shuffle bits of paper … whatever, these days … around and by everyone … tick all the boxes … wait forever for the go-ahead … or until someone else is murdered. Or we can crack on, do it like we used to do in the old days. It's quick. It's effective. We'll catch him. But I'll make a note you're not happy."

She smiled at him, not sure what to say.

He smiled back, waiting for her. Another awkward moment.

And then she nodded her tense agreement.

"You know what, Carrie. This … this Scribbler business … it's an outrage. The way it was all downgraded because it was 'only' gay men being killed. The world's moved on since then, thank God, and the police have, too. But there's still that sense of LGBTQ+ people somehow not being quite as important. The world's got to change more."

He paused, before going on, his voice rising.

"There must be damned few people these days who don't have an LBGTQ+ loved one … son, daughter, brother, sister, friend, work colleague." Gayther stopped, emotional. "… Sorry … rant over … I just hate homophobia and all the harm it does. I had a brother …" Gayther stopped again, struggling for words.

"I have two great-uncles, well one is a proper uncle, the other is his … partner, really," Carrie said, simply. "They've told me what it was like when they were growing up. The discrimination. Things that were put through the letter box. Disgusting."

"My older brother, Mike, was hounded to his death because he was gay. He was in the army in the 1970s. He took his own life, eventually. But that's another story."

They looked at each other, a sense of understanding between them.

A shared anger.

The joint, unspoken commitment to bring The Scribbler to justice.

"Okay, good … look, can you text Peter, the sketch artist. See when he's free so we can get him … no, wait, let's show any pictures they get to Karen Williams first. You and I can run over there this afternoon, lunchtime maybe, catch her on her lunch break. Let's see. Meantime, in case she doesn't recognise any of them and I'm taking us all up a blind alley, what did you manage to dig up yesterday?"

Carrie sat back in her chair, stretching her shoulders. She then leaned forward and fiddled with her phone. "The number of people who go missing, guv. I've not got county figures yet, but nationally, depending on who you read, and I've got this off a missing persons website, … some 180,000 people are reported missing every year. Another 160,000 go missing without being reported, so the site says. In all, 340,000 missing incidents a year. To put that into context, and according to the last census, it's like the whole of Bradford or Cardiff just vanishing. Every year."

Gayther thought of a joke, then thought better of it and just nodded and asked, "What about the National Crime Agency and the Missing Persons Unit? Any joy?"

"Not really, guv, not when I'm not all that sure what I'm looking for. Most of the missing cases, the formal ones anyway, are usually resolved within a week. Most people turn up somewhere, alive. There's a hardcore of about 2,500 people a year who go missing and are never seen again. I don't have numbers yet, but I'd assume lots of teenagers, people struggling with their sexuality, maybe middle-aged men who have just had enough and walked away."

Gayther thought carefully and then said, "I think what I want from you, if you can do it, is a list of middle-aged men who have gone missing each year since, what 1988 to 1990, from around here and who have never been found." He looked across and saw the flash of exasperation on Carrie's face.

"But…" Carrie said and then stopped.

"Go on," Gayther encouraged her to speak further.

She took a moment to formulate her words. "I can see that … if we had a list of, let's say, I don't know, so many middle-aged men who went missing every year from 1988 and we drilled down into what we had on them … not a lot, I think, and only half of the possible total anyway … and so long ago … we may get a lead … possibly. Maybe they all drank in the same pub or borrowed a book from the same library. But The Scribbler … if it's not this Smith … may have simply stopped … or emigrated … or died. I mean, it's all so … vast and endless."

Gayther nodded, sensing she had more to say.

"I mean The Scribbler had a pattern, a clear, unmistakable pattern. He was a young man who picked up … sexually confused middle-aged men in bars. Killed them and left their bodies to rot in ditches. He then stopped … dead in his tracks as far as we can see. So, my question, the one we should be focusing on, in my opinion, is that. Why did he stop? Don't serial killers just go on and on until they're caught?"

Gayther shrugged, indicating he didn't know. Then he spoke.

"It's a myth, from what I've read, that serial killers can't stop. They can go for periods when their urges are subdued, I guess, and eventually they age and their testosterone levels subside and ooze away."

He pondered for a moment before going on.

"Who knows why The Scribbler, in his twenties, in his physical prime, stopped ... it could be for any number of reasons. I'm guessing, maybe, with the ones that got away, he got spooked and thought he might be caught next time and he didn't want to shame his dear old mum and dad. He could have died. Cancer. A car accident. He could have moved overseas. He could even have married or got into some sort of twisted relationship with a goat that satisfied his urges ... whether that would be enough on its own, I'm not sure."

"So, can we do any sort of trace on all those possibilities. From all those years ago?"

Gayther shrugged. "I don't know, Carrie. I'm just trying to spread the net far and wide, then pull it in and go through everything we've got, bit by bit." He then asked, "And the deaths, Carrie, of young men in their twenties, in the three, six, twelve months after the last murder? What did you turn up?"

Gayther saw the quickly covered look of frustration on her face again. He knew that, if he weren't her DI, she'd speak quite sharply to him at times. Instead, she spoke in a calm and measured voice.

"Again, where to start, guv? According to the local council, there were about 7,500 deaths in Suffolk last year. So, add in Norfolk and Cambridgeshire and we're looking at, assuming the same sort of numbers there, maybe 22,000 or more for the year after the last murder thirty-odd years ago. That's 400 or so deaths a week and, I'm guessing now, but if, say, perhaps 10 per cent would be younger males, we'd be looking at 2,000 deaths a year for how many years? … and it's just me … doing this … and we don't know what we're looking for, do we? Not really."

Gayther sat back in his seat, "Points taken, Carrie. If this were a major investigation and we had the resources, we could do it. The answer's out there, all the evidence we need, we just have to find it. One tiny clue. A sudden twist of luck. That's all."

Carrie answered, "If this Smith is The Scribbler, as you say he is, then we have the answer already, surely? And Karen Williams and other possible witnesses at the care home … maybe CCTV footage from roads, petrol stations … and all that happened before, the witnesses, the other victims who got away, that's the evidence and all we need to put him away … we don't need to chase ifs, buts and maybes from thirty years ago."

"You're right, Carrie," replied Gayther. He smiled at her. "As always … look, okay, let's wait and see if Thomas and Cotton turn up some photos. Meantime, go and see if you can find out where … if there are still clothes from the original killings. We need to start thinking DNA. And I'm going to go through the files for the other two victims who got away … see if they are still about. Come and find me when you've got the photos and we'll head back up to see Karen Williams. See if she can put a face to the name for us."

* * *

"Is it sunny today, guv?" Carrie asked, squinting through the car windscreen. "I'm not sure …" She took a tissue from her pocket and wiped at the grime on the inside of the window.

"Very good, Carrie," Gayther replied, accelerating the car up the A12 towards Saxmundham. "In the old days, of course, you could get a trainee to empty your car once a week … clean it … polish it even … but nowadays …" He let the sentence tail off.

"They've invented driverless cars, guv, maybe you could invent a self-cleaning car, make your fortune."

"It's a thought, Carrie. It's definitely a thought."

They smiled at each other.

"So," asked Gayther, "these photos from Thomas and Cotton, to show to Karen Williams. They were quick. What have they turned up?"

Carrie opened the file on her lap and took a sheet of A4 paper out and held it up for Gayther so he could see it.

"Well, he's pretty much how I imagine The Scribbler would look these days. Lean, stringy. Which one's that?"

"Challis, the builder. It's off his website. The 'About Us' page. The two men either side of him are his sons, Toby and Alex. Toby, the bigger lad on the left, is the one who was arrested for the burglary."

"Okay," replied Gayther, taking a closer look. "Hard to imagine Knucklehead knowing a London lawyer. Something to look into. When we get to Saxmundham, fold the page so only old man Challis can be seen."

"And this one is Halom, the drag act. Here's one of him in full regalia strutting his stuff at Great Yarmouth." She showed Gayther first one photo and then moved it to the side. "And here's the other from the files, smirking. His most recent arrest. He's a cocky one, guvnor."

"Quite a difference, Carrie. The master of disguise … mistress of disguise … whatever. I can't see it being him somehow, even though he has a similar look about him as Challis. Show me again? … yes, thin as a whippet, my old mum would have said. And mad eyes, she'd have said that, too."

"And here's Burgess. They had a bit of trouble with that one, ended up getting a photo off his wife's – his ex-wife's – old Facebook page. Not been used for ages. Seems they split up a while back, but

Thomas trawled through her photos. Most photos with him in it have been deleted but there's a family shot with a baby, the first granddaughter, and Burgess is in the middle of the group. A bit blurred as they zoomed in, but you can make him out fairly well. His features, anyway. They did their best."

Gayther grunted as he looked at it. "Another that looks like The Scribbler. How I think he looks anyway. In fact, all three of them, Challis, Halom, Burgess, could be related. Peas in a pod. Three identical strangers. Again, fold the page as best you can so only his face can be seen, no one else's."

Carrie nodded and started folding the various pages.

They drove along for a while, both with their own thoughts, as they approached the turning for Saxmundham.

Carrie then cleared her throat and spoke.

"Shame we've no scissors, guv, we could have cut them and just put the photos on the same page ... a sort of identity parade ... and then asked Karen Williams if she recognised any of them as John Smith ... there, that's done," she added a minute or two later, putting the papers back in the file and taking her mobile phone from her pocket.

"Give them here," Gayther said, taking the papers and folding them up and tucking them into his pocket.

"Of course, if you used your mobile regularly, instead of letting it run down and leaving it wherever, I could have sent photos ... of the photos ... to you."

"Actually, Carrie, Little-Miss-Know-All, I do have my phone on me today and it is charged and working fine ... I just prefer the traditional ways."

They smiled at each other.

Easy together.

A team already.

Gayther signalled, swinging the car across the A12, at the Saxmundham turn-off.

"Could it really be as easy as this?" Carrie asked. "Karen Williams simply pointing at one and saying 'that's him', and we go and bring him in for questioning?"

Gayther nodded as he accelerated the car towards their destination. "Why not? These things don't always have to be complicated. Stranger things have happened. Years ago, we had a robbery down Ranelagh Road way. Really nasty one, killed the pets, took a dump in the bed, all of that. We pulled in every burglar locally who wasn't inside. Long story short, it turned out it was a young kid, first-time offender, eighteen-year old, lived over the road. He'd tried it on with the wife, she rebuffed him two or three times and he seemed to accept it. Then, a week or two later, he did all that. It wasn't a burglary, just his revenge."

"Of course," Carrie replied, "if it is one of these three, the ones they pulled in and questioned and eventually released without charge, there'll be a huge fuss in the papers about letting him escape to kill again."

Gayther shrugged. "Maybe, but there was never enough evidence to charge, let alone convict, any of the three last time round. Chances are, it was one of them. Higher up pulled in the net soon after, unofficially, of course. Young mother went missing. A small child was murdered. Unrelated, but considered more important than gay men at that time. Anyway, this time ..."

"Could they not have kept an eye on them, guvnor, even for a while? See what they did next?"

Gayther exhaled loudly. "Resources, Carrie. And harassment, of course. You can't just tail someone indefinitely. Anyway, the arrests would have been enough to spook whichever one of them did it. After all, that's when the killings stopped."

Carrie nodded as Gayther went on.

"This time, if this Karen Williams recognises one of them, or even if she doesn't and we can still catch him quickly, before he kills again … well, we can't do more. We're acting as fast as we can and even if this is all a wild goose chase as you suggested yesterday, we'll only have spent a few days on it, when all's said and done …"

"Left here," Carrie said suddenly, looking down at her mobile phone.

"I've been here before, Carrie, yesterday; I think I can remember that far back. I'm fifty-five and I'm not yet senile."

"No, guv. Sorry, guv," Carrie smiled.

Gayther huffed theatrically before going on. "Fact is, how can I put this … the media … how big a story is it? Police incompetence is always popular with the media and loved by all the virtue signallers on Twitter, but the killings … from so long ago … to the general public? Back then, it got publicity, but not as much, and as long as … well, if it were pretty young women … cute kids … it would have got a load more and plenty of resources as well. A lot of people in the police force … I shouldn't say it … but it was a different era and … well, there wasn't as much empathy as there could have been for gay men. Anyone LGBTQ+."

"And right, just in here."

"Thank you, Carrie, what would I do without you acting as my carer?"

"That's all right, guv, then left again and we're there." She turned her phone off and slipped it back in her pocket.

Gayther continued talking as they approached the close. "The media, the public, too, won't give two hoots about Old Man Lodge dying, whether he was pushed or jumped, and nor will they care about what happened to a load of troubled, middle-aged men thirty years ago. Dead gays don't matter. And if another middle-aged white man dies. And another. And one more. Well, I doubt that they'd care that much either, truth be told. Not really. But I bloody well do. Knowing what my brother went through ... what the hell is that doing there?"

Carrie looked up. Saw the police patrol car parked outside of Karen Williams' home.

"Shit," exclaimed Gayther, reaching to undo his seat belt and get out of the car.

"Wait," Carrie said, putting her hand on his arm.

Gayther and Carrie watched as a young female police constable got out of the back of the car, leaning back in to help a dark-haired teenager out. Another, older female police officer got out of the front passenger side.

"That's Kai, Karen Williams' son," Gayther said. "What's he been up to? County lines runner? Oh ... no."

They watched as the older female police officer said something to the driver of the car, a younger male policeman, and then, her arm brushing the back of the teenager, she guided Kai up the path to the door with the young female police officer following behind.

"Oh, don't tell me. Don't tell me. Don't tell me," Gayther said. "Something's happened to Karen Williams."

As the female police officers and the teenage boy entered the house, Gayther moved again to get out of the car. Carrie touched him on his arm once more. "Let me go, guvnor. Have a word with Mark, the driver. I know him. I used to play pool with him and his ex."

Gayther nodded his agreement, then sat waiting as she hurried over to the police car and tapped on the window.

He watched as the window was wound down and saw Carrie leaning in. A series of questions and answers. A long conversation. He opened the window of his car, to listen. He could not quite hear what was being said.

Carrie stood up, turned and came back towards Gayther. He studied her face. Their eyes met. She shook her head, a sad, final gesture. Gayther assumed the worst as Carrie got back to the car.

"Karen Williams?"

"She was killed in a hit-and-run accident on the B1119 late last night. Walking back from a pub, the Red Lion, where she'd met a friend for a drink according to Kai Williams. They've just returned from identifying the body. They've got a counsellor coming, and Ali and Sara, the two officers, are waiting until she arrives."

"CCTV?"

"No, not on that road, not from the A12 to until you get to the town centre."

"At the pub?"

Carrie shrugged. "I don't know. Mark's not sure who's handling it yet."

"Did she die at the scene?"

"A young couple driving home from a theatre in Ipswich saw her body by the side of the road at about 10.45pm. The woman went over, the man was too squeamish, and she was dead then. Hit at speed from behind and thrown against a tree, they say."

"Witnesses? Anywhere?"

Carrie shook her head. "I don't think so. Mark says not."

"Who was the friend?"

Carrie pulled a face. "I don't know. Apparently, Kai said his mum went out at short notice to meet someone for a meal at the pub. He thinks she might have been on a date. That's all he knows."

"Anything else?"

"He asked why we were here and I just said we were following up a lead, a few things, in the close. Cold case enquiries. I didn't actually say it was anything to do with Karen Williams. Was that the right thing to say?"

Gayther nodded.

"They're treating it as a hit-and-run. They're checking garages and hospitals and CCTV on the A12 and in Saxmundham to see if they can uncover anything, a damaged car or anyone who was injured. There's no talk of anything else."

"Of murder?" Gayther said.

"Do you think …?" answered Carrie.

"I don't know, Carrie. Big coincidence if it isn't. Look, while everyone is taking care of Kai Williams, you and I can pay a visit to the Red Lion on the way back. Let's drop by and see what we can discover."

7. TUESDAY 13 NOVEMBER, LUNCHTIME

Gayther and Carrie sat quietly at a corner table in the Red Lion pub just outside Saxmundham. They both had a glass of dark fizzy drink, each with ice cubes and a slice of lime, in front of them.

"Tastes disgusting, whatever it is."

"Coke Zero. No sugar."

"Diet Coke, then? With sweeteners … loads of chemicals that'll give you cancer in twenty years."

"No, Coke Zero."

"So, what's the difference? Diet Coke. Zero Coke. I assume they're both sugar-free. And calorie-free?"

Carrie shrugged. "Same drink. Different taste. Good for diabetics paddling about in the shallows."

Gayther huffed and puffed as he pushed his half-empty glass away and looked around him.

It was a quaint, old-fashioned pub, full of low beams, a

mish-mash of dark tables and chairs and a mix of cushions that, Gayther thought as he moved one slowly away from him, had seen far better days.

The pub seemed bigger on the inside than the outside, with more nooks and crannies appearing as they went further in.

It was about a third full, but short-staffed, and the husband-and-wife landlords seemed rushed off their feet serving lunchtime meals. After introductions and brief mentions of Karen Williams, they had shown Gayther and Carrie to a tucked-away table near the back and asked them to wait until the pub had settled down. "Twenty minutes, no more," said the husband. Gayther and Carrie declined the offer of something to eat.

"They've got CCTV," Carrie said suddenly after a few minutes' silence. "Above the door as you come in. That should make it easier."

Gayther nodded. "I've got two questions and we should be able to answer them ourselves from the CCTV. Much easier than half-remembered thoughts and ideas from staff who weren't really taking much notice at the time."

"Who was she with?" asked Carrie.

"Yes, it would be too much to ask that she was with Challis, Halom or Burgess or another Scribbler-look-a-like, though we can but hope. Who knows?"

"And the other," Carrie said, "would be ... why was she walking alone late at night?"

Gayther replied, "Yes, although that's all linked up with who she was with. A man who didn't want to give her a lift home. Why? Because they'd had an argument? She'd knocked him back? I'd like to know if she was drunk ... how much she had drunk ... was she sober or tiddly drunk or all over the road?"

Carrie spoke up quickly. "No crime in a woman having a drink, guvnor. If she did. She could simply have met an old school friend or work colleague for a bite to eat and then walked home for some fresh air and been knocked over. As simple as that."

"Of course, that's more likely than not. Most probably, it's a terrible tragedy. But we have to check out every lead and see …"

Gayther looked up and saw the male landlord coming towards him.

"Barry," he re-introduced himself as Gayther and Carrie got to their feet. "Barry Chapman, sorry to have kept you waiting. We had someone here earlier. PCs Webb and Harris? We went through it all with them. Are you …?"

"DI Gayther, DC Carrie," Gayther smiled, turning towards Carrie. "Karen Wiliams' visit here last night. We just wanted to check, if we may, what you can tell us about it?"

Chapman shook his head. "Nothing much, really. It was busy – curry night – and it was just me and the wife and the chef and a couple of students in helping out, fetching and carrying. Me and the wife were behind the bar, neither of us recall seeing her. One of your PCs showed us a photo. It didn't ring a bell. Neither of us remember serving her at the bar. It was only when we saw the CCTV footage that we recognised the woman in the photo. Clara and Zoe, the two students, may have seen more. They'd have taken the order and served the food to them. They're not in today."

"Them? Who was she with?" Gayther asked.

Chapman stood up. "Come and have a look at the CCTV footage for yourself."

"You still have it?" Carrie asked.

Chapman nodded his reply. "Our licence means we have to keep data for fifty-six days. Your colleague copied it onto a USB or bluetoothed it, I'm not sure which. He told us to keep hold of the original."

Gayther grinned at Carrie as he stood up and she followed. He looked like a child at Christmas, she thought, about to unwrap a big mysterious present, the last and biggest one left beneath the Christmas tree.

* * *

Chapman stood in front of a large black television in a back room that doubled as a rest and storage area. A settee, a coffee table and boxes, stacked here, there and everywhere, filled almost all of the space. He held the remote control in his hand as he pointed it towards the screen that sat on top of an old pine, five-drawer, chest that took up most of the far wall.

"That's live, that is, see there, the bottom half of the screen, and it's still recording …"

"How long have you had it?" Carrie said conversationally, standing behind the landlord and to the left, Gayther to his right.

Chapman shook his head. "It's a new system. We put it in last month, maybe six weeks ago. We had some trouble with a new chef, Nathan, a black lad. Some of the locals were giving us, well him, a hard time. A couple of the old timers thought it would be funny to hide in the bushes and throw bananas at him as he left. It's still a bit 1970s round here. Multiculturalism hasn't quite reached this far."

"Did you report it?" Carrie asked. "Hate crimes are a priority for us."

"No, Nathan didn't want any fuss, just wanted to keep his head down and get on with it. Do his job. He's a good chef. I had a word with one or two of the men we thought it was and talked about barring racists and it seems to have settled down. That reminds me to have a chat with Nathan later on to check he's all right."

"So, you put it in to see who was racially abusing Nathan?" Carrie said as Chapman carried on talking over the top of her.

"We put in the system anyway, after the banana throwing, so we could monitor everyone coming in and out. Only thing is ..." he added, "a young lad, Josh, the local odd-job man, did it and he put it up too far to the left. It only really covers the doorway, some tables to the side and a bit of driveway, so we can't actually see the whole car park, which is what we wanted ... so we could match people up to their cars. We're going to get him to move it or maybe put in a second one further round. Well, hopefully. He seems to have disappeared these past few weeks."

Chapman thought for a minute. Then called out.

"Cath, Cath?"

A moment's pause, footsteps, and she was at the door, looking in.

"Can you remember what the times were when they came in and out?"

Gayther and Carrie looked towards her and smiled as she moved into the room, both thinking how she looked like the stereotypical barmaid: brassy, dressing younger than her age, rather too heavy with the make-up.

She paused. "They came in together at 8.00pm, just past, and she left at 9.30, give or take, and he was out at about 10.00, maybe quarter to. The PC, whatever his name was, this morning, had a good look."

Gayther, standing to the right of Chapman, watched over the man's shoulder as he pressed first one button and then another to bring last night's recording onto the screen, tutting as he did so.

"Give it here," said his wife, "I'll do it, I found it before. When they came in."

"What do you remember of them?" Gayther asked Chapman's wife. "Did you speak to either of them?"

Chapman answered, "I told you. We were busy. Neither of us served them. The girls would have taken orders and delivered food and drinks and maybe got talking to them. You'll have to come back, with your other colleagues. They're on tomorrow at six for the quiz night."

Mrs Chapman stopped, her finger on the button. Gayther could see the screen was about to start showing the footage from 8.00pm last night.

"Actually, Barry, what I said to the police earlier was wrong. I've been thinking … although I don't remember seeing them, I do remember someone shouting out 'cow' at some point in quite a nasty way and there was silence for a second or two … in case there was a slanging match or something … and then everyone ignored it and carried on talking. That was a man and about that time and I think it might have been him … look, here we are, 8.00.52 … 53 … it's exciting, isn't it … that's Jeremy coming in, old soldier that he is. They're in next."

Carrie leaned forward. Gayther did too.

They saw the unmistakable face of Karen Williams coming in, glancing up at the camera as she passed beneath it. A split second, but a full and clear shot of her face.

A second or two's pause.

A hooded man, head down, pulling at the hood so it covered his head more fully as he passed beneath the camera.

"Damn," said Gayther angrily.

"The photo the police showed us this morning matched the freeze-frame of that lady coming in. We had to go back and forth quite a bit to match them," Mrs Chapman said. "We assume that was her man friend just behind her … let me find the bit where they left."

As she pressed more buttons, Gayther reached into his jacket pocket and took out three folded-up sheets of paper, one photo on each, of Challis, Halom and a younger Burgess. He opened them and spread the three sheets out, holding them in front of Mr and Mrs Chapman. "Recognise any of these men?" he asked.

Chapman looked at the photo of Challis. "No," he said. Next, the photo of Halom. "No," he said again. Then the photo of the younger Burgess. He turned his head this way and that. "Him, maybe. But I couldn't say where from. And not recently. He may have been in the pub, but he's not a regular." He paused and then shook his head before adding, "Who are they? The Chuckle Brothers? They all look like brothers."

His wife stopped what she was doing to take a look. She gazed for a moment or two at the photo of the younger Burgess. "I've not seen him before ... nor him," she added, pointing to the photo of Halom. "Although they do look similar, don't they?" She paused as she looked at the photo of Challis. "I've seen him somewhere. No idea where. Who is he ... who are they?"

Gayther shook his head. "We're just trying to establish who was with Karen Williams last night."

Mrs Chapman nodded. Her husband did too. "Come back tomorrow, show the girls. They may recognise one or other of them."

They both looked back towards the screen. "There," said Mrs Chapman. "We think that's her going."

Gayther and Carrie both watched as, at 9.32.32pm, what looked like Karen Williams was leaving.

"She's in a hurry," Carrie said. "Pushing that old man aside."

Gayther nodded, but did not add anything. "Wait," he said, as Mrs Chapman went to fast-forward the footage, "I want to see ..."

"No one leaves straight after her," Mr Chapman said. "We sat through it this morning. Two bikers came in, about three or four minutes later. A couple left, two minutes after that. Dan and Shirley. Locals. Live over the way. Then another of our old boys who comes in sometimes and sits at one end of the bar nursing half a Guinness for hours. He left. He lives over the road. And that was it until the man she came in with went."

Mrs Chapman wound the footage on … by the two bikers … the middle-aged couple … the old boy … and then stopped it at 9.44.22. "There … we think that's him."

Gayther and Carrie watched closely.

Saw the man pulling his hood up as he came on to the screen. "Stop," said Gayther, louder than he meant to. "Rewind and freeze it, please."

Gayther and Carrie looked at each other. They both spoke the same word at the same instant.

"Aland."

"That's very interesting," Gayther added. "Carrie, take a shot of that with your phone … Mr and Mrs Chapman, thank you. You've been very helpful."

* * *

"Your opinion, guvnor?" Carrie asked a distracted-in-thought Gayther as he accelerated the car back up the A12. "Are we now going to the care home again?"

He nodded his agreement and then spoke.

"I can't help thinking this Aland has something to do with all of this. He ran from me … why did he run, really? I'm not scary. And he's been with Karen Williams just before her death. That's too much of a coincidence, surely? Is he The Scribbler?"

She looked as his angry face and then answered calmly.

"I don't see how he can be. He has the look and is about the right age, but that's all. He's only been here, what was it, four months? He hasn't been here thirty years. And he doesn't have a Suffolk accent, which The Scribbler was said to have. So, it's not him, is it, guv? It can't possibly be."

He shook his head. "I guess not, but ... I don't know ... something doesn't feel right to me. None of this does. It all feels wrong."

"He ran from you because he was scared. That's understandable given his background. And why shouldn't he see Karen Williams if they're both single? Maybe they had an argument of some kind – so what? People do. It doesn't have to end in murder. Why would he run her over? It's just a tragic coincidence. And ... come on ... why would The Scribbler, whoever he is, even come back and kill Karen Williams so long after the event?"

"Because Karen Williams was the only person who really saw him and talked to him when he came to check out the care home and discover which room was Lodge's. The only clear witness who could look at a photo and say, without a shadow of a doubt, yes, that's the man ... I don't believe she'd be on a date with this Aland anyway. She was pie-eyed about her dead husband yesterday, not looking forward to a date night."

"For f..." Carrie stopped and composed herself. "Well it's not Aland then, is it, guvnor? Aland can't be ... John bloody Smith ... The Scribbler, can he, the man who came and met Karen Williams and said he was John Smith? The man she'd never met before. I mean The Scribbler can't be two people, can ..."

Her words tailed off as she sat back and got her phone out of her pocket.

He could sense her frustration.

Knew, deep down, that what she said was correct.

"Okay," he answered after a few minutes' silence, "let's look at this rationally. There are two strands to it. First, has The Scribbler, let's assume it's this Smith, come back and killed Karen Williams?"

"I'd say no. I can buy that the vicar somehow saw him at the fete and he returned the next day pretending to be someone's nephew

... that's quite clever ... and then the following evening to commit murder. That's quite risky, but if he was scared and thought he was about to be exposed somehow, well, yes, maybe I can accept that. But why would he kill Karen Williams ... how would he find her ... why would he wait so long?"

"Because he knows we're investigating Lodge's death and he's panicked and decided to kill Karen Williams, too. And because ... maybe, somehow ... he has some other sort of link with the care home we don't yet know about?"

Carrie sat there thinking as Gayther turned the car off the A12 on to the road back to the Kings Court care home.

They drove along in silence as they approached the home.

Both edgy, both tetchy. Trying to work through the ifs, buts and maybes in their heads.

"I don't see it, guvnor, really I don't. I mean The Scribbler took a calculated gamble going back into the care home to find Lodge. There may have been cameras up recording him coming and going. All sorts of people would have seen him. He bluffed them with the Mrs Smith's nephew line, so they'd not link him to the vicar's death. He got away with that. But why come back for Mrs Williams ... so long after. We're ... quite honestly, guv, we're clutching at straws."

Gayther eventually nodded and then added, "Okay, the second strand then, Aland. Quite a coincidence that he was at the care home and acted so suspiciously and, when we look into Karen Williams' death, he happens to be there, too, don't you think?"

"I think Karen Williams simply had a meal with Aland – a work colleague, a would-be lover, someone maybe who was going to fix her car for her for cash, who knows – and then left and was knocked down and killed by ... well, anyone really. A drink or drugs driver. Someone not paying attention. A couple arguing.

Someone nodding off. It's a dark road, it twists and turns. Maybe she'd had a drink … they'd had an argument … she stumbled off a muddy path into the road without thinking … who knows? Shit happens, guv, you know? All the time."

He nodded as he turned the car into the care home's car park.

Pulled up and turned and smiled at her.

"Let's go and find out for sure then, Carrie."

* * *

"Wait, guv." Carrie reached out and touched Gayther's arm as he went to open the car door. "I don't think we should just go steaming in. Mrs Coombes said she'll complain to the chief if we came back. We don't want her coming down hard on us. We need to be subtle here, don't we? We want more of a gentle touch."

Gayther sat back in his seat. "Okay, Carrie, so what do you suggest we do?"

"What exactly do we want to achieve, guvnor?"

Gayther say quietly for a moment before he answered. "First of all, I want Sally and Jen … Miss Bright … Mrs Smith … anyone who might have seen The Scribbler on one of his two visits … to have sight of the photos of Challis, Halom and Burgess … if anyone recognises one of them, is absolutely sure, then we've got our man."

"And if they don't? Can we discard Challis and the others as prime suspects?"

Gayther shrugged. "A clear ID rules them, or at least one of them, in. Not recognising them still leaves them all in the frame. It means he's been clever … or lucky … or they just weren't very observant."

"How about I slip in with the photos? Hope no one knows anything about PACE," Carrie said. "Ask at the reception for Sally and

Jen; chances are one or other will be working today. I can then show them the photos and, if they don't recognise anyone, I can ask them to show the other care assistants and residents who might have seen him. I'll leave them my mobile number."

"Good idea." Gayther handed her the photos. "Tear round the edges really carefully so there's no other information on the page – I know Challis had his sons on there. Right to privacy and all that. No point in asking for trouble," he added.

He watched as Carrie took each picture in turn and tore the edges as neatly as she could.

"Detective work, Carrie. Bet you didn't think you'd be doing this."

She laughed as she finished tearing around the last photo. "All part of the job, guv."

She stopped and looked at the three torn and scruffy pages and thought they didn't look very professional, although she kept the thought to herself.

"Very good, Carrie, very good."

She laughed again as she opened the car door. Leaned back in after she got out.

"Wish me luck, guv. I might need it."

Gayther sat there nodding. Then waited patiently, watching Carrie as she crossed the car park and entered the care home. He sat still a little longer to see if she came straight back out. If Mrs Coombes were on reception, or close by, he guessed that Carrie would not get as far as meeting Sally or Jen.

He thought for a while, wishing that he still smoked, could do with a cigarette now as he mulled over what to do next. He had tried chewing gum, as a replacement, but it had pulled the crown off a tooth and his dentist told him to avoid anything chewy or sticky in future. Something else to add to the lengthening list of things he could no longer eat.

Aland bothered him. He did not know why. He accepted that he was not The Scribbler, could not possibly be, all things considered. But there was something not quite right. It was too much of a coincidence that he was with Karen Williams no more than an hour or so before her death. It niggled away at the back of his mind. There was something obvious that he was overlooking, something right in front of him. He couldn't place it, though.

Gayther knew he needed to step back from Aland and that, if Aland was in some way mixed up with Karen Williams, he had to leave it to whoever was investigating her death. Do no more than tell his fellow officers that the man with her at the pub was Aland, or certainly looked like him.

But then he looked up. Saw Aland driving a van into the car park and around the corner into the staff parking area.

Realised Aland had not seen him.

Gayther dropped down, as if he were reaching for something in the passenger footwell, and then stayed there. He hoped Aland would not recognise his car, which he would have seen the other day as he was weeding.

He counted the seconds, to thirty, forty, fifty and then sixty. Wasn't sure how long he should wait. He knew if he raised his head and Aland saw him there would be trouble of some kind; Aland running to Mrs Coombes and her complaining to the Chief Constable. He could do without that.

He kept counting, to 90, 120, 150 and finally 180 seconds. Then raised his head up slowly. Aland was nowhere to be seen. He was not sure whether the handyman had walked by the car and into reception, or if there was a back-door entrance out of sight near the staff parking area.

Gayther got out of the car, reaching for a pad and pencil in his pocket.

Knew he needed to get the van's registration number noted down to give to his colleagues. Knew too that if he used his phone he'd probably end up photographing himself instead by mistake.

And it was a chance for him to look over the front of the van for any damage that might have occurred last night – putting his suspicions to rest; or confirming them.

He walked out of the visitors' car park towards the staff parking area. Both areas were half-full of cars but empty of people. He saw the van straightaway as he came around the corner. Dark blue and anonymous. Hard to see at night, if the lights were turned off and the van accelerated fast towards a vulnerable woman walking at the side of a dimly lit road. He made a note of the van's number plate.

Went to walk to the front of the van.

Heard a noise behind him.

Turned and saw Aland standing there.

"What the fuck you want?" the handyman said. Gayther noted he was clenching his hands into fists, could feel the anger coming off him, close to striking out.

Gayther stepped back, raised his hands, palms outwards in a conciliatory gesture. "My coll …" he began and then stopped, thought for a second and just said, "I'm picking up my friend … I'm waiting for her."

"Why you …?" the handyman gestured towards the van and then towards the pad and pen in Gayther's left hand. He moved forward towards Gayther, who stepped further back, two or three more steps, so that he was now close to the front of the van. Near enough to check for damage.

Gayther glanced down. The van's bumper was bent and damaged. The paint scratched and scraped. Somehow, it did not surprise him.

But he was not sure if this was fresh or old damage. The van, fifteen years old or more, had been round the block many times.

"When did you do this?" Gayther asked quietly, dropping his hands and pointing to the front of the van.

The handyman moved closer. He was so close to Gayther that he could smell him, a mix of tobacco and sweat. He looked down and then shrugged. "It. How I had it." Gayther took it to mean the van was like this when he got it.

Gayther stepped back one more time, felt his heel now pressed against the kerb by the edge of the parking area.

He looked at the handyman, who stared back without blinking and then raised his finger to his throat, making a cutting motion. "You fuck off. Go 'way."

Gayther shook his head at the ridiculousness of the cut-throat gesture. Raised his hands again, as conciliatory as he could be. "My car's there," he said, nodding towards his car in the visitors' car park.

The handyman moved aside, gesturing for Gayther to walk by him to the car.

As Gayther passed him, the handyman spoke. "Hey." Gayther turned and looked at him.

"You come back," the handyman said, gesturing at his throat again.

This time, Gayther laughed openly at the stupidity of the repeated gesture. He knew he should walk away, sit in the car and wait for Carrie, passing the information he had to the officer in charge of the Karen Williams case when they were back at the station. But the handyman had riled him.

He knew he should keep quiet, say nothing. Not ask the question, "Where were you last night, between the hours of eight and eleven?" He did not need to anyway. He had the answer to that already, from the CCTV camera.

And he wanted to say something better, something that would give him the answer he wanted just by looking at the handyman's face – a carefully prepared mask or a look of sudden shock. So he did.

"Karen Williams. She's dead."

There was a moment's pause. A second or two, no more. The handyman held Gayther's steady gaze, with a look of disbelief, then dropped his head down into his hands. Too fast for Gayther to judge accurately. He realised immediately he should not have made the statement, should have left it to the officer in charge. He could kick himself.

He turned around to walk to his car. Felt movement behind him.

Half-turned back as the handyman thumped him hard with clenched fists on his back, knocking him forwards.

Saw the ground coming towards him fast. Blacked out.

* * *

"Guv, guv, are you okay?" Carrie bent down on one knee. "Guv, guv?" She shook Gayther's shoulder.

Gayther stirred and, after a moment or two, he sat up slowly onto his haunches, groaning a little.

"Funnily enough, Carrie, no, I'm not so good." He touched his forehead gingerly, knocking off two or three pieces of gravel stuck to a bloodied graze. "I seem to have banged my head … and cut it."

"Did you fall over guvnor, have a funny turn?" Carrie reached for a small pack of tissues in her pocket, slipped one out and passed it to him. He took it carefully and patted his forehead. She sat next to him on the ground, picking up his pad and pencil close by.

"I'm not that bloody old, Carrie. I'm not …" he searched for the best word, "… gaga. Aland turned up in his van. I've noted the number … and the front is damaged. Can you text the information to Mark … get him to pass it on to whoever's in charge of the Karen Williams case."

"Yes, sure." She reached for her phone, turned the pad to look at the number and started pressing buttons. "But what happened to you? Did you have a little wobble and fall over?"

He sighed heavily, still feeling slightly dazed. "Give over, Carrie, I'm not that decrepit yet … Aland saw me looking and came across … I wanted to see his reaction, see if he knew about … I told him Karen Williams was dead. Just to see."

Carrie looked up from her phone and made a face at him, "Oh … was that a good idea?" She paused and then asked, "What was his response?"

"He looked shocked … fake or genuine, I don't know. It was so fast. He pushed me as I walked away. Well, hit me on the back as hard as he could, really. I stumbled and …" he gestured at his forehead, "goodnight Vienna."

"There we are, message texted to Mark … so do we go and find him, Aland, and bring him in for assault … and to talk about the van?"

Gayther rose stiffly to his feet as Carrie reached out to support him by the arm. "No, it's not our job … let's leave it for now. I think it might complicate matters … but text Mark again and tell him to get someone over here asap for the van … in fact, take some photos of it now. Just in case."

Gayther stood and watched as Carrie circled the van clockwise and then again anti-clockwise before stopping in front of him.

"Filmed it, guv. All good."

Gayther nodded carefully as he turned to go towards his car. "Anyway, more importantly … How did you get on with Sally and Jen? Did you get through Mrs Coombes?"

Carrie walked alongside of Gayther to the car, her arm on his. It irritated Gayther a little, but he knew she meant well and wasn't teasing him this time.

"Mrs Coombes wasn't there, or at least I didn't see her. I spoke to the receptionist, same woman as last time and asked to see Sally. She wasn't on duty. Jen was, and so this Kaz, on the desk, buzzed her and she came and saw me in reception …"

"Did she recognise any of the photos?" Gayther reached in his pocket for his car keys.

"Do you want me to drive, guv? Let you get your breath?"

He nodded as he gave her the keys and she opened the passenger door and watched him climb onto the seat. "I'm going to have a splitting headache all night … do you have any Anadins or anything … painkillers for your lady things?"

"'Fraid not, guv, but I'll drive you back, give you a chance to shut your eyes … and no, guv, Jen didn't recognise any of them, but I've left photos with her and my phone number … damn PACE, as you'd say … and she'll show them round, to Sally and to Mrs Smith … who's a bit Lady Gaga … and will then text me if anyone does and then bin the photos."

Gayther grunted as he sat down in the passenger seat.

He waited as Carrie got into the driver's side, fastening her seat belt, before speaking as gently as he could. "I'd rather you'd shown the photos to each of them in turn yourself, especially Mrs Smith, in case this Jen doesn't … we can't really rely on her to do our job. Not properly anyway."

Carrie nodded, "I can go back, get the photos, sort it out."

"Leave it for now, let's keep out of the way … give Mark, whoever's dealing with it, the chance to come over and speak to Aland and check the van over … see if Jen contacts you later today or tomorrow. If not, we can go back in tomorrow or the next day."

"So, what's next, guvnor?"

"Home, Carrie. You can play *Space Invaders* or whatever it is these days with your little boy. I can get a good night's sleep. We can start afresh in the morning."

They looked at each other.

Carrie smiled warmly at him.

Gayther smiled back, wincing more than a little.

8. TUESDAY 13 NOVEMBER, 4.55PM

The man with the latex gloves sat on a bench in a back-street park in Lowestoft in Suffolk, close to an overgrown pond and within sight of the public toilets. He had been there most of the after-noon, watching the comings and goings, feeling the screwdriver and the Stanley knife in his pockets, waiting for his chance. Just the one, that's all he needed.

He knew that, in the on-off-on-off drizzle, he must look an odd sight. Wandering back and forth to the pond with his crumpled brown bag of crusts to feed the ducks.

Dropping his head down as if studying his shoes whenever anyone walked by. Not that they did that often, though. And no one spoke to him.

He could not help himself at these times. Had to wait and see if he'd get lucky. The urge getting stronger, more insistent, at each missed opportunity.

He realised that he would be caught one day. A policeman would stop and ask him what he was doing. Or a man he per-suaded to come with him in his van might turn and overpower him at the moment before killing, holding him down as he pressed 9 9 9 on his mobile phone. Or someone, when a man was reported missing, might remember seeing him there or walking to his van with that man.

It was easier at the start, when he was younger and fitter. He could sit in bars and clubs in the city centre, in the corner, for hours on end. Anonymous. Far from home. Invisible. Night after night. Waiting for a sad, middle-aged man to make his nervous approach. So many bodies, so many faces, unlikely to be remembered by anyone – and there were no CCTV cameras nor mobile phones or Twitter and Facebook back then; none of these things he knew so little about.

Even so, he'd nearly been caught. And some of the men had got away. An ever-present spectre just behind him, or just in front and around the next corner, for the rest of his life.

There were too many kills, too close together, too near to home.

He had stopped for a while, had held out for as long as possible. But the urge came back, as it always did, and he started again.

He'd been forced over the years to go further away as he grew older and stood out more in bars and clubs and, eventually, he went to public toilets. Still meeting places for sad old men trying so hard and for so long to subdue their urges and hide their dirty secrets. And he went so far, up the A1 and down to the M25, ever searching. Harder and harder as time passed and, he guessed, so many of these men found what they wanted on the internet.

But there were always one or two. One here, another there. All middle-aged men in suits.

Six, nine months apart, sometimes a year. He once held out for as long as eighteen months.

Never the same part of the country the next time, though.

He had not killed in Suffolk for almost five years. Last time, the man's disappearance made the front page of the local newspaper, as they often did. A respectable man goes missing. Sobbing wife and bewildered children make an appeal. A flurry of publicity and then a sudden deafening silence; no doubt because the man's secret life had been exposed. Assumptions were made by the police and finally the family. A runaway off to start a new life with a gay lover. Or a suicide, as likely as not. The wife and children eventually accepting, in the unending silence, that he had taken his own life.

Only now did he dare to come back, to his home patch of East Anglia, to hunt. Felt it safe to do so. Great Yarmouth, Beccles, Acle and now Lowestoft. He had checked out all of the parks there, one by one, making sure they met all of his criteria before he made his next killing. No speed cameras nearby. No CCTV in or around the park. A public toilet, run-down and unnoticed. Out of the way. And an empty, largely unused park free of mothers with young children, and teens on pushbikes, and families.

Again, as dusk was falling fast, he saw a man walking by. A young man, maybe thirty, thirty-five. Married, most likely. With a pretty young wife and two little children. Blonde-haired girl. Cheeky-faced boy. All oblivious to his other, sordid life of public toilets and casual sex with strangers; men he'd never see again. Thought maybe this was a place where men like this still met.

The young man stopped.

Turned towards the man with the latex gloves. Smiled.

About as obvious as he could be.

The man with the latex gloves watched as the young man turned away and walked into the toilets. A final look back and the young man disappeared inside the building.

He sighed to himself, the man with the gloves, patting the bin bags in one pocket and then the black tape in the other.

He wanted an older man, someone like himself these days, someone who he could kill easily. Not someone young and strong and more powerful than him.

He rose from the bench, looked towards the toilets and then turned and walked away, screwing up the crumpled brown bag in his hand and throwing it angrily towards the ducks.

He knew exactly who he wanted.

For his thirtieth kill.

Someone old who looked like Father.

9. WEDNESDAY 14 NOVEMBER, MORNING

Gayther and Carrie sat opposite each other in the staff canteen the next morning. Gayther had a fabric plaster stuck to his forehead, which Carrie tried hard to ignore.

Both held paper cups of coffee in their hands and shared a packet of three custard creams.

Carrie broke the last biscuit in two and gave Gayther the slightly larger piece. She wanted to tell Gayther he'd look better without the plaster on his head but could not quite bring herself to raise the matter.

"So, what's on the schedule today, guv?"

"Have we got the likely lads in?"

"Likely …? Oh, no, Cotton and Thomas are on a course today. 'Politically Correct Bollocks' I think you'd call it, guvnor. We should have them back again tomorrow, I think, or at least part of it. Did you have something in mind for them, guv?"

"No, not especially, they've given me their notes so far. All of their thoughts. I wanted to arrange for the evidence we had from the original murders to be taken for DNA testing, though. They could have done the to-ing and fro-ing, dogsbody work on that for us. No matter, we can leave it just for the moment."

"Anything they've spotted that we haven't? In their notes. They're bright boys."

Gayther laughed.

"Not exactly. For one of the murders, they found a mention in a statement that Quasimodo, the Hunchback of Notre Dame, they explained, in case I didn't know who Quasimodo was, had been seen lurking in the pub. And for another, there was a reference to Frankenstein being there ... again, they explained the difference to me between Frankenstein, Doctor Frankenstein, and Frankenstein's monster, his creation. Kind of them, I'm sure."

"And what did you say?"

Gayther saw her smirk.

He laughed again.

"Um ... I said to them that it was Norfolk and it's like the *Hammer House of Horrors* up there – Wolfman, Creature from the Black Lagoon ..."

"Count Duckula?"

"Him too ... and I explained the whole inter-breeding thing to them as well ... marrying cousins and aunties and all of that ... and so, for Norfolk, looking like Quasimodo and Frankenstein—"

"Frankenstein's monster."

"Yes, well, it's normal for Norfolk."

"And what did they say, guv, Cotton and Thomas?"

"They seemed a bit bemused, to be honest."

Carrie laughed as she finished her biscuit and cleared her throat.

"So, being serious for a moment, guv, what exactly do we have from the original murders? When I went through the notes, it wasn't clear."

"Not a lot, Carrie. I've just been checking. Long time ago. Another world. You'll have seen the typewritten reports of each case from Hendry, the officer in charge at the time. There were three or four others involved. Hendry's long gone. He passed over back in the 1990s. Lung cancer. I went to his funeral. His wife seemed surprisingly cheerful, if I remember right. The others will have one foot in the grave by now. We'll catch up with them at some point, have a quiet word with those who are still about. Other than that, there are a few exhibits."

"Exhibits?"

"Items of evidence, Carrie. Wakey, wakey. From the deceased victims. There's not much. Most of them were discovered face down and rotting in a ditch six months after they went missing. But we've two or three items. A boot from Marven found close to where the body was discovered in a ditch. Shoes from MacGowan that were pulled off before he was dumped in another ditch. A hair found under the fingernail of Davies; he maybe pulled it out during a struggle with The Scribbler."

"Any good?"

"I think Marven's boot is too much of a long shot. It's likely it just came off as The Scribbler dragged the victim's body to the ditch. He probably never actually touched it. The other boot was found in the water at the bottom of the ditch. MacGowan's shoes might be a possible – it depends on whether The Scribbler pulled them off and, if so, whether he still had his latex gloves on. If he did pull them off, why did he leave them there? I don't think we'll get lucky with them."

"Waste of time then, guv, asking for them to be DNA tested?"

"Maybe, but who knows. I can put it through on the basis that if we can get some DNA we can see if there's a match on the main database. But there's a problem, well two problems really. Back then, we pretty much just fingerprinted items. These days, with DNA, we can retrieve DNA from skin cells left behind when – if – The Scribbler – came into contact with an object such as the boot. But it's a big if, whether there are any skin cells on, say, the shoes that we recovered. If The Scribbler pulled them off, well he was wearing latex gloves, so that's a non-starter."

"And the other problem?" Carrie asked.

The other issue is that we, well some of us, were pretty gung-ho, PC Plod, in those days in the way we handled things. A year or two ago, they looked at the rape and murder of an old lady, in her eighties, walking her dog on old Felixstowe beach in 1979. Funnily enough, they had her boots and reckoned the rapist … the murderer … ripped them off, and so, DNA-wise, there might have been skin cells on those. Nothing … they reckon the way the boots were fingerprinted at the time destroyed any chance of DNA."

"And the hair, under the nail, that's a possibility, surely? Got lucky there," Carrie queried.

"If it's his, maybe. And if there's a root. And if they'll DNA test it. If. If. If. Thing is, without a root, you can't get a full profile, not at present anyway, and upstairs may say no because they want to preserve the little bit of hair they've got. If the hair's rootless, and I'm no expert, you can establish ethnicity, but that's about it. If we get DNA from a suspect and there is a match, it would not be complete, so the evidence wouldn't be … the reality is that, given its age and everything, it's probably degraded so much and will be of too poor quality to do much with it."

Carrie swept up the crumbs of her biscuit and tipped them into the cellophane wrapper in front of her before pushing it into the bottom of her emptied coffee cup. She glanced at Gayther's forehead, paused and went to speak, but then thought better of it.

"So, what are we doing today, guv? Going to see the two victims who got away, Wade the teacher and Wilkerson the bank manager? In case they're next on The Scribbler's 'to do' list?"

Gayther looked at Carrie and shook his head as if to say the 'to do' list comment wasn't appropriate. He finished the rest of his coffee and squashed the cup down into Carrie's and then spoke.

"We're going to cut to the chase, Carrie. We've got Thomas and Cotton's notes and are going to pay visits to Challis and Halom and, in his absence, to the wife of Burgess. One of them's The Scribbler. Let's see if we can find out what they were doing the night of Lodge's death. We'll give them all a little squeeze and see if one of them bursts open."

* * *

"So, which one's first, guv?" Carrie asked, as they sat in the car in a layby on the A12. "Challis … Halom … Burgess?"

Gayther rifled back and forth through the file on his lap in front of him.

"Halom … he's the closest. I've a photocopy of The News of the World front page from … whatever the date was. 1989, I think. Let me show you. Refresh your memory."

He passed an A4 sheet of paper to Carrie and then carried on speaking as she began reading it.

"This is the drag-act guy who … dear God, where to start? Obsessed, for whatever reason, with the case. His bedroom was covered with cuttings about the killings. Came forward to say he thought he did them while in a trance … said he had blackouts … the 'zombie killer' some of the lads at the station called him. Anyway, the desk sergeant initially humoured him and took a statement and filed it under a pile of papers at the bottom of a cabinet and forgot about it."

"So, how did he end up on the front page?" Carrie held up the piece of paper. "With his face all over this rag?"

"Halom kept coming back demanding to be charged with the murders. Made a nuisance of himself, hanging around the car park, stopping the senior officers, the cleaners, anyone who'd listen. He got short shrift. He then went to the newspapers. *The News of the World* ran a front page. God knows why. We were then instructed from on high to interview him under caution, but, well, these days you have to be sympathetic to mental health issues, but then, he was just a swivel-eyed loon they wanted in and out of the building as soon as possible."

Carrie finished reading the piece and then pointed to the photo of Halom on the page as she handed it back. "Not a bad likeness to The Scribbler – if the original sketch was close to the man we're after."

"Well, we think that's what set him off. The likeness being shown on TV. Apparently, his father, a real bully boy, told Halom, Halom junior, they had the same name and middle name too … creepy … that the mugshot was of him … a dead ringer. That put the idea in his head and it escalated from there."

Carrie looked out of the window across the fields to her left. "Okay, so, the guy has, has had, serious mental health issues. But what about the nights of the killings? Did he have an alibi for all of them? Did he drive a car – was he mobile … could he have done them, the murders? Presumably they checked it all out as per usual?"

"Yes, but probably half-heartedly. He said he killed them all, but he was at home, supposedly, for each of the crimes according to his dear old mum. He had a licence and there was a family car, hers – the father was a lorry driver, so he was away for much of the time. There was nothing to place him at the scenes of any of the crimes. To be honest, they just wanted to shift him out of the way so they could focus on finding the real killer. There was no reason to dig deep. He was just another nut. You get them with every case."

Carrie watched as it started to rain, a thin and endless drizzle, before she spoke again. "So, why are we bothering now, all these years on?"

Gayther wiped at the inside of the fogged-up windscreen with the sleeve of his jacket. "There are two ways to look at this one. The first is that he's simply a sad case who had some form of mental illness when he was young and wanted attention at the time. I expect there's some sort of name for it. Look-at-me-itis, probably."

He paused, thinking for a moment, before going on. "Anyway, he's since spent his life doing odd jobs and a drag act around caravan parks, trading stolen goods, living with his old mother in Wickham Market. With her until recently anyway. All a bit seedy and squalid but essentially harmless. And we've his DNA on file and that hasn't matched any crime at any time in any place since. And so, if that's the case, we're wasting our time."

"And the other way?" asked Carrie as she fastened her seat belt ready to go.

"The other is that he is The Scribbler. He did the killings, using his mother's car while she stayed at home and the father was on the road, trucking all over the place. The mother knew it … but lied to protect her precious son … the only thing she had as her husband was a big thick brute of a man. He got lucky. Or was clever. Never got caught. Then came out, did this drag act and that became the outlet for all of his urges. I'm not sure dancing around in frilly underwear would be enough to keep him satisfied, but who knows?"

"How likely is that, guv? Less likely, surely? That doesn't really seem possible to me." Carrie opened her window a little to let in some air.

"I'd agree with you, Carrie, if it weren't for one thing." Gayther started the car, looked back over his shoulder and pulled the car out on to the A12 before continuing.

"His mother moved into sheltered housing in Leiston a while back. She's eighty-something and maybe needs to go into a home now. Leiston to the care home is seven miles. Not that far round here. Maybe, just maybe, young Mr Halom paid a visit to the home with her on its open day to see if she'd like it … and who should be sitting there to welcome him but the Reverend Lodge, the man he tried to murder all those years ago."

* * *

"Welcome to Wickham Market, guvnor," said Carrie as they came off the A12 and passed a sign for the village. "I've never been here before. What's it like? At least it's stopped raining."

Gayther smiled. "Much the same as all of the other decaying villages up and down the A12." He rummaged in his trouser pocket and pulled out a scribbled-on envelope, which he passed to Carrie. "It's the IP13, zero something one. Google Maps it for me please, my phone's dead."

Carrie took the paper, leaned forward and pressed some buttons on the mobile phone resting on her thigh. "I've got reception. Who'd have thought?" She looked closely at the screen and then fiddled with it, turning the picture from side to side. "Bungalow. Looks like it's in a horseshoe-shaped close. All old bungalows. Great long gardens. Then trees and fields behind. Room for a cemetery full of bodies."

They drove along a wide, twisty-turny road, fields stretching out on either side.

By a new housing development. Executive homes. Then the town square, lined with small, mostly empty shops.

And finally beyond, heading out towards fields again.

"Sharp left here," said Carrie, "Sorry, yes ... look, here it is. The close ... just along here."

Gayther turned the car, drove along a little way and then brought the car slowly to a halt by a postbox, looking out across the eight bungalows he counted in front of him.

"Which one is Halom's, guv? Which number?"

"Six, I believe," Gayther replied, counting from his left. "That one there. The one with the weathervane on top of the garage. That's weird. Why would you have a weathervane there where you can't see it from your own home or garden? That's stupid, that is."

"Well he's at home, look, the van on the drive?" she pointed to it and then added, "Do you want me to put the registration into the system, DG05 ... see what comes up?"

He nodded, "Yes, can do ... let's just sit here for a minute and watch for twitching at the windows. These little closes out in the sticks are all the same. Old men and women sitting watching each other's every move. See who's bought themselves a new hat. Nothing better to do with their time."

"Look there," he said after a minute, "to the left of Halom's. There's someone at the window already."

"And there," he added a minute later. "Two doors to his right. They've opened the top bit of that window so they can listen. They're there as well."

He waited a further minute before speaking. "Any second now, and we'll see Halom standing there the other side of the window, dressed up like Norman Bates' old mother in *Psycho*. You wait."

"Registered to his mother, still Maureen Halom," Carrie said after a minute or two. "The van. All clean ... but a bit odd that, the old lady owning it … so how do you want to play this, guvnor? I've been thinking …" She stopped speaking, waiting for his response.

He thought and then replied, "Go on."

"The bungalow is actually listed in the records as Lilac Cottage rather than number six … although it's a bungalow and there are no lilac trees. So, on paper, we're not to know, are we? That he's at number six. I wonder whether we might start with the neighbours, asking for Mr Halom and then striking up a conversation with them after they've directed us to number six … get a bit of background on him, as it were? Have they seen anything strange? Out of place?"

Gayther shook his head. "We need to play this one straight, Carrie. Dead straight. Halom will know his rights … from what I've read of him, he'll scream blue bloody murder if he finds out we're being clever-dicky. And he will. Invasion of privacy. Slander. I want this all low-key, under the radar – until we've got something solid to present to Boss Man."

She nodded and then said, "So we just, what, open the gate, walk up the path, knock on the door and when he answers it, we say … what? Hello, me old mate, tell me, are you The Scribbler?"

"Not quite, Carrie." Gayther opened his car door, undid his seat belt and went to step out of the car. "That's what we want to know, but there are ways and means, Carrie, ways and means. Come and watch. Watch and listen. Listen and learn."

"Guv?"

"Yes, Carrie?"

"I'd, um …" She pointed at the plaster on Gayther's forehead, "… take that off first if I were you."

* * *

Carrie stepped out of the car. Followed Gayther as he pulled the plaster from his forehead.

To the gate. The path. The door.

Watched as he pressed the doorbell, struggling to unstick the plaster from first one finger and then another. Finally, he pulled it off and tucked it into a pocket.

He then turned back towards her and grimaced. Carrie was not sure why. It was a face to suggest he smelled something bad, rotten even. She looked at the faded brown door and dirty net curtains at the windows to either side and then down at the step. An empty milk bottle. Old leaflets tucked behind. And then she saw, on a folded-over tabloid newspaper to the side by Gayther's shoes, a fat pigeon lying there, its neck broken, a thin line of blood from a nostril.

"Uurgh," she said instinctively, under her breath.

She looked across at Gayther. Could see he was stifling a fit of laughter because of her unexpected reaction.

She looked away, biting her lip and digging a thumbnail into her index finger, to stop herself laughing.

For a minute or more, they both avoided each other's eyes, their backs to each other. Gayther glanced down again at the pigeon, which looked as though it had just been killed. He wondered if Halom had done it or whether it was a gift from someone.

Carrie looked across at the van parked in the drive by the side of the bungalow. She thought it was about as grubby a van as she had ever seen. She moved across to check the front for any signs of damage and then, seeing it was all intact, the tyres.

He turned and looked over, steady at last.

"Anything?" he said.

"Below legal minimum this side." She walked round the other side. "One's above, just. The other's worn on the inside quite badly."

She came back and stood on the step next to Gayther.

"What do you think? Start with the tyres?"

Gayther hushed her down, leaning forward, listening at the front door.

The bungalow was quiet and still. The windows all closed. The curtains to the windows on the left, the main bedroom, thought Gayther, were pulled to. He checked the windows to the right, another smaller bedroom, and those were open. He could see through the frosted glass of the front door, watching for movement, the darting of a body from the main bedroom into the hall and away to the rooms at the back of the bungalow.

Nothing. But Gayther sensed someone was there.

In the main bedroom, just behind the curtain, listening too, waiting for them to go.

He rang the doorbell again, then clattered the letterbox with his fingers. Stood back, waiting. A minute passed. Then close to another.

There was movement from the bedroom to the left, the sound of coughing, a door opening and a figure appearing, through the frosted glass, in the hallway. A face, pressed close to the glass, looking out at Gayther and Carrie on the doorstep. Gayther could feel the man's gaze upon him.

"Who are you, what do you want?" A rasping voice, from years of smoking, with a Suffolk accent. Harsh, defensive.

"Mr Halom? It's the police, open up please," Gayther asked politely but firmly.

A moment's pause. Gayther waited for the man to swear at them, to tell them to clear off in as many words. But the rattling of a chain at the door signalled its opening.

Halom stood there in front of them. Mid-fifties but looking older. Sunken-faced and skeletal inside his frayed-brown dressing gown. Cancer, thought Carrie instinctively. Veined and bony-legged, feet in incongruously feminine fluffy pink slippers. Halom looked at Gayther, coughing as he did so. He reached into his dressing-gown pocket and took out an off-white handkerchief, which he coughed phlegm into.

"Police, what do you want?" he said eventually, his words choking out. "I've told you I'm not letting you in any more without a warrant. Snooping and prying. It's harassment. I've told you I'm through."

"We won't take up any of your time, Mr Halom. My colleague and I ..." Gayther gestured towards Carrie, "... are just doing a routine enquiry relating to an incident near Dunwich on the first of October ... van owners in the area ... can you tell me where you were on the evening of the first? It was a Monday."

Halom looked from one to the other. Then bent his head down again and coughed into his handkerchief. Gayther could see globs of white spittle, one left smeared below Halom's bottom lip. Halom looked up sourly at them before speaking. "Wait here," he said, pushing the door to. "This is not an invitation to come in. Stay there."

Gayther watched through the frosted glass, Halom's shape seeming to sway from side to side as he moved further away.

"What are your thoughts, guvnor?" Carrie asked quietly. "Would he have the strength to have killed Lodge?"

Gayther shook his head and put his finger to his lips. "Well, he's coughing and spitting a lot ... maybe for show ... who knows?"

A wait, as if Halom might have slipped out the back and away, but then finally he was back, opening the door, pulling his dressing gown tighter around him and flicking through the pages of a pocket diary. "October ... October ... what was it ... the fifth?"

"The first," replied Gayther, correcting him. He saw Carrie's expression but ignored it.

"Here," said Halom, holding out the opened diary. "See for yourself."

Gayther took the diary as Halom started another coughing fit. Skimmed down one side, then the top of the other and saw the date, the first, and the word 'Bingo' and the letters 'GCP, GY, 6-10' in the small space. "GCP?" he asked.

"Greys Caravan Park, Great Yarmouth. I do a cabaret Friday nights, bingo when I'm needed … if someone's off sick … are you satisfied?" Halom coughed again, struggling for breath.

"Is there much demand for that in a caravan park at this time of year?" Gayther asked.

"The locals turn out for it," Halom answered.

Gayther nodded at him. "Do you do the bingo a lot? Do they just call you in when someone's off sick?"

Halom nodded back, "Now and then. Once or twice a month if someone phones in ill."

Are you still working?" he added, gesturing towards Halom's handkerchief. "What with … everything?"

Halom looked back at him, anger on his face.

"Not this week, no, nor last week, not until I've got rid of this bloody cough." He hacked again. "Next week, hopefully. Is that it, then, are we done?" He looked from Gayther to Carrie and back again.

Carrie spoke up, "Yes, but we couldn't help but notice, on the way in, your tyres … did you know three of them are below the legal tread?"

Halom turned his angry gaze towards her and she held it, thinking that deep down this was an angry man with a quick temper.

"You'll need to get those sorted before you drive it again."

Halom looked at her dismissively. But he said nothing and, after a moment or two, he turned back to Gayther and repeated himself,

"Are we done?"

Gayther nodded his confirmation.

"Don't come back." Halom stepped back and shut the door in their faces.

Gayther smiled quietly to himself as he turned to Carrie and they walked away.

* * *

"Well, it's not him then, is it?" Carrie half-stated, half-asked, as they drove away back through Wickham Market towards the A12.

"Why's that then, Carrie?" Gayther answered as he accelerated the car through the town square.

"Well, he's not well ... on his last legs by the look of it ... and he was at the caravan park that night, he'd have witnesses to that."

Gayther searched in the door well for a half-eaten packet of polos he thought he'd left there. He rummaged a bit more without success. Then he tutted to himself and turned to Carrie.

"He doesn't look good, I'll give you that. But ... it may not be more than a really bad cough. Man flu and all that. Men do suffer badly, you know. More than women. It's worse than childbirth, I'm told." She did not pick up on his teasing comment.

"More like cancer to me, guv. One of my uncles was like that towards the end ... the lung cancer had spread. If he is dying, would he ... well, would he be bothered enough to go to all the trouble of killing a witness even if he were up to it physically? It would hardly be top of his bucket list."

"There's the ailing mother, Carrie. Getting older herself. He might want to stay alive for as long as he can for her ... and to protect his name ... her name ... if he died before her."

"Yes, but still ..." Carrie turned away, looking out of the car window across the fields.

"And the diary entry, Carrie," he went on, "couple of things there. If you did kill someone, I think you'd want to cover your tracks. He could have made that entry before or at any time after in case someone came knocking. He could even have scribbled it in as he walked back to the door to show us the diary."

Carrie said nothing, and just carried on watching the world go by. Something was troubling her, about Halom and his mother, but she couldn't quite think what it was.

Gayther continued, "And he said he worked there Friday nights regularly, bingo when needed. So, I noticed he had noted the cabaret down in the diary for four days later. If you did it every week, week in, week out, would you do that? Would someone make a note ahead of going to church every Sunday? Or that you swam at the local leisure centre, Monday, Wednesday and Friday? No, it's just routine. You don't need to make a note of it. You know your own habits."

Carrie nodded, but she reckoned it was all just too unlikely.

"And answer me this, Carrie," Gayther said, sensing her frustration, "if he got called in on the day, because someone phoned in sick, or texted or whatever, would he rush straight to his diary and make a note of it? Would you? Of course not. A diary like that is for doctor's or dentist's appointments, a nephew's birthday, stuff like that. Not to note something you were doing that very day. It's not like you'd forget."

She turned towards him, as Gayther drove the car back on to the A12. "If you didn't believe him, why didn't you press further, ask him more questions?"

"Because, as it stands, he'll simply take our visit as being routine. He's used to dealing with the police, petty crimes and stuff, and us turning up out of the blue about stolen goods. If I pressed him, even hinted at The Scribbler, we'd spook him. As it is, he's given us a fact that we can check easily. At some point, in the next day or two, I'll ask you to run up to the caravan park, take Cotton or the other one with you, just to double-check that out."

"If he worked that night as he said?" she asked.

"Or not."

"And if he didn't?"

"If he said he did and he didn't … then he lied … why? … we'll want to know … maybe he was at the care home killing Lodge after all."

10. WEDNESDAY 14 NOVEMBER, LUNCHTIME

"Challis then, guv. The moment of truth. What are the chances it's him? Or is this a wild goose chase after all?" Carrie sat in the passenger seat of Gayther's car, sipping at an Americano from a local petrol station. She took the lid off the paper cup, blowing on the black liquid to cool it.

Gayther sat drinking his latte, watching the builder's yard, the Challis & Sons Ltd sign above, on an industrial estate just outside Saxmundham in Suffolk. He shrugged. "Your guess is as good as mine, Carrie. Finding out exactly where he was on the evening of the first of October should rule him in or out, though."

"What time do you expect them to arrive, guv?"

Gayther moved his cup from his left to his right hand and then checked the watch on his left wrist.

"The woman in there …" he gestured towards the yard, "… said they were due back just after lunch to pick up some parts. Someone should appear soon. Whether it's Challis or the sons. Another fifteen minutes, maybe a bit longer."

"Won't she alert them to us, guv?"

He shook his head. "Shouldn't do. I think you'll find she thinks I'm a customer ... not a policeman."

Carrie looked at him doubtfully, but didn't say anything.

Gayther looked around. "Is there anything bleaker than an industrial estate on an overcast and drizzly day?"

"Round here? Kessingland beach is pretty grim with the wind whipping in. Spent the night there once as a teenager, a group of us in a tent. Hard to peg a tent on a shingly beach. It got in a tangle and blew away and we ended up chasing it into the sea. One of the dads picked us up at 2.00am. And, um, anywhere up and down this stretch of coast with the dark mornings and dark nights. All a bit spooky. The beach by the Sizewell power station would be my bleakest place."

"Lit only by the light of its radioactive detritus washing out to sea," Gayther smiled as he finished the dregs of his coffee and crushed his coffee cup, squeezing it down the side of his seat.

"You need cup holders, guv. Between the seats. We could put our cups in them. Newer cars have them, you know."

"Maybe, Carrie, maybe. There's a bit of life left in this one yet. The body's a bit old and battered, but the engine still has some go in it. There's plenty of oomph under the bonnet."

There was a moment's silence.

Both thought of much the same joke, give or take.

Neither of them said it.

"So, Challis, guvnor. Run me through your thoughts on this one please before he arrives ... hopefully." Carrie finished her coffee, put the lid back on and rested the empty cup by her feet.

"Okay," said Gayther, reaching for the file between the seats, "Challis was a plumber, is now a builder with his two sons. He used to drink in some of the pubs where The Scribbler met his victims. Maybe more. Was named by three or four people who saw an appeal on local TV. He had alibis for some of the murders, three of them, but not others. Nothing from forensics."

"The alibis, guv, who provided them?"

"Hold on." Gayther flicked through papers in the file, back and forth, until he found what he was looking for. "For two of them, little old ladies for whom he was doing odd jobs in the evening for cash in hand … installing a washing machine for one, unblocking a drain for another and, for the last one, an old boy, he was fitting a new cistern that night."

"Friends or relatives, guv?"

Gayther shook his head, "No, apparently not, no personal connections."

"Did Challis work alone?"

"He had a young lad with him at the time, Stephen Gill, who fetched and carried. An apprentice in all but name. But there was no mention that he was there for any of these cash-in-hand jobs. He had left by the time of the investigation, went off to college somewhere. He was interviewed but had nothing to say of relevance. We don't seem to have the complete notes on that, though."

"Could they have been mistaken, the old folk? Maybe got confused and got the dates wrong?"

"One old lady wasn't sure … they were interviewed weeks later, of course. Said it has been a Monday or a Wednesday night because *Coronation Street* was on the telly at the time he came round. She then went with the Monday, which was the night in question, and said Challis was there for about an hour after the programme ended. If it was that night, Challis would not have had time to get to Norwich to the bar to meet … hold on … MacGowan."

"And the other ones?"

"Well, this is interesting, Carrie. Digging through the notes, one of the old dears and the old fellow named the days correctly for the respective murders, but both seemed to base their recollection on receiving receipts through the post from Challis, weeks later and dated for the appropriate night."

"So, you're thinking—" Carrie said.

"For those two," Gayther interrupted, "Challis could genuinely have been fixing a drain and a cistern. Equally, he could have been out killing and then, to cover his tracks, issued receipts for the work he'd done the night before or the night after and wrote the wrong date on both of them."

"But not for the first old woman?"

"There's nothing in the notes, but who knows? Maybe he did but she never mentioned it. All three of them were in their late seventies or early eighties. I doubt many of them could distinguish one same-old day from another." Gayther was silent for a moment, lost in his thoughts.

"So, no one at the time picked up on this receipt thing?"

"No, it just caught my eye as they were mentioned in passing in two statements. If he were doing cash-in-hand jobs, why would he give them receipts – and weeks after he'd done the work? Odd that. Hindsight is a wonderful thing, of course. When you're so close to something you don't always see the wood for the trees."

"And, since then, there's been nothing on Challis on the database?"

"No, but there's this business with the son, Toby, and the burglary near Dunwich and the lawyer from London wanting everything deleted from the files. DNA and all. That's so odd, as well. For just a big Suffolk lad. I'd like to have had that DNA to see if there's any sort of match, familial or otherwise, somewhere down the line … take another look at this photo of them, Carrie. Father and sons. I took it again from their website."

Carrie took the A4 sheet of paper offered to her by Gayther and looked down at the three men standing, proud and upright, with arms folded, in front of the Challis & Sons Ltd sign at the yard.

"Thing is, Carrie, you can see from old man Challis in the middle …" Gayther pointed to the photograph, "… well, there's that look again, isn't there? Lean. Not an ounce of fat. Same as Burgess and Halom … and these big lads, Toby on the left, Alex on the right, well, you'd not want to pick a fight with those big buggers. They don't look like him. The mother must have been a colossus."

"Hang on, guv," Carrie replied, looking over to the builder's yard and then back across at him. "Isn't that them in the van over there? … I'll check the number."

Gayther looked over as the van came to a halt and the father got out of the driver's side and one of the sons exited from the passenger side.

He watched as Challis, the father, turned and looked towards him and Carrie, reached back into the van and came out with a sledgehammer. Challis started walking purposefully towards Gayther's car, before breaking into a run.

* * *

"Who the fucking hell are you?" Challis stood aggressively by Gayther's car, bending down towards the car window so his face was only inches from Gayther's.

Gayther looked back blankly at him through the glass. It seemed to enrage Challis further. He moved the hammer from one hand to the other and then spoke again, full of anger.

"Who are you and what do you want?" Challis put the sledge-hammer down and reached to pull open Gayther's door.

Carrie, anticipating the move, pressed a button to lock the car doors.

Gayther spoke in a measured tone. "I am DI Gayther and this is my colleague ... George ... Carrie. We'd like to ask where you were between the hours of six and nine pm on the first of October."

Carrie looked at the man, who seemed to be in such a terrible rage.

"Why don't you fuck off? This is just state harassment again. Police. Tax enquiry. VAT inspection. Speeding tickets. You've not left us alone for months. I'm not talking to any of you any more without a solicitor. So, you can just fuck off and request a meeting in writing."

Gayther nodded and spoke clearly and firmly, "We'll do just that for you, Mr Challis."

As Challis picked up the sledgehammer to walk away, he turned back towards Gayther and looked him in the eye.

Carrie thought for one awful moment that Challis was going to lift the sledgehammer with both hands and slam it into the car windscreen, shattering the glass. Instead he spoke, this time in a lower, more threatening voice.

"You smarmy bastards are all the same. You've not left us alone since ... my boy makes one single mistake ... one mistake, that's all ... and you're all over us. Harassment. Victimisation. That's what this is."

Gayther maintained eye contact and spoke in a louder, firmer voice – but still polite. "Tell me where you were between six and nine pm on the first of October and that's it, over. We'll go away and leave you in peace."

Challis stood still for a minute, searching for words, thought Carrie – although he looked as likely to explode as anything else.

"If ... you ... don't ... fuck off right now, I'm going to put this sledgehammer through your fucking windscreen ... understand?"

Gayther nodded as he started the car and began to reverse it away from Challis.

As he did so, Challis walked alongside the car shouting. "I've got your car number; I'm reporting this to your Chief Constable. I know who that is. Wicks."

Gayther continued to reverse the car, gradually gaining speed, until Challis stopped walking, but then he shouted after them, "And don't fucking come back if you know what's good for you."

Ten, twenty yards further on and Gayther stopped the car, then started to make a three-point turn.

Carrie glanced across at Gayther and noticed he was sweating.

"Well, that was an over-reaction," she said. "What rattled his cage so hard?"

Gayther swung the car back in his second manoeuvre as he answered, "Piss and wind, Carrie. He's blustering and bullying because he's covering up … he has something to hide, simple as that. I doubt it's just his son. Not with that level of anger."

She nodded, "Could he be being harassed? Police? Taxman and all of that?"

Gayther noted her worried face. He smiled at her.

"This isn't Russia, Carrie. There's no state surveillance, not at this level anyway. If … if … it's all true, what he says, it's just coincidence. But I don't believe it." He thought and then added, "We can't harass people anyway … we don't have the resources."

"Should we have arrested him then, for threatening behaviour, taken him in for questioning? That would have got the truth out of him."

Gayther stopped as he was doing the third part of his three-point turn. "No, there's no way he'd have talked voluntarily, and with his son there it would have all blown up out of proportion … it would have ended in an undignified pushing and shoving match. Anyway, I want this all low-key for now. And besides, there's a more important question I want answering."

Gayther put his foot down on the accelerator and roared away.

"Which is?"

"How the hell is it that everyone who looks at me knows immediately that I'm the police?"

They both looked at each other and laughed.

11. WEDNESDAY 14 NOVEMBER, AFTERNOON

"This is it then, guv? The Burgess place?" Carrie looked out of the car window at the ramshackle cottage on its own at the bottom of a wooded lane just outside Aldeburgh. "Hansel and Gretel's old home. Do you think anyone lives there? Just the wicked witch? Look at the state of it."

Gayther, taking the file out again from beside his seat, surveyed the scene.

A tumbledown building, peeling paint and decay everywhere.

An overgrown garden, full of nettles and weeds.

Beyond that, sparse trees, broken and at odd angles, and mud, lots and lots of churned-up, dried-out mud.

"It's long past its glory days, Carrie, that's for sure." He thought for a second or two. "You know, if Burgess is The Scribbler, those woods and fields beyond will turn out to be his burial grounds."

"Would he dare, if he did carry on killing? Bring them back home instead of leaving them in ditches far and wide? What if the local authority gave permission to build a hundred homes over there? He wouldn't take the risk, surely. To look out of his bedroom window one morning to see a crane churning over mud and skulls and bones."

Gayther shrugged. "Who knows, Carrie, but I'd like to see if we can get Kevin and his cadaver dog out for a walk there some time soon. See what Pigflesh can sniff out."

"Pigflesh, guv? Kevin Pigflesh?"

"The dog, Carrie," Gayther laughed. "Kevin called it Pigflesh because that's how he started training it when it was young. To find bits of pig flesh."

Carrie looked back towards the woods and fields. "Imagine being here at twilight with the mist rolling in. Proper creepy, it is. A Halloween nightmare." She shuddered and Gayther wasn't sure whether she was joking or not.

He looked across at the bleak landscape.

A First World War no-man's land. Imagined the horrors that might be buried out there in shallow graves.

Decided she was not.

"According to Cotton's notes," Gayther said, looking down at the papers as he propped them up on his steering wheel, "he has vanished into thin air. Google air anyway. She is now living here on her own. Angela Burgess, wife, or possibly former wife, of Simon Burgess."

"The ungodly creature to be burned to ashes," mumbled Carrie. "Hansel and Gretel."

"Well, possibly. To recap, she wrote to the police in Suffolk when she was living with him in Sussex and he was coming up once or twice a month to deliver baby goods to little shops. She said he was The Scribbler; that he used to make her dress up as a schoolboy and then forced her to have anal sex with him." He grimaced. "I can't help thinking of Jimmy Krankie whenever I read that bit."

"Jimmy Krankie, guv?"

"It's Friday, it's five to five, it's *Crackerjack!*?"

"Not with you, guv."

"Oh, never mind, Jimmy Krankie was a woman who dressed up as a schoolboy and appeared on a children's television programme called *Crackerjack!* years ago."

"Like a transvestite?"

Gayther puffed theatrically ... "No, not really ... Jimmy Krankie was more of a panto act ... oh, never mind." He then went on.

"Burgess was in the area for each of the murders, even though he spent only a few days a month up in this neck of the woods. So that's a strong pointer to him. He just happens to be here every time someone's killed. What are the chances of that if he were an innocent man?"

He coughed and added, "An old boy who talked to The Scribbler on the night one of the victims went missing ... Fotherby was the victim ... saw the police appeal and the identikit drawing and recognised Burgess. He then, by a sheer stroke of luck, saw Burgess in his van a week later and had the good sense to note the number plate and ring in with it."

"Well, that's a good start. So why didn't we nail him?" Carrie suddenly noticed movement at the upstairs window, a fluttering of a net curtain. Someone was there, looking out, watching them.

"It was a start, yes. And we ... they ... came close. But they screwed up. They pulled Burgess in and felt he was near to confessing. They got an extension. Left him alone to stew in his own juices and then set up an identity parade."

Gayther laughed sardonically.

"Big mistake. The old fool who'd talked to Burgess and ID'd him picked out someone else. Unbelievable. It was someone who looked nothing like Burgess – we used to pull them off the streets for a fiver in those days to make up the numbers in a line-up."

"Uh, not so good. Dead in the water, then?" Carrie kept talking, although she had half an eye on the cottage window. No movement.

But the dark shadow to one side could be someone monitoring them, she thought. She looked at it, waiting for the darkness to move.

"It needn't have been if they'd been cute about it," continued Gayther. "If they'd let everyone leave the line-up at the same time and taken Burgess back to the interview room, they maybe could have, with a nudge and a wink to imply he'd been picked out, got him to admit to the killings. But they held back the man the old boy singled out as the rest of the line-up left and that seemed to give Burgess the impetus to hold on."

He flicked through the papers. "And then this clown Halom went to the press, same day, next day, whenever, and confessed, so the focus moved to him as the prime suspect ... he had his confession all written out and presented to the newspaper ... and Burgess just slipped away into the shadows."

"What about the car, the Burgess van, whatever it was, what did forensics get out of that?" There was no movement at the cottage window. Just the shadow. Carrie was sure the movement was coming. Any second now.

"Effectively nothing. Inside the van, nothing of note. Mud, tiny patches of mud, in the footwell that they tried to match up later with mud from where the victims were found. But he was very careful if it was him. Cleaned everything up well. These days, with the victim's flakes of skin and strands of hair and smatterings of blood on him, and him then going back to the van at some point, well, we'd have a better chance."

"Inside the van, guv, you said. Inside the van. What was outside? Mud on the tyres?" Yes, thought Carrie, there it was, the shadow at the window moved back. But still there. Someone watching them sitting there talking.

Gayther breathed out – a long, drawn-out noise. He thought about what he was going to say. "Thing is, Carrie, these days, most members of the public assume the police is some sort of super-powerful organisation with mighty computers and instant access to every database everywhere and CCTV and DNA and so on – and that everything can be solved quickly and easily. Some of it is, but there are still so many variables."

Carrie was distracted. By the shadow at the window. Thoughts and possibilities rolling helter-skelter through her mind. Then, aware of the lengthening silence and Gayther's expectation of her next question, she spoke, "What do you mean, guv?"

"Policing, detective work, solving crimes – it's not just about checking CCTV footage and getting DNA from dandruff on someone's jacket collar. It's not that bloody simple most of the time. It's also about smart policing. Old Man Wilson noticing The Scribbler's mark in a coroner's report.

"It's about lucky policing, too. The Yorkshire Ripper got caught because a traffic cop spotted what turned out to be fake plates on his car. A complete fluke, that was.

"And Dennis Nilsen, who killed and dismembered young gay men at his home in London, was only caught when a Dyno-Rod employee tried unblocking the drains there and found what he thought were flushed-away lumps of Kentucky Fried Chicken. Luck, Carrie, good or bad. That's how so many cases unravel, not through clever-clever policing."

And now the shadow was gone. Out of sight. Hiding? Coming downstairs? Out the back and away? She spoke again, to alert Gayther, "Guv…?"

Gayther sighed loudly once more. "And sometimes, not solving crimes is about careless policing. Human error. Mistakes. Not seeing what's in front of your eyes. Remember The Scribbler always used to go with the victims in their cars. Why? Maybe because there was something about his car that people might notice, that they might remember."

He rifled quickly through the pages for a blurred photo photocopied onto a page. "Burgess had a teddy bear painted on the doors of the van representing his baby goods business. That's been there right through – and I only just noticed it myself when I was going through all of the files at the weekend. A long-forgotten, overlooked photo that just slipped through over and again. Unbelievable, but it's what happens sometimes. It let him get away."

Or coming towards them? The shadow. Whoever it was. Out the front door and towards the car. "Guvnor…?" she said more emphatically.

And still Gayther went on talking, almost in a reverie, thought Carrie as she turned towards him, as if he'd prepared what he was going to say. "And this girlfriend, ex-girlfriend, wife, ex-wife, God knows what, she then retracted her statement anyway. Because she found herself pregnant … so it wasn't all schoolboy sex … and then, who knows?"

He laughed again, ignored Carrie, and went on.

"Those days there was still a stigma … unmarried mothers. They move up there, he becomes a photographer, they have a baby, presumably, Thomas and Cotton have nothing on that, and they end up here. Living their days out in this fairy-tale setting … or not." Finished at last, thought Carrie. About time.

Gayther turned his head towards the cottage.

And pulled back, startled. Carrie glanced over her shoulder and jumped too.

An old woman stood there, a shotgun pointing at them.

* * *

"Fall back, observe, call for support?" Carrie asked quickly in little more than a whisper.

"No time. Stay calm. Make eye contact …"

"Who are you and what do you want?"

The old woman, bloated and dishevelled, with a food-stained black T-shirt, loose grey jogging bottoms and men's faded decking shoes, looked from Carrie to Gayther and back again. She angled the shotgun downwards and gestured for them to get out of the car.

"Do you have a firearms licence for that?" asked Carrie sharply as she stepped out.

The old woman looked at Carrie for a moment before answering. "I've a shotgun certificate if that's what you mean. A .22. Rimfire. For vermin control and rabbiting. You see all sorts up there …" she gestured towards the fields, "with .308s, stalking deer. This is just for my bit of land."

"You can't go pointing it at people, though, can you?" Carrie half-asked, half-demanded, as Gayther walked round from the other side of the car towards them. "Not unless you want your licence revoked."

The old woman shrugged. "I didn't mean anything by it. A woman on her own needs something. You get all sorts here. Up by the woods. Creeps and weirdos. Couples meeting each other. Men usually. Doing things. It's not decent. It's not right."

Gayther stepped forward. "Do you have a gun cabinet for it?"

She nodded, then shrugged again. "I thought you were the police. You have that look about you. Is that what you've come for, to check the certificate?"

Without waiting for a reply, she turned and walked slowly towards the cottage. Gayther and Carrie followed her along the path; once crazy-paved, now dull and overgrown with weeds.

"Stroke of luck," Carrie whispered to Gayther, who nodded his agreement.

They stepped through the doorway. Into a worn and faded living room of dark browns, a soot-black fireplace and swirly carpets, unchanged for many years.

There was an overwhelming smell of damp and decay and something else – something Carrie could not quite place as she resisted the urge to put her fingers to her nose.

"Through here," the old woman said, taking them into the narrow kitchen at the back. A wartime kitchen, thought Gayther, like his old grandmother had when he was a small boy. A rabbit lay dead on the windowsill. He noticed the kitchen opened on to a half-inside, half-outside, lean-to toilet. Door open. Seat up. Unflushed, he thought. He ignored the smell but noticed Carrie wrinkling her nose.

The woman pointed to a metal cabinet on the wall on the other side of the kitchen.

Gayther approached it, tugging to see if it was attached firmly to the wall. It was. He then pulled at the door to see if it opened. It did.

"Do you have a key for it?" he asked as the old woman leaned the shotgun against the sink. "Let me see you put it away before you show me the licence."

The old woman opened the cupboard door beneath the sink and rummaged about inside. A moment or two later, she slowly withdrew her hand, holding a key, which she showed and then handed to Gayther.

"There's not much point having a gun cabinet if a burglar could look under the sink and find the key for it. You might as well leave it on the windowsill," he said.

The woman shrugged.

As if to say, 'who cares', thought Carrie. She looked like she might be drunk or had at least downed a drink or two to dull her misery.

This old, broken woman just stood there, waiting.

"It should be in a safe with a combination lock, at least," Gayther said in a slightly raised voice. "Better still, a key safe with a finger-print lock. This is a dangerous weapon. It kills. Where do you keep the ammunition?"

The woman turned to the sink again, as if in slow motion, bent down, rummaged about.

"Here," she replied, as she stood back up. "Here's the ammunition."

Gayther took the box from her and Carrie could see he didn't quite know what to say next.

"Let's get this locked away properly now," Carrie stepped in. "In the gun cabinet. Then find a good hiding place for the key while you sort out a proper place to keep it. And let's see your certificate, please."

The old woman looked at Carrie, then passed her the gun.

Gayther handed Carrie the key and the box of ammunition, which she put on the draining board next to the sink so she could sort out the cabinet.

The old woman turned and left the room to fetch the certificate.

"Guv?" Carrie asked after a moment, hearing the creak of the stairs as the woman walked up them. "Simon Burgess. There's no sign of him living here." She pointed to the single mug and bowl and spoon left on the draining board to be washed up.

"Ssshhh," Gayther hushed Carrie. "I'm trying to listen."

Creaking floorboards on the landing.

A moment's silence. But no sound of voices, no unexpected movements, no sudden creaks from other parts of the cottage.

And then the faint screech as a drawer was opened. The old woman searching through papers.

Two or three minutes later, as Gayther and Carrie put the gun and the ammunition in the cabinet, the woman was back, a brown

A5 envelope in her hand. She offered it to Gayther.

He took it carefully, fingertips at each corner, and looked down at the word 'Shotgun' written in the top left-hand corner. He then opened the envelope and slipped out the folded piece of paper, unfolded it slowly and looked at it.

"What is your name, please?"

"Angela Margaret Simmons." She paused and added carefully, "Formerly Angela Burgess."

He nodded. "This certificate is in the name of Simon Alan Burgess … and it's out of date … look."

She stood there, searching for words. She seemed surprised, thought Carrie. "I didn't know," she finally answered. "I thought a certificate covered a property."

Gayther shook his head as he put the certificate back in the envelope and gently slipped it into his jacket pocket. "I'll need to hang on to this for the time being, as evidence. Carrie, write Ms Simmons a receipt."

Carrie looked blankly back at Gayther.

"Just write, in your notebook, shotgun certificate received from Angela Simmons by DI Gayther, then date it and sign it and tear it out to give to Ms Simmons."

Gayther then turned back to the old woman.

"Angela."

She looked at him with vague eyes.

"I need to speak to your … ex-husband, Simon Burgess."

"Why?" she asked.

"Because …" Gayther replied, thinking for a minute. He paused for so long that Carrie thought he had forgotten what he was going to say. She was about to prompt him when he spoke again.

"Because, Angela …"

Carrie stepped forward, took out her mobile phone, tapped two or three times and then scrolled down and showed her the photo of the hooded man leaving the Red Lion. "Is this your husband, Simon Burgess?"

She noted Gayther's quick look of annoyance towards her, knowing full well it wasn't Burgess.

The old woman stepped forward, peering myopically at the screen.

She looked up slowly at Carrie and then across at Gayther. "Get out," she said suddenly. "Out. I've nothing to say to you."

* * *

"Out!" the old woman said again, but louder this time, close to shouting, as Carrie and Gayther just stood there. "You've no right to be here, coming in under false pretences. This has nothing to do with my gun. You lied to me."

Carrie looked over at Gayther, as she closed her mobile phone and put it back in her pocket.

Gayther held his hands up, palms outwards in a conciliatory gesture. But he didn't move.

"We just want to speak to Simon to—" he said calmly.

"If you don't get out of this house now," the woman interrupted, "I'll pick up the phone and call 999."

Carrie looked at Gayther, who inclined his head towards the living room, indicating she should leave.

She turned, hesitated, waiting for Gayther to move away from the woman, too. He did not. Instead he took a notebook and pen from his pocket and wrote in it before tearing out the sheet of paper.

"The Scribbler ... you remember The Scribbler, don't you, Angela ... He killed again on the first of October and possibly last night. We're investigating. He'll kill again. We need to speak to Simon."

He turned to his side and placed the sheet of paper on the draining board.

"We're going to leave now, as you've asked us to do, but I'm putting this here, with my name and number on it. We can come back and, as you're obstructing our line of enquiry, we can take you in for questioning ... and forensics can come in here and search the place inch by inch from top to bottom. Turn it all over. Floorboards and all. See what they can find. I think that would be interesting. But I don't think you'd want that, would you?"

He turned away, as if to leave, but then stopped and said, almost as an afterthought, over his shoulder.

"Or you can just text me an address for Simon – that's my personal number – and we'll leave you in peace."

Carrie walked out of the kitchen into the living room and through to the front door.

She thought Gayther was there as well, a step or two behind her.

Stopped and turned back as she heard a groaning noise from the woman.

"I don't know anything," the old woman said forcefully. "I don't know where he is. He left the best part of two years ago and I've not heard a thing from him since."

Gayther turned back to speak to her.

"Years ago, Angela, you said, you told us he was The Scribbler, then you changed your mind when you fell pregnant." He paused. "Is he The Scribbler?"

Carrie looked at the old woman, who seemed to be torn by terrible indecision, not sure what to say next.

"Your child, Angela?" Gayther asked. "What did you have, a boy or a girl? They'd be, what, thirty-something now?"

Carrie kept watching the old woman, seeing her face change

from uncertainty and doubt – on the edge of revealing the truth – into anger and fury.

"If you're not out of this house in ten seconds, I am going to call the police. 999. Get out now!"

Gayther hesitated, watching the old woman move across and take the landline phone from its wall bracket.

She looked back at him as she put her finger on the 9, ready to press it for the first of three times.

Gayther nodded at her and turned to leave, saying "Come on" to Carrie as he passed her. Carrie followed him out, but couldn't help noticing the old woman smiling grimly as she put the phone back on the wall.

"Guv, shouldn't we have taken the shotgun off her?"

Gayther waved her away. "More important things to worry about than that, Carrie. We're chasing a serial killer. Remember?"

Carrie shook her head and bit her lip as they walked to the car.

"Okay, so what do you reckon, guv? About Simon Burgess?" Carrie asked, as she opened the car door and climbed in next to Gayther.

He blew out a breath loudly as he started the car and began to reverse it. "Mark my words, Carrie. It'll be him."

"Oh yes?" she asked, putting on her seat belt.

"I've been a copper for thirty years and after a while you get an instinct for these things. There's something about it that tells me it's him. Simon Alan Burgess … wherever you are, we're coming to get you."

Carrie turned away and pulled a face.

12. WEDNESDAY 14 NOVEMBER, 4.43PM

The man, wearing latex gloves, stood at a urinal in the public toilets in a park in Ipswich as dusk was falling.

He had been there, like this, as if he were urinating, for the best part of five minutes, maybe closer to ten.

He was listening to two other men who had gone into a cubicle at the far end of the toilets.

He knew what they were doing. Had sat on a bench nearby, an old *War of the Worlds* paperback in hand, as if watching the world go by, for close to two hours before he saw them go in.

One man, the one he wanted, mid-fifties, grey and balding, in a dark, ill-fitting suit, went in first. Casting furtive looks around as he did so.

The other, younger, mid-thirties, rougher, maybe a labourer, followed a minute or two later, walking, almost striding in, with more confidence. Only the last-moment, tell-tale look back gave away his intentions.

Now he was just waiting for the moment he hoped would come. He kept his hands in his jacket pockets. Could feel the Phillips screwdriver in one pocket, the Stanley knife in the other.

He wondered, as he often did at such times, exactly what he would say if he were stopped by a policeman, asked what he was doing sitting on that park bench for so long, told to turn out his pockets. Why, the police officer would ask, do you have these tools in your jacket pockets? They could be used as dangerous weapons. And why do you have refuse sacks and tape in your trouser pockets?

Why?

Why?

Why?

He still, after all these years, did not really know what he would say to that. What explanation he could give. He knew he shouldn't carry both, could possibly explain away one, or the other, but not the two of them. Nor the bags and tape. But, in a way, the thought excited him. It added a frisson to what he was doing. And he needed both for what he was going to do.

He could hear movements in one of the cubicles. Back and forth, the sense of some sort of rhythm.

But no words were spoken at all. It was all done in silence.

And then he heard a sudden cry, muffled quickly, and the low voice of one of them hushing the other.

He had thought today that he could have tucked them, the screwdriver and the knife, inside his long winter socks, one left, one right, but he was not sure if he could reach them quickly, especially the screwdriver, if he had to. And if he had to run, to chase, or even be chased, as had happened once or twice over the years, he thought that they might fall out and he might stumble and fall to the ground. And then, one way or the other, he would be done for.

He liked the feel of them, too, as he stood there ready for the moment. The weight of them. The cold strong length of the screwdriver and the thought that he would later, when the time was right, plunge it in again and again. The sharpness of the blade that he would touch occasionally with his thumb through latex glove, imagining it cutting and shaping ageing flesh into some form of likeness.

He heard a low mumble of words from within the cubicle. "It's on the wall," one said.

Then another voice, low, harder-to-hear, "You go, I'll wait five minutes."

He turned to face the urinal and removed his hands from his

pockets, as if now holding himself while urinating.

He heard the cubicle door being opened, another mumble of words he did not catch, and dipped his head as if he were concentrating. He did not want the man who was now leaving to see his face, to even notice he was there.

Good, he was in luck. The first time in such a long time. He could see, out of the corner of his eye, the younger man, the workman, fiddling with his trouser zip as he walked behind him. Quick, brisk, keen to be on his way, to distance himself from what had just taken place. The man's departure thrilled him. It gave him a chance.

It was just a matter of waiting now, for the older man. Tired and flabby, he would, if he showed interest, be easy. Would put up less of a struggle. This old man would do very nicely. Yes, indeed. He would rely on the element of surprise. He just had to decide whether to stand and wait for him to come out of the cubicle or to tap on the door, nudge it gently open and stand there with a smile.

He was not sure if the older man would wait the full five minutes. Maybe not. There was always the chance he might rush by suddenly and be gone, out of the toilets and into the park and away. Or that someone may come in, perhaps young boys, playing with skateboards, and the moment would be lost. Or a policeman. He had always feared the hand on the shoulder. Knew it would come one day. His luck finally breaking after so many years.

He heard the older man, still in the cubicle, coughing now, a smoker's cough, full of mucus and phlegm. He snorted loudly and spat.

Then a strong and steady flow of urine splashing into the bowl. The flushing of the toilet a moment later.

The cubicle door opened and the old man stepped out.

He zipped himself up carefully and then turned to face the

old man. He was older than he first thought now they were face-to-face. Maybe in his sixties. He had had one like this eighteen months ago in Hertfordshire. A brief flurry of news and then, like all the rest, the story faded away.

He checked his pockets, taking pleasure again from the feel of the tools in his hands.

Smiled at the old man.

Stood there hoping he would meet his eye and smile back.

* * *

It was these glorious thirty to forty seconds of delicious anticipation.

Before he plunged the screwdriver into his unsuspecting victim.

That the man with the latex gloves liked the most.

This one, the old man picked up from a public toilet in Ipswich, had been the easiest for ages. Maybe ever. He had returned his smile and made eye contact. A movement of the head to suggest going back into the toilet cubicle. A shake of the head and a mention of somewhere nicer plus a promise to bring him back here later was all that was needed. Then they were walking through the park and out to the anonymous small dark van parked in a shady, tree-lined side street.

Stilted conversation. The exchange of first names, both false.

A short journey. No more than four or five miles.

Down a maze of country lanes into thick woods, where he pulled in and parked among trees. Hidden away.

"It's nice here." The older man looked across at the trees and nodded agreement. He had a thin sheen of sweat on his face and upper lip. Inexperienced, thought the man with the gloves. Can't believe his luck. Two in one day. And him so old and flaccid, a washed-up nobody in his cheap, department store suit. Hanging around filthy public toilets.

"This way," said the man with the gloves, getting out of the car and walking into the woods. "The van's fine here, no one will ever notice it."

He turned and smiled at the older man climbing slowly, reluctantly now, out of the van. "I don't normally do this kind of ..." he tailed off.

"I've been here before; I know a little place. It's nice. Private. Just the two of us. It's a minute's walk, no more."

And so they walked together, one confident, the other less so, through the trees into the deepest part of the wood. The man in front turned on to a little path to the left, led the older man along and then stepped to the side and into a thicket of shrubs. He held the swathe of shrubs back as they moved on to a patch of grass, no bigger than a blanket, surrounded and protected from view by six-foot shrubbery.

"Do you c ... come here often?" the older man asked, trying to sound relaxed and jovial, although the brief stutter gave him away. "This is new to me, this is."

The man with the gloves shook his head.

"Once or twice, that's all. It's good here. Safe. The van's hidden away from the road and I've never seen anyone in this part of the woods."

The man with the gloves sat down on the ground. He beckoned the older man to sit next to him. After a moment's pause, he did so and, side-by-side, they made more small talk, the weather, cold and crisp, and the patch of grass, quite lush and green considering, for a few minutes. Then, as a second or two of silence between them moved towards uncertainty and second thoughts, the man with the gloves gestured to the older man to undress. He hesitated, not sure what to do.

"What do you want …?"

The man with the gloves smiled, "Just take your jacket off and lie it on the ground. Then loosen your trousers and lie down on top of it … on your front. Leave the rest to me."

"I don't want to get anything on my jacket … any stuff."

The man with the gloves smiled again, helping the older man off with his jacket and lying it on its front on the grass. The older man crouched carefully on his knees. "My … wife will want to know why I've got muddy …" The man with the gloves, controlling his excitement, hushed him down as the older man undid the top button of his trousers and then lay forward. "Gloves," the older man said as he did so. "Why do you wear gloves … do you have dermatitis?"

"Ssshhh," the man with the gloves said as he crouched down and put his hands on the older man's trousers. "Lift yourself up a little. Wriggle."

The older man did as he was asked as his trousers and his underwear were pulled slowly down exposing his buttocks.

"Bring your knees up nice and slowly," added the man with the gloves, smiling to himself as the older man did so.

Perfect, he thought as he took a Stanley knife out of one pocket of his fleece and then, relishing every moment, the screwdriver from the other.

He knew, from so many times in the past, that he had about thirty to forty seconds of crouching here, anticipating, enjoying the moment, relishing it. before the old man turned his head with a 'what are you doing?' look on his face.

And he leaned forward and pushed a cloth from his trouser pocket into the older man's mouth at the exact moment that he struck the first savage blow.

* * *

The man with the latex gloves had taken many lives.

This was the thirtieth, something of a milestone.

So many that he knew by now how each would unfold.

The first stabbing, the second, even the third, fourth and fifth, were carried out on the brink of ecstasy. The element of surprise and the fury of attack close to taking the life of the old man. Pinned down by the man with the gloves, he had made a series of squeals and gasping noises with each stabbing blow. Further blows, this time to the middle of the man's back, six, seven, eight, nine, ten and more seemed to extinguish the life from him. As they always did.

Rolled over, the man with the gloves listened to the old man's breathing.

It seemed still, gone, the man was all but dead.

But the man with the gloves pushed the screwdriver into the man's chest several more times. To be sure. Probing, searching for the heart, pressing hard time and again. To be certain.

The man with the gloves then looked at the old man's face. He needed to see what he looked like, this 'Edward', even though he knew that would not be his real name. Reaching out, he lifted up the man's lolling head, tipped it forward to see, really see, how he looked.

Dyed hair, a clumsy ginger, eyes staring and bloodshot, cheeks sunken, he had a hooked nose and protruding ears. The man with the gloves let the head fall back with a thud. He reached for his Stanley knife on the ground next to the body.

Ripped open the old man's shirt.

Wiped at the skin with his arm, scratched the man's likeness, all exaggerated nose and ears, into the fleshy part of his stomach.

Sat back, satisfied.

After a minute, perhaps two, he suddenly began scratching

angrily at the caricature, over and over, until he fell back exhausted, now spent.

It was this time, after he had finished.

That the man with the gloves loathed so much.

A slowly growing, sickening fear of getting caught.

He knew, as the darkness fell, that he had to be business-like, professional – and keep busy. Not dwell on it. There were times in the past, early on, where he had meticulously gone through pockets, wallets, even bags, to find out more about the other man. His name. His age. Where he lived. What he did. To confirm he was like Father.

Leading a double life.

Public respectability.

Private horror.

But he had learned not to do it any more, just to imagine the man's secret life in his mind. He had, as one man took his final breaths, once come across a tiny card, written in a small child's hand, tucked inside his wallet. 'I love you' in a mix of large and little, skewed and straight, felt-tipped letters.

He knew he had to see these men for what they were.

Lying to their wives. Cheating. Shaming their children.

And maybe more, like Father, maybe much more. Monsters.

He started by picking up a button from the man's shirt that was on the ground and a comb that had fallen from his pocket. He tucked these into the old man's bloodied jacket and then struggled to put the jacket back on him, cursing quietly until he had managed it.

He then took folded-up, heavy-duty black bags from one trouser pocket and a small roll of black tape from the other. Pulled one bag over the torso of the body. The other bag, a harder struggle with bent and uncooperative legs, from the feet to the man's waist.

Taped the bags together, then round and round and round with the black tape until it was all used up. An imperfect shroud, with the fingers from one hand stretching the plastic close to splitting, but sufficient for his needs.

He ignored his own dark fleece, spattered with the man's blood, for the time being. He'd burn that, with everything else, later.

The blood on the grass seemed to have soaked through and into the dirt. Nothing else there on the ground around him.

In the failing light, he knew he just had to wait until darkness to go to the van. Check the path was clear. That there was nobody about. Then back to collect the body, up and over his shoulder, and return to the van.

And home. To the cesspit in the old outhouse building.

Tipped in with all of the others. Left to rot and decompose.

And then the burning of the clothes. And the endless washing.

* * *

The man with the latex gloves stood up on the blanket-sized piece of grass and listened long and hard. His ears strained for the sounds of people walking, talking, moving about.

He could hear the wind in the trees close by and the cars on the main road not so very far away.

But nothing closer. No old men and their dogs. Couples in the bushes. Hikers striding out along the path.

No, nothing. He pushed his way carefully out of the shrubbery and onto the path; no more than an overgrown dirt track, really. It seemed darker here, the pathway lined by tall trees seeming to reach up to the sky. Again he waited, listening, looking both ways, for any signs of life.

A rustle.

A clicking noise.

Slight movement in the undergrowth.

Nothing of note. A rabbit maybe, no more. He checked both ways, peering into the fading light. Stood for a moment and saw the dark shadow of a figure down to the left, standing there watching him. He swallowed. Raised his hand in greeting. But the shadow, the dark solid shape, did not respond in kind nor move. A moment longer. Spooked, and as his eyes adjusted to the light, he could see it for what it was. A bush, no more.

Moving now. Striding. As quickly as he could.

Halfway to the van.

But still looking. Listening.

This was the time he feared the most. He was, he knew, analytical before, able to suppress his urges as he assessed the park, the toilets, the possibilities. As he killed, in the midst of ecstasy and release, he had a fleeting sense of happiness. Afterwards, there was a feeling of sickness, the anticipation that, after everything, all that he had done, he might be seen and everything could unravel in seconds.

And then he was there.

At the van, tucked off the road and into the trees.

Close to safety again, just a few strides away.

He stood back, in the dark now, just watching the road, checking the passing traffic. A car going one way, too fast. Another, a minute, maybe two, later, going the other. Not so much, not at this time of the evening, on this back road to nowhere. He would be safe if he were quick.

He doubled back as fast as he could, walking not running, listening and watching.

Back through the shrubbery into the grassy place with the dead body wrapped in bags.

A fireman's lift, dead weight across his shoulders, a struggle these days, but still just possible.

The man with the gloves walked steadily, step-by-step, along the path towards the van. This he thought, he knew, was his last kill. Too many close calls, more in recent times. The vicar at the home. So risky to go back. And now this weight on his back, his knees almost buckling, too heavy for him these days.

But he could see the van, not far in front of him, could make it there without having to stop, falling to his knees, the body lying beside him as he gathered his strength for one final lift and walk. Almost there, just a few more steps.

He stopped briefly, checking the road. All quiet. Could not wait longer, the body on his shoulders close to making his legs give way. He stumbled to the van, the bagged body sliding off his back to the ground as he fell forward onto his knees. Opened the doors, half dragging, half lifting the body up and onto the floor, rolling it in.

He stood up, pushing the doors closed, snatching at breath.

Looked back towards the woods.

A young fair-haired boy, maybe ten or eleven years old, was standing there, holding a lead attached to a Jack Russell dog.

The dog started barking.

PART THREE

THE HOUSE

13. WEDNESDAY 14 NOVEMBER, 6.27PM

The man with the latex gloves drove his van slowly along the main road into the forest. He kept his speed at a steady twenty-seven or twenty-eight miles per hour, had done since he had slammed the van doors shut back in the woods and set off for home.

Knew this drive would seem to take forever.

Breath held. Eyes on the rear-view mirror. Heart thumping.

Some thirty to thirty-five minutes stretching out endlessly.

This was a quiet road that twisted and turned its way through the forest. Cars were few and far between, racing up behind him as often as not, slowing to his pace and then accelerating fast as they turned a bend and saw a long, straight stretch ahead. He watched as the last one disappeared and the next one appeared in the rear-view mirror a few seconds later, still some way off. He checked the speedometer and slowed the van a touch back to twenty-seven miles per hour.

The boy and the dog had troubled him. He had jumped when he saw them, never imagining for a moment that anyone would be there. Looking. Watching him. Seeing everything. It had never happened before. He knew he had always been lucky. Realised his luck could not last forever. But he did not expect it to end like this. The boy with his big saucer eyes. The dog yapping and yelping. He did not know what to do, how to respond.

The car behind was close now, tucked in at the same speed, twenty-seven, twenty-eight miles an hour.

It annoyed him, the car, up so close against his van. He wished it would pass him by.

Leave him alone with his thoughts on his journey home.

His instinct, with the boy and the dog, was to ignore them, to carry on as if what he was doing were perfectly normal. The bagged body, if the boy had seen it, no more than a shot deer. A dead Bambi. As he had stood there thinking, looking at the boy, he finally moved, breaking the moment, towards his van door.

As he got to the door and looked back at the boy, still watching him, and the dog, now quieter but pawing at the ground, he thought he might say something, perhaps making a jokey reference to a dead deer. "Oh dear, a doe, a female deer."

But he hesitated, not exactly sure if that were the best thing to do. Then he thought he might shoo the boy away, gesturing with his arms as if to say, 'Go on, clear off, you bloody nuisance, you shouldn't be here. Be off with you.' But he hesitated again, struggling to form the right words, the correct tone.

The car was still behind him as he turned a bend and looked towards a straightish stretch of road.

So close that he could barely see its lights.

He slowed a little, down to twenty-six, twenty-five, twenty-four, to encourage the car behind to overtake and pull away.

When he had got into the van and sat down, he looked once more at the boy. He could not, in the fading light, quite make out the expression on the boy's face, but he was still there, looking back, taking it all in. He sat there for a moment longer, looking out through the windscreen, staring the boy down so that he would turn away, tugging at the dog's lead, to disappear back into the woods, forgetting about the man and the van and what was in the black bin bags.

But the boy did not move, and the dog settled down, sitting there, waiting for the boy's instructions. The man moved his left hand and turned on the van's lights, adjusting the dipped beams to headlights shining in the boy's face. The boy looked startled, scared even, raising his hands to his face to shield his eyes. The dog moved back, at first frightened and then growling again. Still the boy stood there, as if defiant, refusing to move.

The car was behind him, so precise, adjusting its speed as he moved faster and then slower to shake it off.

He knew that whoever was in the car was playing with him, trying to scare him. Teenage boys going on a night out. Having fun at his expense.

He pushed the car up to thirty, thirty-two and then thirty-five. The car behind came with him, almost nudging his bumper now.

It was at this point, with the boy standing there and the dog growling and pulling at its lead, that he had decided what to do. He would grab the boy and the dog, put them in the van and take them away. He thought about this and decided it was the best course of action. He would not harm the boy or the dog. He would lock them up for the night. That would teach the boy a lesson. A short, sharp shock. To teach him to behave himself. To keep quiet.

But the more he had thought about this, the more it bothered him. The boy's family might call the police when he didn't return home from walking the dog. The idea of bringing the boy back to the place in the woods a day or two later and then leaving him here troubled him more. The boy would be questioned, for sure, and he might well remember all sorts of incriminating things.

So, although it sickened him and broke every principle he had ever held dear, he decided he would have to kill them both and bury the corpses. A terrible choice, but there was nothing else to be done. It was not what he wanted. But he could not risk exposure. It would be the end of everything. He had to do it.

He looked ahead, knowing that his turning was coming up, when he'd move off the main road and into a side lane.

By row upon row upon row of Christmas trees.

He checked his wing mirrors again. The car was still there. He kept watching even as the road twisted and turned. A glimpse of light from the moon, between the trees, and he suddenly saw that it was a police car.

* * *

The man with the gloves knew this moment had been coming for a long time now. Had known, one way or the other, for almost half his lifetime. He had thought, on and off, how it might all end. Being overpowered by someone stronger than him, most likely. Or spotted with somebody who was later reported missing. His van seen, the registration noted down carefully. Two and two put together. The knock on the front door late one night.

And he had thought about what he would do when it did. He'd rush out of the kitchen through the living room to the back door by the vegetable garden to get away. But he knew there would be other police out there, maybe armed, just waiting, in hiding for him.

There were other possible endings. He would fight back if he were overpowered and held down by his planned victim as they called the police on their mobile phone. He'd struggle endlessly for the chance to escape. He'd never give up.

But, of all the various permutations, he had never imagined it would end this way. A police patrol car on his tail, playing with him, toying, as they closed in on his van.

He looked again at the wing mirror, saw the police car was still there, so close to him now that if he braked, it would be sure to crash into his van.

Did not know what to do. A sense of helplessness.

He could accelerate away, racing for his life. But they would most likely keep pace, forcing him off the road. An unseemly scramble as he tried, unsuccessfully, to get out of the van and run. Even if he got away, where would he go? They had his registration number, knew who he was, where he lived.

Brake sharply then. The police driver and passenger, taken by surprise, shaken by the crash. Dazed and bewildered, he could take his chances with them, armed with his screwdriver and Stanley knife. Up and out of his van fast, to the police car, tugging open doors, slashing and stabbing them. It was quiet here, on this road. No one around. Nobody to see. No one to interrupt him. If he were quick, could brace himself for the crash, have the element of surprise on his side, he could just about manage it.

Then what? These days, they'd probably have some sort of recording device, a dash-cam they call it, that would film the van, the crash and his fast approach towards the police car armed with the screwdriver and the Stanley knife. He could take it out and smash it into a million pieces. But maybe the recordings were held somewhere else, perhaps they went straight back to the police's main computer. He did not know. He did not really understand such things. He did not have a computer. Nor a mobile phone. Nothing like that.

His was an old-fashioned life of BBC TV and newspapers, cash and cheque books.

He knew it.

He liked it that way. He did not like the modern world.

The van approached the turning to the lane. A little way along now on the left. And then by the Christmas trees. Or straight on this road, through the forest towards the coast. The police car playing with him, cat and mouse, ready to pounce.

He did not know what to do. Felt paralysed. His mind and body failing him when he needed them most.

All he could think about at this moment was how dry his mouth was and that he did not seem to be able to swallow. And he realised how tight he was gripping the wheel. So inconsequential, such nonsense, when everything was about to end for him.

And then the police car pulled out from behind his van. He kept his eyes fixed on the road ahead, ignoring the sweat pouring down the side of his face, as the car pulled alongside him. A brief second, and he could sense the police car passenger's eyes upon him. He held his breath, five ten, fifteen seconds and more. And then the police car accelerated and moved away, up to forty, fifty and sixty miles per hour, disappearing into the distance.

He turned the van left, on to the side lane, heading towards the Christmas trees.

Breathed out, long and endless, realising suddenly that he had not been breathing properly since he had first seen the police car in the moonlight.

Knew how close a call this had been, the police stopping the van, opening the back doors, seeing the old man's body wrapped in bin blacks. "What's this here then?" signalling the end.

He had not killed the boy or the dog. Was suddenly glad of it. Knew in his heart he could not have done it. He was neither proud nor ashamed of killing the old man, nor any of the other middle-aged men over the years. It was just what he did. He saw it as a culling. Of men who led respectable lives by day and sordid ones at night. And of monsters, like Father. They did not deserve to live. Such monsters. Their families were better off without them.

But he had never killed – culled – anyone else. He had never laid a finger on a woman, young or old. Had always respected them. He had learned much about women from Mother. Their ways. But he had never been with one, physically, at least not for a long time. And even then, not much more than teenage fumblings. He had got as far as the girl's breasts, but they had reminded him of cow udders dripping with milk from when he had worked with farm animals years ago. He had recoiled and gone no further with her, pulling her blouse to cover her breasts and apologising for being so forward. She had laughed, sourly, at him.

He did, at times over the years, think that he would have liked to have been a father. Would have been a good one for sure. He would have raised them well, a boy and a girl, the boy older, the girl younger, perhaps two years between them. He could see them clearly in his head. He would have been a firm but caring father, a proper one. Strong but loving. But for that he would have need a wife and he did not think he could be with a woman with her wants and needs.

The idea – of being a father, with children, perhaps even a young grandfather these days – troubled him. He did not like to think about being a father and having children, Robert and Susan he would have called them, because it made him feel sad. There were occasions when he would cry about it, knowing somehow that something in his life was missing.

He did not like men, not like that anyway. Not in any way, really. He had never made friends easily. There was a boy at school whom he had liked, and they had played together for a while in the playground. But the boy, Andrew, had said that, when they were wrestling, he had been too rough and had hurt him and so he did not play with him again. It did not matter, not really. He had never felt the need for friends. Could not see the point of them.

He looked across as he passed the old familiar rows of Christmas trees. Almost home now.

Two, three more minutes and he swung the car to the left again and pulled over onto a long driveway of gravel and churned-over mud.

He looked towards the trees and saw a man standing there with an axe. Waiting. The man with the axe walked quickly towards him.

* * *

The man with the latex gloves climbed out of the van and moved to the doors at the back. He trod heavily through the gravelly mud.

He looked across at the man with the axe and nodded at him.

The man with the axe gazed back with a child-like expression of hope on his face. A child on Christmas Eve. "Did you get one? Did you get one," he asked excitedly.

"Yes."

"Like Father?"

"Yes."

"A bad man?"

"Yes, very bad."

The man with the axe rested it on the ground next to him, thought slowly for a moment and then carried on with his questions.

"Did he hurt children?"

"Yes."

"Did he touch them in their private places?"

"Yes."

"Did he hit them?"

The man with the axe touched the side of his head as he stared vacantly at the man with the gloves.

Brothers.

"One smart, one simple," as Father used to say.

Before he started his beatings. And more.

"Help me unlock the doors, get the bad man out of the van." The man with the gloves gestured the man with the axe forward.

"Can I see his face?"

"Not yet, help me to get him to the cesspit and you can have a look before we tip him in."

"Promise?"

Between them, they opened the van's doors and the man with the gloves reached in towards the bagged-up body. He dragged it out by its feet, the head and shoulders bumping along the van's floor, over the edge and hitting the ground before the man with the axe could catch hold.

"Sorry."

"It doesn't matter, leave the axe there and pick up that end, share the load."

"Yes I will."

Together they lifted the body, struggling with its awkward bulk and then, once they had got to grips with it, to get into an easier stride. The man with the axe was clumsy and they had to stop once, twice, three times.

"Tell me what happened."

"Not now," the man with the gloves puffed. "Later, when we've tipped him in."

"Was he hurting a little boy or a little girl?"

"Both, he was hurting both," the man with the gloves replied. "He was like Father. He hit them and hurt them, and he made them do things they did not want to do."

The man with the axe stopped and looked across with tears in his eyes. "I hate him," he said. "I hate him. I hate him."

They carried on, walking slowly. Dark now, all they could see was a light from the farmhouse ahead of them. Follow that, and they would stay in a straight line. And come out near the outbuilding with the cesspit.

The man with the axe looked again at his brother. "Tell me what happened. Tell me."

"Stop then, stop here, rest for a minute."

They stopped and laid the bagged body down between them.

"I forgot my axe. I left it at the van."

"Leave it for now. One of us can go back and get it later and shut the doors and lock the van, too."

The man with the axe crouched down by the body. He reached into his pocket for a small tin and a box of matches. With shaking hands, he opened the tin and took out a roll-up cigarette, thin with tobacco at one end, fatter at the other. After lighting two matches that burned down to his fingers, he lit the cigarette with the third and smiled happily to himself as he inhaled the smoke.

"Go on. Tell me. Please."

The man with the gloves sighed as he crouched down, too, reaching across for the tin and rummaging through for the best-made cigarette, which he lit, dragging on the strong tobacco. He looked across at his brother, so similar to him except for the sagging eyelid and crumpled skin to the right side of his face. An accident, it had been said, when burning a field. The reality was a mix of violent blows and a hot iron pressed too hard and too long by Father so many years ago.

"I was walking through the woods …"

"Which woods?"

"I was walking through the woods near Ipswich when I heard screaming. I could not tell if it was a boy or a girl."

"A girl," the man with the axe said firmly. "Girls scream when they are in pain. Boys do not." He touched the side of his face again. "Go on, tell the story."

"I heard screaming and I ran into the woods. There was a man there …"

"What did he look like? The man? Like Father?" the man with the axe asked. "Tell me."

"The man wore a suit. Like Father used to wear when he went to work and for church on Sundays. And he stood there with the boy and the girl on their knees at his feet …"

"What did they look like, the boy and the girl? Were they pretty?"

"Yes, she was a pretty blonde girl with pigtails and he was a handsome blonde boy with curly hair. And the man stood over them holding himself in his hands."

The man with the axe looked down at the ground and shook slightly. After a while, he dragged heavily on his cigarette and then spoke. "He is a very bad man."

"I said to the children, "Go, children, go on, run away and I will deal with this bad man. And they ran off and I saved them by ..." he gestured towards the body.

"He was a very bad man ... can I see his face?"

The man with the gloves finished his cigarette, squeezing the tip with his fingers and then dropping it and crushing it into the ground with his foot. He glanced over at his brother, saw the look of excitement on his face, and then reached for the bagged body. He felt with his fingers across the plastic, searching for the old man's nose and forehead and then down to his chin. He ripped at the bag as it tore, exposing the dead man's face.

"There," he said. "Can you see?"

The man with the axe leaned in, peering at the face, closer to the body than he needed to be.

"He is a bad man."

"Yes."

"The little girl and the little boy will be safe now."

"Yes."

"There will be more bad men?"

"Yes ... but don't worry about that now ... come on, give me a hand ... let's get him to the pit."

One final look from the man with the axe and he pulled the black plastic back over the face. The man with the gloves knew, as they stood and heaved the body up, that they were not yet done with it. Almost, but not quite.

He realised, as they took the body to the cesspit, that the man with the axe would suggest that he alone would deal with the body, that the man with the gloves should go and fetch the axe and shut the van doors and lock the van.

"Yes," the man with the gloves said, a minute or so later, when they rested the body on the ground close to the cesspit. "I'll go and lock the van."

The man with the axe smiled to himself as he turned away to drag the body towards the pit.

"I'll see you in the farmhouse in ten minutes," the man with the gloves said.

"Yes," the man with the axe answered.

"Make sure you're clean and tidy before you come back to the farmhouse. For Mother."

The man with the axe nodded his agreement.

14. THURSDAY 15 NOVEMBER, MORNING

"So," Gayther said, looking at Carrie, Cotton and Thomas around the desk in the portacabin office. "A bright and early start. All well with everyone? We have a busy day. Busy, busy, busy. Lots to do."

Cotton and Thomas nodded and smiled.

Carrie went to say something.

Gayther hushed her down, eager to share out the day's work-load straightaway.

"Cotton, Thomas – jobs for you this morning. I want you to track down the two who got away from The Scribbler. Alan Wade, the teacher at the private school in Ipswich. And the other … Martin Wilkerson, the bank manager from Diss. They'd be retired now. See what you can find. I'd like to have a chat with them. You never know. Every little thing is helpful."

Gayther turned to Carrie.

She went to speak.

He shook his head, silencing her. "In a minute ... busy, busy."

He continued, "Carrie, lots to keep you occupied. I want you to speak with whoever's handling the Karen Williams case ... and Aland ... and bring us up to speed on that as soon as you can ... I think we can dismiss them as Scribbler-related, but you never know. Sally and Jen, whichever one it was you spoke to, contact them and see if anyone recognised the photos. We'll go back in this afternoon if they did. If we get a positive identification, we can move forward fast on that."

"We also need someone to check out Halom and whether he was at the caravan park when he said he was. Probably best to run up there. Carrie, can I leave that with you for this afternoon, please? Take Thomas or Cotton." Before she could answer, he went on. "Burgess ... vanishing like this ... I don't buy it. Something about it bothers me. He's the one my money's on. So, Cotton, Thomas ... one of you ... have another go at that this morning. Dig deeper. See if you can find him. I can't help thinking he'll not have an alibi for the night of Lodge's killing. If he doesn't ... well, maybe the net's closing in already."

Gayther blew out his cheeks, leaning back in his chair and stretching his arms out above his head. He then leaned forward, summing up, "And that just leaves Challis and his completely over-the-top reaction to our visit yesterday. And the son ... getting the records wiped ... the London lawyer. That doesn't add up. None of it. We need to follow that up at some point soon. It worries me. Something's not quite right there either. I just can't put my finger on it. Anyone? Any thoughts on Challis? From what you've seen so far? Is there something I'm missing?"

He turned towards Cotton, who looked pensive but didn't say anything.

Thomas shrugged slightly, "Not sure, sir."

He turned towards Carrie. "Go on then, Carrie, you've been itching to say something. What is it?"

"Boss Man, sir. He popped in five minutes before you arrived. Looking for you. He wants you to go and see him at 11.30."

Gayther shrugged his shoulders. "Did he say what it was about? I'm due to see him at the end of the day anyway."

Carrie shook her head. "No, sir. He didn't give anything away, sir. Just asked if you were in yet and, when I said you weren't, that you should go and see him at 11.30."

"Ask or tell, Carrie?"

"Sir?"

"Did he say, 'Ask Gayther to come and see me' or 'Tell Gayther to come and see me'? Ask or tell, big difference."

"Not certain, sir."

"Did he ask you anything … about what we were doing?"

Carrie paused. "I was sitting here sir, Thomas was there, Cotton was there. Where we're sitting now. The door was pushed open. Boss Man stuck his head round. 'Is DI Gayther in yet?' he said. I said 'No'. He said, 'Get him to come and see me at 11.30'. That was it, sir."

Gayther nodded. "Okay, well, we'll see what that's about."

Carrie looked at Thomas and Cotton. She shook her head ever-so-slightly. Gayther did not notice as he stood up and gathered up his papers and files.

"Okay, everyone, crack on … full steam ahead. Meet back here at, let's say, noon."

He stopped.

"High noon, possibly, depending on what Boss Man has to say."

* * *

"Sit down, Roger ... take a seat."

Bosman gestured Gayther towards the chair on the other side of the desk to him in his small and compact office.

"Guv," Gayther replied, sitting down. He could see a new, thin file on the desk between them. Nothing was written on it.

There was a long pause as Bosman looked at Gayther, who looked back steadily, impassively, waiting for the conversation to begin.

"Roger, so tell me, how are you getting back into the job?"

"Well, thank you, very well, we've hit the ground running."

"So I've been hearing ... tell me what you've been up to so far ... succinctly."

Bosman settled back in his chair, looking relaxed, his hands folded neatly together in his lap. As if he has all the time in the world for me, thought Gayther. Waiting for me to dig a bloody great hole for myself and to keep on digging until I disappear.

"Early days. Going through the old files. Cold cases. LGBTQ+ ... as you know."

Bosman smiled encouragingly at Gayther as if to say, 'go on'.

"And I've got that young Carrie with me, she shows promise. And two of the new DCs, Cotton and Thomas, helping out. Doing desk research and that sort of thing."

Bosman rested his arms on the desk. "So, what have you been looking at first, Roger, which case?"

"This and that. Prioritising. Getting things in order. Getting up to speed. Sorting things out. Setting up a system."

Bosman crossed his arms, sat back and looked long and hard at Gayther. "You've had a tough year or so, Roger. I know that. Annie. Your ... ill health. Recuperation. I'm not unsympathetic. We're very supportive of … mental health issues … in the job these days. Do you feel you're ready to be back in the cut and thrust just yet?"

"Yes, definitely, 100 per cent," Gayther paused, sensing Bosman was leading the conversation somewhere he did not want it to go.

"Then, as you are 100 per cent, and you don't need molly-coddling, don't give me the prioritising getting-up-to-speed bullshit. Since when did you ever set up a system? Or do anything by the book. Or approach anything other than in a zig-zag. Straight question, Roger, straight answer. What case have you been working on?"

"The Scribbler, remember him? The gay serial killer … the serial killer of gay men … from the late eighties. One of the victims … one of the ones who got away, a Reverend Lodge, was found dead a month or so back, came out of a first-floor window at a care home near Dunwich, with The Scribbler's motif … criss-cross scratching … on his stomach. We've been looking at that case first. It's an interesting one."

Bosman lifted up the file on the desk and opened it. Gayther could not see what was in the file but watched as Bosman read through whatever it was. A single page of notes, Gayther guessed.

There was a moment's silence. And more.

Gayther felt Bosman was dragging it out.

That he was about to be pulled off the case. Or worse.

"Roger. How many LGBTQ+ cold case files did we give you?"

"About this many," Gayther lifted his hands, a gap of about four or five inches between them.

"Is there any compelling evidence that gives you a strong reason for re-opening this particular case first and so … enthusiastically?"

"The Scribbler's victim is dead … his trademark scribble on the corpse … The Scribbler may kill again soon."

Bosman dropped the file back on the desk, sighed louder than he needed to as he sat back and then turned to look out of the small office window, thinking.

"Other than a scribbled stomach, which does not seem to have troubled anyone else … the doctors, the coroner … only you … what else do you have? Specifics, Roger."

"Well …" Gayther thought quickly, "we've been to the care home. Checked that out. And we've talked to two of the original suspects that we pulled in, one, the third one, has disappeared. And we're going to talk today to …"

"Enough," Bosman said, his voice rising. "Other than the scribble, do you have anything concrete?"

"Well, it's early days. We've only just started. There are still plenty of leads to follow up."

Bosman leaned forward and re-opened the file.

"We've had a complaint from this care home. A Mrs Coombes. That you were aggressive and intimidating in your manner and that you ended your visit by chasing an employee down the corridor. That you were told to stay away and then went back again to harass that same employee. This was a matter put to bed by Imram Abidi, what, seven weeks ago? Imram's razor sharp, very reliable. You didn't even speak to him first before storming in, did you?"

"No. But …"

"And Barry Johnson's been on to me – he's got the Karen Williams case. You turned up at the house of this Mrs Williams out of the blue, then took it upon yourself to interview – re-interview – the landlords of the pub where she'd been that night and then, to top it all, you went back to the care home to threaten this employee again. So, you've trampled over Johnson's case left, right and centre and pissed him off big time."

Gayther nodded. "I guess I …"

"And, as if that's not enough, I've just heard from the solicitor of Ray Challis in London. Again. Again, Roger. I had to deal with him before when his son was arrested and wanted his records wiping. Pain in the arse know-all. Seems a plain-clothes police officer driving a silver Ford turned up at the Challis workplace unannounced ... well, you know the rest ... you've been hassling him, too ... God's sake, he was interviewed thirty years ago and released without charge. I was on the team, remember? I interviewed him. Me."

Gayther nodded, not sure what to say.

"Roger, giving you the LGBTQ+ cold case files was a way of ..."

"Shunting me sideways into a portacabin office to shuffle files here and there ... back and forth ... until I gave up and took retirement."

"Roger, we go back a long way. To Annie." Bosman paused, before adding quietly, "Best man won ... Look, you're a good officer. We just want to ease you back in slowly."

"Be rid of me for good, more like."

"I'm not having an argument with you, Roger. And you forget yourself. You need to remember I was promoted to this side of the desk, not you. Get over it."

Gayther looked down, not wanting Bosman to see the resentment in his eyes.

Bosman stood up, indicating the meeting was over. "Take the Scribbler file and ..." he held up two hands as if he were holding a thick pile of files, "... put it at the bottom. Forget about it. Unless you have compelling evidence, I don't want to hear any more about this ... Scribbler."

"Or else?" Gayther answered as he stood and turned to leave.

"Roger," Bosman said sharply and was about to add ...

But Gayther had left, slamming the door as he went.

* * *

Gayther sat alone in the half-empty staff canteen, at a corner table, looking out across the car park, nursing a now-cold mug of coffee. He had eaten a packet of three biscuits, knew he shouldn't have, given his diabetes, and had the crumbs from them all down his front. He brushed at them half-heartedly and sighed, not sure what to do next. He could just go out the front doors now and walk and walk and walk until he vanished into thin air. He knew he wouldn't. But part of him would like to. A big part.

There were moments when he felt he could not be a policeman any more. That the new breed of police officers, with their systems and analytics and algorithms, and political correctness and doing everything just so, had somehow passed him by. His policing, mixing dogged perseverance and intuition, was from another age. A time when he knew how the world worked, what was what, and what was right and wrong. Now, it was all topsy-turvy and he was out of place. An oddball. A misfit. An old man on medication. He felt like taking his police pension and selling his house and moving away. They – he and Annie – had talked of retiring to Spain or Portugal. But he knew he did not have the funds, not really, his modest three-bed semi on the outskirts of Ipswich getting him little more than a one- or two-bed apartment on some holiday complex in some obscure resort. And he did not play golf. Nor like the sun that much.

Fact is, he was alone with nothing much to do to occupy himself outside of the job. His high-flying son was busy, getting on with his life in London. An important job in the Met. Birthday and Christmas cards. The odd visit. No partner. No grandchildren. He thought that moment had passed. He had no hobbies or interests. No friends. No other relatives either, apart from the cousin with the horse face who had pretty much disappeared off the face of the earth.

If he dropped down dead tomorrow, no one would really care.

Not even him.

He turned his face to the window and thought he could just about give up now.

"Guv, guv?" Carrie sat down opposite him at the table. "What's going on, what did Boss Man say?"

He turned slowly towards her, forcing a smile. He really wanted to be left alone, to stew over things. "Off the case, Carrie. Unless we have compelling evidence."

Carrie sat there looking at him, could see he was upset. Then she spoke, "Isn't the drawing and scratching out on Lodge's stomach compelling evidence?"

"Not compelling enough, apparently. Maybe I just jumped to the wrong conclusion."

Carrie shook her head. "Someone put them there, the drawing and the scratches, and it wasn't Lodge … remember, you said, there was no knife found."

Gayther shrugged. It was all he could do to show interest.

He wished she would go away.

Then he could go home and go to bed. Forget about it all, for a while anyway.

Carrie smiled as she reached across and brushed crumbs from his shirt. "We'd better go and get some then, guv, hadn't we?"

He looked at her, suddenly touched by her response, but then shook his head. "Bosman will have me out the door. You need to steer clear of Barry Johnson and the Williams case. He's not happy. And don't go back to Sally or Jen at the care home. They've complained too. And don't make that trip to the caravan park. Halom would kick up a storm if he found out."

"So," she asked, sitting back in her seat, "that leaves me with … what … what to do? Burgess. You said it was him for sure. Your instinct."

Gayther rubbed his forehead, could feel a headache coming on. He knew he needed to go home, get some sleep, come back again tomorrow in a better mood. "No, leave him be. Just ... go through the files. See what else there is ... something you can look at online ... that doesn't tread on anyone's toes ... or piss people off. I don't know."

He shook his head and then carried on, "Maybe someone called someone else a big fat fairy at work thirty years and they're both now dead ... that's perfect ... case closed ... write up a report on that saying how we'd press charges if only they were still alive."

"There's no point being ..." Carrie ground to a halt seeing Gayther's expression, but then added, almost defiantly, "Where's that sense of outrage, guv ... your brother, my great-uncles, righting wrongs ... There's a murderer on the loose who might kill again at any moment."

She looked at him, frustrated.

He stared back, now angry and edgy.

They sat there in silence for a moment.

"And give Thomas and Cotton some files to look at ... shuffle them about a bit ... and tell them not to bother tracking down Wade and Wilkerson ... and Burgess for that matter ... although Burgess troubles me. Something's not quite right there."

"That's it then, guvnor, is it? For The Scribbler? We're just giving up?"

He shrugged, knew he was being unreasonable, taking his frustration out on Carrie, who he liked a lot. He couldn't seem to help himself. "Yes, until that compelling new evidence turns up, Carrie."

"And what will that be, this compelling new evidence?"

Gayther got to his feet to go. "Another murder, Carrie, with some scribbling all over the corpse. Is that compelling enough?"

"So, we just leave it then, let the criminals go free … let the families who have never known what happened to loved ones carry on with their suffering … leave them without dignity. Just give up. In spite of everything you said. Just so many empty words."

They looked at each other.

Both angry.

Carrie turned and walked out, slamming the door behind her.

15. THURSDAY 15 NOVEMBER, LATE MORNING

A line of men with axes, each man sweating with exertion, chopping down a row of Christmas trees.

The two brothers, one smart, one slow, were among them, one at one end, one at the other.

"Break!" cried the smart brother, the man with the gloves, the man in charge. Barking instructions like his father used to do.

All of the men stopped what they were doing, put down their axes, and made their way to a trestle table topped with holdalls and carrier bags full of flasks and foil-wrapped sandwiches. They then sat at various fold-away chairs dotted around, stretching, cursing and eating. One or two fiddled with mobile phones.

"Good, this year," one man said, wiping his brow.

"Always is here," replied another.

"Fucking hard work," an older man said.

The men, all bluff camaraderie, barely knew each other. They turned up, for cash in hand, from postcards in local newsagents' and supermarket windows. Ever-changing faces, year after year. Days of cutting, getting the trees ready for various local garden centres, and they were gone, folded notes in their back pockets to be spent in betting shops and pubs.

They knew who the boss was, the smart brother, and nodded respectfully at him, one or two old-timers even touching their fingers to their foreheads as if lifting caps. They were wary. There was something about him. And they knew they had to be respectful of the slow brother, listening to his nonsense and trivia, if they wanted a pocketful of cash to spend without telling the benefits office.

One worker, several years back, not knowing the brotherly connection, had taunted the slow brother, "So, they've let you out again this year then have they ... from the loony bin?", his exact words. Another, more recently, had shouted, "Holy mother of Jesus, it's the Phantom of the Opera." Last year, a man had mocked the collection of men's rings that the slow brother, looking around to check the smart brother wasn't within sight, had shyly shown in his extended hand. "You fucking gannet, where did you get those from?"

The slow brother, answering back, defending himself, straining for a clever answer, rose quickly to inarticulate anger at the continued banter. The smart brother intervened, stepping between his brother and the other men, dismissing them with cash paid up for the day. "What am I going to do with you?" he said afterwards, turning to the now-contrite slow brother. "Every year, every single year, you do this. From now on, you must stay indoors with Mother when we do the trees."

There would be silence, sullen and resentful.

And then, over time, as the tree-cutting then came round again, the shy comments and the hopeful requests and the solemn promises would come.

Until, finally, the smart brother would give in and agree, deciding that, this time round, he would keep a closer eye on him. But he never really did. There was too much to do.

As they gathered around the trestle table, a well-spoken man in a red bobble hat, never been here before and trying to fit in with his rougher co-workers, leaned towards the slow brother, and asked conversationally, "So, do you do this every year?"

The slow brother thought for ages, for so long that the man with the bobble hat had turned away, taking a sip of tea from a flask. Then the slow brother replied.

"Yes," he said simply, "I do it every year."

"It's my first time. Something to do really, keeping busy. I've been widowed … and have just lost my job. I was a sales adviser. Replaced by twelve-year-olds. So, I thought I'd get out and about. Fucking kids."

The slow brother did not reply. Just turned his head away, towards the row of trees that they'd be cutting down.

He glanced over at his brother, who had his back to him and was talking to one of the other men about something or other.

He then went to say something, but, at the moment, his brother shouted, "Let's go" and, as everyone rose to their feet, muttering and swearing and swallowing their final mouthfuls of food and drink, the words he said were lost.

The man with the red bobble hat picked up his axe and walked towards the row of trees.

As he did so, he turned back and smiled at the slow brother.

He got to his feet, lifted his axe, feeling the weight of it in his hands, and followed the man step by step.

* * *

The elderly, bird-like woman, stirring a saucepan full of soup on the ancient Aga oven, looked at the two brothers, her sons, sitting at the table in the kitchen of the farmhouse.

Hats and coats off, hanging by the door, boots left to the side, hands washed. They sat waiting, the smart brother tense and edgy, trying not to show it, the slow brother seemingly distracted, lost in thought.

Even now, at their busiest time of year, they still came in and sat down and ate at lunchtime. Had done, at one o'clock every day, for as long as any of them could remember. Since Father was, well, for many years now. Thirty or so.

She gestured the slow brother over, indicating he should lift the saucepan and pour the soup into the three bowls she had placed on the table, spoons to the side of each. She had put slices of white processed bread, spread thick with margarine and cut clumsily in half, on a plate in the middle of the table.

She eased herself down carefully, through aches and pains, onto her chair and watched as the slow brother fetched the saucepan.

He poured soup first into the mother's bowl, then the smart brother's and, finally, what was left, splashed into his own.

She bent her head forward, clasping her hands together, saying grace through cough and spittle. The two brothers echoed her final amen.

"This is the coldest day so far this year … my bones hurt," said the elderly woman, her voice rasping. She rubbed her arms as best she could and then pulled her worn and faded cardigan across her chest. "And the cold, it gets to me. I hate these winter months. They'll be the death of me, you wait and see. I'll be gone by the spring."

The two brothers exchanged looks as they sipped at their soup. The smart brother shook his head – say nothing – as he reached for a piece of bread and pushed it slowly, folding it over, into his mouth.

She went on, between measured, almost painful sips, addressing what she thought the slow brother was about to say. "I keep telling you … I'm not going into a home … I'm not going into that care home."

"It was a nice home, Mother," the smart brother said reasonably.

"They had cakes there," the slow brother added. "You could have home-made cakes for tea every day." He raised his hand, counting them off, finger by finger. "Fairy cakes and sponge cakes and ..."

"What do you think I am, a child?" the elderly woman answered sharply. "What do I want with home-made cakes at my time of life. I'm eighty-four, not four."

"I just thought, Mother ..."

"Don't. You don't think. You do what you're told ... I'm not well. How many times have I told you? I ache all over all the time." She lurched forward unexpectedly. "But there's nothing wrong with my mind." She tapped the side of her head. "I'm still sharp up here. And I'm watching. Both of you. I know what's going on."

The smart brother rested his spoon by his bowl. "Nothing's going on, Mother; we're just cutting the trees, same as we always do. We've got the men in from the villages to help and ..."

"I'm not talking about the trees. I'm not stupid. I know what you're doing. The two of you." She paused and went on, her voice rising and cracking, "I know."

The slow brother looked flustered, dropping his spoon into his bowl. He did not seem to notice the soup spattering up onto his hand. Head down, he looked up slowly. "We are not doing anything wrong, mother. We are your best boys."

She spoke sharply between sips of soup. "You make sure you are ... both of you ... because I'm watching you ... to make sure ... You can't fool me ... I'm not green, you know." She pulled at her eye. "See, no green there."

The three of them fell silent, working their way through the soup and eating the bread.

The elderly woman looking at them one after the other, tutting to herself.

The slow brother looking up nervously at each tut and then, as if expecting him to do something, at the smart brother.

"What's the matter with you, Sonky?" snapped the elderly woman suddenly, using an old-fashioned word for stupid. The name she often used for her slow son.

"I am not stupid, Mother, do not say that. Please. I am a good boy."

"Don't call him stupid, Mother," echoed the smart brother. "He does his best."

"Sonky and Chopsy. That's what the two of you are, always were. A simpleton and Mr Clever Dick with the gift of the gab. Neither of you are worth that much." She raised her bony hand slowly and rubbed her thumb and forefinger together.

"Do not say that, Mother, do not say that. It is not true."

"Not true?" She stopped as she finished her soup and reached for the last remaining piece of bread. "You should be in a home, Sonky. With your *Jack and Jill* reading books. And your twitching and grunting and forever fiddling with yourself. We'll put you away soon enough the way you're going. Lock you up in the madhouse … and we'll throw away the key."

The slow brother reared up, knocking his chair over in his clumsiness. "Do not say that, Mother, do not say that."

He turned to go. But then stopped, uncertain what to do, as he saw his smart brother sitting there, unmoving.

"Sit down, Sonky," she hissed at him. "Sonky wonky, the old man's donkey." She made a braying noise and then laughed, spittle on her lips.

He sat back down, angry and resentful, head bowed.

The smart brother took a last mouthful of soup. Placed his spoon carefully in his bowl. Wiped his mouth with the back of his hand. Went to get up.

The old woman turned towards him.

He hesitated and then paused, waiting for her final words.

"You two remember. This is my home. Mine. Not yours. I say what happens and when." She coughed suddenly, struggling to clear her throat of phlegm. For a moment, it seemed as though she might choke. They waited patiently until she went on.

"And nothing happens here that I don't know about. As God's my witness. Nothing, do you hear? Nothing. I'm watching you ... every minute, every day ... now go on, get out of here."

The two brothers rose, both taking their bowls and spoons to the kitchen sink.

Then walking back to kiss, one after the other, her proffered cheek.

And to the door to put on hats, coats and boots, one brother subdued, the other angry.

* * *

"I am not stupid, am I? Say I am not stupid." The slow brother strode back towards the other men sitting waiting for them by the rows of Christmas trees.

The smart brother shook his head, saying words he'd said, one way or the other, many times before. "You're not stupid. Mother's not feeling well, that's all. She loves you, really."

"She loves us both."

"Yes, both of us. And she looks after us and ..."

"... we look after her."

"That's the way it always has been ..."

"... and that is the way it always will be."

The slow brother dropped back to walk alongside the smart brother and then, as they approached the waiting men, he whispered quietly, anxiously, "I will not have to go into a home, will I? Say you will not lock me away. Say it."

The smart brother stopped and looked his brother in the eye.

"As long as I'm here, as long as I live, I promise that you won't have to go into a home. I give you my solemn promise."

The slow brother nodded and smiled back, shy and lop-sided.

"Cross your heart?"

"And hope to die."

The slow brother smiled again and then thought of his next question.

"Can I choose the next row of trees?"

"The best row of trees?"

"The biggest and best trees for Christmas."

The two brothers looked at each other and smiled.

They continued walking, but then, as they reached the men, the slow brother stopped smiling and a troubled look spread across his face. He was silent.

"Okay, listen up." The smart brother stood by the men and raised his hands. "I want you … you … you … and you, yes you, big lad … to join me to finish this row of trees …"

"… and you, Where's Wally …" He pointed at the man in the red bobble hat. "I want you to go with my brother up to the … my brother will show you where, to start preparing … he'll choose the next batch of trees, and then you'll clear the path and come back here and help us when you're finished. Okay?"

The man with the bobble hat nodded, throwing his holdall over his shoulder, picking up his axe and walking towards the slow brother, smiling.

The slow brother turned to the smart brother, a look of something close to panic on his face.

The smart brother did not seem to notice as he turned, moving towards the remaining men, shepherding them to trees they'd been working on all morning.

After a moment, as the man in the bobble hat stood smiling and the slow brother stared at the ground, the smart brother clapped his hands towards them. "Come on, come on, lots to do before the sun sets." His father's old phrase.

The slow brother reached for his axe and turned and started walking.

The man with the bobble hat followed him. "Hold on, hold on … not so fast."

The slow brother ignored him and just carried on walking alongside row upon row of trees. On and on he went.

Then he stopped suddenly at a row of trees, seemingly at random. Turned again and walked along them, looking up and looking down, touching a tree here and there with the head of his axe, almost half-heartedly as if lost in thought.

The man with the bobble hat followed him, bemused, trying to keep up, wanting to ask questions, what are you doing, why this row, what do we have to do? But the slow brother kept going and did not stop and did not turn round at all. It was as if he had forgotten that the man in the bobble hat was there.

At last, at the end of the row, they stopped, and the slow brother glanced at the man with the hat and then looked down as he spoke. "You do not like children." Half-statement, half-question, or so it sounded.

The man with the hat laughed uncertainly. An odd question. "Me? Yes, I like children. I've got two of them, boy and girl, ten and eight. They look so alike, people think they're twins."

The slow brother looked up. "People always thought we were twins. My brother and me. We look alike."

"Yes, yes, I noticed you looked similar, I mean apart from your …" He stopped speaking as the slow brother put his fingers to his cheek. "How did it happen?"

The slow brother breathed out heavily and thought for a minute, searching for a long-ago, well-rehearsed answer that he could barely now remember. "It was a fire ... I got burned ... Father ..."

"Okay, yes ... and is your father still here ... or does he have his feet up enjoying a well-deserved rest from cutting Christmas trees? Perhaps he's Father Christmas, is he?" The man with the hat laughed, to show he was being friendly.

"No-oo." The slow brother searched again for the words he was supposed to say. "Father left us ... a long time ago now ..." His words drifted away.

There was another silence, longer this time.

The slow brother thinking, searching for what to say next.

The man with the bobble hat waiting for him to speak, to say what they would be doing.

"You hate twelve-year-olds. You said that."

"Me? My work, do you mean? Oh yes, I hate twelve-year-olds all right ... but, you know, what can you do in this day and age? They're everywhere. Fuck them, that's what I say."

The man with the bobble hat smiled at the slow brother.

Bemused again at the response, a sullen and angry expression across his face. Half-face, he thought to himself. The man with the bobble hat turned away to look back down at the row of trees.

And then the slow brother raised his axe and moved towards the man.

16. THURSDAY 15 NOVEMBER, AFTERNOON

"No!"

The smart brother, appearing by the row of trees and seeing the slow brother raising his axe, shouted at the top of his voice.

The slow brother dropped the axe, startled.

The man with the hat stumbled forward in shock, falling to his knees. "Shit, you could have had my head off."

The smart brother was upon them straightaway. Handing out tools the slow brother had forgotten to take with him. Smoothing over the incident, saying the slow brother was always keen to fell the first tree of a new row … was clumsy … couldn't really be trusted. You know how it is. But, hey ho, no harm done.

"You must never turn your back on him!" A jovial comment.

"No, I'll be more careful in future." The mistaken belief that this was sheer clumsiness, nothing more – no sense of the intent to kill.

"He'll give you a centre-parting if you're not careful!"

Laughter, a sudden sense of relief. And then the smart brother was sending the man with the bobble hat back down to help the other men while he stayed behind. The brothers watched as the man with the hat walked away.

One angry, the other suddenly shame-faced.

The man with the hat turned and smiled as he disappeared out of view. A cheery wave. No harm done. And now the two brothers were alone.

"What were you doing? I saw you go. Could tell something was wrong. What is it? It looked like you were going to kill him."

The slow brother dropped his head, would not speak.

"By God, you were, you were going to kill him … for Christ's sake, why?"

The slow brother raised his head, looked to be on the brink of tears.

The smart brother moved forward, touching arms, leaning his head forward. The slow brother responded, and they stood there, heads bowed close together, their arms on each other.

"He is a bad man. He hates children. He said he does things to them. He said the f word."

"I can't believe ... I don't ... what did he say to you? Tell me. His exact words. Word for word. Can you remember?"

"He said, I go out and ... fuck children ... that was this morning. He just said, kids are everywhere ... Fuck them, that is what I say. He talked like Father."

The smart brother stood back and looked at his brother. "You must have mis ... why would he say that, why would he say such things to you like that? Out of the blue. You only just met. It's just words. He's trying to be funny. Be friends. That's all."

"He is a bad man."

A shake of the head, disbelief, frustration, maybe relief too.

"Yes, but I mean, he'd not say these things to you. A stranger."

"You said we are heroes. We are super-heroes and we destroy bad men who hurt children. Like Father. You said ... you said we are super-heroes."

"We are." He shook his head in exasperation. "We do. But we can't do it here. If you had killed him here, now, what would we have done when his family came knocking on the door ... and then the police. What would Mother say ... we are her best boys, remember?"

"Best boys, yes, we are," he replied, almost absent-mindedly. "We are her best boys."

Another shake of the head, a realisation of how close that was.

The slow brother sat down on the ground and reached for the box of matches and the tin of roll-up cigarettes in his pocket. Hands shaking, he eventually lit a cigarette before passing the box and tin over.

The smart brother lit a cigarette too, leaning his head back and blowing smoke out loudly, something close to a sigh. "You'll be the death of me, really you will," he laughed.

The slow brother looked across. "He said he has two children who look like twins. And he must hurt them. We have to stop him before he hurts them again."

"If he is a bad man ... if ... I'll find out ... we will, but not here, not now. I'll get his name and find out more about him. Where he lives. What he does. And then, if he is bad, one night, next week, next month, when no one will think of him ever being here, I'll go and find him. And then I'll do it."

"Can I come too? I could help," the slow brother said.

The smart brother shook his head. "No, I've told you before. How many times? You can't. You might be recognised. Your face. We nearly got caught ... once or twice before, all those years ago. That pub. Do you remember? ... we can't risk it again. You're too memorable, even if you wear a hood."

The slow brother touched his face as the smart brother went on.

"But I will tell you when I will be going, and you can wait in the trees until you see me get back, and you can come and put him in the cesspit on your own."

"I will do that." The slow brother looked excited. He then thought for a minute and carried on talking.

"You will find him and kill him and save the little children?"

The smart brother nodded.

"You will then bring him back here to me and I will make sure he is dead, and I will put him in the cesspit with the other bad men?"

The smart brother smiled in agreement.

"And the children, all of the little handsome boys and all of the pretty little girls, will all live happily ever after?"

The smart brother embraced the slow brother.

"Because we're ..."

They spoke together, "Super-heroes."

* * *

As the daylight faded, the smart brother raised his arm and whistled. "That's it everyone, finish up, two, three minutes please. Job's done for today."

The workmen, with aching backs and words of relief, finished what they were doing, chopping trees, dragging them towards the piles, getting them ready for the garden centres.

Then made their way to the trestle table, reaching for their holdalls, swigging cans of drink, lighting cigarettes, chewing on chocolate bars.

"Everyone, form a queue, please. You, Roy, at the front ... you, Where's Wally, at the back."

The smart brother moved to the trestle table, pulled up a chair and lifted a holdall onto the chair next to him. He nodded the slow brother over to sit on the other side of that. To do what he used to do with Father. The slow brother unzipped the bag and took out a handful of ten-pound notes, ready and waiting.

"Okay, other bags off the table, please ... make some room ... First one ... Roy? Here's your money ... sign this ..." A moment or two to sign, to nod and smile at each other, to shake hands. "No work tomorrow. We're busy. See you on Monday? We've more to do then. Good ... and the next?"

One by one, the workmen lined up to take their cash and sign and print their names, real or fictitious, it did not matter.

Then, finally, with farewells and checks of their mobile phones and shouts to be at the pub at eight, all but one made their way off, back towards the farmhouse and their cars and vans.

"Sign here," the smart brother said to the man in the bobble hat as the slow brother took out the final few notes and counted them carefully onto the trestle table. "Ten pounds ... and twenty pounds

… and thirty pounds … and forty pounds … and …"

The man with the bobble hat held out his hand and the slow brother, having counted the notes onto the trestle table, counted the notes out again into the outstretched hand. "Ten pounds … and twenty pounds … and …"

"What does this say? Alan? White?" the smart brother asked, looking at the scrawled signature and scribbled, printed name. "I can't keep calling you Where's Wally … because of your hat."

The man smiled and nodded, acknowledging the cash and the question. "It's Whyte. Y. T. E. Adam Whyte. Adam will do … will you want me back on Monday, too? I just wondered … you asked me to get to the back … am I … too slow? I'm not used to rough work like this." He smiled, slightly flushed and embarrassed.

"Your work's fine … I just wondered if you might want some more … keep it to yourself for now, but we might have some work coming up that you might do … if your family … your wife … would be okay with that?" He gestured to the man in the hat to sit down. "If you could write down your address and phone number … Adam … I can give you a call some time?"

The man reached out for a chair, sat down opposite the brothers. Then wrote down his details next to his name and signature on the sheet of paper on the table.

He smiled shyly at the slow brother. Felt perturbed at the brother's unsettling look.

Hesitated, but needed the work, something to do, some sort of prospects. A future.

"I'm widowed … I lost my wife … breast cancer … end of last year. And then I've been made redundant this year, so I've got some redundancy money but that won't last long … and I've two children … as I say …" he tailed off as the slow brother suddenly looked angry, as if he did not want to hear of such matters.

The smart brother spoke. "So, it's just you and your children at home? You don't have your mother or father there with you or a sister ... anyone?"

The man shook his head. "Just us. We live just over the fields, actually, ten minutes through the woods. My parents live the other side of Norwich, well, up near Cromer, really. We see them now and then. My wife's parents live in Stirling in Scotland. We don't really ..."

"So, what do you do ... I mean work ... and going out ... with children? Do you have neighbours who help out ... watch over you?"

The man shrugged. "No, not really. It's just the three of us. There's a young girl with a baby in the village – she's got one of the council houses down by the old watermill – the children go there after school and if I need to go out at all ... which isn't very often, lately. She was a friend of my wife's."

The smart brother nodded. He looked thoughtful, caring even, assumed the man with the hat.

"We've six cottages on the edge of this land. We don't just do Christmas trees. Not much of a living in that. The cottages have always been tenanted, but we've two come up lately, the old boys in each both died ... and they need doing up. We're going up tomorrow, the two of us, to see what we have to do. We'll need some help in a week or two. Clearing out. Painting, decorating, handyman stuff maybe ... cutting wood, drilling ... if you're interested?

The man with the hat nodded, yes, yes, he could do that, he would be interested, certainly.

Daytime would be best, yes, yes, I won't tell any of the other workers.

Well, see you on Monday and then, once the trees have all been done, I'll wait for your call. I can come any weekday. No, I won't tell anyone, yes, the other workers would be jealous.

"Our little secret!" concluded the man with the hat. He smiled, almost a sudden sigh of relief, as if all his troubles were over.

The smart brother stood up and shook hands. "I'll call you … soon."

The man with the hat went to the slow brother to shake his hand. But he had already turned away, picked up his axe and was heading for the farmhouse.

* * *

The elderly woman sat on an old kitchen chair, a blanket wrapped round her, at the bottom of the staircase.

"It's so cold tonight. I cannot feel my fingers. I shall be pleased to get to bed. To wrap up warm at last."

The smart brother stood, three or four steps up, holding the back of the chair.

The slow brother, crouched by the elderly woman's feet, gripped the front two chair legs.

"Be careful, Sonky," the old woman snapped, "you'll have me over."

The slow brother, struggling to raise the chair from below, did not answer as, ever so slowly, he lifted the chair. He smiled at his mother as he held the chair steady.

"Your breath smells. Have you cleaned your teeth?"

He shook his head. Went to say something, to explain, to apologise.

"Don't just stand there, take me upstairs."

The smart brother took one step back, the slow brother one step forward. The elderly woman held tight to the sides of the chair, issuing instructions one after the other.

"Careful."

"Move away from the wall, Sonky."

"Don't drop me."

Halfway up, the two brothers stopped, as they did every night, to get their breath. The smart brother had once suggested that they should move her bedroom downstairs. She'd not hear of it. What do you think I am, she'd said, a cripple? A stair lift, then? But no. That was an unnecessary expense they could ill afford. And they did not really want anyone inside their home.

And so, night after night and day after day, they'd take her up the stairs each evening and bring her down again the next morning. This old, cantankerous woman, who showed little love for her two sons.

The smart son, not so long ago, aware of her increasing frailties and growing belligerence, had looked at care homes in the area. A blessed relief for all of them. But the costs, he had not realised, were way beyond them. And his last visit had been, he searched for the right word, traumatic. Dangerous. He had come close to being uncovered.

"What are you waiting for? Move!"

"Hold me steady."

"Stop. Stop here. I need the bathroom."

The smart brother rested the chair at the top of the stairs. "I can do it myself. I can do it," the old woman said, lifting herself slowly up. "Help me. Help me up. Take my arm, Chopsy."

Between the two of them, the two brothers, they helped the old woman struggle across the landing and into the bathroom, untouched for decades, the 1960s, maybe earlier. She walked slowly, painfully, over to the toilet with the overhead cistern.

"Well?" she asked, looking back at the two brothers in the doorway. "Not you, Sonky. You'll have me over."

The smart brother walked across, lifted the toilet lid and rested the seat down. He reached for the toilet roll hanging from a nail in the wall and, tearing off two or three sheets and folding them over, he wiped marks from the toilet seat.

"Yes, yes," she said impatiently as she stood there, her back to the toilet.

The smart brother leaned forward to unbutton her skirt. It dropped to her feet and he took her arm as she stepped over it and back. He picked it up and put it carefully on the windowsill.

He then bent over and reached for her slip and underwear.

She spoke, looking across at the slow brother, "What are you doing?"

The slow brother pulled the bathroom door to, waiting for her to finish. To do what she needed to do. Dabbing at herself and passing sheets of toilet paper to the smart brother to clean her up if need be.

And then came the long and painful shuffle as they helped her along the landing to her room. The sagging double bed. The faded pink candlewick blankets. The piles of old magazines. The knick-knacks from long-gone funfairs of years ago.

And the bibles and religious pamphlets, from so many different religions and sects, that she had collected over the years and had read from every night until recently.

Now, the smart brother sat on the edge of her bed and read to her, from a thick, old pamphlet, a page or so at a time, as she fussed and fiddled with her sheets and blankets and the bits and pieces on her bedside cabinet. Tissues. Aspirin. Ear plugs. A glass of water.

"Listen to your father who gave you life, and do not despise your mother when she is old ..."

The slow brother sat, in the high-backed chair over by the window, listening to the smart brother's quiet and measured tones, the words little more than a blur. He had heard the same passages read time and time again. Mother's favourites. She had underlined the sentences and paragraphs she liked most. She nodded and occasionally echoed the words.

"Buy truth, and do not sell it; buy wisdom, instruction and understanding."

He looked at the window, smeared thick with dust and dirt, apart from a small, fist-sized circle that had been wiped clear in one of the small panes. He leaned in and looked through the circle, down to the front of the farmhouse and up the driveway and away.

Where the workers parked their cars and vans before walking up to the rows of trees.

Where, in that outbuilding just over the way, there was the cesspit where so many bodies were buried.

Where he had dragged them up the path, stopping for breath beneath the window of his mother's bedroom. All below that little, smear-free circle.

"The father of the righteous will greatly rejoice; he who fathers a wise son will be glad in him. Let your father and mother be glad; let her who bore you rejoice."

And he wondered, in that slow old brain, whether Mother had sat in that chair, looking out of the window at night.

When he thought, they thought, she was fast asleep.

And what, as she rubbed her bony hand back and forth on the glass, she had seen.

17. FRIDAY 16 NOVEMBER, MORNING

DI Gayther sat alone in his portacabin office, looking out of the window. It was overcast and wet; a persistent drizzle had been falling for what seemed like hours. He checked his watch, 10.25am – an hour and thirty-five minutes since he'd sat down at this chair.

It seemed much longer.

He'd done sweet F.A. since then.

Opened files, sorted papers into piles.

Moved them about and back again.

He was on his own, half-heartedly looking for a case that might be as satisfying to investigate as The Scribbler. But most, almost all, looked long dead and buried; one or two serious sexual assaults caught his eye, but looked impossible to progress through lack of evidence then, let alone now. A series of poison pen letters sent to local figures of authority accusing them of sex crimes against children might be a possibility, he thought, what with modern DNA techniques, but cack-handed police from the 1980s had probably destroyed any chances there.

Carrie had stormed off somewhere.

Thomas and Cotton seemed to have vanished. He suspected Bosman may have transferred them to someone else.

He sat there, trying to find a case, maybe two, that he could work on with Carrie when she was back with him on Monday.

And then, as he flicked aimlessly through a pile of papers, he noticed the words 'John' and 'Donkin', common-enough in Norfolk, but notable to Gayther as it was the name of a childhood friend. He stopped, looked through to see if it were one and the same person but saw that it was not – this Donkin had been born twenty, twenty-five years earlier. Not him then. Maybe his friend's father. Gayther looked idly at the photo for a resemblance but could not really remember what the child had looked like, let alone the father.

Gayther worked through the details of the case and then sat up. John Andrew Donkin. Fifty years old in 1991. Worked in an insurance office in Ipswich. Married, to Rita, for twenty-five years, two children, twelve and fourteen, older boy, younger girl. Had been reported missing one Friday evening in September. Never came home from work.

He shuffled through the scant papers; the wife had reported him missing, but then, when interviewed, revealed Donkin had told her not long before that he was homosexual and the marriage was in crisis. He'd met someone else. A man. From what Gayther could see, assumptions had been made but never followed through, and the case had somehow found its way into the LGBTQ+ pile of files. He wondered if this Donkin had returned home or left to start a new life with his male lover or … maybe, just maybe…

He would follow it up himself. See if this might be another victim of The Scribbler.

Then sat back, realising that, even if it were, he had nowhere to go with it. He needed compelling evidence.

He opened other files with renewed vigour, to see if he could find cases like this that had somehow slipped through the net. Maybe the sheer weight of numbers would make Bosman change his mind.

Some thirty, forty minutes later, he had two more cases. A Graham Wellman and a David Nicholas, both from out-of-the-way Suffolk villages.

Middle-aged men who had disappeared over the years. Believed by their wives to have been secretly gay. Reported missing. Two and two put together – and made five by everyone, thought Gayther.

If they'd been reported missing, full stop, the cases might have been linked to The Scribbler, even though they were years later, seven and ten years after the last reported Scribbler case. The post-disappearance revelation that they were gay seemed to lead to these cases being filed away as little more than routine matters.

Gayther wondered whether there was any mileage in checking out these men and their whereabouts himself. Decided, again, that even if they seemed to have disappeared off the face of the earth, it was still some way short of that all-important compelling evidence.

Gayther looked up at the knock at the door and smiled as Carrie entered the portacabin. She smiled back, a file under one arm, holding out a plate with two slices of cut toast with butter and marmalade with the other.

"Got you this, in case you didn't have breakfast today? Carbs and sugar." She smacked her lips. "Lovely."

She put the plate on the desk in front of Gayther, who pulled it towards him, picking up one of the pieces.

"I shouldn't," he said, laughing, "but I'll make an exception for you … just this once … thank you, Carrie, that's kind of you."

He ate the first and then the second piece, one after the other, in rapid succession, leaving two more pieces remaining. He hesitated and then pushed the plate halfway towards Carrie as she sat down opposite him.

"Here," he said, "take one … one each." He picked up one piece and watched as Carrie took the one nearest to her. They both smiled at each other as they ate their toast. As they finished, Carrie spoke.

"You look happy, guv. Have you found a new case for us to investigate?"

He nodded, maybe. "I've found two, no three men, married men, who have gone missing over the years and, because they were later reported as being closet homosexuals, they've … well, the files seem to have ended up here. I don't know why. I'd like to have a look at those, but …"

Gayther looked pained and then added, "Boss Man would have my … whatnots for paperweights …" he tailed off.

Carrie laughed. "We can do better than that anyway." She placed a file in front of him, flipped it open, and then carried on speaking.

"A live case. A report's just come in of a man gone missing the night before last … just down the road … ticks the boxes … Steve

Deacon's been watching out for me ... and he's passed this over."

Gayther sat up. "Compelling evidence, Carrie?"

She nodded.

"Going that way."

* * *

Carrie knocked on the red front door of the neat and tidy terraced house in the back streets of Beccles in Suffolk. She turned to Thomas, standing by her side, and smiled at him. He smiled back nervously. She wondered if this was the first time he'd been out on a case.

"Don't worry," Carrie said. "Leave the questions to me."

He nodded at her. "I thought DI Gayther would want to be here."

"He needs to keep his head down ... don't worry about that for now ... anyway ... look, if you think of a question I don't ask, write it in your notebook and pass it to me."

The door was opened, and Carrie and Thomas stood and looked at the woman in the doorway. Sixty or so, tall and angular, well turned out. She looked like she was sucking a lemon, thought Carrie.

"Mrs Taylor? I'm Detective Constable Carrie and this is my colleague, Glyn Thomas. We're here to talk about your husband, Philip Taylor. You've reported him missing."

The woman seemed taken aback. "Goodness, I didn't expect a detective, I thought you'd send an ordinary policeman ... woman ... and not so soon. I've only just finished my lunch. Has something happened?"

"Just routine, Mrs Taylor. I was there when the report came through and it was given to me and I was coming this way anyway. May I ...?" She said, stepping forward.

The woman invited Carrie and Thomas in. They made their way to the small but immaculate front room, pieces of bone china everywhere, and sat down in two wingback chairs facing a matching sofa. Carrie watched as the woman sat opposite and composed herself, brushing her hands across her skirt. Putting on a concerned face, thought Carrie, and no offer of a cup of tea.

Carrie began the conversation. "We've the basic details from you, Mrs Taylor ... Philip John Taylor, white male, fifty-five years, five foot nine inches, balding, last seen leaving work early, a building society in Ipswich, at about two o'clock on Wednesday ... tell me more, please—"

"Yes," the woman interrupted, "when he wasn't home as usual at six or by half past, I called his mobile ... at about seven. It went straight to answerphone. I thought he might have gone for a drink with a friend from work ... he does occasionally ... and had forgotten we were going out to eat with friends that evening. By the time it got to nine or ten o'clock I was ... disappointed."

"Did you think of reporting him missing that evening?" Thomas asked, ignoring Carrie's look.

"No, I didn't think it was out of the ordinary then ... I rang one of his friends in the morning – just in case he had stayed there overnight ... he has done that once or twice if he's had a drink. I thought, if he had been drinking or maybe his phone had run out of charge, well, I'd have looked silly reporting him missing that evening."

"But you reported him missing the next morning?" Carrie asked.

"Yes, because Brian, the friend I phoned, said that Philip had left work early in the afternoon, about two o'clock, to go to the dentist in Ipswich – our old dentist moved there and, well, as it's close to his workplace, Philip wanted to stay with him ... and he didn't go back to work afterwards, nor come home. That isn't like him at all."

"The dentist's name, Mrs Taylor?"

"Mathias. M. A. T. H. I. A. S. George Mathias. I don't know the practice name or address, I'm afraid. It's in Ipswich, or just outside."

"We can check that," said Carrie, making a note. "Does he know anyone else in Ipswich, Mrs Taylor, that he might have gone to see?"

"No, I don't think so. Not that I know of."

"Has he done this before? Stayed out for a day or two without telling you?" Carrie pressed.

"No, he's always very punctilious."

"When he stays out drinking, does he let you know?" Thomas interjected. Carrie looked at him, but he sat gazing impassively at Mrs Taylor.

"Well …" she smiled mirthlessly, "… he doesn't go out drinking … as you put it … but he's stayed out perhaps two or three times over the past year working for the building society. And no, he doesn't tell me on the night, as we've agreed that he might stay over somewhere if he has a drink or two. He won't drink and drive. He's very careful like that."

The woman paused.

Thomas scribbled a word or two in a notebook, but did not pass it to Carrie as she expected.

Carrie waited a moment and then went on.

"You've tried calling him again on his mobile?"

"Yes, two or three times. It just goes to answerphone every time."

"May we take the number, Mrs Taylor, so we have it … for a possible trace?"

The woman nodded, rose and moved to an old-fashioned telephone table in the corner of the room. She opened a notepad next to the telephone and flicked through the pages.

"It's 07956 …" She passed the notepad to Thomas, who noted the rest of the number on his phone. He then, after Carrie's nod, pressed the buttons to ring the number.

As the woman took the pad back and moved to sit down, Thomas shook his head, "Still the answerphone."

Carrie continued talking, "Mrs Taylor, this may seem an odd question, but I have to ask it. Have you checked to see that your husband is not in the house or the garden?"

The woman looked at Carrie in disbelief.

"It's not as ... there are cases where someone has been reported missing and, on investigation, they've been found in a back bed-room or a shed."

The woman swallowed, taking in the significance of what Carrie was saying. She shook her head.

"May we, Mrs Taylor?"

The woman nodded her agreement

Carrie nodded at Thomas, "Go and check."

There was a tense silence as they heard Thomas's footsteps on the staircase, moving into one upstairs room and then another and, finally, back downstairs again.

He came into the front room and shook his head, all clear, and then went out towards the back door.

They waited, quiet and on edge, as they heard the back door being opened and closed and footsteps disappearing into the distance.

"Just routine, Mrs Taylor. I have to complete a form, tick boxes, to confirm I've covered the basics."

The woman nodded back, to show she understood.

And then Thomas was back, nodding all fine, and Carrie could feel the tension ease out of Mrs Taylor.

"I also need to ask you if any important items may have been taken by your husband ... a suitcase, clothing ... anything to suggest he might have made plans."

The woman shook her head. "No, no, everything is as it should be. I did check."

There was a silence before Thomas spoke, interrupting what Carrie was about to say.

"So, it has occurred to you then, Mrs Taylor, that your husband might have been planning to leave?"

Another silence; both Carrie and Thomas noting to themselves the look on Mrs Taylor's face. A look that screamed yes but whispered I am too ashamed to say so.

"No ..." she answered hesitantly, "I just thought I'd check ... as a loving wife." She stopped, clearly not going to say any more.

Carrie then stared at Thomas, a warning look, don't say anything else, leave it to me. She went on.

"Might he have been in touch with friends or family members at all, Mrs Taylor?"

The woman shook her head slowly. "I've checked, I have rung everyone I can think of." She said it slowly, realising that this was almost an admittance that something was wrong, that others may know more about her husband than she did.

"When we get a missing person report, Mrs Taylor, it's allocated to an officer, on this occasion me, to ... to check the initial details ... and to carry out a risk assessment. I need to ask you one or two more personal questions, Mrs Taylor."

The woman nodded her agreement with a fleeting movement of her head. She did not, Carrie noticed, meet her eye, and was now keeping her head bowed.

"Okay, how would you describe your husband's physical health?"

The woman raised her head, looked relieved. "Fine, generally. The usual aches and pains of getting older. His back hurts from time to time. He sits at a desk all day. But that's about it."

"Is he on any medication at all, that you know of?"

"No, no, he's well."

"And how would you describe your husband's mental health, Mrs Taylor?"

"He's been …" The woman stopped, to gather her thoughts, to say what she wanted to say correctly. Then seemed to think better of it. "He's fine," she nodded.

Thomas started speaking. "Has his behaviour been any different lately? … any reason you can think of why he might go missing?"

The woman glanced from Thomas to Carrie and back.

She's hiding something, thought Carrie. But doesn't want to say.

The woman pulled a not-that-I-can-think-of face and then said no, and then repeated herself once more, no not at all.

Thomas paused, "May I ask about your—"

Carrie interrupted, speaking louder than she meant to, "Okay, that's all good, thank you, Mrs Taylor. We'll need a photo, a recent photo, of your husband and, if you have it, the registration number of his car. We can check the car and mobile phone."

The woman smiled briefly, suggesting they wait there a moment and then left the room.

Carrie turned to Thomas, speaking quietly. "Don't ask about her marriage."

"I just thought …"

"Well don't. Not now," Carrie answered.

There was an awkward silence until the woman returned, holding out a photograph and a sheet of paper.

"Here's a recent photograph of Philip. Taken last Christmas at his office do. He's in the middle. His friend Brian is to his left and that smiling young man, I don't know who he is, someone from work I suppose, is on his right."

Carrie took the photo and looked at it. She passed it to Thomas, indicating he should use his phone to photograph it. As he did so, she spoke to Mrs Taylor. "This is how he looks now?"

The woman nodded. "Yes, he's a little lighter, I think he's lost half a stone this past year … he's taken up walking some evenings … but yes, it's a good likeness."

She then handed a sheet of paper to Carrie, a motor insurance certificate. "And this is his car details, YA … a Nissan Quashqai, a dark grey one …"

She watched as Carrie passed the paper to Thomas, who photographed it. Then asked, "What will you do next?"

Carrie scribbled in her notepad, tore out the page and handed it to the woman, "My number, if you hear anything from your husband … or family and friends … anyone … let me know."

Carrie started moving towards the door. Thomas and the woman followed her.

"We'll conduct enquiries to trace Philip … we'll speak to his colleagues at work … the dentist … see if anything's been reported … trace the car … the phone, of course. We'll do all we can to find him quickly, I promise you."

Brisk handshakes on the doorstep.

Mrs Taylor shut the door.

Thomas looked at Carrie and said, under his breath, "The Scribbler?"

Carrie nodded.

* * *

Gayther watched Carrie, Thomas and Cotton as they came into the portacabin and, exchanging quiet smiles between themselves, sat down around the table. Gayther pushed away the file he was reading and smiled back at them in anticipation. They look triumphant, he thought. Surely not a breakthrough? Stranger things had happened, though. He dare not hope.

"Anything of interest there, sir?" said Carrie, a big grin on her face.

Gayther paused, then sighed theatrically, playing along with her. "No, I've spent the whole f … flipping day trawling through file after file of long-dead cases … victims … criminals … trying to find something worthwhile to do … but what have you got, sitting there grinning like a …"

"Cheshire cat, sir? We all are, sir … we've all got news for you. We've …" Carrie nodded towards Thomas, "… been to see the wife of Philip Taylor, the man from Beccles who disappeared from Ipswich, where he works, on Wednesday night."

Thomas picked up the story. "Middle-aged man … and a bit … respectable married man from a building society … left work for a dentist's appointment down the road on Wednesday afternoon. Not seen since. Disappeared without trace. Classic Scribbler scenario, sir. Absolutely ticks all of the boxes."

"Okay, well, so … what … the evidence, the compelling evidence … what are you saying … you're saying it's The Scribbler?"

"Hold on, sir," Carrie grinned again. "We'll get to that … we've just been to the dentist and Taylor left there at about three forty-five. They've got CCTV, so we have clear images of what he looks like and is wearing. Then he just vanished. His car, we got the plate from Mrs Taylor and put it straight out, has already been found by a park nearby. No CCTV there, but I've asked if we can get it picked up so it can be checked over properly."

"Okay, well, that sounds like a missing person case as it stands. I mean, you know, maybe, I guess. We can but hope. I've known cases to turn on a sixpence like this. What we need to do is—"

"No, sir. That's not all, sir. There's more," Carrie interrupted. She looks fit to burst, thought Gayther, who nodded, go on.

"Cotton's been seeing the cases coming in and yesterday morning, well, two and two usually make four … a boy, a twelve-year old boy walking his dog in woods the other side of Ipswich, saw a man acting suspiciously the night before … a couple of hours after Philip Taylor went missing … loading … well, the boy didn't know what it was … something big and heavy into the back of the man's van. He told his mum and she's been in touch. She thought it might be someone poaching deer."

Gayther laughed.

"While we, me and Thomas, have been up to speak to Mrs Taylor, Cotton tagged along to the … well, Cotton, you say."

Cotton flicked open his notebook.

"I went along this afternoon with Joe White, he sends his regards, and … Sarah, the new liaison officer … to speak to the mother, Laura Wilding, and her boy, Jacob. They live at …"

"Cut to the chase, Cotton. Is it … is it him, The Scribbler?"

Cotton nodded. "The boy described the man and his height and build … and on that basis, yes, it could be The Scribbler. He didn't get a clear view of the man's face, though."

"Well, that's The Scribbler's modus operandi …"

"He couldn't tell the man's age but thought he was old by the way he walked. What's old to a twelve-year-old-boy is pretty subjective … he said the man walked a bit like his grandpa … his mum said he was about sixty."

"Anything else?" Gayther pressed.

"I showed the boy the old picture we had of The Scribbler and he wasn't sure. He said yes at first and then said he didn't think so. I wasn't allowed to press him on it."

"No, fair enough. So …" Gayther turned to Carrie. "We're, what, going to see if we can get some of Dave Green's team up to check out the location?"

"I don't know, sir. I don't think anyone's really joined up all the dots yet. It's not been allocated. Probably Monday, I'd say. If someone higher up thinks it's all a match to The Scribbler ... or not ... just a man who's gone off for the weekend and a lad who's seen a poacher with a muntjac in the woods."

"So," Gayther shrugged. "What's next then, Carrie?"

Carrie pulled out a piece of folded-up paper from the inside pocket of her jacket with the air of a magician about to shout "Ta-Da!". Opened it. Handed it to Gayther, who looked down at a list of car registrations, names and addresses.

"The boy told us more about the van than the man. White. Medium-sized, he said. We showed him pictures and it looks like it's a Ford Transit Connect."

"A lot of them about ..."

"Better still, he remembered the first four digits of the plate, AP55, though not the rest, but ... hey presto ... there are sixteen possible matches across East Anglia ... sixteen vans ... four of us ... two days ... before Boss Man gives the case to someone."

"And not to me, I'd guess," Gayther said.

Carrie, Thomas and Cotton nodded and agreed.

"Well, we can wait for this to be risk assessed and given a number and actioned ... blah, blah, blah ... or we can crack on and catch The Scribbler before someone else is killed."

Carrie, Thomas and Cotton stood waiting.

"First thing in the morning, bright and early, we visit them all one-by-one," Gayther concluded.

18. SATURDAY 17 NOVEMBER, MORNING

The three of them sat around the kitchen table. The mother. The smart brother. The slow brother. Having their breakfast of porridge and toast and marmalade and mugs of tea.

As they did every day. At the same time. In the same way. Heads down, working methodically through it all from beginning to end.

Mostly in silence except for the old woman's clacking teeth and occasional bursts of tuneless humming. The brothers ate quietly, waiting for their mother to start and finish any conversation.

"What are you doing today, Chopsy?" she asked finally, as she raised her mug of tea carefully to her lips.

The smart brother swallowed a mouthful of toast before looking up. Thinking he had not heard her, she went to say "eh?" just as he spoke.

"I need to go up to the cottages again. We carted away Hempshell's stuff yesterday. And Collins … we've not had a chance to look that over properly. But it shouldn't be too bad. I'll do that this morning and we can move anything this afternoon."

"You'll want to get them tenanted before Christmas. We can't manage without the money for long." She laughed bitterly through tombstone teeth. "I'm too old to go out and scrub steps."

"You do not need to do that, Mother," the slow brother said, taking her comment at face value.

The smart brother nodded his head, agreeing.

"They'll need some work over the next week or two. Bring them up to standard. I'll get on to it the week after, once we've got the trees sorted. We're all right for money for a while longer."

"You see that we are. We can't make do much more. We can't go without anything … there's nothing left that we can go without." Her voice rose, cracking, "We shouldn't have to live in this … filth. Honour thy mother … that …" She stopped to think of the precise words, "… thy days may be long upon the land which the Lord thy God giveth thee."

She nodded to herself, yes, that's about right.

The slow brother shifted uncomfortably in his chair. Struggling to find the words to say. He looked pained.

"We honour you, Mother. And we take care of you. And we look after you as you looked after us when we were little. Because we are your boys, Mother. We are your best—"

"Shut up with your nonsense, stupid." The old woman put her mug of tea down on the table. "Your silly homilies don't put food on the table … clothes on our backs … they don't pay the bills … we'll have bailiffs at the door next. It won't be the first time."

"We won't have bailiffs," the smart brother said quietly. "We don't have much, Mother, but we have enough."

"Not with the cottages standing empty, going to rack and ruin. That's where we'll end up. Rack and ruin." She sobbed suddenly, angrily. "It shouldn't be like this. I worked hard, morning, noon and night, after your father …"

The slow brother glanced nervously at the smart brother.

The smart brother ignored him. Reached out instead to put his hand on the old woman's bony fingers. She shook it off.

"And look at us now," she said bitterly, "living off rents and Christmas trees once a year. Everything else … you've lost everything else. This was a good farm once. I made it so. It made money. A living. More than a living."

"That was a long time ago, Mother," the smart brother spoke soothing words. "It's not been easy … since Father … since before Father. He had to take that sales job to make ends meet … and Europe … and subsidies being cut all the time."

She shook her head dismally as he carried on.

"And we had … so much bad luck … every year there was something. All through the 1990s. And the land, no one wants the land. Over at Woodbridge, the Hensons sold up and they built … so many houses. Set them up nicely. We're too far off the beaten track. Nobody wants to live this far out, so far from anywhere," he added sadly.

"It will be the death of me, all this. I won't make it through this winter. Not if it's a cold one."

"Yes, you will. You wait. Once we've got the money for the trees in, we'll go over to Ipswich and buy you a new coat. And a bigger heater for your bedroom. Whatever you want."

She smiled, unexpectedly, to herself. Mopping at the spittle from her mouth with her fingers. "And we'll have a slap-up meal upstairs at the Co-op, like we used to do."

"Mother, the Co-op is not—"

The smart brother finished the slow brother's sentence, before he could say "not there any more".

"Not the talk of the town any more, Mother. But there's a new place to eat. Where you can have a proper three-course meal, roast beef and all the trimmings. Served by proper waitresses, all dressed up nice and proper in their black and white uniforms."

The old woman pretended to lick her lips, her thin, probing tongue somehow grotesque.

The three of them fell silent again, thinking their own thoughts as they finished their mugs of tea, had one last scrape of their bowls and spread a final smear of marmalade on the corner of their pieces of toast.

"I shall make shortbread this morning. I have plenty of sugar and flour and butter," the old woman said emphatically, suddenly more cheerful. "You can have it with your lunch."

The slow brother smiled. He liked shortbread. His favourite.

"And what will you do this morning?" The old woman turned towards the slow brother.

"I am taking the gun and going ratting."

"There's a nest of them somewhere behind the outhouse," added the smart brother. "We'll need to put poison down once we're done with the trees."

The old woman reached into the pocket of her overall, pulled out her purse and opened it, checking the contents.

"Bring me the tails and I'll give you a shiny gold coin for each of them."

The slow brother mimed loading a gun, cocking it, taking aim and firing.

The smart brother made a squelching noise at each imaginary shot, "There'll be nothing left but tails mother, he's the sharpest shooter …"

"The smartest shooter …"

"The rooting-tooting …"

"… super-duper …"

"… best-ever shooter in town."

The three of them laughed. A moment of peace, if not quite happiness. The smart brother then rose from the chair, clearing away the breakfast plates and mugs. The slow brother went towards the cupboard by the door to the staircase to get the gun and ammunition. The mother thought for a while and then spoke to the slow brother.

"Before you start ratting, go up to the fields and get me a big strong rabbit for the pot. We'll have ourselves a rabbit pie."

The slow brother, loading the gun and feeling its weight in his hands, nodded and smiled.

"The biggest, strongest rabbit … for the shiniest, brightest gold coin," he said cheerfully.

* * *

The slow brother moved carefully through the Christmas trees and out towards the fields. His gun was cocked, ready to use.

He crouched, the Christmas trees behind him, and looked over to the boundary of their land to the edge of the forest.

Knew that if he waited there for a while, probably not too long, rabbits would appear. And if he stayed still, they would come across the field towards him. He could shoot them easily. Whichever he wanted.

He did not shoot the baby rabbits with their fluffy tails.

Nor the mummy rabbits. The baby rabbits needed their mummy rabbits.

Only the big rabbits, the older, slower ones that no one loved. The father rabbits.

As he waited, he remembered when he shot his first rabbit. It was here, or close enough to it to make no difference. It was his seventh birthday. Father made him crouch down between his legs and he could feel his breath upon his neck and the smell of tobacco from his lips.

Father had made him hold the gun, finger on the trigger, and had then wrapped his big hands around his own smaller ones. He felt Father's body pressed against his, the hardness of it, although he did not really understand it at the time nor his father's heavier breathing.

He remembered the shot, the smell, the power of the gun in his hands. And, after crossing the field, the bulging-eyed rabbit that lay twitching by their feet. "Mix a my toes-ees," was what he thought his father had said.

Myxomatosis, the reality, with the two of them, and the smart brother and the mother, shooting rabbits for what seemed like forever after that. Maybe just the summer, he thought, but he could not be sure.

He sighed. Sad suddenly.

At the memories of his father.

So many of them. Forcing their way into his mind.

The nights Father would bathe the two of them. Soaping away softly and carefully, at first, until their bodies were covered with lather. The careful drying and attention to detail so they'd avoid chafing and sores.

And then the stories at bedtime, with Mother downstairs darning and sewing by the fire. The acting out of stories. Of dragons and knights. The boys kneeling and bending before him. On and on.

And the burning. With the iron. The day he had fought back, the brother, the smart brother, standing there horrified, unable even to scream. And the lies. A fire in a barn. A brave boy burned.

It was the 1960s. Another world. No one investigated, nobody cared. A respectable father. Compliant children. A silent mother. And children were seen but not heard then. Life carried on.

He felt sudden anger. Raised his gun. Ready to shoot.

And he recalled the end. When he was grown up.

The words mostly. He remembered each one. Could almost say them as a rhyme.

Father, old now, a man in his late fifties, taunting and mocking the slow brother as he stood, in the outhouse, struggling, all fingers and thumbs, to skin a rabbit.

Stupid. Ugly. Good for nothing. Waste of space. Homo. Thick as shit. Mummy's boy. Only good for fucking up the …"

And he remembered stabbing him. In the throat with the knife. Over and over again. Until he fell. Calling the smart brother. Hiding the body. The first in the old, long-since-unused cesspit.

The story the smart brother dreamed up. Rehearsed. Repeated. On and on. For ever and ever. Say this. Say that. Never anything else. Pretend you don't understand. Nor know what to say. Act dumb if you have to. That should be easy enough.

He saw movement in the trees in the forest. Rabbits.

Swung the gun in that direction. Watched closely.

But there was nothing there, just his imagination. Wind in the trees.

They saved children like them. Abused by fathers who presented one face, happy and smiling, to the world and another, of fear and loathing, at home.

At first going out together, until the smart brother said the slow brother would be recognised one day. That they would be caught. Imprisoned. Mother left alone. Then the smart brother went out on his own, until he almost got caught and stopped for a while.

And then, in recent years, more occasionally, and far and wide, the slow brother waiting patiently among the trees for the smart brother's return. To do what he did with the bodies.

And they had got away with it. All of it. For all these years. The two of them here at the farm with Mother. The smart brother out and about. The slow brother at home looking after Mother. And, in turn, Mother taking care of them.

A sudden noise behind. Rustling. The sound of a rabbit. He turned, raising his gun.

A little girl there, blonde and blue-eyed, the sweet child of his dreams.

She looked at the man with the melted face and screamed as he fired the gun.

* * *

The shot went up and over her head.

His instinct, to recoil as he shot the gun.

A moment's silence as she stopped screaming then turned and ran, screaming again.

The slow brother stood for a second or two, as if dazed by what had happened. And then he was after her, running between the

Christmas trees in a straight line following her footsteps, without thinking or hesitating.

And now he could not hear her screaming.

She ran silently. And not in a straight line.

Left to right. Running for her life.

He stopped for a moment, listening now, the gun at his side, struggling for breath. He could not hear her footsteps crunching and crackling as he might expect on dry land, nor squelching in the muddier patches.

Wondered suddenly, whether she might have taken cover.

Dropped down. Hidden somewhere between the trees.

Lying low. Waiting for him to walk slowly by. Then up and away again in the opposite direction.

He sat on his haunches, listening for the slightest noise. He could hear voices, off in the distance, his brother maybe and someone else, a man, somebody who had come to the farm that morning.

Unexpectedly, for something or other. Two men talking, maybe one looking for work. Helping with the trees.

He rose to his feet. Walked steadily, step by step, towards the farmhouse.

Deliberately making a noise, much louder than he needed to be.

Then stopped again suddenly, unexpectedly, turning around quickly, looking back into the silent woods.

A noise. A movement now. Two children, a handsome boy, that pretty girl, rising from a dip in the ground as if by magic. Turning to look at him, horror on their faces. The boy, a touch faster, wriggling to get away as the slow brother's hand reached for his arm. The girl, too timid, wincing in pain and fright as the slow brother grabbed her arm instead.

She went to scream again. The slow brother clamped his hand over her mouth, dropping his gun as he put his other hand to the back of her head so she could not pull away.

The boy stopped, looked back, too scared to run, too frightened to help his sister. He stared at the slow brother's damaged face and then at his sister and went to speak. But no words came out. The slow brother spoke instead.

"Hello," he said and then stopped, searching for words, suddenly realising that for all his dreams and imaginings and thoughts of super-heroes saving children, he had not spoken to a little boy and a little girl for years.

He could not remember when. If at all. So many years ago. He felt shy, unsure what to say.

"What is your name, little boy?" he asked.

There was silence.

"What is your name, little boy?" he asked again, louder this time, wondering if the boy had heard him clearly.

Again, the boy did not speak.

The girl, sensing the slow brother's hands were loosening, started wriggling and pulling.

"You're hurting my sister," the boy shouted suddenly, "You're hurting her. Get off!"

The boy dashed forward and pushed at the slow brother who, off-balance, stumbled backwards, letting go of the girl.

And the boy and girl were off and running towards the farmhouse.

The slow brother shouted after them. "Stop, little children, stop. Come back!"

He picked up his gun and, worried that he had frightened them, ran after them to tell them they had nothing to be scared of. That he was a good man and would do anything for them. That he loved children.

This time, the children ran in a straight line.

Towards the farmhouse.

Both of them screaming, both of them terrified.

As the slow brother broke through the trees and down along the path and on to the driveway, he saw his brother and the man with the bobble hat standing there. He slipped the gun into his jacket pocket as he approached them.

The two children ran straight into the man's arms, now squealing and babbling over each other, as he crouched down and hugged them, telling him their story of fear and terror.

The slow brother stopped and looked at the smart brother, who glared at him and shook his head, say nothing, and then spoke to the man with the hat and his children.

"I'm so sorry, Adam, my brother was up at the fields, shooting vermin. He must have scared your children, with the gunshots. He wouldn't have realised. He's not … you know … we don't have any children."

The man with the bobble hat looked up from comforting his two children, their heads down tucked into either side of his shoulders.

"No harm done," he said, getting to his feet and holding his children's hands. The children looked at the slow brother, almost reproachfully, the girl still sobbing slightly to herself.

"I shouldn't have let them run about … I forget this is a working farm. You've work to do … I'm sorry," he added, turning to the slow brother. "My fault, I hope they didn't bother you too much."

Bewildered, the slow brother smiled back uncertainly. "I was shooting a rabbit for supper."

The man with the hat pulled a slightly disgusted face, but then corrected himself as he spoke again. "I was telling Zoe and Luke that we were cutting Christmas trees … and I promised we'd have one of them for ourselves … I, we just came over so I could show them the trees and, I don't know, pick one. Zoe, Luke, show the nice men what you've got."

Slowly, shyly, the two children reached into the pockets.

The little girl pulled out a red ribbon, which she held up to the slow brother.

The little boy took out a green ribbon, but hung back, not wanting to hold it outwards.

The smart brother spoke, remembering how polite his father could be in company, "Well, come on then, Adam, Luke, Zoe … let's go and pick you a Christmas tree. We'll find you a nice one and you can put your ribbons round the branches and your father can chop it down himself on Monday."

They smiled at each other, the smart brother, the man with the hat and the two children, and then turned and went towards the trees. Excited now, the children, with the thought of their own tree to choose. And Christmas too. Not so very far away.

The slow brother followed. A surge of something, he wasn't sure what, he could not articulate it, inside of him. But he knew he did not like the man with the hat and what he did with these children behind closed doors.

And he thought, maybe, that he loved these pretty children. That he would like to look after them and care for them. If only this horrible man, a nasty man just like Father, wasn't around any more.

The slow brother felt the gun in his pocket.

Rallied himself, at what he knew he had to do. And be. A super-hero.

And he followed the four of them up into the trees.

* * *

They had a nice time among the trees, the children, running back and forth, excited.

Stopping to look at one tree. This one! And then another. No, this one – it's bigger!

The man with the bobble hat smiling to himself and the two brothers standing there awkwardly, not quite sure what to say. Both of them so unfamiliar with children.

"It's …" the man in the hat started to talk and then stopped, suddenly emotional. He gathered his thoughts. "It's so nice to see them happy. They've had a tough old time since their mum died. It's not been easy."

The smart brother nodded his agreement, not sure how to answer.

The slow brother looked at the man in the hat, a still, almost resentful look.

The man did not notice, his eyes transfixed on his children.

At last, after a squabble and some shoving and some words muttered under their breath to each other, the two children had made their choice. Almost. This tree or that tree, they could not decide.

The two trees, next to each other. Almost identical to an inexperienced eye.

The smart brother moving in to suggest a choice. He ummed and aahed, looking them up and down, pretending to measure the height and spread of the branches with his hands.

This one, he said finally, look at the shape, it's perfect, that's the best one. Well picked, children. Well picked!

A sulky face from the girl, soon transformed as the man with the hat invited her to be the first to twist her ribbon around the branch closest to them. Then the boy's, at the same height, not a centimetre higher, not a centimetre lower, on the branch next to hers.

"Shake hands, children," the man in the hat said. They moved towards each other and hugged reluctantly.

"Stand by the tree, I'll take a photo."

And he did, the two brothers quietly at the side.

And then the man with the hat, standing there with the phone in his hand, smiling, gestured for the two brothers to join in. One to one side. One to the other. The children in between. They shook their heads, no not us, and the slow brother turned away, covering the damaged part of his face with his hand.

But the man with the hat, jolly, laughing now, persisted. No, no, you must. A memento. A souvenir of the first Christmas tree cut by my own hand. A pause. Then, with further encouragement, the two brothers moved slowly into the photo.

Come on, guys! One this side, one that! And so they moved into position and smiled as the man with the hat took his photo. The smart brother looking straight at the phone, a slight smile on his lips. The slow brother, instinctively, turned to the side to mask the burned part of his face.

And then the man checked his phone, zoomed in on the children's faces, declared himself happy and that it was time to go.

They walked, the three men, back down through the trees, to the path and to the long driveway, the children hopping and skipping about in front of them.

Like baby rabbits, thought the slow brother to himself. He felt again the gun in his pocket. The sudden surge of anger towards the man in the hat. What he would like to do. What he was going to do. When he got the chance. He would save these children and love them himself.

"Well," said the man in the hat as they got to the car. "Thank you." He shook the smart brother's hand. "Children, what do you say?"

"Thank you," said the little girl.

"Thank you," echoed the little boy.

The man in the hat opened the car door for the children to climb in. "I'm not sure why we drove here, we could have walked it, really. We're only just over there."

"You're welcome," the smart brother said, not sure what else to say. He was not good at small talk. The other man didn't seem to be either.

The man in the hat went to say goodbye to the slow brother, but saw that he had already turned and walked away into the farmhouse, the door shutting quietly behind him.

"I … say thank you to your brother for me … for us."

"He's …" The smart brother stopped, not sure what to say.

"I know," he paused and went on carefully. "When I was young, I had an aunt who had, they call it Down's syndrome these days. She wasn't quite … she was nice, lovely, really, but, well, I understand anyway. It must be hard for you."

The smart brother nodded, not wanting to say any more. That it wasn't that. Down's syndrome. Nothing like it at all.

"I'll see you Monday, first thing?"

The smart brother nodded again, offering a handshake.

Then smiled at the children and turned and made his way back into the farmhouse, where he stopped and gave one final wave as the man drove away.

"That was rude," the smart brother said to the slow brother as he walked across the kitchen to pick up a kettle.

"He is a bad man, a very bad man. He hurts children."

"Keep your voice down, you'll wake Mother. Is she still napping?"

The slow brother nodded, watching as the smart brother filled the kettle and clicked a switch for it to boil.

They both stood, neither speaking, as the kettle heated the water.

The smart brother flicked the switch off as the kettle started to make its wailing noise. Reached for mugs, milk from the fridge, sugar from the side.

"He doesn't seem like a bad man to me … they aren't scared of him." He hesitated and then added in a quieter voice, "Not like we were of Father."

"He told me … things … things that he did," the slow brother answered in an angry, raised voice. He took his gun from his pocket. "I want to kill him … and save the children … they can come and live with us … and Mother."

"Oh, listen to yourself. Don't be so …"

They both stopped and turned as they heard a knocking at the kitchen door. Loud and assertive.

Bang.

Bang.

Bang.

The slow brother looked across. A savage lopsided smile of excitement on his face. He whispered, "It is Where's Wally. He has come back."

The smart brother moved by him, hushing him down. "I'll get rid of him." He could not risk the man coming in now. Alone. With his brother fired up and holding a gun.

He opened the door and smiled, the word, 'Adam' forming on his lips.

Stepped back, surprised.

"Hello, my name's Georgia Carrie, from the police, may I come in and have a word?"

PART FOUR

ANOTHER VICTIM

19. SATURDAY 17 NOVEMBER, LUNCHTIME

The three of them stood awkwardly in the kitchen.

Carrie, looking around, thinking this was the kitchen that time forgot.

The smart brother edgy. The slow brother uncomfortable, his hand on the gun tucked back into his pocket.

After a moment or two's silence, Carrie turned and looked at the slow brother. He would not meet her eye, like a naughty child. There was something about him, his look, that bothered her, but she couldn't quite think what it was. The burned face and the way he brought his hand up to it, as if brushing the hair away from his forehead. It reminded her of someone.

"Hello," he muttered.

No more, no less.

Keeping his head down, waiting for his brother to speak, to lead the conversation, to get her out and away.

She turned towards the smart brother. It struck her that this could be The Scribbler standing before her. Lean. Whippet thin. Rangy. All the words used to describe The Scribbler were a perfect match for this man. And the lines drawn by Gayther on the Mr Potato Head picture, to the forehead, to the sides of the mouth, were all there, too. And the old-man hairs sprouting everywhere.

"What can we do for you?" he said briskly.

She smiled, hesitating suddenly.

Stumbling to say anything.

She had come here, for the second of the four vans she was checking, all alone. She had been quite breezy about it all. It was as if she were doing something of little consequence, neither here nor there. Something academic. A university project. Ignoring Gayther's advice to simply sit nearby and look and listen. And then, if it seemed like a possible line of enquiry, they'd follow procedures, fill in forms and go back together later and do an interview. "Do it properly," he'd stressed. But she'd ignored him.

Instead, she'd walked up to the first door, knocked on it, realised the man who answered it and owned the van looked nothing like The Scribbler and, to be sure, checked he had an alibi for the night in question. The man was chatty, friendly even. Trevor. A lonely widower. She had a cup of tea. Two, then three biscuits. Decided this was easy enough. And so she did the same here, arriving at this rundown farmhouse in the back of beyond, looking over the van, taking a couple of photos, and then rat-a-tat-tatting on the door.

But now, right now, as the smart brother asked her what she wanted, first once and then again, the tension clear in his strained voice, she realised why the slow brother, his head bowed and face covered, bothered her. It was his melted face. The talk from Thomas and Cotton of Quasimodo being seen with The Scribbler at one pub. The lurking presence of Frankenstein's monster at another. The sense that maybe there were two people working together on the killings. Now here they both were in front of her.

The Scribbler to one side. Ready to act the moment she said the wrong thing.

The monster to the other. A lurking, threatening presence.

She felt as though she were going to be sick. From her foolishness and fear.

"What can we do for you?" the smart brother repeated a third time, glancing first at the struck-dumb woman and then at his slow brother. He shook his head slightly as if to say to him, 'don't say anything, don't do anything, just wait'. He then looked again at the woman and added suddenly, "Do you feel all right?"

That Suffolk accent.

Gayther had drawn attention to The Scribbler's voice. Sloightly on th' huh, witnesses has said.

They were right. It was.

"Come, over here." He really wanted her gone, but he gestured her towards a chair at the kitchen table instead. It would seem odd otherwise. Not to show sympathy. Cause unnecessary suspicion. "Sit yourself down, catch your breath." He looked up at the slow brother and pointed him towards the sink, go on, get a glass of water.

The smart brother and Carrie both watched as the slow brother went to the sink and picked up an empty glass standing upside-down on the draining board. He hesitated, holding the glass to the light momentarily to see if it was clean. It was, or clean enough, anyway. He filled the glass half-full from the tap and walked slowly back towards Carrie. She smiled at him, teeth stuck to gums, as she took the glass and sipped at the water. She hoped they did not see her hand tremble. She then looked again at the smart brother.

He wondered what she wanted. Something and nothing most likely.

Perhaps he'd forgotten the tax on the van. MOT maybe. He wracked his brains, wondering if he'd insured the van again this year.

But still, that sudden stab of fear was there. Couldn't help but think this was something more serious. About that boy and the dog. Maybe this was the beginning of the end.

"I'm ever so sorry," Carrie said, as she put down the half-drunk glass of water. "I suddenly felt faint." She paused and then added, "I'm just going to call my colleague to come and collect me. He's waiting for me with the dog. Down your driveway." She reached slowly, painfully slowly, into her pocket and took out her phone, then stopped, the phone in her hands, as she heard a sudden noise and saw the door into the main part of the farmhouse being pushed open.

Carrie half-smiled automatically at the old woman who was standing there, thin as a stick, and looking confused, as if she had fallen asleep and woken up in a panic, not knowing where she was. Carrie felt, suddenly, as though all the pieces of the jigsaw were falling into place. The Scribbler. His mad brother. The old lady they were looking to put into a care home. The Kings Court care home. Where The Scribbler had stumbled into Edwin Lodge. And gone back later to kill him. Everything Gayther had guessed at was correct. Give or take. More or less. As he would say.

Carrie watched as the old woman used a stick to move slowly, painfully, across the room, towards her and the two brothers. Carrie wondered what babbling, dementia-driven nonsense was about to be said as the woman moved close to her, closer than was necessary. Carrie thought the old woman was about to take her arm for support, to stop herself falling over.

The old woman raised her stick and brought it crashing down on the phone in Carrie's hands. Carrie recoiled in pain.

"I've been sitting upstairs watching her. She's been snooping round like a thief … looking at the van … taking photographs. She's trouble."

She turned to the two brothers, standing there looking shocked. "Exodus 22: 'If a thief is struck so that he dies, there shall be no bloodguilt' … deal with her."

* * *

As Carrie struggled up from her chair, the smart brother stepped forward instinctively and hit her across her face with the back of his hand. She tumbled backwards, hitting her head on the floor.

Dazed, she tried to sit up, but the smart brother was upon her, banging her head against the floor, one, two, three times, until she was still.

The smart brother stood there breathing heavily, wiping his mouth with his hand. The slow brother held his hands to his open mouth, stunned by the sudden, unexpected savagery. The old woman stepped forward and put her heel on the mobile phone, crushing it into the floor.

"Is she on her own?" asked the old woman looking at the smart brother. "Did she say?"

He looked across at her, wide-eyed, as if shocked into silence by what she had said and how he had reacted without thinking. Fear and panic and Mother's orders had made him do it.

"Listen to me. Is she on her own?" the old woman repeated. "Be quick." She gestured the smart brother towards the body. "Check her pockets, take her keys ... and the gun ... Sonky, give it to him ... go and check she's alone. Move her car into the outhouse for now and lock the doors. Give me time to think."

The smart brother, almost in slow motion, turned to the slow brother, holding out his hands for the keys. "Hurry," he said finally, as the slow brother struggled endlessly to get the gun out of his pocket. "Hurry."

The smart brother turned to the old woman as he was about to leave.

"What shall I do, Mother ...?" he asked, sounding like a lost little boy, "... if there's someone else in the car? She said she was with a man and a dog."

"Do what you have to do ... God permits the taking of a life if one's own is in danger ... go, go now."

"But Mother ..." said the slow brother, suddenly finding his voice. He paused, looking down at Carrie on the floor. "We do not do bad things. She is a lady. We do not hurt ladies."

"Don't do bad things?" the old woman laughed sourly. She looked at him through watery eyes. "I know everything that happens here, Sonky. Everything." She raised her voice, crackling with fear and anger. "I sit at my bedroom window and I see it all. All of it, do you hear? You bringing everything back here to my home."

She raised herself up with her stick as the two brothers stood there watching and listening to her in shame-faced silence. "You did all of this. The two of you. You brought this trouble to our door." She gestured towards the lifeless body of Carrie laying by their feet. "Now you deal with it."

"The Lord's curse is on the house of the wicked ..." she sobbed suddenly, angrily. "He blesses the dwelling of the righteous ... This is my home. My home, do you hear me? I was born here and I live here and I want to die here in my own bed ... you'll not put me into a home ... or worse."

She paused, her voice seeming calmer now, but still urgent. "We must do what we have to do. Chopsy, go and find her car and do whatever you need to. We have to hope she's on her own."

She stood silently for a second or two, in the utter horror of the moment.

"Sonky," she gestured towards Carrie's body, "take her and put her in one of the barns ... the barn up ... nearest to the fields ... do what you have to do if she's still breathing ... take a shovel from the outhouse with you. Chopsy, you go and help him when you're done."

"And you, Mother, what will you do?" the smart brother asked as he moved to open the door.

The slow brother stood still, looking from the smart brother to the old woman almost reproachfully. Then he spoke, calmly and with certainty. "Mother will think, and she will tell us what to do for the best. For her best boys."

She answered them, after a moment or two's thought. "I'm going to sit here and pray this doesn't bring all of the police to our door. I don't know what we'll do if ..." she stopped for a second, seeming lost for words. "Go," she added angrily.

The smart brother nodded as she moved to sit down in a kitchen chair. Slipping the gun into his pocket, he left through the kitchen door, leaving it ajar for his brother.

The slow brother reached to lift Carrie, her head hanging back over his arms. He looked at the old woman, as if to say something more, some simple words of regret and sorrow, but she had already sat down, her head bowed, and ignored him as he followed his brother out into the yard.

The old woman sat there, in an ancient, high-backed corner chair, thinking things through in her mind. Eventually, she sat up and spoke out loud as if someone were there listening to her, "Those who bring trouble on their families will have nothing." She shook her head sorrowfully. "And nor will I ..." she added sadly and then sobbed.

* * *

The slow brother walked, with Carrie in his arms, away from the farmhouse and up towards the main outbuilding and fields. He knew what he had to do but did not want to. Not really.

This is not right, he thought, what his brother had just done. What he was now doing. What Mother had told them to do. It was not right at all.

They were super-heroes. They killed bad men. They saved little children. They did not hurt ladies.

He stopped on the other side of the outbuilding with the cesspit and looked down at the lady. She was a pretty lady, he thought. She had a kind and friendly face. He laid Carrie out, gently and respectfully, on a grassy stretch of ground and then straightened her legs and folded her arms neatly across her chest. He said a few words quietly to himself and then added, "Amen".

The slow brother wanted to think about things. He sat down next to the body and reached into his pocket for his tin of tobacco, papers and matches. There were no ready-made cigarettes left so he carefully took out a piece of rolling paper and dropped tobacco into it, rubbing it back and forward with his big clumsy hands.

He knew he wasn't very good at this, the rolling of hand-made cigarettes. It wasn't his fault, his brother had said. He had what his brother called sausage fingers. Like Father. His brother had slim fingers, like Mother. He wished he had thinner fingers. It would make it easier to roll a cigarette. One end would always be fatter than the other. His brother was better at it. Always was, always will be.

The slow brother finally managed to get the tobacco spread as evenly as he could. He lifted the cigarette to his lips, running his tongue along the edge of the paper, half on the paper, half on his fingers. They tasted sharp and bitter. He did not know why. He lit the cigarette and inhaled the smoke. He liked this part the most, tasting the smoke for the first time, feeling it in his mouth and then blowing it out. His brother could blow smoke through his nose and make smoke rings, too. He could not. He wished he could.

He looked around as he sat there, thinking about where he was going to put the body.

He did not want to put it in the cesspit with the bad men. That would be a horrible thing to do. It would not be respectful.

He wanted to put her somewhere nice and clean. He searched for the word he meant ... special. Yes, that was it. A special place for a lady.

He thought about this as he smoked his cigarette. He did not want to put her in among the trees. He knew that next year when the men came to chop down the next lines of trees, they might come across the mound of earth. He did not want to put her in the fields behind the trees and out towards the forest. That was not right in the wind and the rain. And he knew what the animals of the forest would do.

The farm had other unused, rundown buildings from when Father was alive. A cow milking shed full of old machinery. Two storage buildings that were once a sawmill and a workshop. Two barns, one larger, one smaller. An air-raid shelter from the Second World War. He had not been in some of them for years and wondered whether they'd now be over-run by mice or rats, maybe even foxes.

He wished he had the gun on him that he had given to his brother. He liked to shoot vermin. Knew he was good at it. He was what was called a sharp shooter. The best, his brother had said. The sharpest shot in town. When he went back to the farmhouse to get the shovel, he thought he'd get the old spare gun from the upstairs cupboard at the same time. Keep that on him so he could use it later.

He decided, as he finished his cigarette and pinched the tip with his fingers, that he would put the lady in the smaller barn. He had always liked the small one. It was, what was the word, 'cosy'. Yes, that was it, cosy. He would lay her down on any straw that might still be in there. He would clean the barn up and make it nice for her. He would then come back down and get the shovel and the gun and, well, he would do what needed to be done. He did not like the thought of it. Not with a lady. A nice, good lady.

The slow brother looked up as he heard the sound of a car engine.

At first revving and then more steadily, more slowly.

The smart brother bringing the lady's car into the outhouse with the cesspit.

He wondered, suddenly, whether his brother had had any trouble. The lady had said she was with a man and a dog. But he did not know if that were so. He did not think a lady would lie about something like that, but he remembered that mother had thought it might not be true. It may, he thought, have been what was it, a little white lie. Yes, that was it. Not a proper lie. Not a bad thing to say. Not properly bad.

He wondered a moment or two longer. Then realised that there had been no gunshots. If there had been a man and a dog there would have been shots. At least two. One for the man and one for the dog. His brother was a good shot. Not as good as him. But he was fast and he was accurate and he would have needed only two shots.

One to the man's head. And then the other to the dog's. He did not really care about the man. But he felt sorry for the dog and wondered what type it was. They had had a Jack Russell when they were boys, but Father had made them kill it when it got old. "Too old and too useless," Father had said.

Take it outside and shoot it. One kill. The other watch and bury it. Toughen you up. Make men of you. Proper men. That's what Father had said. He had cried tears of anger. His brother, his face set, had shot the dog and helped him bury it. The dog was just 'dog', it never had a proper name. Father had said it was soft to give a dog a name. A dog was just a dog, that is all. He would have liked to have given the dog a name. He would have called it Bernard. When it was a puppy it looked like a Saint Bernard.

He thought he had better hurry. That his brother would have parked the lady's car by now, hidden away in the outhouse with the cesspit. Cleaning it over. Making sure he had not left any fingerprints anywhere. His brother always wore gloves for this sort of thing. Because of the fingerprints. He would then be striding up to make sure the lady was buried properly. Somewhere safe. Where she would not be found. Somewhere proper, though. Then they'd have to go back to the farmhouse and see what Mother had to say and what she would tell them to do next.

He reached for Carrie, sliding his arms beneath her.

Lifting her up as he got unsteadily to his feet.

Her head lolled back and, suddenly, she groaned.

* * *

The old woman was down on her knees scrubbing the floor when she heard the kitchen door creaking open.

"Sonky?" she said, glancing up. "Oh, it's you," she added, looking at the smart brother. "Good."

"You don't need to do that, Mother, I'll do it." He reached to help her up, taking the brush from her hand. "You sit down."

She made her way painfully to the high-backed chair and sat back in it. She wiped her hands absently on the armrests, distracted by the horror of what was happening around her.

"We need to clean this place," she said, her voice cracking. "From where she came in the door to where she stood to where she fell." The old woman thought for a moment. "Fingerprints on the door handle … on that chair … hair, skin, blood … where she fell."

"I know, Mother, I know," he answered. "I'll finish cleaning the floor and then I'll wipe …"

"There's some Dettol under the sink," she added. "Wipe everything over with that. Then pour the dirty water away in the outside drain and burn the cloths round the back."

She watched as he reached into the cupboard.

Cloths. Dettol. Some sort of antiseptic spray. Sponges.

He set about cleaning everything thoroughly.

"When you've done that, go up and find Sonky, make sure he's done a proper job of it … that he's buried her somewhere no one will …" She stopped, close to choking on her words, and then was silent.

"I've moved the car into the outhouse; there was no man or dog," he said matter-of-factly as he continued cleaning.

"I put my gloves on and wiped the seat and the pedals afterwards. I did it carefully and thoroughly," he added.

"It's now in the outhouse and I've locked and bolted the doors." He stood up and arched his back.

"Eighty-four years I've lived here," the old woman said, finally. "Eighty-four years. I've buried my father, God rest his blessed soul. And my mother with her long, beautiful hair. And two dear brothers. Wallace and Charles. Good boys they were, decent … your father. May God have mercy … and on yours, both of you, for all that you have done."

He bowed his head. "I'm sorry, Mother. Truly I am. I never meant to—"

"All that you have done," she interrupted, her voice rising, "you have bought it all to my door, to my home … and … suffer little children, and forbid them not, to come unto me: for of such is the kingdom of heaven." She took a deep breath. "I'll not see my days out here. Not now."

He nodded his head. "It will be all right, Mother, I promise. You just have to help us to get through this."

She sighed and then shook her head sorrowfully.

"Your father, well …" she shrugged, as if to say 'well, I understand, he was a monster'. "But the rest. You're not … neither of you … you're not normal. Like father, like son. God help me, what have I done to deserve this …"

He shook his head. "Don't, Mother, don't. Please. I promise this is the end of it. Please help us."

"I have been thinking. You must move the car. It's not safe here. If they come looking. Take it far away and hide it somewhere. Deep in the forest. Do it now in case the police come looking soon. Then walk back through the forest and sweep the road up to the outhouse."

He nodded then stopped, embarrassed, as he heard his brother at the kitchen door.

"That was quick," the smart brother said. "What did you do with her?"

The slow brother shifted uncomfortably from one foot to another on the doormat.

"She is in the barn." He looked from the brother to the mother. "Like Mother said I was to do."

"Have you buried her? You've not had time to dig a proper grave. It needs to be done properly. Dug deep."

The slow brother bent to take off his boots. Pulling first one and then the other. He struggled a little with the second boot.

"I forgot to take the shovel. I will take it up later." He crossed slowly to the sink to wash his hands.

"Did you do what you had to do, Sonky?" The old woman looked towards him as he finished at the sink and turned towards the larder. "Did you deal with it?"

"Yes, Mother." He looked away. She did not notice, distracted. And he had his back to the smart brother, who simply echoed his comment, dig her deep, you must dig her deep, so she'll not be found.

"Go now, Chopsy, you must move the car far away, like I told you to do." The old woman looked at the smart brother and then at the slow brother. "And you must go back and bury her properly. Say a few words for her soul. And ours. For this terrible thing that we have done."

She hesitated and then bowed her head and clasped her hands. In a quiet but crackling voice, she spoke, "The Lord is my Shepherd, I shall not want. He makes me lie down in green pastures. He leads me beside quiet waters. He restores my soul."

Both brothers stood quietly where they were, their heads bowed, listening and waiting for Mother to say what she needed to say.

The old woman searched for the words.

The brothers waited patiently until they both thought that she had finished. Then she carried on.

"He guides me in the path of righteousness. Even though I walk through the valley of the shadow of death, I will fear no evil, for You are with me. Your rod and Your staff, they comfort me."

She stopped again, her head still bowed, her hands clasped together.

This time, the brothers shifted uneasily.

It seemed to them that Mother was crying softly. Then she finished what she was saying. It was if she were talking now about herself.

"You prepare a table before me in the presence of my enemies. You anoint my head with oil ... my cup overflows. Surely goodness and love will follow me all the days of my life, And I will dwell in the house of the Lord forever. Amen."

"Amen."

"Amen."

The two brothers stood waiting for Mother to sit up and tell them again to go, to hurry. After a moment, a minute, maybe more, she opened her eyes and loosened her hands.

The smart brother looked at her, despairingly. Not sure what to say.

The slow brother stood there waiting patiently.

She sat up. "And then ..."

"And then, Mother?" the smart brother asked.

"And then we have to sit and wait and hope that the police didn't know she was coming here. If they didn't … you must solemnly promise me that you will bring no more trouble to my door."

"I promise, Mother," said the smart brother.

"I promise, Mother," echoed the slow brother.

She mused for a moment, looking from one to the other.

"But if they did know she was coming here … If they did … it's only a matter of time before they come to my door. Police in cars. And police with guns. We need to be rid of the car … and the girl … and be ready for them."

20. SATURDAY 17 NOVEMBER, EARLY AFTERNOON

Gayther sat by the portacabin table, feet up, leaning back in his chair, eating a Pot Noodle with the only utensil he could find – a badly stained teaspoon with a serrated edge. He hated Pot Noodles, usually, but it was all there was to eat, what with the canteen being closed and the local petrol station stuck in the 1970s food-wise. And he was really, really hungry.

Even so, he didn't particularly like the gooey mess he was spooning carelessly into his mouth. He checked the outside of the pot to see what it was meant to be. Beef something or other. He'd never have guessed. Had assumed it was something spicy, that's all. But it was warm and filling and so he finished it before starting, without pause, on a bag of cheese Nik Naks.

Three or four minutes later, with his fingers a bright orange and already regretting what he had eaten, he reached into his pockets for a tissue. Out of luck, he wiped his hands clean inside his pockets and decided he wouldn't test his blood sugar levels that day. They'd be off the scale. Gone twenty, he reckoned. Danger territory.

He looked up through the window on the sunny side. Saw Thomas out the front of the police station, standing by the wall checking his phone.

Waiting, Gayther assumed, for Cotton and Carrie to arrive. They'd come in together. The three stooges.

Place still looks like a builder's yard, thought Gayther, looking out the back window. A never-ending mess.

He sat up, rummaging through his notes. Four vans for him to check. Two done this morning. Two to do this afternoon after he'd caught up with Carrie, Thomas and Cotton. If any had uncovered a possible, he'd go back with them later. Do it properly.

Nothing suspicious so far, not from the first two he'd visited anyway. One van was parked up on the drive of a semi-retired window cleaner on the other side of Ipswich. He'd knocked on the front door to talk about having his windows cleaned. The man – a William Harrison – was black with grizzled grey hair. Not The Scribbler then. He withdrew as politely as he could.

The other, a chimney sweep this side of Ipswich. About to go out as Gayther pulled up alongside in his car. A tall, broad Irishman who'd never have been picked out of an identity parade for The Scribbler, not in a million years. Another struck off the list. Another polite withdrawal. Two down, two to go.

And now Cotton appeared at the front of the police station, exchanging a few quiet words with Thomas.

Comparing notes, no doubt. They looked subdued. Downcast. No joy then, thought Gayther, from their respective van checks.

They both stood there, fiddling with their phones, waiting for Carrie.

Gayther wondered if this were all a waste of time and effort. This whole Scribbler thing. Most police investigations were, he thought. Charging blindly down wrong avenues, twists and turns, fits and starts before, as often as not, stumbling across the truth, if they ever did, as much by luck as judgement. He rubbed his face with his hands, ground knuckles into his eyes. It had all been a dead loss so far. The Scribbler. Chasing shadows and ghosts. This will-o'-the-wisp figure.

He thought, for a minute or two, about The Scribbler and whether he'd got it all wrong. All of this. Edwin Lodge. Everything. The marks on the stomach were the only evidence, such as it was, to indicate that this was the work of The Scribbler. He wondered whether there was some way Lodge could have learned of these cartoonish marks and, in his torment, had inflicted the wounds on himself. It was possible, for sure.

But no, he decided finally, there was the knife, or rather the lack of it. No knife was found near Lodge's body, nor in his room. So where was it? In The Scribbler's pocket. That's bloody well where. The only place it could be.

Even so, was this whole van and the boy with the dog something and nothing? A poacher most likely. A deer, maybe. There were plenty hereabouts. The boy's identification of the old iden-tikit image no more than hit and miss.

Gayther groaned. Boss Man will have my balls for this, he thought.

What a bloody shambles. A right old mess.

Still, go down fighting. All guns blazing. Out with a bang not a whimper and all of that.

He swivelled round in his chair as he heard the door to the port-acabin opening. Smiled first at Thomas, leading the way, and then Cotton, a step or two behind. They stood there awkwardly, not sure how to greet Gayther. He nodded at them, "Thomas … Cotton," and gestured to them to sit down in the chairs opposite him.

"No sign of Carrie?" asked Gayther to neither of them in particular.

"No, sir," replied Cotton. "Not yet."

"We'd agreed to meet outside about one o'clock," Thomas added. "But she's taking her little boy to a birthday party after so she may have …"

Gayther checked his watch. "Well, she's only fifteen minutes late. She'll be in a layby somewhere, shovelling down cheesy chips as fast as she can."

"Chips with curry sauce, sir," Thomas commented.

"Curry sauce, Thomas?" Gayther queried.

"Her favourite, sir, chips with curry sauce. She gets them up at the crossroads, sir, Captain Haddock's."

There was a moment's silence.

No one seemed to quite know what to say.

And then Gayther moved the conversation on.

"So, Thomas … anything?"

"No, sir. The first two vans, on the way to Norwich, they weren't there, at the addresses. I sat and waited, just like you said, but nothing, sir. I can go back tomorrow. Might be more likely to be at home on a Sunday, sir? These two and the other two I'm due to check out this afternoon?"

Gayther nodded, "Yes, you may have a point … maybe … and Cotton, what about you?"

"Same as Thomas, sir. They weren't there, the vans. I waited and the first one, the one up at the Gainsborough estate, turned up after an hour. He's a carpenter, sir, John Alan Simpson, according to the van and I've checked him out online, sir, and it's not him. He doesn't match the description of The Scribbler. I don't think he …"

"And the other one, Cotton? Did you see the owner of the second van?"

"No, sir, no sign of that. I can go back this afternoon, sir, or tomorrow, like Thomas, sir. They're more likely to be at home then. We could do them all together, sir?"

Gayther leaned back in his chair, checked his watch again.

"Okay, I'm happy to call it a day for now … It's been a long week and we've been going nowhere fast … Carrie, have either of you heard from her?"

"We've been texting each other, sir, all morning, sharing ideas, sir," Thomas answered.

"And …?"

"She'd got lucky, sir, with the first two. Both at home and she spoke to them and texted …" He looked down at his mobile phone, pressed a button and scrolled. *No. No. Rendlesham. Beware UFOs!*

"When was this, when you last heard from her?" Gayther asked.

"Um … 11.28, sir. I'm not sure if she texted as she was leaving the second van or when she arrived at Rendlesham. Hard to say, sir."

Cotton then spoke. "We texted her when we were out the front, sir, but it just goes to answerphone. If she's running late and has nothing to report, she may have gone straight to this kids' party."

Gayther smiled, "That's the farm out at Rendlesham. She drew the short straw. Bit of a journey, that. She'll be ages and I doubt there's any signal out there either … at the farm … or on Mars … or Jupiter … if the UFOs have taken her." He wanted to do a Uranus joke but couldn't think how to work it in naturally. Thomas and Cotton would probably look blank-faced at him anyway. Or tell him it wasn't pronounced like that in these PC days.

Cotton looked hopefully at Gayther.

As did Thomas. "We'll catch up with her, sir, after this party. Let you know if she's found anything."

Gayther could see they wanted to get off home.

"Okay, look, let me know … text me … I'll make sure my mobile's switched on. If there's a possible anywhere in there, Carrie and I can go over and follow it up. Until then, Mr Thomas … Mr Cotton … have a good afternoon and evening …"

21. SATURDAY 17 NOVEMBER, MID-AFTERNOON

The man wearing the latex gloves drove Carrie's car steadily along the road that cut through the forest.

He kept it at thirty miles per hour. A habit now. Always careful not to stand out. To be noticed.

He drove as if he knew where he was going. But wasn't in a particular hurry. Just an ordinary man going about his humdrum business.

He was driving a dark and nondescript Smart car. A woman's car, he thought. Not a man's. A mother's car. A booster cushion sitting there on the seat behind him. He knew he was safe from CCTV and speed cameras on this road. There was nothing like that out here. But it worried him that, as cars passed, the drivers and passengers might look across and see him and wonder why he was driving a car like this. That they might remember him later, if or when the car was found and it was shown on television.

"Doris, dear? Come here quickly," an old man watching the television might call out to his wife preparing their tea in the kitchen.

"This young policewoman's gone missing and they've found her car in Rendlesham Forest …" The old man would ponder for a minute as his wife stood behind him watching the news, too.

"Isn't that the one we saw on the Rendlesham road with that man driving it? Doris, call the police … I remember what he looks like."

The man with the gloves dipped his head down whenever a car passed. He did it three or four times. One or so a minute. All they would see, anyone who looked across, would be the top of his head. Balding now. Like so many men of his age. In his haste, he had forgotten to put on a cap and he regretted that.

He knew where he was going to take the car. He had thought of setting fire to it, but decided that was too risky. He would just hide it. Three or four miles from home. Deep in the forest. He'd been there once or twice before. A dark, almost impenetrable, place. Through trees, down a slope and into bushes. Not somewhere hikers or dog walkers would go, nor even stumble across. A mile down this road. Then left. And left again. Off the road, down a track and, finally, into the densest part of the forest.

Not far enough from home. Not really. But he knew he needed to walk back. Had to do that through the forest. So he would not be seen. He realised he should take the car farther away. Ten, twenty miles. But he did not know where he would hide it. And the longer he spent in the car, on main roads, the riskier it was. CCTV and speed cameras were everywhere closer to the towns of Woodbridge and Ipswich.

He had to get back as soon as he could. To sort everything out properly. He had not intended to kill the policewoman. Had panicked and lashed out. Acting on Mother's instructions. Had managed to control himself quickly enough, though.

He did not think the policewoman was dead. He had not finished the job. Alive and conscious now, most likely. His brother would have put her somewhere, tied up, in one of his not-so-secret special places. He would have to deal with it, with her, when he arrived home. He did not want to, but what else could he do? What choice did he have?

Take her somewhere quiet.

Shoot her painlessly. Through the back of her head.

Bury the body deep.

But he did not kill women. Only bad men. Men like Father who pretended to be respectable. Family men who led double lives. In public toilets with other men while their wives and children waited patiently and unknowing at home.

He did not want to kill this woman.

But did not know what else to do.

They could not keep her locked up forever.

If the police came, it would be better if she were found alive than dead. He knew that well enough. But there were so many bodies at the farm that one more hardly mattered. They would go to prison forever either way and Mother would be left at home to die alone.

He knew in his heart that it was likely that the policewoman had told someone that she was going to the farm. Someone would come looking for her soon, he thought.

Today.

Tomorrow.

Monday at the latest.

He reached into his pocket, felt the gun there. One person, another policewoman or man, he could deal with. But then more would come. And dogs. And police with guns, and it would all be over. One way or the other.

He would go down fighting, he decided, rather than spending his remaining days in prison. There was a chance, he thought, if he wrote a confession when he got back, that his brother and mother would be spared. That everything that had been done had been done by him and him alone.

But he could not trust his brother to stand up to the police, knew he would say, in his slow and simple voice, that he had buried the bodies. As if that were right and decent and no more. And Mother knew, too. They would all be implicated to some degree or other. Perhaps it would be better if they all went together. There were plenty of bullets.

One for his brother while his head was bowed down as he smoked one of the cigarettes he loved so much.

And another for Mother while she slept, her mouth hanging open. When she was at peace. In sweet dreams.

And the last one for him, shutting his eyes and putting the gun into his mouth and pulling the trigger. One moment there. The next, gone forever. He did not know where. If anywhere. He did not really believe in heaven. Not for him anyway.

He looked up. Checked the rear-view mirror. Nothing. No cars behind. Hadn't been since he turned on to the main road. He'd got lucky. Looked ahead. Towards the side road he was going to take on the left. Just there in the distance. Not far now. He accelerated the car.

A layby on the other side of the road. A car in it. Facing towards him. A police car. His luck suddenly breaking unexpectedly. The man with the gloves had no time to think. He could not stop, do a three-point turn, go back where he came from. That would look odd. Attract attention.

He could drive on by. Head fixed straight ahead, looking into the distance. Nice and steady speed. Calm and relaxed. Or turn left as planned. A man in a woman's car, though. The number plate noted and easily checked. A car that belongs to a police officer. A young woman.

He drove up to the police car. His eyes met those of the policeman in the passenger seat.

Turned left instinctively. Then drove on. Did not look back.

Knowing full well that the police car would appear in his rear-view mirror at any moment.

22. SATURDAY 17 NOVEMBER, LATE AFTERNOON

Carrie was on her back, laid out flat, gazing upwards. Her eyes focused slowly. There was a roof up there, she thought. No, a ceiling. No, not a ceiling … what was it? It was … no, it's gone … whatever.

She came round again a few minutes later.

Maybe longer.

Looked upwards once more. It bothered her, this … this whatever it was.

It was made of something that was … no, she couldn't think. Wood, was it? Wood? The sky was made of wood. It made no sense.

She felt sick. And was wet somewhere. Down between her legs. Her brain hurt. And she didn't want to move in case it made the pain worse. In her head, it was. The pain. She had to lie here. As still as she could. In the wetness. Until the pain went away.

She lay there a little longer, just a minute or two more. She would think about things soon. But not just yet.

She drifted in and out of consciousness. Trying to think about something … she wasn't sure what … whenever she was awake. It was there, what she wanted to mull over, just beyond the edges of her mind.

And then it was gone. Whatever it was. And she thought maybe she had fallen asleep again. Did not know how she could do that with the pain inside her head. And the feeling of sickness.

Now she could hear noises. Birds, that was it. In the trees. Bird song. Was she outdoors? Was it the morning? Was she late for … what was it … no, it was gone again.

She lay there, still unmoving. This time she was going to stay awake and think what it was she needed to think about. Something bad, it was. Not good. Something … no, she couldn't remember.

And now she was dreaming. Some monstrous thing was behind her. In her mind. Just in the shadows. A nameless shape. An unspeaking presence. But a monster.

Something that scared her.

Wanted to hurt her. If it caught her.

She needed to get away.

She jolted awake. The pain in her head did not make her wince. It had before, she thought. She was sure of it. Now, the pain was still there. But it was … she searched her mind … scissors … that made no sense.

She could not find the word she wanted. Scissors … nails … sharp. It suddenly came to her. Just like that. Sharp. That was what the pain was. No, it was not sharp, it was … blunt.

What was she thinking?

A blur.

Everything out of focus.

She just needed to lie here. Until the pain had gone. And she could think straight. It was just inside her head. The pain. Nowhere else. But she felt uncomfortable. Her arms stretched out. Behind her and above her head? That made no sense. She went to move her arms. To wrap them around her chest. To comfort herself. But could not. Her hands were stuck together. They didn't feel right.

She wondered for a moment if she had legs. A sense of panic suddenly. She remembered a story about a man who woke up in bed and had no legs. Bader. The name came to her suddenly. Douglas Bader.

She had drunk in the pub. The Douglas Bader.

Somewhere near Woodbridge, it was.

What made her think of that? Had she been drinking? Was that why she was wet?

She tried to move her hands to reach her legs but could not. She realised suddenly she was lying down flat. On a rack in a torture chamber. Her arms stretched up and out behind her. Her hands. Her arms. And they were tied to something. Why was that? Why was she tied up? Had she been bad?

Her legs. She could feel them, but they felt as though they were one. One leg. That made no sense. To have one leg. One big leg? Why did she have one big leg? She should have two legs. Not one. What a puzzle this was. A conun … dumb … no, it was no good.

She lay back, exhausted.

The pain in her head. Her uncomfortable arms. Her big, strapped leg. The dampness.

She was gone again, back into her uneasy sleep.

It was dark, wherever she was. A tunnel, maybe. So black. And she could not move. Her head ached. Her arms and legs hurt now. She still felt sick. But she needed to move. To go. To run. But she was paralysed.

The presence was there again. Nearby. In front of her this time. And coming closer. She could hear, no she could feel, the heavy footsteps. The boom … boom … boom getting ever nearer.

Boom. Boom. Boom.

Boom. Boom. Boom.

The footsteps stopped and she could see a shadow in front of her. A silhouette against the darkness. Almost blotting out the little light there was. Moving closer. Until there was nothing but blackness. And she could feel and smell hot breath on her face. Rancid breath.

She awoke.

The monster, the man with the melted face, loomed over her. She screamed.

* * *

The slow brother knelt on his hands and knees, his head bowed.

In the farmhouse kitchen, by the feet of his mother in her high-backed chair.

Bent forward, her bony hands clasped together tightly, saying the Lord's Prayer.

"Our Father, who art in heaven, hallowed be thy name. Thy kingdom come. Thy will be done. On earth as it is in heaven."

She paused, looked up. Clasped his hands in hers.

"Say it with me … let us pray together."

He joined in, at first slowly and quietly, and then more loudly. He enjoyed the Lord's Prayer. Could remember every word of it.

"Give us this day our daily bread. And forgive us our trespasses as we forgive those who trespass against us."

She stumbled, hesitating, as if suddenly choking on her words.

The slow brother kept going, now leading the prayer.

"And lead us not into temptation but deliver us from evil. For thine is the kingdom, the power and the glory, for ever and ever. Amen."

"Amen," the old woman said once and then again, "amen."

She looked at the slow brother. Nodded. Eyes full of tears.

"Forgive us," she whispered. Urgently. "Deliver us from evil."

The old woman leaned forward, struggling to put her arms around her son. He sat there quietly, uncomfortable with her unexpected touch and not moving, even as she rested her head against his in an awkward embrace. He felt her crying. Did not know what to do.

He thought instead about the young woman in the barn who had slept for so long and had woken up as he bent towards her. He was pleased that she was not dead. But did not like it that she screamed. He did not want her to be frightened. He did not like the idea that they might hurt or even kill women. Because they were super-heroes. They killed only bad men. The baddest of all. Men who hurt children. Men like Father.

He did not like to think about Father and what he had done. What he had made them do. He tried very hard to forget. But sometimes he could not.

It was why he did not carry the lady into the large barn. It was where Father would take them from time to time. Sometimes him on his own. More often his brother. Now and then the two of them together.

He felt the old woman stroking him.

Her hands across his back and shoulders.

He kept as still as he could.

He had put the lady in the small barn, a warm and comfortable place. Found some rope and twine from another outbuilding to tie her hands and her feet. Tightly so that they were secure but would not hurt.

Knew that he must not let her go. That he had to keep her safe. Until his brother got back. He would decide what they should do. But he would not let his brother hurt her. They would keep her there. Look after her.

He thought, perhaps she might become a friend. A sister to them. A daughter to Mother. He would like that. He had always wanted a sister. He did not know how this would come about, but he hoped that it would.

He felt his mother close to him.

Her face almost touching his.

He felt her sweet, sickly-smelling breath on his cheek.

After the lady had screamed, he had stopped her and then gone back towards the outbuilding with the cesspit to get the shovel. To pretend to Mother. So she would not know. That the lady was alive. As he opened the outhouse door to pick up the shovel, he looked over and could see Mother sitting by the kitchen window of the farmhouse, watching him.

He lifted the shovel up to show her. She nodded. He then went towards the farmhouse and into the kitchen to go upstairs to get the old gun from the cupboard on the landing.

She barely looked up from her chair by the window as he came in. She was lost in thought. As he came back down, tucking the gun into his pocket, she turned slightly and nodded at him again and smiled a little. She looked sad. It made him feel sad too.

"Do not worry, Mother," he had said. "Your best boys are doing good work."

She went to say something to him, but then stopped and looked out of the window, keeping watch. "You're a good boy," she said finally, as he waited there. "Always be a good boy for your poor old mother … come … come and sit with me and pray."

And now he wished he had not.

Because mother was holding him, embracing him, their faces, their mouths, almost touching.

It did not feel right.

He looked at her wet dripping mouth and did not like it.

* * *

Carrie knew where she was now. And what was going on. That she had wet herself. Not that that really mattered, all things considered. She was in an old barn. Her arms and legs tied together. Strapped to some sort of wooden post, part of the wall. She'd been put there by the man with the melted face. The brother of The Scribbler. To be killed by the man with the melted face. Or kept alive until The Scribbler returned. For him to do whatever he wanted with her. She did not know which.

Either way, she thought she was almost certainly going to die some time soon.

And that made her angry. Mostly with herself. That she'd been so stupid as to walk into the farmhouse.

And with Gayther, too. She had let herself be swept up by his outrage and gung-ho attitude.

When she had woken from her dream and screamed, the man with the melted face had clamped his hand over her mouth. Made her promise, in his oh-so-slow and simple voice, not to scream if he took his hand away. She nodded. He took his hand away. She screamed again. Louder this time.

He had covered her mouth with his hand again, more in sorrow than anger. Had pulled a handkerchief from one pocket, some sort of string-twine-rope thing from the other. Then set about making sure she wouldn't be able to scream any more.

She had stared furiously at him as he did this, but he would not meet her eyes. He was almost shame-faced. Then she twisted and turned, close to petulant rage. But he simply held her down, almost apologetically, until she slowed and then stopped.

He had cut the cloth that held her hands. Sat her up. Put her back against the barn wall. Retied her hands, just as tight behind her, to a huge wooden post by the wall.

Legs still tied together, stretched out in front of her. He had then left her there. Unable to move or call out.

She had pulled as hard as she could against whatever it was that held her hands tight. Some sort of rope. But it did not show any sign of loosening or weakening. Neither the rope nor the post. She tried to arch her back, putting her weight behind it, but could not move much at all. Not far enough anyway. She could twist her legs and turn her body, but that was about it. She was stuck fast and she knew it.

Now she was exhausted and was waiting for the man to come back. Strangely, she did not fear him. Or at least not as much. She could see and hear he was what her mother would call "not all there". Grandpa would have called him "a simpleton" from a distance or "Simple Simon" if he knew him well. The way he did what he did – the material in her mouth, the untying and tying of her hands carefully, almost gently, was almost respectful. And he did not notice, or comment, on her damp trousers.

She feared the other brother more, much more, the one who had struck her and then knocked her out. He was harder, more calculating. Had those staring eyes that witnesses had talked about. He was The Scribbler, she thought. No doubt about that. Not this one.

And the mother. Who looked so old and brittle. She was even worse. The Scribbler had acted on her instructions. The brother with the melted face troubled her, though. She did not know how he fitted into all of this. Nor how she was still alive. She should be dead already.

She thought suddenly of Noah. His soft smile. Giggling laughter. His sweet innocence.

And it was all she could do not to break down and sob.

She had to be strong. Not give in to anger or fury. Had to be ready to try and talk her way out of this when the man with the melted face came back. Hoped that it would be him rather than The Scribbler.

That she would have a chance. To talk her way out of it.

She sat quietly, her head still aching, her body exhausted, thinking what she would say.

And hoped, more than anything else, that the next person she saw would not be The Scribbler.

23. SATURDAY 19 NOVEMBER, EARLY EVENING

Gayther laid back on his sofa at home, feet up on the coffee table, eating a ready-made, microwaved lasagne meal for one that he'd picked up from the Co-op over the road.

Watching some early Saturday night programme on ITV. Endless fake bonhomie, inane nonsense, load of rubbish, really.

Plastic container, knife, fork. Tin of indeterminate fizz.

Fast food. Straight into the bin when he'd finished. All of it. Then back to work. Nothing much else to do when all was said and done.

He put the half-eaten lasagne on the coffee table and reached for the file by his side. Flicking through the papers. Scanning notes. Running through ideas. Round and round and round, going nowhere fast.

He feared that this – checking out the remaining vans with Carrie, Thomas and Cotton the next morning – was his last chance to progress the case. Even then, it was a long shot at best.

The possibility that one of these vans belonged to the man seen by the boy with the dog in the woods seemed unlikely. The child, as likely as not, he thought, guessing at the numbers and letters and make and model of the van. He was twelve, for Christ's sake.

And the chances that the missing Philip Taylor was somehow bundled up in the bin bags over the man's shoulder seemed even more improbable. And that the man was The Scribbler was ... just so ... he searched for the right phrase ... a million-to-one shot, surely. Then again, stranger things had happened over the years. Time and again.

The Scribbler, he thought. If this doesn't come off, it has nowhere else to go. He had nowhere else to go. There was nothing in the other files as big as this. Bits and bobs. Leftovers. He'd be sidelined. Where Bosman and all of the others wanted him to be. He might as well take his pension and go off into the sunset.

Rat.

A-tat.

Tat.

Gayther shook his head. All he wanted was a little bit of peace, time to mull things over, think things through. And his feet hurt. Toes really. He did not know why. He wondered if it was to do with the diabetes.

He decided to ignore the door. Reached for the TV remote control. Turned the sound down. To pretend nobody was in.

As they were knocking, he suddenly realised it meant his doorbell wasn't working. He'd need to get some new batteries for it. Something else to remember. Household stuff had been, well, Annie had dealt with all of that before she died. Since then, it was rather hit and miss. More miss, actually. He never seemed to have any toilet paper. Or kitchen roll for that matter. It wasn't easy at times.

It was a light rap on the glass part of the door. Whoever was there was trying to be friendly. He had fallen for that before, of course. Turned out it was someone who wanted him not only to donate to some charity or other but to sign up to a monthly direct debit. He signed, the lowest amount possible, just to get rid of them. A young Rastafarian girl with a funny hat and an eager face.

Rat-a.

Tat.

Tat.

There it goes again. He was just going to sit here and stay quiet until they went away. If it were anything important, Carrie, Thomas or Cotton, they'd have texted. Or knocked loudly and repeatedly. Carrie would have hammered away with some daft rhythm, no doubt. As if she were in *Riverdance* or some such show. Not this timid, oh-so-polite (but persistent) tapping.

He checked his mobile phone, almost out of battery again. Nothing. No messages. All quiet. He'd text the three of them first thing in the morning. To get things sorted. Out and about by mid-morning. To wrap up this line of enquiry. And then what? He did not know.

He looked around the living room. It was all old and faded. He didn't mind that so much. It was comforting in a way, he thought. The familiarity. But he now noticed the dust and the dirt. A smear of something white and crusty on the coffee table. Mud from his shoes trodden into the carpet by the fireplace. A stack of mostly empty Chinese takeaway cartons over by one of the two armchairs. God knows how long they'd been there. He couldn't remember when he'd last had a Chinese.

Bang.

Bang.

Bang.

Oh, for Christ's sake. Am I ever going to get any peace? Gayther got up and walked out of the living room, along the hallway and to the front door. He pulled it open, "Yes?" Loud, not quite a shout, but getting there.

He knew he sounded edgy and even aggressive, but you needed to be when dealing with these charity collectors. He'd once been chased down the length of Ipswich's high street by a shaven-headed chugger because he'd smiled and been vaguely polite.

A skinny, middle-aged woman, the spit of Carrie, and a small, mixed-race boy of about five. Cheeky-faced. Gayther knew straightaway who they were and what their unexpected arrival on his doorstep meant. Carrie hadn't gone to a children's party as everyone had automatically assumed. She was missing. He felt sick.

* * *

"When did you last hear from her?" Gayther asked, smiling at the woman and boy now sitting politely on the sofa opposite him. He didn't feel like smiling, but knew he had to for them. He must not show the sudden, growing alarm he felt.

"We haven't. Not since this morning. When she left for work," the woman answered simply.

She had seemed calm enough, thought Gayther, as they introduced themselves to each other on the doorstep. They shook hands awkwardly, knowing each other vaguely. They'd met, he thought, once or twice before. He then invited them through to sit down in the living room.

She was in control as she spoke her carefully rehearsed words, explaining that Georgia hadn't come home as expected … not like her at all … no contact from her since … they were worried something might have happened.

An accident perhaps?

If only. Gayther suspected it was worse.

Having mentioned the word 'accident', he thought she might start crying. He hoped she wouldn't. He didn't handle that sort of thing very well. He never knew quite what to do. He wasn't someone who hugged, not even people he knew well. He could pat her on the shoulder, but he'd need to kneel down to do it and it might look odd.

He smiled more encouragingly at her as best he could. Then at the boy, who sat there grinning cheerfully. He's no idea what's going on, thought Gayther. Poor lamb.

"She's not answering her phone, either. That's not like her. And she's not replying to text messages." The woman sounded tense and worried.

"She's gone over to a farm in Rendlesham Forest," Gayther answered, reassuringly – more reassuring than he actually felt.

"The mobile coverage is patchy there … and her phone may have run out of battery."

"I don't think it would have," the woman answered. "She plugs it in with a lead in her car … so it's always topped up close to 100 per cent. Her phone's … part of her … she has it there all the time." She pointed to the back pocket of her jeans. Then she went on.

"When Noah was small, smaller than he is now … I looked after him a lot and I'd send her pictures and videos of him … doing things … just silly stuff … the first time he ate a Cadbury's Creme Egg, things like that. She always keeps her phone close, and charged and turned on, always. Always," she added for emphasis.

"So, you've had no texts or emails or calls since she left for work … when did you last try to contact her?"

"She said she'd be working most of the day, but that she'd pop back for lunch if she could … I texted her at about twelve-thirty and then about half an hour later … we had some baked potatoes … Noah likes baked potatoes with beans …" She smiled briefly at the little boy, who smiled back as she talked on.

"Nothing. I assumed she was busy, so I didn't try her again. But I then took Noah to a little birthday party round the corner from ours from two until four. Georgia said she'd meet us there later on if she could and sing happy birthday. She didn't turn up. I've called her two or three times since, but nothing. Georgy wouldn't … she would have been in touch. I wouldn't normally come and bother you, invade your privacy. But …"

She looked up at Gayther.

Still assuming an accident.

Gayther wished it were only that simple.

He knew what he had to do. He had to reassure Carrie's mother and son. That he'd get on to it straightaway, saying he'd visit the station, check if anything had happened, follow up on everything.

He then had to get them to go back home and wait. Do what they'd normally do. Have their tea, watch television, read a story, go to bed. He'd take her mobile phone number, give her his number, too. Promise to text her just as soon as he had some news. Good news, he'd stress. She just had to be patient.

He then had to go to this farm, this out-of-the-way place that Carrie had last visited. He could not believe that Carrie would have blundered in. Stumbled naively into The Scribbler's lair. And was now … it didn't bear thinking about. He hoped that it was as simple as he had suggested. That her car had broken down and she'd been walking ever since back through the forest. It could be so, he thought. Unlikely. But possible. He had to cling to that hope.

He thought, no, he knew, that he should go to the station and pass this upwards. Do it officially. But he realised where that would lead. The inevitable over-the-top response. Cars galore. Gung-ho coppers. Police marksmen. An unpredictable outcome. If he texted Thomas and Cotton as a heads-up, just in case something goes wrong and you don't hear back from me in half an hour, call in the cavalry, he could check it out alone more quickly. Quietly, sensibly, ready to call for reinforcements as necessary, he could maybe come out of this okay.

With Carrie.

And The Scribbler. Brought to justice.

He had to act fast.

24. SATURDAY 17 NOVEMBER, MID-EVENING

The man with the latex gloves walked slowly through the forest. Exhausted now, but close to home.

He had left the car deep among the trees and bushes. Four or five miles away was what he'd intended.

But he had been walking for hours now. Six, seven, eight miles, maybe more, and getting ever slower with every mile.

He had been lucky. Had turned left and driven along the side road. Waiting, any second, for the police car to come up behind him, flashing lights, siren wailing, the officers gesturing furiously at him to pull over and stop. He'd tug the gun from his pocket. A last, desperate act to escape. To get back to the farm.

But the police car did not appear. As he turned left again, a mile or so down the road, he glanced back once more. There was nothing to be seen. And he found himself breathing again. Great big gulps of air. Had not realised he had been holding his breath for so long.

He had buried the car down a slope in a saucer-shaped dip full of bushes surrounded by trees. Thought, if he were lucky, that it might not be discovered for years, maybe never. Had wiped it all clean, wheel, seat, floor, door handle, and then scouted round, making sure it could not be seen from the path, even from within the circle of trees. Maybe from above, a police helicopter, but he could do little about that.

And then he started walking home. Through trees, row upon row of trees, going on forever.

Feeling sick, not knowing what to expect when he arrived back.

And tense, worried that he could not get there faster, help in some way with whatever was happening.

He had thought of running off. Just taking the policewoman's car and driving away. But he did not know where to go. He had no passport. No credit card. Nothing but the cash in his pocket. No change of clothes. No place to go. No idea how to disappear into thin air. No family or friends to help him. He was not of this world.

This modern, unfamiliar world. He did not understand how it all worked.

And he knew he could not leave his brother. Nor his mother. Could not desert them to deal with the police, who would come knocking some time soon, perhaps were there already, wanting to know where the policewoman was.

Had she come to the farm, they'd ask. Have you seen her? Mother would shake her head, say no. But his slow brother would shuffle from one foot to the other. Head down. Shame-faced. Guilty. May we have a look around, they'd ask. Just to check. And they'd go into the outhouse and the barns and wherever she'd been hidden. And then. And then he needed to be there for that moment.

He hurried on, as best he could.

Not far now.

A mile or two, maybe a little more.

Whatever was happening at the farm when he returned, he had to deal with it. If the policewoman were still alive, he would have to dispose of her. He had thought things through. There was no other way. They could not keep her prisoner forever. He would do it cleanly and quickly. As soon as he saw her. Then they must sit and wait and see if or when the police came. Hold tight. Keep their nerve.

If they came when he was there, he would keep his brother and his mother hidden away beyond the kitchen. Say no, he'd not seen anyone. Now please leave, my mother is seriously ill. She needs peace and quiet. He knew how to do that. Would then watch them leave. Breathe a sigh of relief.

If they were there already, the police, he'd have to decide what to do when he arrived. One policeman or woman, just following up, looking around, opening doors to barns, and he would deal with them. He felt the gun in his pocket. Was ready to use it.

More police? Swarming all over the farm with dogs and marksmen. He could not run away, leaving his brother and mother behind. He would fight his way through somehow. Get to them. End their lives together. How it should be. For a mother and her loving sons.

The man with the gloves reached a plain. Looked out across the fields of a neighbouring farm. Beyond that was the farm. His home. All his life. His brother's too. And Mother's, of course. He stood and watched for a minute or two, getting his breath back.

He blinked once, then twice. He would have sworn he could see the lights of a car coming down the lane towards the farm. Distant. Far away. But he wasn't sure of what he was seeing.

He took the gun out of his pocket. Checked it. He was ready to deal with whatever he was going to face. Kill or be killed. He started to run. Fast and hard.

25. SATURDAY 17 NOVEMBER, EVENING

Carrie leaned back against the wall of the barn trying to look as calm and relaxed as she could. Like she'd been trained to do in tense and difficult situations.

About as calm and relaxed as you can, she thought, when you're gagged and bound to a wall. And a madman is standing over you about to kill you. Because his mother told him to.

Most likely with his bare hands. Unless he had a knife in his pocket that he'd pull out and use to cut her throat. She felt a sudden, sobbing sense of despair. She'd never see Noah again, nor her mum. She tried to speak. Calm and rational words. Mumbled desperately through her gag.

The man put down the lantern he was carrying and reached into his pocket.

Pulled out a knife.

Moved towards her. Carrie looked up, terrified.

She was not going to let him see that, though. She met his gaze, her chin jutting out, her eyes steady, strong and defiant.

She thought her final words. Noah. I love you with all my heart. Mum, Dad, I love you, too. Dad, I remember you always.

The man lurched forward, cut at the gag at the side of her mouth. Opened her mouth. Removed the handkerchief. "Do not scream again," he said quietly. "I will put it back on if you do."

"Please," she said as calmly as she could. He must be able to hear the shaking in her voice, she thought. "Let me go … it's not too late."

The man with the melted face shook his head.

"Let me go now, just untie my arms and legs and let me walk away. You don't have to do this."

The man shook his head again, more emphatically this time.

"It's not too late. We can sort this out. I'll speak up for you and help you. Just let me go now."

The man with the melted face reached into his pocket and took out a hip flask.

He held it up to her lips.

"It is water," he said. "You are thirsty."

She drank from it, once, then twice, and nodded her thanks.

"I must take you somewhere else. Before my brother gets back. He will know you are here." He spoke so slowly, almost methodically.

"Why? What will your brother do? Where's he gone?" She tried not to let him hear the panic she was feeling.

The man crouched down next to her. Then sat down, reaching for his tin of tobacco.

"He is hiding your car in the forest," he said slowly, opening the tin. "He will be back soon."

"What will he do then? To me?" Again, she could hear her voice wavering. Wished she hadn't said it. Knew she shouldn't sound like a victim. Should sound calm and measured. And she had to take charge of this situation somehow. Be in control. Act fast too.

He was just sitting there. Calm as you like.

The brother on the way back.

Here at any moment. God knows what then.

The man took out a cigarette and a matchbox from his tin. With thick and clumsy fingers, he tried to light the cigarette. He dropped the burning match. Pressed it out with his foot.

"Here," she said, "untie my hands. I can do it for you. Let me help you." She smiled as best she could.

He shook his head as he had another go. The match burned down to his fingers before he dropped it and trod on it. Once more, and the cigarette was finally lit.

There was a moment's silence. She wondered whether a lit match might set fire to the straw, the barn going up in flames. Her and him with it. Whether he would untie her then or walk away and let her burn to death.

He smoked his cigarette carefully. He held it like a child smoking for the first time, she thought.

She wanted him to hurry, before the brother returned. To do whatever it was he could not bring himself to tell her about. But she also knew this was her chance to engage with him, to somehow win him over.

"Please may I have a cigarette?" She had not smoked a cigarette for years. Not since she was at school. Even then, only the once. She had coughed and spluttered and thought she was going to throw up. But she had to bond with him somehow. This was her only chance. All she could think of to say.

He stopped smoking. Held his roll-up cigarette away from his mouth. Thought and then mumbled his reply.

"I do not have proper cigarettes. Only these." He gestured the roll-up towards her.

She smiled. "I'm like you. I smoke those."

He looked at her curiously, thought again for a moment, and then answered, "Ladies do not smoke roll-ups. They are for men … working men," he added with emphasis.

She went to say, "I'm no lady."

Thought better of it.

Asked his name instead.

The man with the melted face dragged on his cigarette. He thought for a while. So long that she thought he was not going to answer. But then he did.

"Dennis," he said. "My name is Dennis. D. E. N. N. I. S. Dennis with two n's not one n."

"Georgia," she replied. "Georgy to my friends." She smiled at him. And then added, "You can call me Georgy if you like … We should shake hands. Now we've been introduced properly."

He looked at her for a second, no more than that. He turned away as she looked back at him as steady and as encouraging as she could.

"I am going to move you to another place. You will be safe there."

"Safe from your brother?" she asked quietly.

He nodded.

"The Scribbler?" she asked carefully.

The man looked blank-faced.

"The Scribbler," she repeated, watching him closely.

"My brother," he answered finally.

Carrie wanted to have this conversation before he finished his cigarette and moved her. This was her best chance of understanding. Making a connection. Getting this child-like man on her side. Surviving and getting away. She had to be quick – but careful as well.

"Your brother … the man who hit me …"

He nodded slightly, glancing at her and away.

"He …" she searched for what to say. She wasn't trained for this. "He kills … he takes the lives of gay … homosexual men."

He looked at her for a long time and then answered quietly, almost a whisper. She had to lean forward to hear him.

"Bad men … bad men who hurt children." He stopped. As if he shouldn't have spoken.

"Gays or paedophiles?" she pressed. "They're not the same at all."

He seemed uncertain, as if he had not quite heard what she'd said.

"Paedophiles. Small boys and girls?" The thought made her feel sick. She had to blank out thoughts of Noah.

He nodded again, then looked down, dragging on his cigarette.

"Do you help him? Do you kill the bad men who hurt children?" She spoke softly, as conversationally as she could. As if she were talking about going shopping or some other humdrum matter.

"I did once …" he answered before touching his scarred face. He sighed suddenly, unexpectedly, long and hard. "Now I bury them. The bad men. The baddest of bad men."

Carrie was not sure what to say to that, thought perhaps she should ask where he buried them. But guessed it was somewhere on the farm. Maybe even the place he had talked about moving her to. She struggled to quell a rising sense of panic again. Knew she must not show it.

He finished his cigarette, stubbing it into the ground with his boot as he stood up.

"We are good boys. We are Mother's best boys. We are super-heroes," he said firmly, as if he were proud.

Carrie looked up at his slow, simple face, still not sure what to say to this man who spoke in such a measured, child-like way.

He moved towards her, taking out the knife and then a cloth of some kind from his pocket.

Gagged her again. Cut her arms free from the post. Retied her wrists, a little tighter this time. Pulled her up and over his shoulder in a fireman's lift. Bent down again to pick up the lantern with his right hand. And then headed out of the small barn.

She wondered if he was now carrying her to her grave.

Had a terrible vision of being buried alive. By The Scribbler when he returned at any moment.

Made to dig her own grave. Climb down into it and lie still as he shovelled the soil on top of her.

* * *

"What is this place?" Carrie asked, after the man with the melted face had put the lantern on the ground, sat her down gently against a wall and removed the gag from her mouth.

He did not bind her to the wall this time. That was good, she thought. She could take advantage.

She could move about a little. On her bottom. And she could roll over. She could probably stand up if she used the wall behind her for balance.

Even though her arms and legs were tied tight, it gave her a chance, she thought.

He shrugged. "Father used it." He looked round the now-derelict structure, maybe twelve foot by fifteen foot. A rickety wooden staircase led to an upstairs area. Carrie could see moonlight, assumed there were windows up there, or maybe the roof had just rotted away. It stank of dirt and decay.

"No one comes here. Except me. I come to smoke and think. My brother will not know you are here."

"What do you think about … when you're here?" said Carrie. The light from the lamp shone on the undamaged side of his face. She thought, seeing mostly that side, that he had a surprisingly kind face.

He looked shy suddenly, dipping his head down.

"When you come here for a smoke, what do you think about?" she pressed, making herself look as interested as she could. Knowing she had to win him over, gain his trust.

"Things," he said eventually, still shy. Carrie sensed he wanted to talk, to say more.

"What sort of things?" she pressed.

He did not answer. Would not meet her eye.

"Nice things?" she added.

Still he did not say.

"I'm going to think about nice things when I sit here," she said. "Sit down next to me. I'm going to think about my little boy. He's called Noah. He's five."

The man with the melted face sat down next to her. "Noah," he said. "That is a nice name. A Bible name. He is five." He repeated Carrie's comment, as if to himself. "Five," he said once more.

"Yes," Carrie replied, hesitating for a moment, deciding what to say next. Which way to go. How hard to push.

"Is he handsome?" the man said unexpectedly.

"Yes," Carrie answered, looking at the simplicity, the innocence, in the man's face.

"I like children," the man said.

"You'd like Noah," Carrie continued. "And he'd like you."

"Would he?" the man looked surprised and then pleased.

"Yes. Do you know why?"

"Why?" the man asked eagerly.

"Because you are a kind man who is being nice to his mummy. He'd love you for that."

The man looks beside himself, thought Carrie. She was not sure how to handle this. Make him feel guilty? Get him on her side?

"He's having a birthday party soon. Perhaps you can come to it."

"Will there be cakes?" he asked.

"Yes, cakes and crisps and sausage rolls and sandwiches and orange squash and Ribena."

"And games? Will there be games?" he asked eagerly.

"Yes, all sorts of games. Hide and seek. And the one with chairs and music. Um, you stop and start the—"

"Musical chairs!" the man interrupted, "That is what it is called. Musical chairs. I played it once." He laughed suddenly and Carrie joined in.

He stopped laughing. So did she. They fell silent for a second or two.

Carrie was not sure what way to go with this next.

The man then looked at her excitedly, struggling to find the words to say. And then he spoke, in something close to a whisper.

"Will there be a party bag to take home?"

"Yes, of course," she replied. "There will be a piece of birthday cake in it and a drawing pad and some crayons and some stickers and a toot-toot whistle."

He looked at her, plainly puzzled. "A toot …"

"Toot-toot whistle. That's what my mum calls them anyway. It's like a boiled fruit sweet shaped like a whistle so you can blow it … toot, toot … and suck it as a sweet, too."

He stared at her in amazement. It was hard, even now, in such terrible circumstances, not to laugh. She pressed on.

"Let me go," she said suddenly, trying not to show her feelings in her voice. She spoke firmly suddenly. Like a mother to a naughty child. "Now. Dennis. We'll say no more about this silly nonsense and you can come to Noah's party ... as a special guest. I'll do you a badge with Dennis on it. Dennis with two n's."

He said nothing, his head dipped down.

"You can sing happy birthday ... with the other children."

Still he did not speak.

"And join in all of the games ... I bet you'll win some of them and get prizes."

He did not look at her.

"If you're really good, Noah might let you blow the candles out on the cake."

He was silent.

"You're such a good boy, Dennis, such a sweetheart," she said, and then wished she hadn't. She'd pushed too far. Got it wrong. She knew that.

He roared, a sudden angry sound, as he clambered to his feet.

She looked at him in his inarticulate fury. Feared that he would lash out.

"Stupid," he said furiously. "Stupid."

"No, Dennis, it's ..."

"It is stupid. I cannot come." He leaned towards her, his face twisted in sudden anger. "I do not have a present for him."

And with that, he turned and stormed out of the building, slamming the rickety old door behind him.

* * *

Carrie tried with all her strength to loosen the material tied tight around her wrists behind her back.

She flexed her wrists back and forth to try and slip a hand out.

Then pulled her hands outwards as hard as she could. To rip the material. All to no avail.

She sat back, thinking about how to free her arms and legs and get away, and suddenly realised the lantern was still there, just in front of her. A light bulb. Some heat. A chance. If she could jiggle around on her bottom and take the lantern cover off with her hands, she could maybe press the material against the bulb. Burn it through.

Started jiggling.

Backed up to the lantern.

Felt for the cover.

Wondered suddenly whether a forty-watt bulb would give off sufficient heat to burn through cloth if she held her wrists there long enough. Probably not. But she had to try. She struggled to remove the cover. Had to unscrew it with one hand while stopping the base from moving with the other. Too hard to do. Thought she could maybe smash the lantern cover and bulb, and use a shard of glass to cut through the material.

Held the lantern.

Dropped it on the floor.

It didn't break. Not a far-enough fall.

Carrie held the lantern behind her back. Struggling up onto her knees. Thought of sitting back suddenly as hard as she could on the lantern to shatter it. Debated. A second or two. No more. Then struggled up further, leaning against the wall, onto her feet. Still bound together, still so tight. Letting the wall take her weight, she stretched first one foot and then the other to try to loosen the binding round her feet. No luck. There was no give at all.

She dropped the lantern again.

Higher up this time.

The cover cracked open and the light bulb shattered.

She was in darkness now. Could see a little, though, shapes and shadows, from the moonlight streaming in through the roof. Looked at the door in front of her. Where the man had gone out and might come back at any moment, full of anger and rage. God knows what he might do. This child-like man having a furious tantrum. Or the other brother, The Scribbler, might appear. He would kill her in seconds. Knifed to death, most likely. She had to get away now.

Carrie lowered herself onto her knees, lost her balance, and fell forward onto her face. She shook her head, still so painful, and rolled over and back onto her bottom. She searched gingerly behind her with the tips of her fingers for a piece of glass from the cover. She found one, a large-ish chunk, touching the edges carefully and picking it up and holding it against the cloth between her wrists. Up into a crouch. Started cutting backwards and forwards.

Heard a noise outside the door of the building. Footsteps. A pushing at the door.

Stopped cutting. Was silent. Watching carefully. Breath held.

This was it, she thought, my final moments, as the door creaked slowly open.

She swallowed, subduing the sob in her throat. Thought suddenly again of Noah and her mum and dad. Then, defiant, started slashing as hard as she could with the shard of glass at the cloth between her wrists.

She sobbed now.

In anger and frustration.

And fear too.

If she could free her hands, at least she'd have a chance to cut her legs loose or to slash The Scribbler across the face in self-defence as he went for her with the knife. She looked back up to see the man now in the doorway, silhouetted against the moon.

Breathed out jagged breaths.

Close to tears.

And then she spoke, in stuttering words.

"Nice to s … see you, guv … what kept you?" She could not disguise the joy and relief in her shaking voice.

"This and that," Gayther answered, looking across at her crouched down in the shadows. "Had to have my tea first. Obviously."

She sobbed again. "Anything nice, guv, for your tea?"

She thought he said the word 'Pot'. Expected him to complete the phrase 'Pot Noodle', but, as he finished the word 'Pot', two shots rang out.

There was a moment's silence.

Gayther's head seemed to shimmer and shake in the moonlight. A haze of brain and bone and he fell forward, dead before he hit the ground.

Carrie screamed and screamed again.

Looked back at the doorway.

And saw The Scribbler standing there holding a gun.

PART FIVE

THE OLD BARN

26. SATURDAY 17 NOVEMBER, 11.25PM

Carrie knew she was about to die.

Wanted to say something profound. Or at least think about something important. Could do neither.

She did not seem to be able to say or think or do anything.

She stared through moonlight and shadows as The Scribbler stepped forward and studied Gayther's corpse laying on the ground in front of him. He pushed at the side of Gayther's head with his foot. Watched as it tipped slowly to one side. He seemed to think for a moment. Then nodded to himself. Job done. He stepped over Gayther's body and looked at Carrie. After a while, he spoke.

"Who was he?" he nodded back towards the corpse.

She looked up at him. Struggled to say the words.

"My … g … guvnor," she stuttered, eventually, close to sobbing.

She knew she was in shock. That she could not function properly. Unable to talk clearly. Nor defend herself. If she struggled up, she would fall down. If she sat back, she would stumble over. So, she just stayed there, crouching. Waiting for him to raise the gun and shoot her in the head. Same as Gayther. Gone in an instant. She tried to compose herself in the long silence.

"A bad man," he said finally.

Another long silence. She tried to frame the words in her mind before speaking. Was not going to let him see her cry.

"Good man … very good," she said finally, unable to say more.

He shrugged, as if to say, 'no matter, he's dead now anyway, good or bad. It makes no difference.' She thought, her mind slowly unravelling, that this is what the other brother had said, about bad men. That they were heroes, killing them.

"You're no hero," she said suddenly, the words coming to her unexpectedly easily. She felt sudden anger. It seemed to revive her, help her think straight.

"I rid the world of bad men," he answered. "Men with loving wives and little children. Men who lie and cheat and hurt their families and make the beast with other men … other men … men not women … Men who force themselves on their own children. Make them do things … dirty things. Terrible things." He thought for a moment. "The world is a better place without them. They are monsters."

She looked at him now, hearing the emotion in his voice. His justification. His reasoning. His logic. The sick assumption that gay men and paedophiles were one and the same. It somehow gave her courage, to talk, to speak, to answer back. To try to save her life. This was her chance to reason with him. Take control. But the anger was rising almost uncontrolled in her.

"You just shot a good man. Roger. My friend." Her voice wavered and she paused to try to steady herself.

"His name was Roger Gayther and he loved his wife and his son and he was a good man. A kind man to me. A loving man. He brought bad men, men who kill wives and children, to justice … He was the best of men.

"You just killed him for no good reason. You shot him from behind. You did not even give him a chance. You're not a hero. You're a coward, that's all you are."

He did not answer her.

His silence encouraged her to go on.

She rose unsteadily, arms and legs still tied, to her feet, her weight pressing against the barn wall.

"Cowards kill from behind. That's what you are. A coward. And now you're going to kill me. Tied up. Defenceless. Big man you are. Shooting someone who can't even defend themselves."

He did not speak.

She could not see his face clearly in the shadows.

Waited, letting the silence go on and on. Until he finally responded.

"I don't kill women," he said quietly. "Not unless—"

"You tried to before," Carrie interrupted. "In the kitchen. You hit me and knocked me out. What was that then? A big oops?"

"That was …" He stopped speaking, the words tailing away as though he were ashamed of himself and what he had done.

Carrie knew this was the moment. It was in the balance. This was the tipping point. If she said the wrong thing, he would kill her. Regardless of what he had just said. The right thing and she would live. For now, anyway. She didn't know how she was going to get out of this alive, though. It was only delaying the inevitable.

"Your mum," Carrie said. "It was your mum who told you to kill me, wasn't it? Do you always do what your mum says, or do you sometimes do what you think is right?"

He was silent.

She pressed on. "Was it your mum who told you to kill all the men … and Edwin Lodge at the care home … you killed him too, didn't you? Did Mummy tell you to do that?"

"Shut up," he said quietly, close to a whisper, almost under his breath.

She needed to do this. "You don't need to do what Mummy tells you, all the time. She's a bad person. You're not. I can tell. You're a good person. Your mother's a monster."

"Shut up about Mother," he shouted back and stepped forward.

Carrie shut her eyes. Expecting a blow across the face. Striking her into unconsciousness. And then the bullet. Some sort of blessing that. But there was silence.

And she heard, in the distance, down towards the farm, gunshots.

She opened her eyes. To look at The Scribbler.

But he had already turned, had stepped over Gayther's body, and was moving quickly to the door of the barn.

* * *

"What's that? What's happening?" Carrie shouted across to The Scribbler, who was standing by the door, looking out and listening, his head at an angle, as if he might be hard of hearing in one ear.

"My brother. He'll be shooting at the police. They'll all be dead. He's a sharp shooter. The sharpest shooter in town."

Carrie did not know what to say. Knowing Gayther, he'd have come alone or brought Thomas and Cotton and made them wait in the car while he scouted around. Please God, she thought, don't let the man with the melted face have seen them sitting patiently in the car. Creeping up on them. Pulling the door open. Shooting them at point-blank range. Those two sweet young boys.

They were both silent, listening intently.

For more gunshots. Other noises. Shouts. Yells. Anything. Signs of life.

But there was just silence, the stillness of the night.

"What can you see?" Carrie asked, her voice cracking.

"From here?" The Scribbler replied. "The barns. The farmhouse. Part of the drive. Your boss must have parked further down, just too far to see. He'd have had other police with him. Yes?"

She nodded. "Two new detective constables, I think, yes. Thomas and Cotton. Both about twenty. All their lives ahead of them." She stopped, knew she had to be strong now.

He shrugged as he turned towards her as if it were of no significance. "Two, yes, that's right. Two shots. That's all my brother would have needed. That's what we heard." He nodded, as if satisfied. "They'll both be dead," he added as a matter-of-fact afterthought.

She swallowed, composing herself as best she could. The horror of it all. Then spoke in a measured voice. "What will your brother do now?"

"There's an outhouse with a cesspit. It's where he … he'll put the bodies in there. Then he'll check on Mother … she'll need putting to bed … then he'll come here …"

"You have to stop this," Carrie said. "Give yourself up. You can't go on."

He didn't reply. She thought he was thinking. Weighing the odds.

"I'll speak up for you. You and your brother." She had to keep the desperation out of her voice. "I'll say you were good to me. That you didn't hurt me. That you let me go. That will help you. Just set me free now. Untie my arms and legs. I will go and …"

"No," he shouted, wanting her to be silent. "No!"

She hesitated. This man was dangerous, so much harder than the slow brother.

She tried a different approach. Quiet and reasoning.

"You could go. You and your brother. Leave me here. Just take off through the forest into the night. Disappear."

"Mother," he said simply. "We cannot abandon Mother. This is her home. She will not leave it, no matter what. She would be better off in a … I did look … at places for her … she was not happy about that. But she could not manage here on her own. She needs her boys. Her best boys. She needs us. And we need her."

"Go and be with her, then. Now. Leave me here. You and your brother go and put her to bed. Make her comfortable. See her to sleep. I'll still be here in an hour. We can talk about things then. Sort things out."

She felt the shard of glass still in her hands.

Knew that, given time, she could free herself.

Be running off into the night.

He stood and looked down at Gayther's corpse again. Carrie could not follow his gaze. Had to look upwards and away. She knew that if she did see Gayther's body and his shattered face that she would crack, her heart breaking for the sad, kind old man she'd got to know a little. That she'd expected to work with day after day for years to come. His life taken from him so coldly.

"I'll need to get rid of this first," he said, as if it were a nuisance, a bother, no more than a dead mouse found on a doormat. Not a once living, breathing man with thoughts and feelings and love in his heart. Carrie knew she had to switch off, blot out what she was thinking, and focus on practicalities. On getting The Scribbler out. On cutting the cloth round her wrists and feet. On running hard and fast away from here.

The Scribbler tucked his gun into the waistband of his trousers and reached down towards Gayther's body. He stepped over the corpse and around it, getting into a better position to lift Gayther up by the shoulders. Carrie looked away as The Scribbler dragged Gayther backwards to the door. He stopped close to the doorway, breathing hard already, and looked back towards Carrie and was about to speak. To tell her to wait there.

In that moment, The Scribbler and Carrie both froze into silence.

The sound of heavy footsteps and jagged, panting breath.

The Scribbler pulled Gayther to the side, reached for his gun and turned to fire.

* * *

The slow brother stopped just outside the doorway. In that instant he was about to be shot.

Carrie expected him to throw his hands in the air and shout, "No!".

But he just stood here, waiting. The smart brother drew in his breath loudly, stepped back, did not shoot.

"What is it?" the smart brother snapped.

"I went to my room," the slow brother said in his careful, steady voice as Carrie watched, willing him to speak faster, to get to the point. "To get a toy for the birthday party."

He turned towards Carrie.

The smart brother turned too, confused.

"But two policemen were taking Mother away. In the back of their car. She looked at me as they drove off. She was sad. She was crying. I ran after the car and shot at the two policemen in the front. To stop them taking Mother." He dipped his head down. "But it was too fast. I missed."

The two brothers looked at each other.

The smart one stepped forward, put his arm on the other's shoulder.

"I missed," the slow brother repeated himself. "And now Mother has gone."

A silence. Then the slow brother spoke again.

"Why have they taken Mother?"

The smart brother did not answer.

"What will they do with her?"

The smart brother did not reply.

"How will we get Mother back?"

The smart brother looked at the slow brother.

Carrie could sense the helplessness and the despair between them.

"We'll get Mother back. Don't worry. I will think of something."

And he turned and looked at Carrie.

She guessed what had happened. Gayther had come ahead, scouted round. Taken an age to find her. A police car there as back up or arriving when Gayther didn't return on time, most likely. Two local officers going to the farmhouse. The old woman there telling all or falling ill perhaps. Taken off, either way. Out of the line of the coming fire.

No matter. Carrie knew what came next. After the shots at the car. The police officers already radioing through. For the teams that were always called for in a hostage scenario. Negotiators. Marksmen. For Gayther and her. Except Gayther was dead. And she would be next. Before they even got here. She had no idea what these two brothers would do at any moment.

She looked back at the smart brother and spoke quietly, sensibly. Taking charge. As fast as she could.

"The police will already be on their way now. With dogs. And guns. And helicopters. They will surround the farm. They will move in closer and closer, searching and using sensors to find us in this barn. Then they will give you one chance to come out with your hands up. One chance only. And if you do not take it, they will storm in and shoot you both dead."

She watched the slow brother look from her to his brother and then back again. She could almost hear him swallowing.

She waited. For the smart brother to respond.

He was about to speak. But she pressed on, saying much the same as before to see what the slow brother might say and do. To set the brothers against each other.

"Give yourself up now. Let me go. I've said I'll speak up for you. You two can wait in the kitchen. In the farmhouse. I'll make sure they don't shoot you. I'll save you. Make certain you get a fair hearing."

She watched as the slow brother looked at the smart brother. She could win him over, no doubt about that. The promise of a party and a slice of birthday cake, that's all he needed. This simple, child-like man. The other one was different. A hard man. Difficult to predict what he would do.

The smart brother shook his head.

She tried again.

"Then go, go now. Run into the forest and away. But be quick. They will be here soon and then you will be trapped. Leave me here and run, before they arrive. Save yourself. I'll say you didn't hurt me."

The slow brother looked again from one to the other, and back again. Uncertain what to do.

The smart brother spoke finally in a rising voice.

"I have told you. This is Mother's home. She has lived here all her life. She does not want to leave it. She wants to die here in her nice warm bed."

The slow brother nodded. "Yes," he said, "with us. Her best boys."

The smart brother agreed. "Her very best boys."

Carrie came close to shaking her head in disbelief. At the nonsense of it all. The complete detachment from reality. Of what was about to happen to them. To engulf them all.

The smart brother went on. "The police can come here. And they can surround the barn. And they can give us one chance. But I will give them one chance, too. One chance only. To bring Mother back and return her to us here."

The slow brother nodded, yes, yes, that's right, that's what we'll do.

"And when they don't?" Carrie asked.

"Then we will stand you by the door of the barn. And we will ask them again nicely. Very nicely. And if they do not bring Mother back, we will shoot you dead."

The smart brother looked at Carrie unblinking.

The slow brother seemed uneasy, looking from one to the other and back again. Not meeting Carrie's eye.

Carrie tried to swallow, but found that she couldn't. She was scared. Whatever he'd said about not hurting women, she knew, from the kitchen, that he would if he thought he had to do so.

27. SUNDAY 18 NOVEMBER, 12.26AM

Carrie sat herself down and edged back along the wall of the barn while the brothers hurried to prepare for the siege. Tense, nervous, yet somehow excited. The slow brother, anyway. Like it was a game of cowboys and Indians. One where nobody died.

The slow brother ran back to the farmhouse for supplies, food, drink, more ammunition. Three times he came and went. Each time saying they're not here yet, they're not here yet, they're not here yet. As if the police would just roll up the driveway, would not think of doing anything less obvious. Might actually be here already, encircling the farm.

The smart brother was quieter, more serious, as if he knew and understood exactly what was coming. He secured the barn as best he could. Pulling the door to and fastening it. Dragging Gayther further to the side. Climbing the rickety staircase to peer out into the night, his gun cocked and ready to use. Like he was a sharp shooter. The sharpest shooter in the town. She'd have laughed to herself if the situation weren't so desperate.

Carrie studied the barn, taking it all in. Broken down. Wide-open upstairs. Ready to be attacked from all sides.

The thought of a kitchen sieve came to her. Even the wood of the walls was rotting in places. She could see through gaps in the roof.

This wouldn't last long, she was sure. Once the police arrived en masse. She just had to make it out the other side.

She knew she had to huddle down, stay out of view. Get her back against the only sound wall in the barn. Make herself as small as possible. Hope that the two brothers would leave themselves open, vulnerable. Would walk around not realising that the police would soon be there, hidden and waiting. Marksmen at noon, three o'clock, six o'clock and nine o'clock.

Carrie was not sure exactly what the police procedures would be. She knew they could not just storm in unless there was a real and imminent threat to life. Nor shoot the brothers through an open window, even if they provided an easy target. Could do that only if someone were about to die. A madman holding a hostage in front of him, while waving a gun around. No other choice then.

They would have to engage first. With the brothers. Try to reason with them. Assess the risks. She wondered if they'd assume both she and Gayther were alive. Were being held hostage. That would slow things down. But she thought maybe the mother may have said she was dead. Only Gayther then. Roger Gayther, who was already dead. But the police would not know that. God knows what they would do, she thought.

She knew she had to do it.

Look at his dead body lying there towards the front corner of the barn.

Decide what to do.

She wanted them to move his body, lay it out somewhere quiet and peaceful, respectful, in another barn. Feared though that, if she asked, the smart brother might just dump it unceremoniously outside of this barn, to show the police what they were capable of.

Carrie thought that, if the police saw Gayther's body and had been told by the mother that Carrie was already dead, they might just storm the barn after no more than one or two peremptory warnings. And that she might die in the crossfire.

So, she sat there and waited for what was going to happen. Knew it would all end here. That the brothers were not going to run. They had nowhere to go. Would not give themselves up. To spend the rest of their lives in prison. Would not move anywhere else, somewhere more secure and easier to defend. That they clung to the madness that they could trade Carrie for their mother. The insanity of it.

She knew all of this. And that, at some stage, the police would attack.

All she didn't know was which of them was going to live. And who would die.

She thought, one way or the other, they all would.

* * *

The smart brother was busy, checking his gun, the supplies of ammunition, going up and down the staircase, deciding where he was going to sit and wait for the police.

He chose upstairs, near the front of the barn. Turning to the slow brother as he went, "Watch her." Tense and anxious; "twanging," thought Carrie. So unpredictable.

Now out of sight, Carrie could imagine him lying down at the front, working a hole in the rotting wall, looking out, taking aim. Ready. Waiting. Trigger happy. Like he was with Gayther.

She looked across at Gayther's body again. Felt a sudden overwhelming sense of sorrow. Knew, in her heart, it was better if his body were inside than out. The longer the police thought he was alive, the more they'd hold off, and the better her chances of escape. She felt the shard of glass still in her hand. Jagged and rough.

The slow brother sat down carefully beside Carrie.

She looked to the side, waiting for him to speak.

He smiled shyly at her, reached into his pocket.

She looked down at what he took out. A small, threadbare teddy bear folded over and tucked into his pocket. One eye, no more than a roughly sewn-on button. Its limbs thin and flaccid. It looks more like a bald rat, thought Carrie, although she did not say so.

"That's nice," she said instead. "What is it?"

He sighed almost happily, and she thought he seemed somehow proud.

"This is Charlie," he answered.

"Who's Charlie?" she said.

"Charlie is my pal." He held the bear in one hand and ran one fat finger from his other hand over the bear's eye, where the other eye should have been, and down and across the nose and mouth, long since faded lines of black.

"He's an old boy," she said, as conversationally as she could. "A good old Suffolk boy."

He nodded. She thought he was going to say something, but he didn't. He just stroked the bear's head as if it soothed him.

"Is he yours?" she asked. "From when you were young?"

He jiggled suddenly on his bottom, like a small child, turning towards her. She could see the excitement in his face. "Yes," he said simply, looking at her. Little boy lost, she thought.

She nodded. "That's nice," she said, "that you've kept him so long. Looked after him." She paused. "I hope you look after me as well." She tried to sound jolly.

The slow brother glanced at her. Then upwards, as if checking on his brother. To see if he was watching. Or listening.

He looked back at her. She thought he nodded, only ever so slightly, but it was definitely a nod of agreement.

And then he spoke. "This is for you," he said, putting the bear carefully beside her legs. "For your best boy. So I can come to the party." He nodded again, more firmly this time, as if to say, 'there, a present, now I can be there'.

She smiled at him.

"I'd love to hold Charlie," she dropped her voice.

"Untie me and I can give Charlie a cuddle," she paused, judging the moment. "And you too, Dennis, if you'd like me to."

He looked bewildered, confused. She realised she had mis-judged it. Offering a cuddle to a man who, most likely, was not used to affection. A brute of a father. A hard-faced mother. A brother who went out and killed men. It was no surprise he almost recoiled at the thought of kindness and a gentle touch. She changed her approach.

"Hold Charlie up to my face, Dennis."

He looked uncertain but did as she asked. She breathed in. The bear smelled of dirt and dust and decay. It had probably been kept at the back of a drawer in a chest in a damp bedroom for years. She knew she had to look pleased, though. She pretended to kiss the bear.

"He's so sweet, Dennis, so lovely."

"He is for your best boy," he repeated, as if making sure she knew. "For his birthday party. So I can come." He sounded excited and anxious too, wanting confirmation.

"Of course you can come, Dennis. With Charlie. You can play all the games, and have some cake and—"

"Blow the candles out?" he interrupted in a quiet but urgent voice.

"Yes … and bring a party bag home with you, too," she whis-pered back. "But you have to keep me safe and well. Will you do that, will you promise?"

Another glance upwards.

A flickering of the eyes back and forth.

Another nod, more emphatic this time.

She thought about asking him again to free her hands. Knew that this might be a step too far. Was pleased that he might, just might, protect her if – more likely when – the other brother turned on her as he surely would. Meantime, holding the shard of glass, she could continue working on the material that bound her wrists so tight.

A noise above, rustling, footsteps.

The Scribbler. Carrie expected him to shout, "What are you whispering about?" Suspicious, he'd come down, pull them apart, find the shard of glass, her best chance of getting away or at least defending herself.

Instead, he simply said, "They're here. The police."

* * *

"Bring her up. Where we can see her," the smart brother instructed.

The slow brother stood up and moved towards her, bending down and pulling her gently over his shoulder in a fireman's lift. She did not struggle, just focused on covering the shard of glass with her hands. No matter what, she had to keep hold of that. And keep it hidden, too.

"Then go back and get your gun."

Carrie looked around the upper part of the barn where the slow brother had sat her down. There was a window with broken panes at the front, towards the farmhouse. The smart brother stood to the left side of that, just out of her sight, peering through one of the broken panes, his gun ready.

To the back, another window, six small panes, all thick with dirt. She saw the slow brother knock one pane out with his gun, then crouch to see through, covering the back towards the trees and the fields.

She sat in the middle, to the side of the barn and against a solid enough wall, halfway between the two brothers. Below her, the floorboards, part-covered with straw, felt soft and spongy and she could see parts had simply rotted away. Easy to fall through, she thought, in the shadows. The moonlight, streaming in the holes in the roof, was all that lit the barn. It was chilly now, and she could see her breath. The brothers' too. Cold as a morgue, she thought, then wished she hadn't.

"They're at the farmhouse," the smart brother said, almost as if he were thinking aloud. "Two police cars. The headlights are on. Full beam."

"I will come to the front," the slow brother replied.

"No," snapped the smart brother. "There will be more of them. At the back."

"They cannot get in at the back," the slow brother said, as if he needed to explain. "There is no door there."

"They'll circle around. Surround us from all sides." The smart brother hesitated, wanting to clarify what he'd said. Make the other brother understand. "Like Custer and the Indians ... in that cowboy film we used to watch when we were small ... remember? Custer in the middle with the Indians on horses, all running around him, shooting at him with bows and arrows."

Carrie looked at the slow brother, could see him thinking slowly, remembering, working things out in his head. Eventually, he spoke. "Custer died," he said sadly. "The baddies killed him when he ran out of bullets."

"They won't kill us," the smart brother answered. "We've plenty of ammunition. And we're sharp shooters."

"The smartest shooters ..." echoed the slow brother before they chanted together.

"The rooting-tooting ..."

"… super-duper …"

"… best-ever shooters in town."

Dear God, thought Carrie. They think it's some sort of game. She wanted to tell them again, over and over, to give themselves up. That this was it, their last chance. The final chance for all of them. Her too. But she knew they wouldn't give in now. And that, with the police outside, they could not run either. Not that they wanted to do that. They wanted a shooting match. Some sort of heroic shoot-out as they'd see it.

She sighed. This is hopeless.

Sat back.

Shut her eyes. The madness of it.

The smart brother, as if sensing her mood, spoke to her, almost over his shoulder, as he kept watch towards the farmhouse.

"We will trade you for Mother," he said firmly. "You won't be here long. A policeman will approach soon and he will shout up at us, what do you want, he will say, and I will tell him. Mother! That's what we want. Bring her back home. Our mother! And the policeman will reply, what do you have to trade, to trade for Mother? And I will tell him we have you …" He looked towards her, almost nodding, as if asking for her name.

"Brenda McButton," she answered, surprising herself with the savage edge to her words. He did not seem to notice.

"And I will tell him we have Brenda McButton to trade. And they will go and fetch Mother from wherever they have taken her and bring her to us. And I will see her and shout, Mother, we are here for you, your best boys—"

"Best boys," the slow brother interrupted, moving away from the window at the back and coming towards his brother. Carrie could see the look of excitement on his face.

"We are here for you," the smart brother repeated. "And I will tell the police to let her go, let Mother go. To come to us here in the barn. And my brother will take you down. He will take you downstairs and let you out and he will bring Mother here into the barn with us. Mother and her best boys. And we will be together again."

"Mother and her best boys," the slow brother repeated slowly, as if in astonishment, the undamaged side of his face all shiny with pride.

"And then what?" Carrie said bluntly. "You, what, live happily ever after? In this barn?" She knew she should go along with this charade. The stupidity of it. And keep her big mouth shut. But she couldn't. She knew her loose tongue would be the death of her.

"Mummy's boys," she added. Then wished she hadn't. She saw the sudden rage on the smart brother's face. The look of bewilderment on the other's. The smart brother turned towards her. She bought her head up, defiant.

And then he stopped.

She could see him swallow.

At the sudden loud clanging noise from behind the barn.

28. SUNDAY 18 NOVEMBER. 1.35AM

The smart brother rushed by Carrie and the slow brother.

Moved to the side of the window at the back.

Fired his gun, once, twice, randomly, into the night. Stepped back, watching.

Carrie ducked her head down, waiting for the return of gunfire, back and front, the police then storming the barn. She snatched a look at the slow brother, her only possible protector, but he had moved to the back window, too, standing behind the smart brother looking out. She scratched desperately once more at the material between her hands with the shard of glass.

"Get away," the smart brother snapped. "Don't give them a clear shot."

The slow brother stepped backwards.

"I've got this side covered," the smart brother whispered quickly. "Crouch down. Go and cover the front."

Carrie saw the slow brother, bent over, move hurriedly to the front window, peer through the broken pane, then put his gun through it, ready to shoot.

Waited for the police response.

A trigger-happy brother at the back.

A slow-witted brother at the front.

The moment stretched into a minute, then longer, more minutes, and towards an unending and uneasy silence.

"What do you see?" the smart brother suddenly called over to his brother.

"Nothing," he answered matter-of-factly.

"The two police cars with their lights on?"

"There are no lights. It is dark."

"Farmhouse?"

Carrie saw the slow brother nod. The smart brother, still keeping watch at the back, did not. He spoke again, a hardness to his voice.

"Are there lights on in the farmhouse?"

"No," the slow brother answered simply. "It is dark."

"Keep watching. Say if you see anything," the smart brother said, looking out the back of the barn.

The slow brother grunted slightly, half crouching by the window.

All Carrie could hear beyond that was the wind in the trees.

"What do you see?" she said eventually to the smart brother in a quiet voice.

He shook his head as if he wanted her to be silent; was still watching and listening intently.

"What was that clanging?" she asked a minute later, still speaking softly.

"I don't know," he answered, after a long pause. "I don't see the police. Probably foxes by one of the other barns or the bins. We sometimes get thieves at this time of year. For the Christmas trees. They'd have been scared off now, though."

Another silence. Longer this time. Seeming to stretch on forever.

The brothers stood still, as if they had been doing this for years.

Carrie guessed, if they had had thieves before, that maybe they had stood guard many times like this through long winter nights.

Carrie thought she could a creaking noise, then a rustling, the pitter-patter sound of someone creeping towards the barn. And then away.

More silence.

Then other movements. Further away this time. A crackling of leaves among the trees. The swish of a branch.

Silence again.

And voices. She was certain she could hear low, urgent voices. Whispering out there in the trees. Insistent whispers. Instructions. You stay here. You – over there, spread out. Lie low. Await the order to fire.

Even then she thought it might be her imagination.

Her ears straining for the sounds of police marksmen moving into place. She knew they were coming, the marksmen. Would circle and be ready, just as soon as they had worked out which barn they were in. Not that hard with the equipment they had these days and the two brothers moving continually to and from the windows and pretty much in plain sight.

Silence.

On and on.

Into the night.

All she could hear now, she thought, were the two brothers. The smart one at the back was taut and tense, ready to explode any second. Noises rumbled and whirred incongruously from his stomach.

The slow brother at the front kept moving his right foot back and forth, as if steadying himself ready to fire. Back and forth. Back and forth. Back and forth. A slippery, sliding noise, almost a squeaking, on the rotting floorboard. Over and over. Stop-start. Again and again. This rhythmic endless noise.

"Shut up," the smart brother shouted.

The slow brother jumped and then turned slowly. "What?" His simple face, uncomprehending.

"We need to be quiet and listen … watch for the police," the smart brother said quietly.

"I am," the slow brother replied.

"Keep still then," the smart brother said.

"Like a statue," the slow brother answered. Thought for a few seconds and then added, "I will not blink."

Another long silence.

The slow brother's foot began again. It was all Carrie could hear.

Front to back.

To and fro.

Back to front.

Carrie waited for the smart brother to explode in fury. Thought what he might do. This trigger-happy man with his loaded gun. An argument. Brother against brother. Two guns. She wondered whether the slow brother might fight back or not. Was not sure.

It was all she could hear now. The slow brother's foot. And all she could see. The smart brother's back, arched and tense. Each slide of the foot another torture. Every slip forward another movement towards the explosion.

"I see them," the slow brother said suddenly.

"Don't …"

But it was too late. The slow brother fired his gun, once, twice, three times.

* * *

The smart brother was across to the front window.

Pulling the slow brother back by the shoulders.

They tumbled to the floor, the slow brother struggling to get to his feet.

After a brief tussle, they stood there, like two wrestlers facing each other, both panting. Evenly matched, thought Carrie, in a fight to the death.

"Don't shoot at them," the smart brother said. "They will shoot back. If you're by the window, they will kill you. They've been trained. It's all they do all day. Shooting. They have lasers and things."

"You shot …" the slow brother went to say, out of the back window.

"I shot high. To scare them back. Warning shots. You shot down to kill. If you kill one of them, they will come for us straightaway. They will not wait. There will be too many of them for us."

There was a moment's silence.

"Wait," said the smart brother.

He crawled on his knees to the front window.

Carrie held her breath as he slowly moved to the right side of the window frame, the opposite side to the broken pane of glass that he had shot through. He wiped with his fingers at the dirty pane of glass to the right, raised his head, peered through.

"What do you see?" the slow brother asked. "Are they dead?"

"Ssshhh."

The three of them were quiet as the smart brother looked out.

Eventually, the smart brother looked back, gesturing to the slow brother to check the back window.

"Slowly ... head down, like I did."

The slow brother crept across, adopting the same opposite-side, head-low position as the smart brother.

He shook his head, no, no one out the back.

"There's no one here," the smart brother said finally. "Out the front. You shot at ghosts."

"I saw policemen and I shot at them," the slow brother responded, slower to anger than his brother, but it was definitely there, thought Carrie. Down deep inside. Ready to rumble up. "I am a hotshot shooter."

The slow brother stood up and, without thinking, stomped across to the front window.

He bent and looked through the broken pane.

Carrie shut her eyes, waiting for a shot to ring out, to see the slow brother stagger back and collapse dead on the floor.

She pulled and tore at the material between her wrists with the shard, one more attempt to free her hands before the smart brother, screaming in anguish, turned on her to kill her.

But nothing happened.

The slow brother just peered out. Carrie could see him checking slowly all around.

"They have gone," he said finally. "The police cars have left."

"What did you shoot at?" the smart brother asked.

"Over there," he answered. "By the big barn. There was someone behind it. A policeman. And someone behind him."

"You imagined it," the smart brother replied. "Moonlight on metal ... a padlock ... or a fox running across ... the corner of your eye ... there's no one there."

The slow brother shook his head emphatically, a sense of anger that his brother would not believe him. "I shot the policeman. And now they have gone. The cars. We have won. It is over."

The slow brother sounded delighted. He dropped his gun to the floor on the other side of the barn from her, Carrie noted.

The smart brother looked disbelieving as he turned to Carrie.

She shook her head slowly as if to say to him, 'it's not over, it's only just beginning. This is the quiet before the storm.'

* * *

The slow brother sat down on the floor by his gun and reached into his tin of roll-up cigarettes. Carrie could see him visibly relaxing.

He held the tin up to his smart brother as if to say, 'do you want one?'

The smart brother ignored him, moving back and forth between the front and back windows looking out. Agitated. On edge. Expectant.

"Could they have gone, the police, for a while?" the smart brother stopped and looked at Carrie.

She shrugged, not sure what to say. "They might have retreated a bit, but not far ... once you shot at the police ... when they were taking your mother off ... they won't have gone away."

"Why have they taken Mother?" the slow brother asked in a steady, concerned voice, as if it had only just occurred to him.

"Because it's dangerous here and they need to get everyone out of the way. Your mother will be at the police station. She'll be safe there."

"What will they do next, the police?" the smart brother asked more urgently, now looking out the back. She thought he'd shoot at anything that moved in that moment. He was that twitchy.

"The first lot of police who arrived were probably local officers. They'll be waiting for reinforcements … someone to take charge … firearms … specialist, trained police. It takes a while to get everything into place … and they will want to talk to your mother too … see what she has to say."

"She won't say anything," the smart brother snapped back. "Mother would not betray us."

"Mother wants to come home," the slow brother said patiently, lighting a cigarette successfully for the first time. "To be with her boys. And we want Mother home."

Carrie nodded.

"They know you have guns … so they will evacuate and cordon off the area first."

The smart brother nodded back, yes, I realise that.

"They will then scout around to see where we are. That may take some time. Once they have done that, they will try to engage with you, to talk you into giving yourself up and letting me go."

"We will let you go; we will exchange you for Mother. If they do not bring Mother back, we will not release you," the smart brother said.

"You've fired shots." She looked across. "So they will want to know that you are serious and will let me go."

"They will want to know we are serious?" the smart brother asked.

"Yes," Carrie nodded.

The smart brother thought for a second or two and then looked across at his slow brother as if reaching a decision.

"We'll show them we're serious … watch her carefully," he said, looking at the slow brother and nodding towards Carrie.

He moved towards the staircase.

"I'm going to drag the body out and down towards the drive. Then they'll see how serious we are. And what we will do if they don't bring Mother back to trade for you. We'll shoot you, too."

And with that he was down the stairs.

Carrie sat helplessly, listening to the smart brother creaking the barn door open, imagining him holding his gun up and peering out into the night. Checking. Watching. Waiting.

Then back for Gayther.

She heard the smart brother heave Gayther up, hands under his shoulders, straining for breath as he dragged the body away, the feet trailing on the ground.

And out of the barn.

A silence – ten, fifteen, twenty seconds – Carrie hoping to hear gunshots, knowing that the slow brother, listening intently, would not kill her.

And then the smart brother was back.

"I've propped him up against the old tree stump near the top of the drive. They'll see him there when they come back … they'll know we're serious all right."

He looked at Carrie.

"That we want Mother back in exchange for you."

Or else, she thought.

29. SUNDAY 18 NOVEMBER. 2.37AM

Time passed slowly. Minutes turned towards the hour. And then more. The brothers kept watch, going back and forward and then finally settling in an uneasy silence.

The three of them now sat in a circle, more like a triangle, on the top floor of the barn.

Moonlight still streaming through, breath like puffs of smoke in the cold air.

"They are not coming," the slow brother said, lighting up another roll-up cigarette. Carrie noted his gun was on the floor behind him, up against the wall. Unnoticed. Forgotten about. For the moment anyway.

"They will," the smart brother answered abruptly. He reached for the cigarette tin, laying his gun in his lap as he did so. "It's only a matter of time. They will bring Mother back. We will then talk to them."

Carrie knew that the police would arrive soon, at any moment. Most likely, a cordon was already in place around the farm. They were still questioning the mother. Working out where the brothers would be. What they might do. Getting the team in place. Marksmen too. Then it would all unfold – and fast.

She had to try to get away before that.

Once the police arrived anything could happen.

This gun-happy man and his half-witted brother.

Carrie felt the material between her wrists. She had been pulling and tearing at it with the shard of glass at every opportunity. Her hands, her wrists, she knew, were scratched and torn with her cutting. But the material did not seem to have loosened or ripped and she wondered whether she had actually been cutting at the right part of it at all.

She stayed put, her back against the wall opposite where the slow brother sat. If she stood up, she would wobble and stumble and was worried that, if she fell, the shard of glass that she'd been holding so carefully might stab into her wrist, cutting her veins. Or that she might drop the shard and they would see what she had been doing. They'd then gag her and tie her against something so she could not move at all and any chance she had of escaping would be gone.

She kept watch on the two guns. If she could somehow free her hands, and get one of them, she had a chance. The smart brother held his loosely on his lap or by his side. Moving it back and forth as he smoked and stubbed out his cigarette – but always conscious of it and never really letting go. If she grabbed at it, he'd be up and ready to shoot her in an instant.

She looked at the slow brother, who, now and then, would glance shyly back at her and smile his wonky-faced smile; more of a grimace, really. She smiled, too, but did not talk to him the way she had done, as a friend and confidante, because the other brother, with the hard face and staring eyes, would see through her. Would understand what she was doing. Might punish her in some way.

The slow brother seemed to have forgotten about his gun. Carrie hadn't. She knew she had to go for it.

She wondered, if she got the slow brother's gun, whether she could hold them both off. Or if she could shoot the smart brother before he shot her. If she had to. Life or death.

She had to try something. To avoid the oncoming slaughter. Pondered a while. Then decided to put a plan she'd worked out into action.

She started by pushing the shard of glass carefully into the straw just behind her, so it would not be seen, and then sat upright.

* * *

"I need to go to the toilet," she said firmly, almost insistently. The only thing she could think of.

The slow brother looked troubled. She could see from his face that he was embarrassed, felt awkward.

"You'll have to wait," the smart brother answered.

"I can't," she replied.

"You'll have to. We don't have a lavatory here," he said, taking one last drag on his cigarette.

A second or two's silence.

The slow brother looked bewildered.

"So, you what?" she asked. "You want me to … just go … as I am … here … now?"

The smart brother shrugged, as if to say, 'do what you like, I'm not untying you'.

She looked at the slow brother for help, but he would not meet her eye. She sat, waiting.

Then the slow brother spoke. "I can untie her hands. Watch her."

The smart brother leaned back, blowing the last puff of smoke out of his mouth.

"You'll have to keep an eye on her. I don't trust her," he said.

"You can turn your back," she answered sharply. "You're not watching me." She paused and then added, "You'll need to let me go downstairs. I need to go to the toilet properly."

A moment or two as they both took in the meaning of what she was saying. The slow brother looked uncomfortable. The smart brother barely concealing his disgust.

Not really, she wanted to say, not really. I just want to get away from you up here and be downstairs with my hands and legs untied. And this is the only thing I can think of. What else can I say? How else do I create a chance?

The smart brother spoke clearly to the slow brother. "Untie her and walk her downstairs. Stand by the door. Aim your gun at her. Turn your head to the side to give her some privacy."

He stared at her. "We don't have anything for you. You'll have to sort yourself out after. And if you try to run, we'll shoot you. Won't we?" He nodded towards the slow brother.

The slow brother looked unsure. "I do not …"

"When the police arrive," she said, "the first thing they will do once they see … DI Gayther's body … is to ask to see me. Alive. If I'm dead, they will just storm the barn and kill you. You'll never see your mother again."

The smart brother paused and then nodded. "If she tries to run, shoot her in the legs."

"I do not …" the slow brother tailed off. They all knew what he was going to say. *I do not shoot ladies.*

And that was what Carrie was banking on. That he'd half turn away as she crouched down. That she could somehow run at him, push him aside, maybe catch him off-balance, and be out of the barn door and running before the smart brother could react, coming down the stairs and shooting her.

The smart brother thought for a second or two. Then he spoke. "Untie her and take her downstairs. Put her at the back of the barn and go to the front and turn your back. I'll stand by the top of the stairs so I can see the barn door. If she makes a break for it, I'll shoot her down."

She looked back at him and knew he meant it.

Changed her mind.

Thought it better, safer, to stay as she was.

But the slow brother was already up, pocketing his gun and moving towards her. He lifted her up, steadied her and turned her around as he reached for a penknife in his pocket.

"Your hands are all bleeding," he said, looking down. "How did—"

"The material's been too tight, it's been chafing and cutting into my flesh, the blood's from that."

She waited for a moment for the smart brother to say, stop, let me see, and to get up and come across, peering in the moonlight at her wrists and hands and seeing the cuts. Then declaring, she's been cutting with something, she's got a knife. Searching and finding the shard of glass. Taking it away. Strapping her up tight after that so she could not move at all.

But he did not even glance over. Just waited as the slow brother looked from Carrie's wrists to her face and back again and she smiled at him and slightly shook her head as if to say, 'no, don't say anything'. He seemed to understand as he cut her ties and then took her arm gently and led her towards the stairs.

The smart brother stood and called after her. "If you try anything, I'll aim for your kneecaps."

She swallowed, could not help but think he would do just that. She looked back at his cold, hard face as he finished his words.

"You'll live, but you'll wish you hadn't. You'll be a cripple for the rest of your life."

* * *

"Please turn around," said Carrie quietly as she loosened her trousers.

The slow brother did as she asked, over by the barn door, his gun in his right hand.

As she squatted down, she tried to listen to the smart brother upstairs. She heard nothing. Assumed he was watching the door, waiting, half expecting her to try something. Wanting her to, most likely.

She started peeing, realising as she crouched there that she really had to. Had not been since she wet herself in the afternoon. Did not seem to need to. Adrenaline, she supposed. That, and fear, had got her this far.

She did not need to do anything more, although the brothers didn't know that. So she had, she thought, two or three minutes more squatting here to figure out what to do.

She could finish and then run at the slow brother, fast and unexpected, trying to spin him round as he was off guard so that his body was between her and the smart brother and his gun.

Considered this for a moment and decided it was too risky. If the smart brother was watching like he'd said, he could fire at her legs or, more likely, into her back and head as she got to the slow brother to twist him round for cover.

Shoot her dead like Gayther. She thought of Gayther, his sudden death, the terrible waste of it all. Knew she did not want to take such a chance with the odds stacked against her.

Remembered Gayther's body, his large, lifeless corpse, arms and legs at odd angles. She had not really seen his head and was glad of that. Knew that the sight of it would have sickened her.

"Have you …?" the slow brother turned his head slightly towards her.

"Not yet," she answered. "Give me a moment … women take longer than men, you know," she added, assuming he didn't.

He turned away. Shuffling and twitching. The thought of a woman's basic needs unsettling him.

She thought maybe, if she stopped and stood up and gestured the slow brother to come over, to speak to her, that he might approach her and, if she was quick, she could snatch his gun off him.

Or she could whisper to him, something about the birthday party and his invitation. And she could ask to see the teddy bear again. Make a move as he shuffled about, reaching into his pocket for the bear.

She could just ask him to help her. To let her go. That her little boy would miss his mummy, like the slow brother missed his mother. That her little boy would be scared, not knowing where she was and what was happening. Get him to stand up to his brother. While she made her escape. She hesitated, not sure what to do. Had to come to a decision.

"You've got two minutes."

She jumped as the smart brother shouted downstairs. "Okay," she answered.

"And then you're coming back up, come what may."

The barn wall behind her was soft, more damp and mould and rot than solid wood. She felt it with her fingers then pushed at it with the palms of her hands, trying to find the softest spot, wondering whether she could somehow force her way through it and away. It was so rotten.

Looked across at the slow brother in front of her, his back to her. Awkward. Uncomfortable. She did not think, if push came to shove, that he would shoot her. If he turned, as he heard the soft rotting wood giving way and saw her scrambling out, he would not fire, she thought, at least not straightaway, would hesitate for a second or two.

And then she would be gone, around the side of the barn, away from the line of fire from the windows at front and back, zig-zagging into the night. Her hands held high, no mistaking the surrender gesture, as she ran towards the police cordon that must by now surely be surrounding the barn.

She shuffled slowly to the left, feeling the wall. It was harder there, impossible to break through.

Back and to the right. Again, the wall was hard, and she knew it would not give way here, even with all her weight against it.

Now back where she started, the softest part. Here, then, her best chance. She took a deep breath, steadying her nerves, searching for confidence.

She knew if she did not do it now, the chance would be lost. That she'd be tied back up, taken upstairs, sat down and told to wait. Would sit there, ready to be caught in the crossfire.

Pressed hard against the wood, such as it was. More sponge than wood. Felt it give against her hands. This was it. Now. She changed position, pulled her trousers up, fastened them, and leaned her body against the wall. Felt it move. Clear and definite.

Stood up, pushed back harder this time. Yes, definitely some give here. She heard footsteps above. The smart brother moving. Looked at the slow brother, about to turn. This was it, she had to do it now.

She stood tall, ready to throw herself back against the wall as hard as she possibly could.

Then staggered, holding her hands to her face.

As the barn filled with sudden, blinding light.

30. SUNDAY 18 NOVEMBER, 2.51AM

All hell broke out, all sudden panic.

Carrie dropped to the ground, expecting gunfire.

The two brothers running back and forth.

In the confusion, she thought she might escape. Pushed hard with her back, then scrabbling with her hands, at the wall behind her. It gave a little but not enough. Went so far, but no further. Her hopes of breaking through dashed. She stood, half up, half down.

Looked across, towards the barn door, thinking she might run to it and out, her arms held high, praying that none of the police marksmen out there were jittery. Feared one might instinctively shoot at an emerging figure.

The slow brother was there, twisting and turning. First this way, then that, holding his gun up, not sure what to do, which way to go, where to turn. She tensed, ready to tackle him if he loosened his grip on the gun or even dropped it.

"Bring her upstairs, cover the back window," the smart brother shouted down.

She moved forward, saw the smart brother, shielding his eyes, looking at them.

"Let me go," she gabbled as the slow brother came at her, ignoring her words, pulling her towards him in his haste.

She thought that she might struggle, fight back, push at the slow brother, demanding that he free her. But she hesitated, knowing that the smart brother would shoot her where she stood or as she ran out through the barn door.

She let the slow brother carry her upstairs over his shoulder. Suddenly angry at the indignity of it. That she should be used like this. An object. Something to barter over. To trade.

She knew, as he tumbled her clumsily to the floor and moved to the back window, that she had to control her anger. Her temper had always been quick and hot, and it had cost her dearly in the past, with friendships and relationships. If she were not careful, this time it could cost her everything, her life.

"Anyone there?" the smart brother at the front called to the slow brother at the back.

"No," the slow brother shouted back.

"They're at the front. Behind the light. It may be a distraction to sneak up on us at the back," the smart brother called again, at the side of the window, shielding his eyes, peering out, careful not to provide a target. "If they come from behind, shoot at them. Over their heads first. Warn them off. Shoot to kill if they keep coming."

Carrie watched the two brothers. Scared. Engrossed. Ready to fire their guns.

In the turmoil, they had forgotten her and her untied hands and legs.

She crouched down quickly, as if sitting waiting. But really, she was feeling carefully behind her for the shard of glass.

The smart brother turned to her as if alerted by her sudden movement.

"Do anything and I'll shoot you. I've told you. You know that," he said.

She stood up slowly, her hands behind her back, and leaned against the wall as nonchalantly as she could. It took all her powers not to show she was shaking. She did not speak. The fear would be heard in her voice.

"Stand there and wait," he added. "Move unless I tell you to and you'll be shot before you've taken a step. The back of your knee-caps. You'll not walk again."

She nodded, yes I understand, and stood there silently, moving the shard of glass carefully from her left to her right hand, ready. It gave her a chance; to use in self-defence if – more likely when – the smart brother turned his gun towards her.

And so they all stood, motionless.

The smart brother at the front. The slow brother at the back. Carrie in between.

All waiting for something to happen.

* * *

They all jumped at the same moment.

A voice, a woman's strong and steady voice, calling through a megaphone.

Blurred and somehow distant, though, blown in the wind.

The smart brother turned towards his slow brother, then to

Carrie, before edging back to the side of the front window, peering out in the direction of the voice.

"Who was that?" asked the slow brother, moving away from the back window and forgetting he was keeping watch. He sounded puzzled. His brain turning it all over, working it out, making some sort of simple sense to it all.

The smart brother moved his head dismissively, ssshhh, I'm trying to listen.

"It was a lady," the slow brother continued, taking a step or two towards his brother, his voice full of curiosity. "A lady was calling to us."

The voice called out again. A little clearer now.

Ronald. Dennis. Talk to me. Then something else. Some other words lost to the wind.

That was the gist of it, though, thought Carrie. Talk. Engage. Let's find a way out of this.

"Is it Mother?" the slow brother asked, taking another step forward, the astonishment clear in his voice. "Is Mother calling to us?"

A pause and then another comment. "Does Mother want us to pray with her?"

It would be funny, thought Carrie, if it weren't so stupid. Tragically funny. The utter nonsense of it.

"Shut up," the smart brother replied, his voice rising.

Carrie watched the slow brother move even closer to his brother, wanting to see out of the front window, to look at Mother.

"Mother is talking to us. Let us both listen," he said. He sounds suddenly joyful, happy, thought Carrie.

"Get back." The smart brother pushed the slow brother away with his arm. "It's not Mother. Don't give them a clean shot."

The slow brother stepped back, bewildered.

"What does Mother want us to do?" the slow brother asked, as if he could not understand what he was doing wrong.

Another pause. One more comment. "We are her boys. Her ..."

"She wants us to shut up and listen to what's being said. Be ..." The smart brother stopped suddenly, listening to the voice again.

Carrie strained to hear all of the words.

"Talk to us."

That was about it. All that mattered.

The slow brother approached the front window again. He was pressed close to the smart brother, up by his elbow, providing a clear target and preventing his brother shooting back.

"Where is she? Where is Mother?" the slow brother asked, pushing forward and peering out of one of the dirty window frames. He wiped at it with the back of his hand.

"For God's sake." The smart brother swivelled and pushed the slow brother back as hard as he could. "Get over there and be quiet."

The slow brother took two, three steps back, turning to Carrie, who had taken a step or two towards the stairs to get away.

The smart brother turned, too, saw Carrie moving, and fired his gun once, then twice.

* * *

Carrie stumbled forwards and fell to the ground.

One shot way above her head, the other closer.

She dropped the shard of glass on the floor behind her.

"Only chance ..." the smart brother shouted at her, turning fast to the slow brother. "Tie her up. Her hands. Find the cloths you used before ... over there."

He moved back to the window, shouting into the wind, "It's all right, it's all right." The fear that his gunshots might have been heard and would trigger an immediate police attack.

Silence, though.

Except for the slight grunting of the slow brother as he tied Carrie's wrists, tight as before, and then sat her back down against the wall. Carrie could feel the shard of glass jabbing into the outside of her left thigh. Where she had dropped it. She moved slightly to the side.

Waiting.

The slow brother made his way, ducking down, to the back window. Seemingly chastened by the smart brother's warning shots. He stood to the side, looked out, put his gun through the broken pane.

Nothing.

The smart brother peered out, half-shielding his eyes, into the light. Knew there must be several police out there, if not many more. And all around.

Half-expected to see two or three break cover, running through the light and to the barn door. Did not know if he would shoot to kill or to scare, as he had just done with Carrie.

Wound maybe, if he could. To bring them down. Cut them to their knees before they got to the barn door.

"All is well. All are safe," he shouted into the cold night air, an almost echoing, empty sound. "We want Mother. Bring us Mother."

A pause.

"Let her come into the barn. To be with her boys."

Thinking what to say.

"And we will let the policewoman go … You can have her." He stopped now, waiting for the reply from the woman with the megaphone behind the lights.

The longest pause. As if that was that.

Then more blurred shouts from the police.

The smart brother shouting back, exchanging thoughts, reaching some sort of agreement, assumed Carrie, too far away to hear clearly.

"They want to see you," the smart brother said. "To show you're alive. That you are safe."

"We do not hurt ladies," the slow brother said.

"Your brother did … would," Carrie answered. "He hit me hard across the face and banged my …"

"Shut up," the smart brother shouted, the tension twisting his voice. "I could have shot you, couldn't I? Just now. But I didn't. I will next time."

He dragged Carrie up and to the window.

Shouts from the police. Checking she was well. Being treated properly.

She called back, her voice breaking, all good, bring back their mother and they have promised to release me unharmed.

Another long pause. The brothers and Carrie waited.

Silence from the police.

Just the unending light and the eternal quiet.

And then, after more shouts back and forth, it was agreed.

Between the smart brother and the police.

The mother was sleeping, resting right now, but would be brought back.

At daybreak.

Wait. Be patient.

An uneasy truce until then.

31. SUNDAY 18 NOVEMBER, 4.11AM

The three of them sat quietly on the top floor of the barn, up by the front window, the two brothers leaning against one wall, Carrie resting at the other. Close to peaceful, almost dozing, despite what was happening.

Waiting for the police to arrive with Mother. A lull. The calm before the storm.

The smart brother stretched up and moved occasionally, looking through the bottom pane of glass, checking. Just in case. Now and then, he'd send the slow brother to watch the back.

It was still dark. And cold. There was a sharp crispness to the air. And the light, lights really, two or three of them, continued to shine in and illuminate much of the barn. Light and shadows. Even so, there was a sense of stillness, a ceasefire, with both sides waiting for the real business to begin, the negotiations, on Mother's return.

The two brothers had finished their cigarettes. Had papers still in the tin, but no tobacco. The slow brother rat-a-tat-tatted his fingernails on the top of the tin over and again. Some endless rhythm to a long-forgotten tune. The smart brother eventually reached out and touched the slow brother's hand, hush now, to quieten him.

Carrie found herself fighting sleep, could not believe it in the circumstances. But she thought she had nodded off once or twice, soothed by the brothers talking. The smart brother's stronger voice, explaining, clarifying, instructing, and the slow brother's slower, monotone voice, listening and agreeing. Then waking at any sudden movement.

The smart brother was up. Across to the stairs.

Moving downstairs for a pee.

She could hear him below them at the back of the barn, the strong flow of urine hitting the wall.

Carrie looked over at the slow brother, who met her gaze shyly. He smiled back.

"You look tired, Dennis," she said, yawning.

He yawned too, an instinctive response, and rubbed his left

hand across his face. His right hand rested gently on his gun, she noted.

"I am," he said simply.

"You'll be glad to get to bed," she said.

He nodded, "I will."

"Not long now hopefully," she said, smiling.

"When Mother comes home, we will sleep then. Up the stairs to Bedfordshire."

She smiled again, not sure how to reply to that.

"What time is it?" she asked.

"I do not know," he replied. "It will be a while. Before sunrise."

"Do you have a watch?" Carrie pressed.

He shook his head.

She saw a possible opportunity.

"Can you tell the time?" she asked quietly.

He seemed awkward, looking down, thinking for a moment or two before answering. A stuttered answer.

"I know all the hours … the big hand. One o'clock," he said, moving his right arm to the one o'clock position and then moving it to two, three, four o'clock as he gave the times.

She nodded, smiling and pretending to laugh as he went through to twelve o'clock and said, "Midday."

"Or midnight," she replied.

He thought about that. "Midday in the day … midnight at night." Then added, for emphasis, "Mid … day. Mid … night."

She laughed, properly this time, at his serious, childlike expression. And he laughed too.

"Noah's birthday party starts at two o'clock. You must remember that. You don't want to miss the fun and games or the tea or the take-home goody bag."

The slow brother put his arm into the two o'clock position.

"Not at quarter to two," she said.

He sensed oh-so slowly that Carrie was joking, having a little bit of fun.

Thought a while. Moved his arm back a touch, to where quarter to two might be. Give or take.

She laughed.

"Nor at quarter past two," she added.

Thought again. Then moved his arm forward, quicker this time, in on the fun. But still not quite where it should be.

She laughed again, almost delightedly.

"Not at five o'clock," he said, laughing loudly as he moved his arm sharply to the five o'clock position.

They laughed together.

Then fell back into silence.

She knew her moment was coming.

She listened, for a while, until she heard the smart brother zip himself up downstairs. She hesitated, expecting to hear his footsteps on the staircase. But, after a pause, she could hear him moving about down below, checking this and that and making certain the barn door was secure.

"Do you have a watch?" she asked again.

He shook his head.

"I have one you can have … if you'd like it … and I can teach you to tell the time … the big hand and the little hand. Not just the hours, but all of the minutes, too. You can show people how clever you are, knowing all the different times of the day."

He looked at her, a sudden glimpse of pleasure on his shattered face.

"Would you like that?" she whispered urgently, hearing the smart brother coming to the bottom of the stairs.

A slight nod, shy, not wanting to seem too keen. Yes, yes, he would. As much for her attention than the exact telling of the time, she suspected. He'd not had much, after all.

"I have a watch in my car … just outside … it's in the glove compartment … you can have that … if you let me go and get it."

He looked at her, and she could see the excitement on his face.

"It's nice. It's a Walt Disney one. A blue strap with Mickey Mouse on the watch face. His hands are the big and small hands."

He looked back at her, thinking, taking it all in, making sense of her words. He seemed confused. The talk of hands.

"Mickey Mouse," she said. "You know Mickey Mouse?"

"Yes," he nodded, "Mickey Mouse lives with his dog Pluto in a nice house. His …" he smiled shyly, "… girlfriend is Minnie Mouse. She's pretty."

"That's right and his watch is yours if you'd like it. Just cut me loose and I can go and get it for you later … when your brother falls asleep."

A long silence. She was sure he was about to move forward to untie her hands. He was that close.

But then she saw the slow brother's face cloud over with sudden uncertainty and doubt.

She knew it was too late, and why, before she heard the harsh voice.

"No one's going to any birthday party … not him anyway … and you're not getting yourself untied. You're staying put," the smart brother said brusquely, taking the stairs two at a time.

"And he doesn't need to know the time," he added, checking the back window. "He gets up at seven and has breakfast. Dinner's at one o'clock, tea at six and supper at nine. He goes to bed at ten o'clock. That's all he needs to know."

He went to the front window, "We're all just going to sit here nice and quiet and wait for Mother. Until it's light. He doesn't need a Mickey Mouse watch to tell him when the sun's coming up."

Carrie glanced at the smart brother and then away from this hard and dismissive man. Unfeeling.

Then she saw the look on the slow brother's face. Anger, plain and simple anger. That he couldn't go to the party nor have the watch or be taught all of the different times.

She wondered what might happen if this simple man worked himself into a rage. And whether that might be enough for him to turn on his brother. She knew she had to try before daybreak.

* * *

It seemed to be on the hour and half-hour. Over and again. As regular as clockwork.

That the woman with the megaphone shouted out. To be shown Carrie. To check she was okay.

The smart brother dragging her up. Shouted exchanges. Carrie was safe. All was well. Mother was coming. Not long now. And then sat back down again until next time.

These insistent checks.

And ragged sleeps.

In between each round of shouting.

"So," Carrie asked, looking at the smart brother and thinking what to say, how to begin, "your mother comes here when the sun comes up. You exchange her for me and then the three of you are left here in the barn together?"

The smart brother looked up and nodded, yes, that's about it.

"And then the police go away and leave you to live happily ever after," Carrie sighed dramatically. She knew she was playing a difficult game. But it was one she had to try.

"No," the smart brother answered. "We just want to be together again, that's all."

"Mother and her best boys," the slow brother chipped in. "Together forever, never to—"

"The three of us together here in our home," the smart brother interrupted. "Mother loves her home. She has lived here all her life. She wants to die here. And she will. Because we love her."

Carrie nodded, working through possibilities in her mind.

Deciding which way to go.

To pitch brother against brother.

"If your mother loves her home so much, why did you want to put her away in a care home?"

She looked at the smart brother. He held her gaze and then looked aside, thinking how to answer. The slow brother looked at him, too, a worried expression on his face.

The smart brother sighed suddenly, unexpectedly. A vulnerability. A weakness. Something Carrie could maybe exploit.

"We thought it was for the best. It was a mistake," he said, starting slowly, before clearing his throat and carrying on. "Mother has not been well for a while. She has had falls when we have been out. She hurt her arm. And her face was bruised another time. Like Father had …" he stumbled to a halt.

"And she burned herself," the slow brother added carefully. "On the oven."

"Have you called the doctor … an ambulance?"

The smart brother turned his head. "No. We take care of ourselves. We don't want people here in the farmhouse … snooping about. Mother would not like that. But she cannot really manage on her own unless one of us is here to watch her. Not for long anyway."

Carrie nodded. She pressed on.

"So, you went to the care home to see about putting her away."

The smart brother breathed in deeply. Searched for words, explanations.

"Mother has … times of confusion and she had … has … become incontinent on occasion. We did not think she would want her best boys to—"

"We are Mother's best boys," the slow brother interrupted, "and we would do anything for Mother and Mother would do anything for us. Say it, Ronnie, say it."

"We love Mother and …"

They joined in together, "… Mother loves us."

A second's silence.

Carrie sensed emotions, something akin to love, from the two brothers as they stopped and did not seem to know what else to say. She recognised that two late-middle-aged men changing their elderly mother's soiled underwear and clothes would be difficult for them all; probably unbearable for the mother.

She waited. And then the smart brother went on.

"So, I went to, all over the place, it must have been four or five care homes. Just to talk. Get help. There are different sorts. I did not know. And they are expensive. We could not afford any of them. Not one."

"Mother was angry," the slow brother said. "She said to us, how dare you, she said, how dare you." He spoke the words as if he had learned them word-by-word, like they were somehow deep in his heart. "This is my home and you are my boys, my best boys, and we will all live here together until the day we die."

"And so we said we were wrong and that we were sorry, and we have been looking after Mother and nursing her ever since," the smart brother spoke. "We have changed and cleaned her and she has accepted that, for there is no other choice for us and we have promised we will live here together …"

The slow brother suddenly joined in and they chanted the final words together.

"For ever."

"Never to part."

"Until death do us part."

And with those words it came to Carrie suddenly. What the smart brother intended to do.

Exchange her for Mother. And then shoot first his mother, then his slow brother and finally himself.

The only way out.

* * *

They sat there for a while after that. Each of them with their own thoughts and tiring slowly as they approached the dawn, snatching now and then at restless sleep.

Another half-hour passing. More shouting. Carrie calling that all was well. A shout back that the mother would be there soon.

The brothers then getting up, checking front and back. Edgy again, ever restless, at each round of shouting and as the time of Mother's arrival drew near.

Eventually they sat back down. Settled. Waiting for the time to pass.

A sense of something between them. If not camaraderie or kinship, at least acceptance then. Of their shared circumstances.

"So," Carrie said, looking at the smart brother, "tell me about Edwin Lodge at the care home, the vicar."

The smart brother paused, thinking for what seemed an age. Carrie had the feeling that, with Mother coming, he was close to a confession. And she was correct.

"We both saw … and recognised each other … at the same time at an open day. He was much older, of course, but looked much the same. He seemed terrified and went to call out but could not. I think he was too frightened. I left straightaway without looking back."

"But you went back ... later ... and killed him?"

"I did not intend to. I was going to leave it. But ... it worried me. It nagged away. I kept thinking of what I had done, who I had spoken to there, what I had said, whether I had given my name to anyone ... my van may have been seen ... so he might somehow uncover ..." The smart brother stopped, trying to find the words to describe his fears.

"So, I went back at visiting time, the next night I think it was, perhaps the one after. I held on for a long as I could, but I could not bear it any longer, not knowing what might happen. I found his room and went in ... he knew who I was ... what I had to do."

"'Have you told anyone?' I asked him, but he would not speak. 'Who have you told?' I said. Still he did not answer. I gave him every chance. He did not take one of them. So I dealt with him. I had no choice. I have been waiting for that knock on the door ever since."

"How many have you ... killed ... over the years?" Carrie looked him in the eyes.

He drew in his breath slowly. Held it for a moment. Breathed out. Then spoke. "Thirty," he said. "The last one was thirty."

"Bad men," the slow brother said, "only bad men."

"We used to go out together at the start, but it got too dangerous ... Dennis ... stood out ... so I went on my own and then brought them back here. We put them in the cesspit in the main outbuilding, mostly," the smart brother added.

"Where the bad men belong," the slow brother said, and then added, almost proudly, "I put them there."

"Philip Taylor," Carrie replied, pressing on, "the last one ... a married man, happily married, a loving wife who missed him, no children. He had no children. Loved his wife. Never hurt anyone in his life. Would not hurt a fly. He may have been gay but he wasn't a paedophile. The two aren't linked at all. You do know that, don't you?"

The smart brother stared at her. She felt, perhaps for the first time, a sense of doubt in him. Perhaps even sorrow. Or maybe that was just what she wanted to see. Remorse.

The slow brother seemed uncertain, trying to remember what his brother had said about the man.

Knew that the man had been with children. That his brother had stopped him. Had saved the little children. That's what super-heroes did. And that's what they were. Super-heroes.

The smart brother twitched his shoulders. "He was with a man, making the beast, in a public toilet. He was a bad man."

The slow brother nodded, agreeing, "He was the baddest of men."

"That doesn't mean he deserves to die, does it?" Carrie stopped, full of angry frustration, before finally going on. " ... You were seen by a boy with his dog, putting Philip Taylor into your van."

The smart brother nodded. "I saw him. He was a handsome fellow. He had a dog like we used to have."

"My brother saved the little boy, yes, he saved him," the slow brother explained.

"He gave us part of the number plate on your van ... that's how we traced you ... how I came knocking on your door."

The smart brother shrugged. "I know. I knew it would happen like that. But I could not bring myself to do anything with him. I would not hurt a little boy. I am not a bad man. I am a good man."

The slow brother spoke. "We protect and save children. We are super-heroes." He looked from his brother to Carrie and back again, nodding as if to say, 'yes, there, we have agreed'.

"It's my downfall," said the smart brother.

"Yes," Carrie said.

And then, before she could say any more, the police called out again, another check and another step closer to the end.

32. SUNDAY 18 NOVEMBER, 6.53AM

They waited there.

The three of them.

As the sky turned slowly from night towards day.

The smart brother woke, barely sleeping anyway, just nodding on and off with tiredness.

He nudged the slow brother, leaning against him. "Mother's here soon," he said quietly.

The slow brother sat up, looked around him, remembering where he was, and smiled across at Carrie.

Carrie, already awake, smiled back, her hands, raw and torn, holding the shard of glass as she tore steadily at the material round her wrists.

It snapped.

She looked across at the smart brother, who had his fingers resting lightly on the gun on his lap.

Always ready.

"I meant to ask," she said to the smart brother, "the papers called you The Scribbler ... why do you draw a likeness on the chests ... the stomachs?"

He sat there, looking back at her for a while. Then put the gun carefully to one side and pulled at his jumper and the vest beneath.

Lifted them up so she could see the white lines of ridged skin across his chest; age-old scars of a rough-hewn face.

He shrugged and said hesitantly, "Father ... we both have them."

The slow brother moved his gun away from the side of his leg. Reached and pulled up his jumper and vest too.

Carrie felt a sudden pang of sadness.

The two of them like awkward children, lifting their tops, showing their matching, etched-in scars, all these years later.

"Why?" she said simply, not trusting herself to say more.

The smart brother pulled down his vest and jumper.

"Father was … an angry man … frustrated."

"Ronnie wanted to be an artist," the slow brother said.

"I told him one day," the smart brother continued, "when we were in the small barn, that I wanted to draw. That it would be my job when I grew up. Mother had given me a pad and pencils at Christmas … Caran d'Ache they were called … I was good at it. I enjoyed it. It made me happy."

"You drew everything," the slow brother said. "The farmhouse. The dog. Charlie." He pulled his clothes down too and reached into his pocket and took out the teddy bear. "You were very good."

"Father flew into a rage. Said it was stupid. I was needed on the farm. There was no living to be made from drawing … I defied him … said I was going to be an artist when I was older. And then …" The smart brother stopped speaking, struggling for words.

"He taught us a lesson." The slow brother reached out and put his hand on his brother's arm. "So that we would remember his words … Do nothing out of selfish ambition or vain conceit." He paused, remembering. "In humility value others above yourselves."

"So, he did this … to both of you … because …" Carrie stumbled over her sentence.

And as they sat there, lost for words, they heard the police calling again, not asking to see Carrie this time, but shouting that Mother was on the way.

The smart brother grabbed his gun and went to the front

window to answer.

The slow brother picked up his gun and went downstairs. Emptying his bladder against the barn wall.

Carrie sat there, shard of glass in her hand, deciding what to do.

* * *

Carrie heard them first. Somewhere off to the left. In the distance. But coming closer.

The noise of children, running through the trees.

Happy shouts. Sudden bursts of laughter.

She looked over to the front window, where the smart brother stood crouched, gazing out, gun in hand, waiting for Mother's imminent arrival. The spotlights were off now so close to daylight. There were police officers, mostly armed, spread out in various protected positions in an arc in front of him.

"What's that?" she shouted urgently.

He tipped his head at an angle, listening. He answered slowly, as if it were of no significance. "Children coming for a Christmas tree. They're not supposed to be here now. They must be over-excited, coming here before breakfast."

"No, but I mean …" she struggled to get to her feet.

"Their father will be with them. They live on the other side of the fields. The father's been helping to cut the Christmas trees. We promised them one. They have come early, that's all. They have chosen their tree and put their ribbons on it."

"Yes, but …" she stood up, with a sense of almost overwhelming unease.

"I'm not going to shoot them. And the police won't. They'll just gather the children up when they get here."

He stopped and turned towards her. "Look," he said, pointing the gun down to the floor. He seemed close to smiling, "they're safe. I told you. I'll not shoot them."

Carrie heard the children again, closer now.

Laughter. Lots of ssshhhing. More giggles.

By the side of the barn, up alongside it and towards the front.

She waited for the police to call out. To shout to the children. Stop. Stand still. A woman PC, maybe two, running over to fetch them. Take them away from any danger. All under the watchful eyes of the waiting armed police.

But all she could hear were the children.

Now at the front of the barn.

Shouting and excited. Almost beside themselves with expectation. An incongruous, joyful noise.

Carrie saw her chance, moving carefully towards the smart brother and the front window. Slowly, so he would not notice. She felt the shard of glass in her hand and was ready to use it.

She could hear a girl clearly now, very close and giggling loudly.

The smart brother watched as Carrie approached, standing back so that she could move up and see out of the window. He seemed to have no sense of danger.

She stopped, though, before she got there, could hear a boy calling, "Hello-oo. Hello-oo," at the top of his voice. He must be just below the window. It reminded her of someone, a cartoon character Noah liked on the telly.

Expected to hear shouts and movements from the police. Going to get the children. Taking them to safety.

Instead, she turned in sudden shock, hearing the slow brother below moving to the door, wrenching it open and running out of the barn. She felt a surge of fear.

"Children!" he shouted, running towards them as they stood bewildered, midway between the barn and the arc of police. "Little children, come unto me."

As he moved, he fired once, twice, three times towards the police.

Then turned himself and his gun to the two children as he ran to save them.

The first shot fired by the police hit him in the chest. The second went into his heart. The third shot missed, although, by then, it did not really matter either way. The slow brother was already dead on his feet and sprawling to the ground.

* * *

Carrie heard the gunshots, the split-second silence, the screams of the two children. Guessed what had happened. Brother shot. Children saved.

The anguished, animal cry of The Scribbler as he moved to the window to see his dead brother fall confirmed it. He started firing randomly at the police. Downwards. To kill.

She moved suddenly, one, two, three steps towards him, raised her hand to slash at his gun hand with the shard of glass.

He saw her. Out of the corner of his eye. Just in time.

Turned and hit her across her face with the back of his gun hand.

Sending her sprawling. The shard of glass flung far from her hand, out of sight. Over there somewhere, deep in the straw. Too far away to reach. No time to scramble towards it.

The Scribbler felt quickly in his pocket, reaching for ammunition. Reloading the gun. She thought he would shoot her. But he went back to the window. Firing again now in raging heartbreak. Three, four times.

Stepped back. In the nick of time.

As the police returned fire.

Flashbangs and smoke.

Carrie could not tell, as she scrabbled desperately to find the piece of glass, whether they were shooting to kill him.

Or whether they were simply returning fire to keep him busy, distracted, while other police officers stormed the barn.

Guessed they'd move the children first and then, under cover of more fire to the front and the back, they'd head to the building.

She found the shard of glass and turned to face The Scribbler one last time. She was ready to attack as he turned to shoot her in his wild rage.

But he was crouching now, his head down. Ignoring her. He looked up slowly as she moved towards him.

"My brother," he said, sobbing angrily, "they shot him as he went to save the little children."

She stopped and looked back at him, hesitating for a moment. Knowing she had to get him to drop the gun so she could arrest him. Bring him out alive to face justice for all he had done.

"I know," she answered simply. Not sure what else to say in that instant.

They gazed at each other then. For a second or two. In silence. It was a moment of balance, even surrender, she thought. This is it. No more deaths. The end of all the carnage.

She was about to ask him to hand her the gun, give himself up, was just phrasing the words, the sentences, in her mind before she spoke. One final time. To make the arrest.

Heard, at the same moment, the two of them, police officers rushing through the barn door and, before either of them could say or do anything, heading up the staircase.

The Scribbler reacted fastest, sitting up, full of tears and fury, and firing his final two shots.

As the police reached the top of the stairs.

Carrie was hit first once, then twice, by The Scribbler's shots and fell to the ground.

And then the police returned fire. Five, six times. And shot The
Scribbler dead.

EPILOGUE

MONDAY 10 DECEMBER, 11.25AM

Sharon Carrie stood in the garden of the crematorium at Nacton, a mile or two outside of Ipswich. She held the hand of her restless grandson, Noah, jigging from foot to foot, as they looked across the garden to the huge, swaying trees that surrounded the site.

She could still hear the roaring traffic from the road, the A14, and its endless procession of lorries to and from the docks in Felixstowe.

She turned back to look at the crematorium. An odd, wooden building behind a nondescript car park. This could be anything, she thought, a supermarket, a truck stop, some sort of country warehouse that sold remaindered books, outsized clothes and cheap garden furniture.

What a place to say goodbye to a loved one.

Miserable and soul-destroying.

Like being cremated in the shower and toilet block of a campsite.

She put her arm around her grandson's shoulders and looked down at him. He stopped moving about and smiled up at her. She smiled back, pleased that he was settling.

They then both turned towards the crematorium as they heard organ music playing to mark the end of the funeral service and, within a minute, the doors had been opened.

They put on a good do, she thought, when one of their own dies. Is killed. Murdered. Police officers lining either side of the road up to the crematorium. A guard of honour. The Constabulary drape over the coffin. Bearers. The attendance of the good and the great, including the Chief Constable herself.

The full works. For all the world to see.

More for themselves, she thought, than for Roger Gayther or his loved ones.

To show how kind and caring they all were.

She watched as the mourners came out of the crematorium. The family and personal friends first, no more than half a dozen by the look of things. The police officers inside, who would have filled most of the building, holding back.

A vicar to one side of the doors, commiserating, shaking hands, saying a few words. Opposite him, a tall, fair-haired man in a charcoal grey suit echoing the vicar's words and actions. He looked familiar.

She suddenly saw Georgia pushing herself out in a wheelchair – her "rocket chair", as she called it. The latest model, for sure.

The vicar bending, saying a few words, shaking Georgia's outstretched hand.

Then an unexpected embrace from the sandy-haired man, a long conversation, so it seemed, as the police officers inside the crematorium lined up waiting to file out. And then Georgia was through and away.

"Mama!" the little boy spotted his mum and called out.

Sharon Carrie hushed him quiet and raised her hand towards Georgia, who steered her wheelchair towards them.

The little boy broke free and ran to his mum. She wrapped her arms around him and hugged him tight.

"I've had to park over the road," Sharon Carrie said to her daughter. "You can't move for police cars round here."

Georgia laughed. "Hope you don't get a ticket."

Sharon Carrie smiled back and then, after a moment or two, looked more serious. "We've been reading some of the wreaths and things while we were waiting for you. From the other funerals. There's one over there, from this week I think, with just one wreath, from the funeral director. Margaret Stenning. Is that the …?"

"Yes," Georgia replied, "that's her, the mother. Died of a broken heart, they say … although I don't believe she had one personally. I think it was a council funeral, so Glyn Thomas said. No one attended."

"No more than she deserved. What have they done with the brothers?"

Georgia shrugged. "Don't know. Lou Cotton reckons they've been cremated already, all very secretive. So as not to attract the ghouls."

"They deserved nothing. All those bodies. Monsters. Both of them."

"The younger one wasn't so …" Georgia's words tailed off. "I don't suppose it matters now."

"The older one could have crippled you for life, shooting you like that."

"Maybe." Carrie thought for a while as she moved her wheelchair to go up the path and on to the road and back to the car. "But I'm not so sure … I was thinking about that during the service."

"He was so close to me, he could have …" she dropped her voice so the little boy could not hear, "… blown my head off if he'd wanted to. But he didn't."

She continued, "If he hadn't shot me, I could have been killed in the crossfire. Between the police and him. So …"

Sharon Carrie pulled a face as if to say, 'so what are you saying?'.

"He shot me in the legs so I'd fall down out of the line of fire and he could be shot dead by the police."

Sharon Carrie made an instinctive snorting noise. "That's just … silly."

"Is it?" Georgia asked. "I'm not so sure."

They both stopped for a minute, each with their own thoughts.

Watching the little boy, now jiggling again, impatient to go.

And they turned to leave the crematorium.

"And that man was Michael Gayther, Roger Gayther's son? The one who hugged you. He seemed very pleased to see you."

"Mu-um ..." Georgia answered in a long-suffering, please-don't-start-matchmaking-again voice. "He's just ... you know ... because I worked with Roger ... on his last case."

"Is he in the police? He's another one that looks like a policeman. Like father, like son."

"He does something undercover in the Met, but there's talk he may be coming to Suffolk to set something up. I don't know. He asked if we could meet up for lunch to talk about his dad and I said I'd love to ... once I'm out of this chair."

"Do I see romance in my crystal ball, Georgy?"

"No," Georgia answered, "you do not. I've no time for that ... I've got to recuperate, get on my feet again ... then there's my course work ... loads of that ... and Christmas ... and New Year ... and Noah's birthday party to sort ... busy, busy, busy, Mum. No time for romance. None at all."

They looked at each other.

A long pause.

Georgia held her mother's gaze.

Sharon nodded and smiled, taking her grandson's hand. "Come on then, let's get back to the car, get you unpacked and loaded up ... I've promised Noah we can pick up a McDonalds on the way home."

The older woman and the little boy went ahead, one walking slowly, the other hop-skippity-hopping along.

Georgia Carrie sighed, turning back towards the crematorium.

Saw Michael Gayther standing there looking at her. As if he

had been like that for an age, just watching, and waiting to see her leave.

He broke into a sudden smile, raised his arm and waved at her.

She felt herself blush unexpectedly and waved back. Then chuckled to herself as she followed her mother and son out of the crematorium.

THE END

AUTHOR'S NOTES

So, I'm sitting in a Soho restaurant having lunch with my literary agent Clare and talking about writing – the stuff of dreams for so many would-be writers – and we're having an enjoyable time.

And then Clare asks me, 'What's next?' So far, I've written a couple of memoirs, *Dear Michael, Love Dad* and *Out of the Madhouse,* about my eldest son's battles with mental health issues, and two dark literary thrillers, *Sweet William* and *Mr Todd's Reckoning.*

I hesitate and say I want to write a thriller series featuring two detectives.

Clare laughs. Take a look at this. A million-selling detective novel is on the table in front of me.

We both had the same idea at the same time.

Thing is, there's a big difference between what I'd been writing and what I now wanted to do. I've always just kind of done my own thing. Written what I liked and hoped other people would like it too.

I flick through the detective novel. It's really good. I'd love to write something like this. Strong characters, gritty and exciting, a plot that rattles along to a great ending.

I'd never written anything like this before. I wasn't sure I could do it. The characterisation, the twists and turns, the ratcheting up of tension over 300 pages or more.

I'll have a go, though, I said.

I'll start writing.

See where it takes me.

I knew from the beginning I wanted to make this a buddy-buddy book where I could run the partnership through a series. An older, world-weary man, something of a maverick, and a younger, keen and enthusiastic woman. He's a step behind the times in his thoughts and language. She's not.

I didn't want to give him a bionic eye or a wooden leg or to have her as a shape-shifting alien with psychic powers – none of that sort of thing just to try to make them stand out. I wanted to write about ordinary people doing their jobs.

Those of you who are *Doctor Who* fans, as I have been all my life, may recall the relationship between the Third Doctor, Jon Pertwee, and Jo, Katy Manning. It's like that, warm and respectful. No funny business, thank you very much.

So, I had the characters in my head. Sorted.

Then the names.

Easy. Roger Gayther and Georgia Carrie.

Roger was the name of my uncle. He died of meningitis when he was twenty and I was five. I remember him clearly. And sitting in a car by green railings outside the hospital. Asking, "Where's Roger?" when we visited Nan and Grandpa's, I guess, a week or two after he died. And my nan's face. Always my nan's face. I doubt anyone remembers Roger these days. I do. And he is the hero of my book.

Georgia? My son Michael had eight years and more struggling with mental ill health. He spent time in hospital, and five months in the Priory, and lost pretty much everything. Coming out of that, as if waiting for him at the end of a long road, was Georgia. And now he is happy and his life is on track. And I never thought that would happen. So, there's the heroine.

I set the book in Suffolk.

I always do. Probably always will.

I like to see locations, real or close to it, in my mind as I write.

And then the plot. I didn't have one yet. I spent some time thinking of ideas that would spark my imagination.

I didn't want to write a novel based on something as recent and raw as an unsolved murder still in the news. Loved ones, broken hearts, respect; all of that.

But I couldn't help thinking about how many unsolved crimes of murder there are – depending on what you read, 20 per cent or more are never solved. About half of those cases are closed down.

Once I started looking into some of these stories, I had a growing sense that crimes against the LGBTQ+ community have often been taken less seriously, especially going back in time. So, my story started to take shape.

Unsolved crimes going back over the years.

In the LGBTQ+ community.

Closed down – cold cases.

Another theme that stood out was how so many investigations started off going in one direction – plod, plod, plod – and then suddenly turned on a sixpence with a lucky break. The Dennis Nilsen case and the Yorkshire Ripper – both referenced in the book – are prime examples where this happened, with the investigations then going in a totally different direction. I wanted to get that 'twist' into *The Scribbler* as well.

And so I began writing. As ever, as I start work, there comes a moment when the book kind of takes on a life of its own and it runs ahead of me. That's usually when I get inside the mind of the lead character – in this case the wounded and impulsive Gayther with a point to prove – and everything sort of falls into place.

This is the first of a series of Gayther & Carrie books. As well as Gayther and Carrie, working on LGBTQ+ cold cases, I have introduced two fast-tracked detective constables, Glyn Thomas and Lou Cotton; a gay couple who are new to the force. They take a back seat in *The Scribbler* but will come to the fore in the next book. Gayther and Carrie and Thomas and Cotton will be back sometime soon in *The Key Man*.

Iain
March 2020

AUTHOR'S ACKNOWLEDGEMENTS

I'd like to thank …

Saraband for publishing *The Scribbler* – it's been another wonderful experience.

Sara, my third book with you – here's to more!

Tony Conry for reading the MS to make sure the psycho-dynamics of The Scribbler and other characters were as accurate as possible. You made a big difference, Tony. Thank you.

Neil Boast MBE for reading the MS from a police perspective to ensure procedures matched the realities of what would actually happen. I could not have asked for more, Neil. Thank you.

A quick thank you, too, to Jules at Woodbridge Emporium for introducing me to Neil.

My other MS readers who helped to check and double-check facts and figures. Any errors to be found, artistic licence aside, are mine and mine alone.

Ali Moore for copy-editing the MS and helping me turn it into the best book we could. I could not ask for a better copy-editor.

Rosie Hilton for a forensic proof-read and for giving me a heads-up on one or two LGBTQ+ issues. And another sensitivity reader; you know who you are.

Ken Leeder – a brilliant cover again!

My fab, possibly long-suffering, agent Clare who not only guides me and sorts out all the contractual stuff but also steps in when needed to stop me doing anything 'dramatic'.

Georgia, Glyn and Sophie – my children's partners – for letting me use the names Carrie, Thomas and Cotton for my main characters.

Tracey, Michael, Sophie and Adam, my family. You are always in everything I do.

ABOUT THE AUTHOR

Iain Maitland is the author of two previous thrillers, *Mr Todd's Reckoning* (2019, optioned for television) and *Sweet William* (2017), both published by Contraband, the crime, thriller and dystopia imprint of Saraband. He is also the author of *Dear Michael, Love Dad* (Hodder, 2016), a book of letters written to his son who suffered from depression and anorexia, and writer of the script of its television adaptation; and co-author (with his son) of *Out of the Madhouse: An Insider's Guide to Managing Depression and Anxiety* (Jessica Kingsley, 2018). Iain is an ambassador for Stem4, the teenage mental health charity, and talks regularly about mental health issues. A writer since 1987, as a journalist he has contributed to the *Sunday Times, Financial Times* and *Guardian* as well as writing many books on management and business.

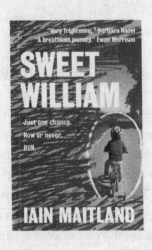

A father desperate to be with his young son escapes from a secure psychiatric hospital, knowing he has just one chance for the two of them to start a new life together. His goal is to snatch the three-year-old – a diabetic who needs insulin to stay alive – and run away to France … but first he must find the boy, evade his foster family and stay well clear of the police, already in pursuit.

A real page-turner cut through with pitch-black humour, *Sweet William* zeroes in on a potent mix: mental illness, a foster family under pressure, and an aggrieved father separated from his precious child. The result is a breathtakingly dark thriller that spans forty-eight hours in the life of a desperate father and a three-year-old child in peril. Brilliant and terrifying, this is a debut novel that will stay with its readers long after they finish turning the pages.

"Extremely well written and very frightening." BARBARA NADEL

"A breathless journey through fear and love that explores how interdependent those two extreme emotions are." EWAN MORRISON